The
Blood
Jaguar

Michael H. Payne

A TOM DOHERTY ASSOCIATES BOOK
NEW YORK

This is a work of fiction. All the characters and events portrayed in this book are either products of the author's imagination or are used fictitiously.

THE BLOOD JAGUAR

An earlier version of this book ran as a serial in www.tomorrowsf.com electronic magazine.

Maps by Kandis Elliot

A Tor Book
Published by Tom Doherty Associates, LLC
175 Fifth Avenue
New York, NY 10010

www.tor.com

Tor® is a registered trademark of Tom Doherty Associates, LLC.

ISBN: 0-812-56675-0
Library of Congress Catalog Card Number: 98-23496

First edition: December 1998
First mass market edition: October 1999

Printed in the United States of America

0 9 8 7 6 5 4 3 2 1

The
Blood
Jaguar

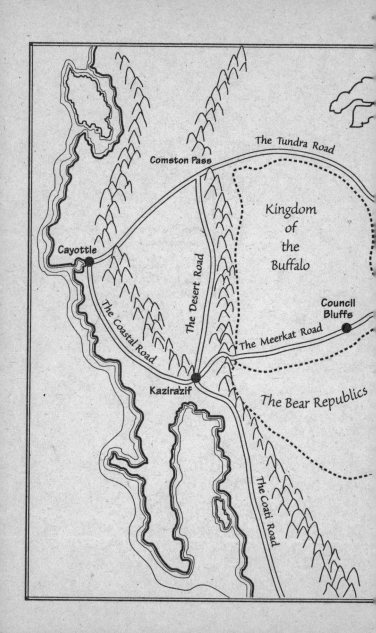

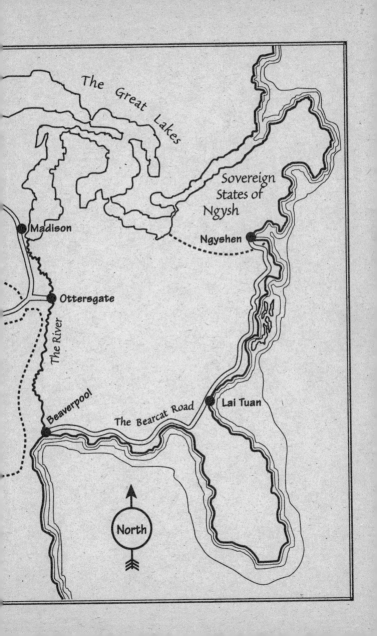

Chapter One

Skink's Luck

The morning sun shone bright over the forest, cool and tangy with the snap of early spring. Bobcat lay in the doorway of his tree stump and blinked for another moment. Then, with a yawn, he stretched himself outside onto the grass along the riverbank.

The River flowed quickly here, rocks tickling the shallow water and making it trip and laugh. Bobcat smiled at the leaf shadows dancing with the morning breeze over the River's surface, at the smell of the flowers' first bloom in the woods around him, at the birds just starting to call out, wishing one another a happy equinox and wondering if they could borrow each other's brooms to start their spring-cleaning.

He took a breath and puffed it out. A nice morning to be out without a hangover.

"Well, well, well," came a familiar voice from behind him, and Bobcat turned to see Garson Rix hopping out from the trees. "Usually when I pass here in the morning, all I get is snores. What, no catnip last night?"

She settled in the grass next to him, the sunlight catching the white swirls in her black fur, dazzling from the tips of her ears to the nub of her tail, and Bobcat suddenly wasn't sure if he was breathing or not. Oh, yes, definitely a nice morning to be out without a hangover.

He realized he was staring when Garson cocked her head at

him. "I don't know, though; you *are* looking a little glassy-eyed." She reached up a paw, pressed it to his nose. "Are you off the catnip?"

"Me?" Bobcat got ahold of himself and gave a laugh, but quietly, hoping she wouldn't pull her paw away. "Never. Though I haven't had a roll in three days, I'll have you know. You're a bad influence on me."

"Do tell." A smile spread through her whiskers, and a tingle spread over Bobcat's spine. "Well, if you're not busy tonight, I've got some more of that eggplant." She gave his nose a little tap. "I know it's not rabbit stew, but you seemed to like it last week."

He winced. "You're never gonna let me forget that stew crack, are you?"

Garson put a paw to her chin, seemed to consider for a moment, then shook her head. Bobcat let out a little growl. "Shouldn't you be at work, bunny? I understand they can't run the Farms without you."

"Just on my way, kitten." She stood and stretched, her ears spread, her nose twitching, her dark eyes half-closed. "Mmmm. Lovely morning, isn't it?"

"Yeah," he said, drinking her in. "Lovely."

She rubbed her whiskers, licked a paw, and started down the riverbank. "I'll see you tonight, then."

"If I'm not busy!" he called after her, but she just gave her cottony tail a flick, leaped to the first stepping-stone, and scurried from one to the next till she reached the opposite bank, Bobcat watching till she was lost in the trees.

Well, this morning just kept getting better and better. He yawned again and figured the best thing to do right now would be to wade across the River; find the biggest, laciest fern leaf he could; fold it into a net; fill it with mud, rocks, moss, and maybe a little tree sap; carry it up to Ree's Meadow; pick a bright yellow daisy to lay gently on top; carry the bundle through the woods to Rat's house; sneak inside; and dump the whole mess over the rodent's head. Bobcat was sure Rat wouldn't be up yet, and it would be a real shame for him to miss such a lovely morning.

Bobcat chuckled, moved down the bank, and slid into the

River. The stones in the bed slipped a little under his paws, but since the water here barely reached his chest, he just watched his step, leaned against the current, and enjoyed the coolness rushing through his fur. Out onto the other bank he waded, then shook himself, whole body first, then each paw—front, front, back, back—a quick flick of his tail, and he settled onto the warm rocks to lick his fur down.

But as he started on his left flank, he began to notice a strange little noise under the River's rushing and the leaves' rustling and the birds' warbling: a dry, whispery noise, like the wind sighing through an old and dying maple tree. Bobcat stopped, focused on the sound, and found that it was coming from a big, flat rock just down the bank.

Bobcat tapped a claw against his nose. Did he really want to know what Skink was up to this time? Sure, most of the words the lizard used went in one ear and out the other, but his weird stories were usually good for a laugh or two. . . .

So why not? Bobcat rose, padded over to the rock, and squatted down beside the mailbox to peer under. And there lay Skink curled around a pebble, his claws stroking it, his eyes closed, the dry, rustling moan Bobcat had heard keening from his parted lips.

For a while, Bobcat just watched, but finally he clicked his tongue and asked, "There some kinda problem here, Skink?"

Skink's eyes drew open. "Ohhh . . .," he said. "Ohhh. . . ."

"Ah." Bobcat nodded. "Well, that sure clears it up."

Skink was shaking his head. "Oh, Bobcat," he whispered. "It's terrible, just terrible. . . ."

Bobcat waited, but Skink only moaned again. Bobcat blew out a breath. "OK. Fine. Be that way. I got things to do, so I'll see you—"

"My luck, Bobcat. It's gone, just . . . gone. . . ."

"Your what?"

"My luck." Skink's voice broke, and a few drops trickled from the corners of his eyes. "Look." He grasped the pebble in his claws and held it up.

Bobcat looked at it. He looked at it again. He looked at it with one eye, then with the other. Each time, he saw a pebble, a small, not quite round pebble.

"See? My luck is gone." Skink let go another moan and wrapped himself around the pebble again.

"Uh-huh." Bobcat eyed the lizard for a moment. "Skink, you been under that rock too long; why don't you just come on out and get a little spring air into you? Believe me, you'll feel a lot better."

Skink was moving his head back and forth. "No, you don't understand. My grandmother, she said . . . she said that to lose your luck . . . She said it was too terrible, too terrible to contemplate, too terrible for everyone. She said—" And Skink's eyes sprang open, his whole body stiffening. He jumped up, shot out of his cave, and jerked to a stop pointing straight at Bobcat. "Ohhh!" he cried. "Ohhh!"

Bobcat stared, the fur prickling at the back of his neck.

"Bobcat!" Skink squeaked. "Bobcat! You've got to be careful! You've got to hide! You've got to go home right now and stay in bed for . . . I don't know, for a long time! If I've lost my luck . . . oh, Bobcat, you've got to!"

"Wait a minute; I what? What're you—"

"My grandmother, Bobcat! She said! She said that when she lost her luck something awful happened to Bobcat! And then, oh, then she said the worst thing in the world happened! The worst thing in the world!"

Bobcat rolled his eyes. "Ah. Another story."

"No, Bobcat, this comes straight from my grandmother! We've got to do something!"

"Skink, I—"

"Right now! Before it's too late!"

"Look, Skink; I've gotta—"

"No, Bobcat! You've got to listen! She said—"

"Lizard?" Bobcat let his claws spring out, crooked one till it just touched Skink's neck, and Skink froze, his eyes wide. "Now, you can have all the little fantasies you want; I don't care. But you leave me out of 'em, OK? The last thing I need is you mixing me up in some weird reptile story." Bobcat ran his claw slowly along Skink's side, but the lizard stayed just as cold and still as a stone. "Now, I got better things to do with my day than listen to some crazy lizard, so you have fun under your rock, OK? I gotta go."

Bobcat stood, turned, and padded back up the bank toward the woods, just shaking his head when Skink called to him. Then he only heard the birds singing, the River behind him splashing, the morning breeze rustling warm in the trees. And a dry sobbing now, very quiet, just underneath it all.

"Feh!" Bobcat snorted. He moved through the undergrowth and into the woods, the rushing of the River fading as he wound between the trees. It was still a nice morning, and he was determined not to give Skink another thought.

The forest floor spread cool and shady around him, spots of sun dappling the loam where they'd managed to dance down through the tree canopy. Birds practiced their spring melodies in the trees above him, and Bobcat started humming along. The scents of the forest wildflowers drifted past, spicing the air just the way he liked it.

After he'd finished with Rat, maybe he'd head upriver to Ottersgate. On a morning like this, Lorn Gedolkin would be setting up one of his water polo tourneys; Bobcat could spend the morning at the game, win a few bets, maybe check out the catnip at Jaybirds' Emporium. Or he could even head out to the woods around Donal's Lake, pick some of his own. Both Garson and wild catnip, what an evening *that* would make!

But first things first. The edge of the Brackens would be coming up here in a minute with its thick tangles of briers and blackberries and, most important, the best fern leaves north of the grottoes around Beaverpool. Then it'd be on to Ree's Meadow and the raw materials, up to Rat's house, and there the start of a perfect day.

Warned by the smell of blackberry blossoms, Bobcat slowed his pace. A few more steps, and he came out from under the tree canopy; the forest floor ended in an abrupt but fairly gentle drop-off, and Bobcat was looking out over the shallow brier-choked valley known as the Brackens.

The sharp sea of underbrush made him smile. He knew this place pretty well, had chased plenty of rabbits out here before

Garson had, well, before the two of them had come to an understanding, and the ferns he had in mind were just north of where he stood. So he started along the edge of the bluff, took another lungful of blackberry scent . . .

And stopped, the fur along the back of his neck prickling.

He shook his head, sniffed again . . .

And got nothing. No smell. At all. The blackberries, the wildflowers, the tree sap, the mulch of the forest floor, even his own scent, they were all gone.

Bobcat blinked, sat down, wiped at his nose, but it didn't help. There was just nothing in the air.

A little thought gave him the answer, though: he must have stirred up a lot of dirt on his way through the woods, and it was clogging his nose. That was it. He smiled. When he got to the ferns, he could use a few to blow the ol' sniffer clear, and then everything'd be back to normal.

That settled, he was about to stand and get on his way when he noticed how quiet it had become; the breeze wasn't rustling the leaves anymore, and in the silence not a chirp, not a whistle, not an insect's buzz nor a lizard's scuffling. He twitched his ears back and forth, but he couldn't even hear his own breathing, the silence thick around him, heavier and deeper than the silence of those long winter midnights when he was too wasted to sleep and too tired to move and could only stare at the walls and wait for the dawn. . . .

Bobcat shook his head. Could everyone have gone somewhere? But where? And why? He would have smelled a forest fire, and the birds would be calling alarms from every treetop. The same with a flood, and the River had seemed calm enough earlier. It just didn't make sense.

He stood and blinked, trying to think, and slowly began to notice something else. It was happening so gradually that he had to stare hard before he was sure, but . . . but . . .

Everything green, the wild grass, the leaves overhead, the sprouts and buds and every tiny berry, all were changing color, were fading to a dull, overcast gray. And as all the green seeped away, Bobcat watched the blue of the sky become a sickly white, like the white in the eyes of a boiled fish.

Panic tickled his chest, but he pushed it down with a swallow. A catnip flashback, that's what this had to be. Sudden dizzy spells, fits of uncontrollable laughter, manic twitching, he'd had them all, and this couldn't be anything but some new, weird kind. He forced another swallow. All he had to do was sit in this gray, scentless silence, breathe evenly, and it would pass after a while. It always did.

So when the leaves and sprouts and buds kept changing, their dank gray continuing to deepen, Bobcat blew out a breath, settled back, and waited for the green to return.

But it didn't. Instead of green, as Bobcat stared the forest around him slowly turned a thick, dark red, a tide the color of blood washing through the trees and over the ground.

That was it. Heart fluttering like a sparrow's, nothing left in his mouth to swallow, he only wanted to run back to the River, run back and throw himself in and wash the silence from his ears and the redness from his eyes; he'd even leaped to his paws, ready to take off into the woods, when a sound reached him, the first he'd heard in minutes.

A smile pulled his whiskers. Was the flashback over?

But the sound seemed odd, a low rumbling behind him getting louder every second, getting louder and more coherent till he recognized it, his hackles rising and his pupils going wide. It wasn't a rumbling; it was a growling, a deep and angry growling. And it was coming closer.

Breath quick and shallow, fear an acid taste on his tongue, redness pouring into his eyes and growling into his ears, all thought of running vanished. He sat frozen, his whole body trembling, nothing left in the world as far as he could tell but this vast, red, disembodied anger.

And it wanted him to turn around. How he knew that, he had no idea, but in a way that he had never known anything before he knew that the thing behind him wanted him to turn, was demanding that he turn and face it.

He couldn't stop his paws. He inched around and raised his head and looked back along the edge of the bluff. . . .

And it was there.

A blinding yellow-orange it blazed, a solid mass of fire brighter than the sun standing at midday but spotted all over with black rings as charred and dead as burned tree branches. Mind spinning, he heard the growling deepen, and the flames flowed into the figure of a huge cat, towering over him, its tail lashing the bloody undergrowth and its eyes, oh, its eyes, searing down with the deep and raging reds of an onrushing forest fire.

The fire of those eyes swept over him, and with a roar like thunder the thing sprang. Ebon claws flashed from a paw bigger than his whole head and slapped him aside with a force that knocked the wind out of him, sent him tumbling and gasping, and pitched him over the edge of the bluff down into the brambles, thorns snagging and tearing his fur, till he hit the ground under the bushes with a splintering crash.

A stink of blood and singed fur filled his nose, made him sneeze, and shocked him to awareness, the afterglow of fire and claws and terrible burning eyes flashing before him every time he blinked. He was lying on his side, and when he moved to drag himself into a sitting position the dirt rubbing into what felt like hundreds of cuts made him grit his teeth almost as much as the pinpricks of circulation returning to his paws. He forced several shaky breaths, then raised his head and traced the path of his descent back up the slope through the litter of broken branches to the top of the incline.

Birds sang in the trees, he could hear, the leaves green and rustling in the morning breeze once more. The sky shone blue, the air again sweet with blackberry scent, but mixed now with the sour stench of his own fear.

Most important, though, that impossible, horrible cat thing was gone.

Bobcat wanted to go home. He wanted to go home, pile all the furniture against the door, and stuff his nose with any scrap of catnip he could find, just turn his mind off, not have to think, and go far, far away for a very long time.

But he stayed crouched under the brambles. That thing could be hiding somewhere, waiting for him. It could even be waiting back home, waiting because it knew he would want to get all cat-nipped up. He would be completely defenseless then, and it would tear him to tiny shreds.

That was it, Bobcat was sure; those eyes still burning at the back of his head made him feel certain that the monster was play-ing with him. And here he was, cowering like a rabbit in the brier patch.

He almost laughed at that, but the sound caught in his throat, those eyes boiling it away to nothing and fear locking his mind up again. What could it have been?

No. He shook his head, tried to clear his thoughts. He needed to think, needed a plan, but the pain in his sides made those eyes blaze up, made the shaking start; it was out there waiting, waiting for him. . . .

"Stop it!" he hissed, pounding his paws against the ground. He had to get ahold of himself, had to think about something else, *anything* else: about the trees, which might turn red again; about the breeze, which might disappear at any moment; about the flashing claws, the horrible eyes, the angry growling of that fiery monster—

"No! No! No!" he shouted, grasping for anything in his head that wasn't that giant cat, . . . and there he found another giant cat, someone he hadn't thought about in years. He grabbed at the memories, pounced and held them fast, pushed out every other thought, forced himself to be there, two decades ago, slogging through the snow. . . .

The snow of his first winter after running away from home, a winter that had turned into the worst in generations. Pushing through the drifts, soaked to the skin, knowing that the dark clouds creeping up the valley behind him held another storm, he had staggered on, and just as the wind began to grow wet he had stumbled into a cave, sprawled onto the floor, not even seeing the huge paws in front of his nose for a minute or two. But when he had and had raised his head, had found himself staring up at a tawny cat ten times his size . . .

He had cowered there while the old lioness muttered about throwing him out, but she'd finally picked him up and set him beside the fire. Shemka Harr she had called herself—it meant "ancient teacher," Bobcat later learned—and she had dubbed him Ghareen, the word for snow where she came from.

During that whole long winter, they had played riddle games, caught cave fish, and foraged whenever the storms let up. She had taught him some of the language of her homeland, the great southern Savannah, and had filled the cave with stories of the Twelve Curials and the heroic folk of earlier times. Everything flooded back to Bobcat crouched there under the brambles: her rumbling voice, her musky scent, the way she would cock her head as she told him about the Lady Raven and the phases of the moon, about the Lord Lion's mane shining down over the earth by day, all the stories she had spun by the fire.

And he heard her say, as she had after every tale, "But you want to know the truth?"

That was when she would tell him how the sun was actually a star like those in the night sky only a lot closer, how the moon was really a giant chunk of rock, how all these stories about the Curials were just stories. She would get this sour look on her face and poke a huge paw at him. "There aren't any Curials to come bail you out," she would say, "so you have to learn to do it yourself, you hear me, Ghareen? In this whole world, there's nothing you can't do if you set your mind to it, take it step-by-step, and think it through."

Think it through. Bobcat blew out a breath. That advice had saved his life more times than he could count, and holding close to Shemka Harr's memories, he swallowed and turned his mind to that cat thing again.

First off, what could it have been? Some sort of creature, some wild animal he'd never heard of before? Creatures did attack folk sometimes, but usually only to eat them, something that monster could have done easily. No, there had been something behind those burning eyes, something that had known what it was doing, something that was neither creature nor folk.

But what else was there? Whom could he go ask? Who would

even believe what had happened to him? He had told a few wild stories in the past when some bad catnip had gotten hold of him, so who would believe him now?

The answer came to him at once, and his hackles rose. "Skink!" he shouted. He clawed his way out from beneath the blackberry bushes, the thorns gouging his torn-up fur, scrambled to the top of the slope, pulled himself over the edge, and took off into the forest toward the River. Skink had said something terrible was going to happen, had *known* that monster was going to be there, and Bobcat was going to find out how.

Through the trees Bobcat ran, the pain digging at his sides with every leap. Soon he could smell the River, hear its rapids, and the trees fell away as he clattered out onto the rocky riverbank. Racing along the stones to Skink's rock, he bounded up, stuffed a paw underneath, and wrenched the lizard out. "All right," he growled. "You tell me. Now."

Skink's eyes bulged, his legs wheeling frantically. "Bobcat!" he squeaked. "What . . . what . . . ?"

"Now! You tell me what that thing was!"

Skink stopped flailing. "You mean," he whispered, "you mean it happened?"

Bobcat squeezed harder. "Do I start tearing off legs?"

"No! Please! I don't know! You have to understand!"

"You knew enough earlier!"

"I tried to warn you! I did! Please! I . . . can't . . . breathe. . . ."

Bobcat considered, then relaxed his grip a bit. "All right, you did. So tell me the rest."

"I will! I will! But please . . . set me down. I'll . . . I'll tell you what I know, what my grandmother said. . . ."

Bobcat looked at the lizard for a moment, then set him on top of his rock. Skink sat very still, only a slight fluttering of his sides showing that he was alive. Bobcat waited a minute, then said, "So start talking."

Skink blinked once. "It was a long time ago," he began, "back when I was just a hatchling. You see, every month, my family gathers at the kiva by Donal's Lake for the Semurlyenn, the festival celebrating the Lord Eft's explanation of—"

"Do I look like I care? I wanna know—!"

"And you will, Bobcat. For it was on those festival days that Grandmother would tell us her stories. Before dinner, my brothers and sisters and all my cousins, we would go into the kiva to the fire pit where Grandmother sat, and she would tell us about all the things she had seen and done. She was very old, you see, old even among my folk, and she would tell us about the early mouse clans, about the coming of the otters, about Ong Gedolkin and the founding of Ottersgate, about her adventures all up and down the River." Skink paused. "She was quite remarkable."

"Uh-huh. But what about—"

"I am coming to that, Bobcat. Late one winter night, Uncle came to our house and said that Grandmother was very ill. She wanted to see us all one last time, so my parents woke us, and we followed Uncle back to Grandmother's house. The rest of the family was already there, and we all stood in Grandmother's room as the adults sang the Final Welcome song.

"When they were done, Grandmother asked the adults please to leave, for she had one more story for the children. My parents and aunts and uncles all bowed and went out into the front of the house, and my brothers and sisters and cousins and I all sat down around Grandmother's bed and waited. I can still remember I've never heard anything so quiet as the silence in that room that night.

"Finally, Grandmother raised her head and spoke, and her voice was so gray, it made me shiver. And she said, 'There's one last story, my little ones, one last story, the story I wish I never had to tell. It's an old story about three folk and a failure that leads to death. It's a story I once had to live and a story one of you may someday have to live, though I pray the Lord Eft that it might pass you all by. . . .'

"For a long while she was silent, and I remember wondering if she had already died, but she spoke up again. 'I will tell you how it begins,' she said, 'in hopes that you might somehow change the ending. If you should lose your luck—and I pray it may never happen, for it is too terrible to contemplate, too terrible for everyone—but should you ever lose your luck, watch for Bobcat. An awful thing will happen to him, and after that will come the worst thing in the world. You will have to go to Fisher to try to stop it from happening, and I pray you do better than we did. Remember this well, my little ones. I love you all. . . .'

"Her voice faded away and dropped to nothing. My eldest sister called out for our parents, but by the time the adults arrived, Grandmother was dead.

"And then this morning, I woke to find my luck was gone. I was so distraught, I could not think, but when you came along I remembered the rest of Grandmother's words and tried to warn you. But now, we'll have to go see Fisher."

Bobcat closed his eyes. "Fisher. I shoulda known that witch'd have something to do with this." His anger and fear had dribbled away during Skink's story, and all he had left were his aches.

"Bobcat?" he heard Skink say. He let his eyes roll open and saw the lizard standing at the edge of his rock. "You should wash those cuts, or they may become infected. When we get there, Fisher can put something on them for you."

"Yeah. . . ." Bobcat pushed himself up, his sides throbbing with every breath, and padded down the riverbank into the chest-high water. It did feel good, and he bent back to lick at the cuts. The water rushed past, dirty hair and blood swirling away downstream, and the pain in his sides slowly lost its biting edge, still a sharp pain, sure, but now at least it was a clean one.

When he was finished, Bobcat pulled himself back onto the bank and gave one quick shake, his head too light for more than that. Settling down on the warm stones next to Skink's rock, he let the morning sun work into his fur and tried not to wince at those burning eyes flashing with each blink.

But a moment later, he heard Skink's voice saying, "Well, are you ready to go?"

Bobcat looked over. The lizard stood perched on the edge of the rock, a satchel slung over his back, his head cocking from one side to the other, the motion making Bobcat's stomach roll. "Stop that," he said, looking away.

"Stop what?"

"Never mind. What're you talking about? Go where?"

Skink made a clicking noise. "Weren't you listening? Grandmother said we have to go see Fisher."

This struck Bobcat as funny, so he let a little laugh start up in the back of his throat. "Can you gimme a minute here? It's not every day I find out I'm a key player in—what?—some kinda ancient reptile prophecy." The laugh got bigger, so he let more of it out. "I mean other than go see Fisher, what're we s'posed to do?"

"Grandmother was less than clear on that, I admit, but—"

Bobcat laughed louder and hauled himself up. "OK! Long as we know what we're doing! And . . . and we have to see Fisher to do this?"

Skink nodded again.

"Great! That's great! Oh, and . . . and don't tell me: she'll be expecting us, right?"

"I don't think so." Skink cocked his head. "But I'm sure that once we explain—"

"Explain? Right! That's it! Explain! Maybe someone can explain it to *me* sometime!"

"Bobcat, I already told you what Grandmother—"

"Yeah! OK! I'm ready!" The laughter shook him so hard he could scarcely keep on his paws. "I mean my day's shot, giant flaming monsters trying to eat me and ev'rything! So, yeah! Let's . . . let's do something stupid instead! Let's go see Fisher and tell her . . . tell her all about it, OK? What a trip!" He gasped around the laughter. "Whadda I need catnip for?" And Bobcat laughed and laughed and laughed till his eyes dripped and his cuts clanged like sharp steel bells.

Skink was staring. "Are you sure you're all right?"

Bobcat tried to answer, tried to take a breath, but the laughter just stripped it away. His eyes wouldn't work and his nose had gone dead and his sides were on fire and that monster was waiting for him somewhere, and all he could do was laugh louder and louder. Those horrible eyes burned in his head, set his brain sparking and fluttering, twisting him around as only his worst catnip flashbacks ever had.

Flashback? With his last thought, Bobcat threw himself forward and slammed his head against Skink's rock once, twice, a third time. The pain made him gasp, and before his laughter could snatch the breath away he let fly the loudest scream he could, clenching his body and shrieking till the forest echoed with it, till the birds stopped singing in the trees. The scream emptied his lungs, cleared his eyes, and Bobcat lay where he'd sprawled, waiting for the laughter to come back; the last time he'd had a fit like this, it had taken another couple of good bashes to settle him down.

But a quiet minute went by, so Bobcat got to his paws. "No," he said to Skink, staring frozen from atop his rock. "No, I'm not all right. Let's go, huh?"

Skink stayed still, a few birds starting to call again in the trees before he blinked. "It will be faster if I ride on your back," he said.

"Yeah, whatever." Bobcat crouched down beside the rock. "We'll stick to the River till we get to Ottersgate, then cut inland. And don't tell me it'll be faster going past the Brackens 'cause I don't wanna hear it." Bobcat glared until he felt Skink clamber up and settle in the fur between his shoulder blades. "You ready?"

A small "yes" from behind him, and Bobcat grimaced, stood up, and started north along the River.

It was usually one of his favorite walks, and he tried to let his mind wander into the blue of the morning, to enjoy the warmth of the sun and the tumbling of the River, but those eyes burned their way into everything. The green of the trees only reminded him of the redness that had seeped into them; every time the birds took a break or the leaves overhead stopped rustling, Bobcat would tense up, thinking that awful silence was falling over him again, and of course he couldn't ignore the throbbing of the cuts all up and down his sides.

"I hate this!" Bobcat snapped when he couldn't keep quiet another second. "You know that? I mean this was gonna be a nice morning! I had stuff to do, plans to make, folks to see, everything! This whole thing just makes me twitch!"

He felt the lizard stir between his shoulder blades. "I do not understand. We are only doing what we must."

Bobcat growled. He should just dump the lizard off right here and go home; there was probably a quarter-roll of catnip in a cupboard somewhere, enough to smother the fire of those eyes for a couple hours at least. But then they flared into his thoughts again, made him stumble like a sudden blast of wind, and he knew he couldn't go home. That cat monster had put its eyes in his head to watch him, to let him know it was still out there waiting for him, that he couldn't ignore it.

He growled again. But he kept on walking.

Soon the River began to widen, and Ottersgate rose up in the middle, the Bailey Oak towering from the center of the island and covering the houses and shops along the whole west side of town with its shadow. The blankets and umbrellas of folks claiming their spots for the water polo to come already dotted the grass and sand of the park at South Point, laughter floating across the water to Bobcat's ears from young otters and mice and birds scampering away from their parents and splashing into the River.

Bobcat followed the curve of the riverbank, and the rocks became the sandy shore of the West Channel. Along the beach sat the warehouses of the Ottersgate Transport Service, all but one closed and locked today, their barges up in dry dock beside them. The only open warehouse had a group of otters lolling around in front of it; one of them looked up, gave a shrill whistle, and bounded over the sand toward Bobcat.

"Bobby, Bobby, Bobby!" The otter slid up beside him. "I was afraid we'd have to start without you!"

"Sorry, Lorn. I . . . well, I guess I got caught up in some other stuff." Bobcat saw Lorn's brow wrinkle, saw his gaze tracing the cuts along Bobcat's sides, and Bobcat tried not to wince. "Trust me—you don't wanna know."

Lorn Gedolkin flashed his famous smile, but his eyes were still worried. "Trust you? Bobby, at all times. Now that you're here, though . . ." The otter let off another shattering whistle. "Let the games begin!"

The group of otters tumbled down the sand and splashed whooping into the West Channel. A ball popped out of the water, and the otters began passing it around, batting at it with paws and snouts and tails. Trec Sinpatclin, still in his orange straw boss vest, came out of the warehouse with a goal box made of wood and old nets, and Bobcat could see Desh Rennif across the Channel on the Ottersgate side fastening a similar box to the sand.

"Oh, Bobby. . . ." Bobcat swung his head back to Lorn; the otter nodded toward Bobcat's back. "Who's your friend?"

"Oh, yeah. Lorn, this is Skink. Skink, Lorn Gedolkin."

Bobcat felt Skink shift around. "It is an honor to meet you," the lizard said, "not only a descendant of the famed founder of Ottersgate, but also its current mayor. May the peace and prosperity of the Twelve visit you and your city."

"It is an honor to meet *you*," Lorn answered, "a follower in the ancient and noble line of the Curial Lord Eft. May his luck and longevity come to you and your family." Lorn smiled again. "So much for the formalities. You come to watch the games, Skink?"

"I'm afraid we cannot," Skink said. "Bobcat and I have some business elsewhere we must attend to."

The otter turned back to Bobcat. "Bobby! You're skipping out on us?"

Bobcat's sides were itching. "Yeah, well, something weird's come up. Just believe me, I'd rather be here."

Lorn shook his head. "You're really going to miss it, Bobby. Coll Belverdeen's up from Beaverpool, and Ewell swears she's gonna keep him to under three goals."

"Belverdeen?" Bobcat winced. "Well, wish her luck. Or better yet, put fifteen on her for me, will you?"

"Fifteen?"

"Hey, I'm good for it."

"You? Since when?"

Bobcat flicked a paw at him. "Lorn, when have I ever—"

"I know; I know. I just don't want you throwing my money away; the bookies have her at—"

"Stuff the bookies. If anyone can hold Belverdeen, you know it's Ewell." Bobcat smiled. "Trust me on this one."

Lorn laughed. "Well, that settles it. Fifteen on Ewell for you, and fifteen on Ewell for me." He turned to face Skink. "I'm sorry you couldn't stay, Skink. Perhaps some other time?"

"I would like that, Mayor Gedolkin. May the Twelve watch over you and your city."

"And may the Lord Eft keep and follow you. You take care, too, Bobby." He poked Bobcat's shoulder, and with another whistle, the otter was over the sand and into the water.

Bobcat watched him go. "Belverdeen," he said, shaking his head.

"Hmmm?" he heard Skink ask from behind him. "Did you say something, Bobcat?"

Bobcat turned away from the otters warming up. "No, I didn't say a thing."

He'd padded up the beach and was passing between the warehouses when Skink spoke again: "The mayor seems like a nice fellow. I just hope he wasn't too embarrassed."

"Embarrassed? Whadda you mean? By what?"

"Well, it's just that, according to proper etiquette, you should have introduced me to him before you introduced him to me."

Bobcat had to stop. "What?"

"I'm sure he saw that you were distraught, and—"

"Etiquette? Did you just say etiquette?" He twisted around to glare at Skink. "I'm missing the greatest water polo match since Willa Maferty went head-to-head with Sif Apperton, and you're talking to me about etiquette? This is all your fault! If you hadn't started in with your lost luck and your weird story and your 'worst thing in the world,' I could be at that game right now! I hate this! Have I told you that? You and your grandma and your stories, none of it makes any sense! None of it! Any! At all!"

Out of the warehouses Bobcat stalked, still grumbling, and weaved through the crowds coming down the Meerkat Road into Ottersgate. He crossed the road and was halfway across Ree's Meadow before Skink asked, "But if you don't believe Grandmother's story, why are you coming with me?"

Bobcat stopped in the middle of the meadow. The flowers shimmered in the midmorning sun, their perfume softening the breeze that ruffled his fur. He could hear cheers from the polo match, vendors shouting, laughter and singing from the folks crossing the West Bridge into Ottersgate.

But Bobcat shivered, those eyes smoldering inside him. "I don't know," he said at last. "Whatever happened to me today, it . . . it just keeps on happening, like it got stuck in my head or something; I don't know. But I've gotta get rid of it, get some kinda handle on it anyway, or it'll drive me crazy. It was . . . was . . . I don't know what it was, but I've gotta do something about it. When you told me it was gonna happen, I didn't listen. Now you say go see Fisher." He shrugged. "So here I go."

Skink didn't respond. Bobcat turned away from the sounds and scents of Ottersgate and set off for the woods above town.

Chapter Two

Plague Year

Bobcat knew where Fisher lived, but he'd never thought he'd actually be going there. The way she looked at him always made him feel itchy, like she wasn't looking at him so much as *through* him, straight down to his innards.

North and slightly west through the woods he padded, Skink a slight weight gripped into the fur between his shoulder blades, until they came out into a clearing with a gnarled sycamore clumped down in the center. "This is the place," Bobcat said, waving a paw at the tree.

He felt Skink clamber up onto his neck. "I see. Then we'd best announce ourselves."

"No problem." Bobcat cleared his throat and shouted, "Hey, Fisher! You got visitors!"

Branches rustled about halfway up, and Bobcat saw Fisher's dark face peering through the leaves. "Bobcat?" he heard her mutter; then she shouted, "Whadda you want?"

"Oh, don't get me started!" Bobcat yelled back, but Skink gave a hiss into his ear.

"Bobcat, please!" The lizard then raised his voice and called out, "A good day to you, Fisher! I'd be more than happy to explain why we're here, but I think it might be easier on us all if we didn't have to shout at one another! Should we come up, or would you rather come down?"

Bobcat saw Fisher lean out of the foliage and her brow furrow. "Skink? What the . . . ?" She was silent for a second. "OK, sure. I'll be right down."

The branches rustled again, and her face disappeared from the leaves. Bobcat could hear the scritch-scratch of her making her way down the trunk; then she dropped to the ground and sauntered over to them. "This is unexpected."

"You're telling me," Bobcat muttered, but Skink had already started speaking.

"Unfortunately," the lizard began, scuttling down Bobcat's leg to stand in the grass in front of Fisher, "this is not entirely a social call. We have need of your professional advice and perhaps even your assistance."

Bobcat could see that Fisher was trying not to smile. "Do tell," she said. "In what way?"

"Well, you see, I've lost my luck."

All trace of Fisher's smile vanished. "Your luck? How?"

"That I do not know. But," he opened his satchel and pulled out his pebble, "as you can see, it is certainly gone."

Fisher crouched down, stared close at the pebble for a moment, then nodded slowly. "That's weird. It's almost like it'd never even been there." She stood and shrugged. "I'm sorry to hear it, Skink, but I don't see how I can help."

"Oh, but it's not just that," the lizard went on. "Something has happened to Bobcat as well."

"Really?" Fisher's eyes moved to Bobcat's, and he saw her almost-smile came back. "I find that hard to believe. How could anything possibly happen to Bobcat?"

Her voice made Bobcat's sides itch, and that made his cuts hurt. "And whadda you mean by that?"

Fisher shrugged. "Nothing. Just curious is all."

"Yeah, right. Look, witch; I've had it up to here with weirdness today, OK? I didn't wanna come out here; I coulda lived my whole life without coming out here, but—"

"But here you are," Fisher cut in. "So whadda you want?"

Bobcat took one look at her and closed his mouth. She wouldn't believe him; he almost didn't believe it himself anymore.

Maybe the whole thing had been some really vicious sort of flash-back. Maybe he'd just plain panicked and thrown himself into the Brackens. That made a lot more sense than Skink and his grandma did. Maybe he *had* imagined it.

He was vaguely aware that Skink had stepped in and was telling Fisher his whole Grandma story, but Bobcat wasn't really paying attention. Those eyes had sparked up again, glowing like coals inside his head, and he knew there was no way he could have imagined them. That monster and its eyes, they were burned too deeply into him for that.

Bobcat shuddered and tried to listen to Skink, but those eyes, those eyes, those . . . eyes . . . Not in his most twisted catnip dream had he ever seen anything as awful as those eyes. He didn't want to think about them, but they wouldn't go away, flaring up like a summer brush fire slashing through the undergrowth. He could almost feel them, their heat whirling around him, their flames licking into his fur. . . .

And then fire was shooting out of the ground and into the sky, roaring enormous up the sides of the trees, crackling through the grass, the smoke billowing in clouds of black blood, filling the air and making him choke and cough. He wanted to run, but there was no place to go; the smoke clawed at his eyes and the air was too hot to breathe and there was nothing anywhere but sheets of flame—

Except now tiny pinpricks, sharp and icy, were digging at the sides of his head, and the molten fire surging over him was pierced by two spots of dark coolness. Bobcat grabbed at the spots and pulled, the sharp points seeming to guide him toward them. Bigger and bigger they grew, quenching the flames and resolving themselves into another pair of eyes, but eyes as deep and calm as mountain pools. And he heard a voice now, growing with the eyes, a voice saying, "That's it; just slow down: slow breaths, in, out, in, out, that's right. . . ."

Bobcat could hear himself panting wildly. He tried to shake his head, to get some kind of grip on himself, but something had hold of him. He blinked once and realized he was staring straight into Fisher's face, their noses almost touching, her claws the sharp points beneath his ears. A second blink, and he saw that his front paws had just as tight a grip on the sides of her head.

A third blink went by before Bobcat could make himself let go, and by that time Fisher had loosed her claws and was taking a step back.

Bobcat could hear Skink rustling and squeaking somewhere: "See? See? I said it was something awful; didn't I say it was something awful? Just like Grandmother said; didn't I tell you? And then the worst thing in the world! What'll we do? What'll we do?"

"Do?" Fisher said, her eyes wide and staring at Bobcat. "First, you can hush up. And second, you can sit still."

Bobcat had to blink a few more times before he could cough out, "No more, please, no more. It's gotta stop; I don't know, but it's gotta, that's all." The fire was still burning all along his cuts, and he just wanted to collapse somewhere. He forced his head to stay up, though, his eyes to stay on Fisher. "You gotta do something; I don't care what, just . . . something., . . ."

Fisher nodded. "Can you climb?"

"I don't know; gods, what a question." That bubbling laughter wanted to start up in the back of his throat, but he clamped down on it. "Whatever. Just point me the right way."

"All right. Skink, up on my back. Straight ahead, Bobcat; we'll be right behind you."

Bobcat stumbled forward, his legs prickling like they were asleep. Then he was at the sycamore and climbing up its trunk. Fisher's voice came from below: "The patio. To your right." He looked, saw some planking among the branches, and pushed himself over onto it.

It smelled nice, the patio did, sycamore leaves draping overhead, and Bobcat settled down to let the quiet seep into his fur. He heard Fisher's claws scrabbling against the bark, heard her and Skink say a few words to each other, but he wasn't really listening: the eyes had shrunk to the back of his head, and he was concentrating on the breeze that whispered through the sycamore's branches, on the shadows that stirred over his fur, on keeping those awful flames contained.

* * *

Hey," came Fisher's voice from in front of him. Bobcat let his eyes roll open and saw Fisher taking a glass jar out of her satchel. "I'm gonna put some of this on your cuts. It might sting a little, but it'll keep 'em from going septic."

"Sure, whatever."

The stuff went on cool and smooth, and the pain in his sides sank slowly, the fire of those eyes lessening a bit more. He took some deep breaths and somehow managed to unclench everything.

Fisher came around in front of him again and stretched herself out along the planking, her elbow cushioned on her satchel. Bobcat avoided her gaze. After some silence, she asked, "So what happened?"

Bobcat almost laughed. "Uh-uh. I'm not gonna do that again. I leave it alone, maybe it'll leave me alone."

"You sure 'bout that? You talk it out, there'll be the three of us here instead of just you—"

"No way. Not again."

"I'm telling you, Bobcat—"

"Just drop it!" Bobcat snarled, leaping to his paws. "I don't need this! Any of it! Any of you or that lizard or his stories or his grandma or any of it! Nothing makes sense anymore! Nothing! And if I think about it, it'll all come back and maybe it'll get me this time, see? So no, I don't wanna talk about it, OK? Not now, not ever! So just drop it!"

Fisher blinked once. "Whatever." She turned to Bobcat's right, and as Bobcat lay back down, he saw Skink crouching on the patio next to him. "Skink, about this stuff your grandma told you, this 'worst thing in the world' and all, she said she had lived through it, right? So when do you figure it actually happened to her?"

Skink didn't move for a second or two; then his head snapped over to look at Fisher. "I've given this a great deal of thought over the years, and I've come to believe that the actual time at which it took place is of no real importance."

"Really? And why's that?"

"Well, you'll understand that this is just a theory of mine, but I believe that what Grandmother told us is some form of a previously unknown Cyclical Myth."

Fisher rubbed her whiskers. "OK, I can see that. We've got—what?—the signs to be watched for and the things to be done? And I guess the final unifying action, but—"

"Wait a minute," Bobcat cut in. "Did we switch to another language here?"

Fisher sighed. "Is there a problem?"

"Problem? Yeah, I'd say that. What in the bright blue above you're talking about, for one thing."

"I'm sorry, Bobcat." Skink twitched his head over. "You see, I'm adapting some principles from the Philosophy of History. Perhaps you remember from your school days how—"

"My school days?" Bobcat coughed out a laugh. "Lizard, I was only in school till I could outrun my mom and pop, and I haven't been near a school or them since."

Skink's mouth stayed open, but no sound came out, his stare unblinking and focused on Bobcat.

Bobcat stared back, and the silence went on for a moment; then, "OK, look," Fisher said. "The Cyclical Myths are old reptile stories about how and why things work. Basically they say that everything in nature is patterned in cycles and these cycles are controlled by the Twelve Curials. You have heard of the Twelve Curials, haven't you?"

"Course I have," Bobcat snapped. The stories Shemka Harr had told him so many years ago drifted into his mind again. "You mean like how the Lord Leopard comes around at the beginning of autumn to put his spots on all the leaves? Or how the Lady Dolphin swims through the clouds to make it rain? Those stories?"

"Yeah, those're some of 'em. See, the Lord Eft explained how things worked to the first Elders of the first kiva just after the world was made, and they've handed the stories down since then. As time went on, the stories got outta the reptile communities, and folks really liked 'em. They told 'em over and over until they got to be just stories—y'know, bedtime and fireside tales to keep the cubs amused."

"Wait a minute." Bobcat narrowed his eyes. "They *are* just stories. You . . . you're saying you believe that stuff?"

"The stories?" Fisher shook her head. "Most of 'em are the bunk. The Curials, though, I've met a couple of 'em."

Bobcat stared at her. She wasn't smiling. But she couldn't be serious, could she? Bobcat hadn't believed in the gods even when he was a kitten; could Fisher be crazy enough to think she'd actually met them?

He still hadn't made up his mind when she spoke again: "Anyway, these stories all have a certain shape to 'em, certain ways you can tell you're dealing with a Cyclical Myth. Even the real complicated ones, like the Lord Tiger's pursuit of the Justice Beast, have the same basic structure as all those two-minute Lady Squirrel stories. What Skink's saying is that his grandma's story has some of the same elements as a classic Cyclical Myth." She shrugged again. "For all that's worth. I just don't see that it helps us any."

"Oh, but it does," Skink piped up. "If we *are* involved in a Cyclical Myth, it will prove the case for Curial intervention. Many in my own kiva argue against the Curial powers involving themselves in the affairs of earthly folk; they state that the Curial powers keep the world turning for their own benefit, that our devotions to the Lord Eft are pointless. But since all Cyclical Myths involve the Curial powers, if Grandmother's story continues to follow the pattern, then the powers will have to involve themselves, especially with the worst thing in the world coming. I would even say—"

"Yeah, OK," Fisher cut in, "but I don't care about proving anybody's theory. I just wanna know what this 'worst thing in the world' is and how we fit into it."

"Wait a minute." Bobcat could see he'd be saying that a lot with these two. "You don't know? I thought . . . Aren't you s'posed to . . . Isn't that why we came here? Isn't that what Skink's grandma said?"

Skink raised an arm. "Not exactly, Bobcat. Grandmother merely said we were to go to Fisher."

"But . . . but why else would we come out here?"

Fisher was tapping her claws on the planking. "If you'd just keep quiet for a couple of minutes, I might be able to figure that out. That OK with you?"

Bobcat bristled, then pulled his mouth shut and nodded.

"Good," Fisher went on. "OK, Skink, we're gonna need some background info on your grandma."

"Certainly."

"Now, she was an adventurer, right? The skink Ong Gedolkin talks about in his books about founding Ottersgate?"

Skink smiled. "Yes, Grandmother had quite a collection of stories to tell, and most of them concerned adventures she had participated in."

"So what was her earliest adventure?"

"Earliest? Well, I recall a story she told us concerning her being washed down River in the floods when she was six; that was the first time she crossed paths with Red Chilliri, the River pirate. She always said that from that day on she knew she was supposed to be an adventurer."

"And her last adventure?"

Skink rubbed his chin. "That would be the avalanche story; she was exploring some caves up north for a mining interest, and they collapsed. She said she made a deal with the Lord Eft that if he would let her live through it, she would settle down for good. He did, and she did."

"So, how many years are we talking from first to last?"

"Well, the floods were in 1577, and the avalanche was just before my clutch's hatchday in 1707. That makes 130 years, all told."

Bobcat gave a low whistle. "When you said she was old, I didn't know you meant *old.*"

"Oh, yes," Skink said with a nod. "She died just after her 140th hatchday."

There was a short silence; then Fisher started in again. "But the real question is: was there a time in there when she didn't go adventuring for a while?"

Skink blinked a few times. "Didn't go adventuring?"

"Yeah. I mean think about what she said. She'd had a chance to stop the worst thing in the world from happening. But she said she'd failed, so whatever this worst thing was, it must've happened. Now, that'd make me slow down, at least for a couple months."

"That's very true. . . ." Skink looked into the distance. "Well, the only time I can think of was after she married Grandfather and hatched their first clutch. She always said that she wasn't really sure how to do things that first time, so she stayed home and performed all the proper matronly duties. But after that, she'd just swing by, drop the eggs, and pop out again; she said she was lucky Grandfather was so good with children. That's the only break I can remember."

Fisher smiled. "I'm sorry I never got to meet your grandma. So what years are we talking here?"

"Let's see. Grandmother married Grandfather in 1624, and their first clutch hatched out in 1630."

Fisher's brow furrowed. "Sixteen twenty-four . . . ," she muttered.

Bobcat stared at her. "What?"

She held up a paw and shook her head. "Something I read once was written that year, something . . . Be right back," and she was past Bobcat and into a large hole in the trunk of the sycamore. Bobcat could hear scufflings and scrapings and Fisher murmuring; then there was a crash from inside. Bobcat leaped up, a wall of dust cascading from the hole, and a small metal tube clattered out across the patio and lodged against his left front paw. Then everything was still.

After a few seconds, Bobcat called out, "Fisher? You all right in there?"

A little more dust drifted from the hole, and Fisher emerged onto the patio, two books clutched to her chest, the look in her eyes making Bobcat's fur prickle. "What?" he asked. "What is it?"

"Sixteen twenty-three." She set the books, red-bound and cracked with age, down on the planking. "My great-great-grandfather . . . his books . . . they were the last books my mother had me read before she took me on my spirit walk. . . ."

Bobcat couldn't make out titles on the worn covers of the books. "But what are they? What do they say?"

"Sixteen twenty-three," Fisher said again. "Sixteen twenty-three was the Plague Year."

"The what?" Bobcat was about to say, but he stopped himself when he heard Skink gasp.

"Of course," the lizard whispered, his eyes wide and staring at nothing. "I am a fool. I never connected it. . . ."

Bobcat held up both paws. "C'mon; let's not start that again. Remember me? What's all this 'Plague Year' stuff?"

Her face still tight, Fisher picked up one of the books, flipped to near the end. "Here," she said, and read: " 'By my reckoning, at least 50 percent of the population died in the first ten months. After that, the plague seems to have run its course, but the following months saw thousands more, weakened by the disease, die of pneumonia, influenza, and other normally treatable maladies. Over half the population dead in one year, and not merely in the Ottersgate area; from Lai Tuan in the east to Kazirazif in the west, the figures are similar. Every second being, both creature and folk, has died on this continent, possibly on this whole planet, in this past year.' "

She looked up from the book. "The worst thing in the world, I'd say."

Bobcat could only stare. Questions whizzed through his head, but they went by too fast for him to ask any of them.

He heard Skink clear his throat. "I blame myself for not having seen it earlier. What must we do?"

Fisher closed the book. "First thing, we get us some serious help. How soon can you get the Elders together for the Kesshurmeshk?"

Skink blinked at her. "The Kesshurmeshk? But that's a leave-taking ceremony, only to be convened—"

"I know what it is. How soon can you get 'em together?"

"Tomorrow morning, I should think. But where—?"

"I'm not sure yet. I got some ideas, but I need to check 'em out. You just get down to the kiva and get the ceremony set for dawn. Send word if it's not gonna come off; otherwise, Bobcat and I'll meet you there tomorrow morning. We've gotta get moving on this, and I'd really like the Lord Eft's blessing before we get in any deeper."

"I agree. I fear the situation is much graver than I had foreseen. If you will take me to ground level, I shall start for the kiva at once."

"Wait," Bobcat said. "What're you—"

"In a minute," Fisher answered, and with Skink clinging to her back, she was over the edge of the patio and gone, leaving Bobcat alone with his spinning head.

It didn't take Bobcat long to decide that things still weren't making a lot of sense. Sure, this Plague Year thing sounded awful, but it had happened in 1623, over a hundred years ago; why get so excited about it now? The way they were talking, you'd almost think that they . . . that they . . .

He heard the scritch-scratch of Fisher's claws on the tree trunk; then she was on the patio and gathering up her books. "C'mon inside," she said.

"Wait a minute." Bobcat crooked a claw at her. "You and Skink think this Plague Year's coming back, don't you? You think that's what his grandma was talking about and we're s'posed to do something about it, right?"

"Yep." Fisher turned and walked into the tree trunk. "C'mon in."

"That's crazy, you know that?" But Fisher had vanished into the darkness inside the tree. Bobcat waited, but she didn't come back out. So he rose and padded after her. "I mean we're talking a disease, right? I'm no doctor; what'm I s'posed to do?"

The darkness closed dry and musty around him, but before his eyes could adjust he heard some low mutterings ahead, then the scrape and fizz of a match, a little flame appearing in the darkness. It rose up, grew larger with a crackling hiss, and the room glowed out in the light of the red candle Fisher was turning away from.

Bobcat gave a low whistle at the room brightening into view. It wasn't a big room, but on every inch of the curving walls, over every spare bit of floor space, even hanging from the ceiling in a few places, were bookshelves and bookcases, all nearly bursting.

"Have you really read all these?" he asked, staring around. Even the table the candleholder was standing on was thick with books.

"Never mind that." Fisher had unslung her satchel and was pulling a padded lounge chair out from under the table. "We're in deep serious here, and I'm betting you've got the one last nasty puzzle piece I really don't wanna see."

"Me? I don't even know what's going on! What've I gotta do with any of this?"

"I wish I knew." She lay back on the chair. "Now, I'm gonna ask you, and you gotta answer me true, 'cause if I'm right on this . . ." She stopped, and for the briefest of seconds in the candlelight her eyes held the look of a rabbit whose last exit had just been cut off. The look was gone almost instantly, but Bobcat knew it when he saw it, and he suddenly felt very cold.

"This morning," Fisher went on in the silence of the room, "this thing that happened to you, was it . . . Was there a fire, a fire in the shape of a giant cat?"

The candle crackled in Bobcat's ears, and the scene flooded over him again: the growling, the eyes, the claws, the whole huge flaming thing as it roared and leaped. Then it was gone and he was back in Fisher's room, his throat dry. "How?" he finally got out. "How did you know?"

Fisher closed her eyes and rubbed her forehead. "Sometimes I wish I'd gone into forestry . . .," she muttered.

"You know what it was," Bobcat whispered. "Don't you?"

Fisher nodded.

"You gotta tell me. I . . . It's been driving me crazy all day. I don't know if it was real or a dream or what, but you gotta tell me, Fisher; I hafta know. Fisher? Fisher!"

When Fisher finally opened her eyes, they shone like black stones in the candlelight. "She has many names," she began, her voice slow and quiet. "She is the Shadow in the Grass, the Stalker After Midnight, the Raging Fire That Burns Cold. She is the Strangler of Laughter, the Darkness on the Sun, the Claw That Stops the Throat's Last Rattle. She is Mayhem, Slaughter, Destruction, and in all things she is Death." Fisher blinked, and her eyes focused back on Bobcat. "She is the Blood Jaguar."

Bobcat could only stare, the name triggering more memories of Shemka Harr's stories.

"There are the Twelve Curials," Fisher went on, "and she is the Thirteenth. They're on opposite sides of things, the Twelve in charge of the aspects of life and the Thirteenth in charge of the aspects of death. That's a little simplistic, but I don't wanna get into all the jargon. But if she's involved, I'll bet we've got another Plague Year coming. And, well, like you said, we're supposed to do something about it."

Bobcat still couldn't say anything. It wasn't that he doubted Fisher; in fact, and this was even scarier, he believed every word she had said. That monstrous cat thing couldn't have been anything but the Death Queen of Shemka Harr's stories, the fiery Soul Slasher who rules the Shroud Islands far to the south of the world, the glades where the Just find eternal rest and the pits where she torments the Guilty.

Of course, Shemka Harr had also told him it was just a way of personalizing the wearing out of the body, that there was no Blood Jaguar, that she was just a story, something Bobcat had never had any reason to doubt. Now that he'd *seen* her, though . . . "But why me?" he blurted out at last. "I don't know any of that stuff you and Skink were talking about! Why'd she wanna jump out and kick me into the Brackens?"

Fisher shrugged. "Like I said, I wish I knew."

Bobcat rubbed at the throbbing between his eyes. "It doesn't make any sense . . . ," he whispered.

"You're telling me." For a minute, the only sound in the room was the crackle of the candle; then Fisher cleared her throat. "Well, I got some reading to do, and you might wanna get yourself some sleep."

"Sleep?" Bobcat barked a laugh. "Yeah, right! And besides, it's not even noon yet."

"True, but you've just had a bit of a shock, and—"

"A bit?"

"And we're gonna be leaving before sunup tomorrow, so—"

"Uh-uh. No, thank you." Bobcat ran his tongue over his teeth; he needed a little catnip, just a roll to calm him down. "Look;

I'm . . . I'm just gonna take a walk, maybe run over to Donal's Lake, OK? I'll be back by sundown, and you can get your reading done without me underpaw. OK?"

Fisher narrowed her eyes, then glanced over at the table where the candle sparked and snapped. "Well, I'd rather you stayed in this room, if it's all the same."

"What? Why? What's so special about this room?"

"The candle. It's the best ward spell I've got, but you hafta stay in its radius. It won't stop her if she really wants to get in, but it might make her think twice."

Bobcat's fur prickled. "Her? You . . . You mean . . . You . . . You think . . . she might come back? Might come here?"

"Nah. Not her style. But then kicking folks into the Brackens isn't her style either, so I figure better safe than shredded." Fisher shrugged. "But it's your life." She took up the second of the two books she'd been holding and began leafing through it.

Bobcat stared at her, then started inching along the floor till he was next to the table. He lay down on the polished wood and tried to close his eyes, but it didn't work; the Blood Jaguar, all huge and fiery, kept flashing in behind his eyelids, and he would start up with a cry, leap backward, and slam into the bookcases.

After he'd done this four or five times, Fisher folded her book closed. "This is not going to work," she said.

The air felt hot and solid around Bobcat. "Sure," he snarled. "You're used to this! You prob'ly have big flaming monsters in for lunch ev'ry weekend! 'More tea, anyone?' 'Oh, no, thank you; we've got to go find some idiot to kick into the Brackens.' 'Ah, well, have a good time.' Why are you doing this to me? Why can't you just leave me alone?"

Fisher rubbed her whiskers. "Y'know, tea sounds like a good idea. You want some?"

"What?"

"I've got some mint tea in the kitchen. You wanna cup?"

Bobcat's ears had clamped themselves tight against his head, his whole body shaking, his heart crashing at his ribs. "Tea? What are you talking about? Don't you understand? The Blood Jaguar is trying to kill me! And I haven't done anything! Why are you doing this to me? Nothing makes sense anymore! Don't you understand? Nothing—"

Fisher rolled off her lounge chair and grabbed Bobcat by his scruff. "The world doesn't make sense!" she hissed into his face, her eyes cold and black, her claws digging into his neck. "It never *has* made sense! It's a strange and twisted place that works on rules you have to work to read, let alone understand, and if you ever came down outta that catnip cloud, you'd maybe have a better handle on it! Folks like you are worthless in the real world, Bobcat, absolutely worthless, and I'll be damned to the Strangler's claw if I'll put up with your whining in my house!" Her dark eyes burned into him, and Bobcat felt every hair on his body bristle up.

Then she was stepping back, undoing her claws from his fur, and blowing out a breath. "Sorry. But you're not doing anyone any good sitting here complaining. So something weird happened to you. Live with it. Sure, normally I'd be happy to help you through this—I mean your first Curial experience and it had to be with the Strangler herself. But there's nothing normal here, and we just haven't got the time." She gave him a thin smile. "Now, I'm gonna get that tea. You want some or not?"

Bobcat's fur was drifting back into place, but he was still frozen to the spot. He found his tongue somewhere. "Uhh, yeah. Sure. Thanks."

"Be right back." And she went out through a small doorway among the bookshelves. Bobcat could only stare after her, his mind defrosting as his senses opened back up.

The candle popped on the table next to him, and he jumped halfway across the room. He realized he was panting like he'd run the Circuit race around Donal's Lake and his legs felt just as shaky. But he managed to sit down and get a tentative grip on himself. Fisher was right about one thing: he had pretty much been acting like a whiskerless kitten here. He just needed a little relaxing, that was all, a good catnip roll or something to calm him down and let him start thinking. Mint tea would be better than nothing, though.

In another minute, Fisher was back with two steaming cups.

"This'll do you," she said, handing one to him. The stuff smelled softly of mint, and it went down smooth and warm, Bobcat draining his cup dry in three swallows.

His shoulders unclenched then with a sudden snap, and a lazy wave rolled down his back. His eyelids started to droop, the aftertaste spread over his tongue, and he realized the tea had had more in it than just mint. His knees buckled, and he sank to the floor, Fisher's voice ringing in his head: "See you in the morning, Bobcat."

Then he was being shaken awake, the same voice saying, "What? You're not up yet?"

He rose slowly, shook his head to clear the muck from between his ears, saw Fisher with two backpacks on the floor next to her and a plate of toast balanced in one paw. "You'd better eat something," she was saying. "We've gotta get going pretty quick." She held out a mug. "Coffee?"

Bobcat's tongue felt thick and sticky. He wrapped a paw around the mug and was about to swig it down when his first thought struck him. "Wait a minute. What's in this one?"

"Just coffee." Fisher took a swig of hers, then held the mug out. "We can trade, if you like."

Bobcat took her mug and sipped it. It was good coffee, better than his ever was, not that that was too difficult a feat. He fumbled for the toast, and after he'd stuffed three slices down his throat he grumbled, "You didn't hafta put me out, y'know."

"Yeah, I did. You'd never've gotten to sleep on your own, and we've got traveling to do today." She took another slice of toast. "I didn't have time to argue with you yesterday, and we don't have any more time for it this morning. Now finish up; we've gotta get moving."

Bobcat took the last piece of toast. "I hope I snored."

"You didn't."

The bottom of the mug had some grounds in it; Bobcat rolled them around on his tongue and thought dark thoughts. The worst part of it all was that she was right. He'd needed a long and dreamless sleep, and whatever Fisher had slipped him hadn't even left a hangover. He spat the grounds back into the cup. "So where are we going?"

"To the kiva out by Donal's Lake." Fisher took his mug and the toast plate and tossed them through the little doorway among the bookshelves. "I haven't heard anything from Skink, so I guess everything's set." She slung one of the packs over her shoulders. "You get the heavy one."

"What?" Bobcat hefted the bag she'd left on the floor. "What's all this stuff?"

Fisher was standing in the doorway, looking out over the patio. "Trail mix, pots and pans, canteens, first-aid kits, the usual." She turned back to him. "You ready to go?"

"Go? Go where?"

"I already . . ." She sighed. "Just put that on and let's get moving. I'll meet you down on the ground." And she was gone from the doorway.

"But what—" Bobcat started to say.

"And blow out the candle, will you? We won't need it anymore. Not where we're going."

Bobcat looked from the candle to the doorway and back again. He gave a little snort, struggled into the pack, aimed a breath at the table, and made his way from the darkness inside the tree to the grayness outside. Fisher wasn't there, but her voice came up to him through the leaves: "Bobcat! We got places to be!"

So Bobcat clambered down the trunk of the sycamore, his pack trying its best to pull him to the ground more quickly, and padded across the clearing to where Fisher was waiting, tapping her claws against a tree root. "I still don't know what's going on," he said. "But don't let that stop you."

"I won't. Let's go."

She started off at a quick pace through the trees; Bobcat followed along till the coffee buzz behind his ears got his tongue working. "It's not that I'm the type to complain," he said to the back of Fisher's head, "but would it really be too much for you to tell me what in the bright blue above is going on here?"

He heard her laugh. "You? Complain? Now I've heard everything." She slacked her pace and fell in beside him. "You wanna know? OK. See, I did some reading last night about your friend— you know, the big fiery one?"

Bobcat's sides started itching, but he didn't say anything. Those eyes had sunk to a mere shimmer, and he didn't want to chance waking them up.

Fisher gave him a sidelong look. "Not interested?"

"Just get on with it," he said through gritted teeth.

"Bobcat, you can't keep on being so uptight about this. She'll eat you alive that way without her having to lift a claw. Believe me, I know it's hard, but you've gotta keep a sense of humor about all this stuff."

Bobcat stared at her. She was crazy; that was the only explanation. "A sense of humor? About the Blood Jaguar herself trying to kill me?"

"She wasn't trying. You'd be dead if she'd been trying."

"That's not the point!"

"Actually, it is. Well, maybe not *the* point, but *a* point certainly."

"Stop interrupting me! Every time I start something, you cut me off! Don't you think I've got anything to say?"

"I know you don't have anything to say. You don't have the vaguest idea of what's going on, so how can you? Watch your step now; we're here."

Bobcat looked forward and saw that they'd come to the bank of the River. The water rushed by quick and cold in the predawn grayness, the River especially turbulent here where Mackinaw Creek brought down the meltwaters from Donal's Lake. A little way up the creek across the River, Bobcat saw smoke drifting out from a low earthen dome settled among the trees.

He turned to ask Fisher if that was the place, but Fisher wasn't next to him anymore. Bobcat looked around and saw her jumping from rock to rock across the River's roiling face. She turned around halfway there and shouted, "Come on! We haven't got all day, y'know!" Then she was on the other bank and scurrying up toward the dome.

Bobcat stared after her, then started to pick his way across. He kept the extra weight on his back in mind and reached the riverbank without getting more than a paw wet—no thanks to that witch, of course. If the Blood Jaguar didn't get him, Bobcat was sure Fisher would. He shook his paw to dry it and started up the bank.

The wisp of smoke showed above the trees to mark his destination, and Bobcat kept his eye on it as he climbed. At the top of the rise, he could see the dome itself, and he stepped out into the clearing that surrounded it. Fisher and Skink were both standing there, and Bobcat was about to call out to them when Skink turned, put a claw to his lips, and pointed back toward the dome.

Lizards were coming out through the hole in the top. One after another, newts and geckos, salamanders and chameleons, reptiles and amphibians, all swaying down in some sort of procession. The first dozen or so wore red fringed collars with black spines that arched up over their heads and rattled counterpoint to their steps. They moved with a rhythmic slowness, first one front leg held suspended, then a few rustling steps scuttled them farther into the clearing and the whole train stopped, each with its front leg cocked in front of it.

Bobcat noticed that Skink was swaying in place to the rhythm and when they all held their claws raised his came up as well. Fisher gestured with her head for Bobcat to come over next to them, so he padded across the clearing, a question forming on his lips. But Fisher shook her head and nodded toward the lizards; Bobcat looked and suddenly realized that the lizards were moving to surround them. He could make out a sound now, too: a low, thrumming chant that shivered with the same uneven rhythm set up by the rattling of the lizards' collars.

The sound made Bobcat's throat go dry; he swallowed and wondered what was going on. Skink and Fisher, he noticed, had closed their eyes and seemed to be caught up in the disjointed skittering and humming in the air around them. Bobcat didn't see how they could shut their eyes with all this happening; he couldn't stop swallowing, the rustling voices of the lizards seeming to settle at the base of his throat.

But as the rustling settled in, it seemed to roll around his ears, to buzz and chime with other tones than those that he had heard before: dry and whistling, something seemed to whisper there beneath the thrum. "Yes," it murmured, "yes," it tolled, "yes," it rumbled, deep and low, a voice that somehow drifted in behind the chant and touched his ears from places Bobcat couldn't see. Except . . . he could, or thought he could, the sound so solid it took shape, began to stir and raise its head, a lizard curving through the chant but huge, beyond it, colored gray, its eyes aspark like dawn's first touch upon the billowed clouds of morning.

Then the sun burst into Bobcat's eyes and the lizards let out a whoop that sent him stumbling back. His paws didn't end up where he thought they'd be, though, and he fell onto his tail with a thud. "Brains and eggs!" he shouted.

Slowly his eyes cleared, and he saw the courtyard emptying, lizards going off in groups and chattering in that weird rustling language of theirs. Fisher and Skink sat chattering, too, with one of the lizards wearing a big red collar, but Fisher turned at Bobcat's shout and sighed. "Problem?" she asked.

"Yes!" Bobcat got to his paws. "You! You're the problem! You and all these weird things you keep dumping on me!"

The lizard with the collar scuttled over, the black fronds chiming above her head. "Please," she whispered, her voice like an evening breeze, "there is no cause to argue. Some things you have seen, they have disturbed you?"

"Disturbed me?" Bobcat laughed. "Yeah, I think it'd be safe to call giant flaming Death Goddesses sorta disturbing."

"That one. She is indeed." The lizard raised a claw. "But the one you have seen here this morning?"

Bobcat stopped and thought a minute. "Well, no. I mean it wasn't . . . It didn't . . . I didn't really see anything. It was more like . . . like I heard a sound underneath the chanting, and I looked over to the other side of the kiva there, and . . ." He waved a paw at the creek rushing past the dome to the River. "And I saw the sound. Not what was making it, but the sound itself." Bobcat shook his head quickly. "But that's crazy."

Skink had come up next to the other lizard. "No, Bobcat. It was the voice of the Lord Eft. He speaks with shapes, shapes which the chant brings forth."

The other lizard raised a front leg, her collar clattering. "You are touched all three with the sounds he shapes, the shapes bespoken long ago. Here the story starts again, yours the telling, yours the living, yours the claws and pads that pace it." She touched Bobcat's knee, then rested her claws on Skink's upraised leg and Fisher's upturned paw. "I have done all I know to do," she said quietly. "Go now. The Lord Eft's blessing is upon you."

Skink and Fisher held their pose, each with one paw suspended; Bobcat looked from one to the other, then turned back to see the lizard scurrying away up the side of the kiva, her neckpiece giving one final rustle before she disappeared down into the hole at the top of the dome.

"Well," Fisher breathed out a moment later, "let's go. I packed everything I think we'll need." She looked down at Skink. "You ready?"

"I can hardly say I am," Skink replied, "but there are some things we cannot change. Shall I ride upon your back?"

Fisher nodded, and the lizard clambered up to settle on her neck above her backpack.

Bobcat watched them, his mind slightly numb. "Wait a minute," he said, a little surprised at how calm he sounded. "You're telling me that I just saw one of the Curials, aren't you? That I'm walking off into a world of storybook characters, is that it?"

"Yeah," Fisher said. "That a problem for you?"

Skink raised a claw. "Fisher, please. We must remember Bobcat's lack of proper schooling." The lizard turned to him and smiled. "I will be more than happy to explain, Bobcat."

Fisher sighed. "Fine; go right ahead. But can we get going before you start orating?"

"Of course," Skink said. "Where are we headed?"

"West," Fisher replied, waving a paw toward the River. "Down to the Meerkat Road, then west."

Bobcat looked in the direction she was pointing. All he saw were trees. "Why? What's over there?"

"Can we just get moving?"

"Certainly," Skink said. "We can talk as we go. If you will lead the way, Fisher?" He looked over at Bobcat. "Bobcat? Shall we?"

"What? I don't even get to say good-bye to anyone?"

Fisher gave a snort and began to pad down the slope. Bobcat looked south toward the Brackens, toward where Garson would just be starting her rounds, assigning duties to her field hands, maybe even wondering why he hadn't shown up for dinner last night.

Oh, well, at least all this would give him a good, weird story to tell her when he got back. He breathed a silent good-bye in her direction, blew out a breath, shrugged his pack into a more comfortable position, and followed Fisher.

Chapter Three

At the Crossroads

Now lemme see if I've got this straight," Bobcat said, leaping in before Skink could start up again.

It had been hours since they'd left the kiva, Ottersgate long ago disappearing behind the wooded hills that the Meerkat Road wound through on its way west from town. Bobcat had been surprised when they'd hit the pavement to feel that same stirring in his middle that had kept him on the roads for years before he'd settled in Ottersgate and had all at once found himself looking forward to this trip, wherever they were going. . . .

Except that Skink had been talking the whole time, rambling on and on, subjects pouring out of him, defining long words Bobcat didn't know with other long words Bobcat didn't know. Fisher hadn't been any help at all, not giving so much as a snort during Skink's whole monologue, and Bobcat was sure he didn't understand any more now than he had when Skink had started. He had to interrupt, though; he couldn't take listening to the lizard for one more minute. "So you're telling me that the Twelve Curials are real, actual folk—"

"Not folk, Bobcat; you see, their Curial Privilege—"

"Yeah, OK, so they're gods or whatever. But you're saying that they really *do* wander around and do things like in the stories, right?"

"Well, on the most basic level, yes."

Bobcat blinked at him. "Wow."

At that, Fisher did snort and stopped so suddenly that Bobcat nearly ran into her. " 'Wow'? Is that it? You've just heard one of the most thorough and scholarly discussions of the aspects of the Curial powers that I've ever come across, and all you can say is 'wow'?"

Bobcat shrugged. "Well, I meant it."

She watched him for a moment. "You didn't understand word one of that, did you?"

"Not really, no." Bobcat managed to get a hind leg around his backpack to scratch at an ear.

Skink's gray head appeared over Fisher's shoulder. "Bobcat! You should have stopped me! I would have happily given you more complete definitions if you—"

"No, no, no!" Bobcat held up his paws. "That's OK! Really! I've got enough to chew on right now, thank you very much. I mean if the Twelve are real, and if the Blood Jaguar is real . . ." He stopped, Skink giving a little cry, and he could only blink at the lizard making some quick motions with a front foot, his eyes clenched shut. "We're in some kinda trouble here, aren't we?" Bobcat finished after a minute.

Fisher gave him a sideways grin. "I take it all back. You do understand."

Before Bobcat could reply, a loud cry echoed from the road ahead of them. He looked past Fisher and saw, cresting the next hill, the lead wagon of a freight caravan, the otters in harness belting out a haulers' tune in roughly parallel harmonies while the straw boss up topside let the verses fly in a baritone rumble that rang through the trees.

Bobcat heard the straw boss give a shout, and a whoop burst from the hauling otters. They leaped up onto their beams, the wagon seeming to hang at the peak of the hill until, with many a creak and holler, it began rumbling down into the valley, another wagon appearing at the crest behind it, its crew breaking off their song and leaping up in the same way.

"Uhh," Bobcat said, watching the first wagon speed down the slope into the little valley before them, "this might not be the best place to stand. . . ."

The others seemed to agree, and they scurried to the shade of the oaks alongside the road. The first wagon, Bobcat saw, its load of otters clinging to every part of it, had reached the bottom and was halfway up the next slope when the straw boss gave three quick shouts and down the haulers tumbled. Paws flashed on pavement, and the wagon sailed past, the straw boss waving his hat as he started up the song again.

Bobcat looked back into the little valley and saw two more wagons racing down the slope, a third topping the hill. "Brains and eggs. This's an eastern caravan day, isn't it? And of course we hafta be heading west."

Fisher shrugged. "It's time for a break anyway. Sling that pack off, Bobcat; we might as well eat something."

So Bobcat wriggled out from under his backpack, and the three settled down beneath the oaks with some of Fisher's trail mix to watch the otter caravan stream by. Bobcat gnawed some dried berries and took a swig from his canteen before asking, "So, do we have a plan here, or are we just stumbling around?"

Fisher was leaning back against her own pack. "A valid question." She recorked her canteen and began rummaging through one of her pack's side pockets. "I've got some ideas and a few things that might be of interest, specially to you, Skink, what with all you were saying earlier about the Syzygy of Material Concepts."

"Indeed?" The lizard scuttled over. "I have always been fascinated by the subject. Chiard's work on conceptualization ratios opened whole new doors—"

Bobcat was beginning to wish he'd brought a whistle. "Wait a minute; let's not start all that again."

Skink looked down. "I am sorry, Bobcat. I often become carried away."

By this time, Fisher had pulled a familiar red-bound book from her pack. "Maybe we can talk about it later, Skink, when the kids are in bed."

The lizard looked confused. Bobcat opened his mouth to complain, his sides itching, but Fisher had already started. "Anyway, I went through my library last night, trying to find anything that might help us out here, and there was basically nothing. The only book on the Plague Year I could find any reference to at all was my great-great-grandfather's, the one I showed you yesterday; it's in my pack here somewhere. It seems to be the only book on the subject."

Skink raised a front foot. "Forgive me for interrupting, Fisher, but what about Salamander of Churfos Kiva? His account is the one I read while in school."

"Yeah, but Salamander wrote in the 1680s, sixty years after the Plague Year, and he basically admits that since he was something like two years old in 1623, he had to get most of his facts from other sources. The only *written* source he mentions, though, is Great-great-granddad's book. You'd almost think no other scholar lived through the plague, but we know that's not true. It's just that nobody else wrote anything. Kinda weird, I thought."

"Yeah," Bobcat offered, "unless maybe this Plague Year wasn't really as bad as he made it out to be."

The look Fisher gave him was dark and cold, but she went on without answering. "Granddad calls it *A Journal of the Plague Year,* but it really deals with what he found as he went from place to place just after the thing had run its course, so even this book isn't really about the Plague Year itself. And nowhere does he mention either Skink's grandma or whoever the bobcat was that went with them."

"Wait a minute," Bobcat said again. "What's this about a bobcat?"

Fisher closed her eyes and leaned back onto her pack. "OK," she said after a minute, "I'm only gonna do this once, so if you don't get it now, you're eggs outta luck; got it?"

Bobcat blinked at her. "What? What're you—"

"In 1622 or maybe early 1623, Skink's grandma lost her luck."

"And that's another thing," Bobcat began.

"Shut up and listen. Around the same time, some local bobcat had an awful experience: got himself kicked into the Brackens by a giant flaming cat monster or something like that. Sound familiar?"

Bobcat stopped chewing. "Wait a minute—"

"Just listen. Skink's grandma and this bobcat both went to see my great-great-grandfather, who was the local fisher back then, and what they did after that I don't really know. But somehow they found out that the Plague Year was coming, and from what Skink's grandma said, it sounds like the three of them set out to stop it.

"Well, whatever they did, it didn't work, and the Plague Year came. We know that Skink's grandma came back to Ottersgate afterward and basically retired from adventuring for a while, and my great-great-granddad traveled around and wrote this book." Her eyes took on a faraway look. "It's something I didn't notice the last time I went through it, but in every line you can read just how . . . how responsible he felt. He died about six years after finishing it." She shook herself and looked back at them. "And the bobcat, whoever he or she was, we don't hear anything at all about."

Skink rustled in the leaves. " 'A failure that leads to death.' That's what Grandmother said. And she told us the beginning in the hope that we could change the ending."

Bobcat looked from one to the other. "So . . . now, now wait a minute—"

"So that's it," Fisher said, settling back onto her pack. "It's happening again, see? Only it's us this time. Now, can I get on with what I was saying?"

"But how do you know—"

Fisher was rubbing her eyes. "It's all there, Bobcat, all of it in what Skink's grandma said. There was a skink, a fisher, and a bobcat involved in this 'worst thing in the world' quest last time, and here we all are again. Now, if I can get to the plan?"

Bobcat decided he probably shouldn't ask any of the other questions that kept poking at him, so he just waved a paw for her to continue. Maybe things would get clearer, but he sort of doubted it.

"So anyway," Fisher went on, "since Double 'G' Granddad was the only one who wrote about the Plague Year, I read the whole thing last night, hoping I could pull out some clues even though he didn't seem to wanna talk about it any more'n Skink's grandma did. And the only thing I found was in the part where he's talking about Kazirazif, the city of the meerkats in the western desert. See, he gives these overviews of the cities and folk in an area before he gets to talking about the effects of the plague there, and his overview of Kazirazif is pretty much the same as the overviews he gives for Beaverpool and Lai Tuan and Cayottle and the rest.

"But in the Kazirazif overview, he gets into some detail about the Ramons, the spiritual advisers to the caliphs there. He tells some of the stories he heard while in Kazirazif and winds up by saying that the Ramons display a greater understanding of the darker aspects of the Curial powers than any other folks he's met. You with me so far?"

Bobcat wasn't sure he was, but he saw Skink nod, so he figured he'd better keep his mouth shut till Fisher finished. Fisher gave him a sideways look, then continued.

"Well, the phrase 'aspects of the Curial powers' struck me. See," and she held up the book she had in her paws, "that's the title of this book, Great-great-granddad's second and last. In this one, he devotes a chapter to each of the Twelve Curials, talks about the rites associated with each, their spheres of influence, stuff like that.

"What makes the book so interesting to us, though, aside from Granddad's ideas on Material Concepts," she shot another glance at Bobcat, "is that the book actually has thirteen chapters. I don't think I need to tell you who the thirteenth chapter is about, do I?"

Skink was muttering and making his little gestures again. Bobcat felt his cuts heat up; he didn't want to say the name out loud, didn't want to take the chance of making those eyes flare up. "Yeah, OK," he whispered.

Fisher had opened the book to near the end and was leafing through. "Not a whole lot about the Strangler, really. But he does say, right here at the beginning . . ." She turned a few more pages and poked a paw into the book. "Here: 'She of the Cold Fire is the embodiment of all that is Death and Destruction, all that is Ruin and Decay, all the darker aspects of the Curial powers.' " She looked up from the book. "Since these are the only two places he uses the phrase 'darker aspects,' I think, whether he meant to or not, he's pointing us toward Kazirazif. That seem logical?"

Skink twitched his head to one side. "The Ramons of Kazirazif are rumored to know the certain rituals abolished long ago by the Elders on instructions from the Lord Eft himself. Your plan has a great deal of merit."

The caravan continued to rattle past, Bobcat's cuts tickling at his sides. "Yeah, OK," he said, taking a pull from his canteen, "so that's where we're headed. I can follow that. But what're we really *doing?* I mean, fine, we go and we talk to these meerkats. Then what? If the thing I saw is the Blood Jaguar, lemme tell you, I don't think there's much we're gonna be able to do to stop her."

Fisher was giving him the cold eye again. "So we should just quit?" she asked quietly. "Just go home and wait for folks to start getting sick?" She dug into her pack and came out with the other red-bound book. "You want me to read you some more? About the bodies piled in the streets 'cause there weren't enough folk left to carry 'em to the bonfires? About the mouse kit Granddad found standing in an empty town east of Beaverpool, just standing there listing names, his parents and grandparents and aunts and uncles and cousins, the entire town, all dead? Or d'you think Granddad just made it up, just wrote this book out of some twisted sense of humor?"

"C'mon, Fisher; I didn't mean—"

"So maybe we haven't got a chance." Her voice was still quiet, but every word bit into Bobcat's ears. "Maybe the Blood Jaguar's waiting for us over the next hill to tear our throats out before we even know she's there. Maybe we were dead before we started. But we got the warning, and I'll be damned if I'm gonna just sit by and let half the folks in the world die again. You can do whatever you want, Bobcat."

The last wagon in the caravan rattled past, and the haulers' chant sank away behind the hills, the ringing baritone of the straw bosses fading into the rustle of leaves in the morning breeze.

Fisher slipped her books into her pack and strapped it to her back. "Let's go," she said.

Skink snapped to life next to Bobcat and scurried through the grass to where he'd left his satchel. Bobcat sat still for a moment, the Blood Jaguar's terrible eyes sparking with dull fire at his sides. "You think so?" he asked as Skink clambered up onto Fisher's back. "You think I can do what I want? Is that what you think?"

Fisher wasn't looking at him.

With a growl, Bobcat leaped forward and grabbed her paws. "Damn you, Fisher, listen to me!" Her eyes snapped over, cold and black as river ice; Bobcat glared into them. "I don't care what you think about me, witch; I *know* I'm dumber'n dirt! But you aren't gonna ignore me or stare me down or make me shut up! I'm not here 'cause I believe all this crap about plagues and Curials and ev'rything! I'm here 'cause I got no choice! That Blood Jaguar of yours, she picked me out for this, left her eyes in my head so I wouldn't forget about her, and I wanna know why! So don't talk to me about saving the world, Fisher! I've got problems enough of my own!"

Skink was rustling and squeaking from his perch on Fisher's neck, "Please, Bobcat, Fisher, please don't argue! We can't afford—"

"Argue?" Fisher's voice was calm, and her eyes never left Bobcat's. "Who's arguing? I just said, 'Let's go,' and he just said, 'I'm coming.' Where's the argument there? I mean it's not really me he's mad at." She made no move to pull her paws away. "Is it?"

Bobcat stood where he was, his breath shaking its way in and out of his throat. At last, he let Fisher's paws loose.

"Don't forget your pack," she said.

It took Bobcat another minute or so to slip into the straps; then he was following Fisher back down the Meerkat Road heading west. They wound their way over the hills, through the meadows bright with spring flowers stretching their petals into the midmorning sun, over the brooks that chattered their stony teeth at the meltwaters flowing past them, but Bobcat wasn't paying them much attention. He was wondering just who he *was* mad at.

Not Fisher, he had to admit, and he couldn't make himself get mad at Skink, even though the lizard and his grandma had started this whole thing up. And how could he be mad at the Curials? He didn't even believe in them.

The Blood Jaguar, then? Sure, his brain froze up every time he thought of her, but she was the one who'd thrown him into this for no reason; even the threat he felt from her fitfully glowing eyes couldn't make him deny that.

So he would be mad at her.

That settled, Bobcat let himself swing into the rhythm of the road, the heft of the pack and the sweet scent of someplace new pushing those eyes to a simmer at the back of his thoughts. It was still spring, after all, and Bobcat had spent many a worse day on the road, his paws taking him from one nowhere to another. Even if all this Plague Year stuff was true, it was still nice to have a def-inite thing to do. And having other folks along to share the road made a lot of difference, too.

They walked on for some hours, until the sun reached the top of the sky; then Fisher turned her head back to Bobcat. "You feel like some lunch?"

Bobcat nodded. They had crested a hill and were making their way down some switchbacks into a valley with a river tumbling along the bottom. Buildings sat along each side of the river, and some sort of festival seemed to be going on among the trees off beside the Meerkat Road. Tents and booths fluttered with paper flags, and an amphitheater had been set up at the base of a big rock slumped in a field on the opposite bank. Bobcat could hear laughter and snatches of song coming up from the folk who sat at the tables and under the trees and wandered between the tents.

"That's Flatrock, isn't it?" he asked, nodding toward the town.

"Yeah," Fisher called back. "I was hoping we'd get here by noontime. We can actually buy something and not have to waste any hardtack."

Down the trail they went, drawing closer and closer to the

town. Then the slope leveled out, and they were walking between fields of wheat and various sorts of vegetables. The fields fell away after a bit, and the tents and stands were all around them, mice and squirrels in colorful hats roaming about with plates of food or musical instruments, wrens and sparrows, otters and weasels, hawks and foxes, and all manner of folk calling from the booths or tossing rings over posts or waiting in line for the Tilt-A-Whirl or the parachute drop, the whole place bursting and bustling under the spring sun.

Skink was peering over Fisher's shoulder. "A vernal equinox festival, no doubt. A pity we missed the invocation rituals; these rustic ceremonies can be quite moving."

Bobcat came up beside them. "You pack any money in here, Fisher? Or are we gonna volunteer to wind up the merry-go-round if they feed us?"

"Don't worry." Fisher patted her pack. "I've got some otter scrip. Let's take a look around."

The place had everything, the best spread Bobcat had seen since the last winter fair in Ree's Meadow. One whole row of booths seemed to be devoted just to food: cabbage rolls on a stick, corn on the cob, every sort of insect and fish prepared in ways Bobcat had never even considered, almond roca, fried ice cream, casseroles and cobblers made of everything from apples to peanuts to string beans.

After some discussion, the three agreed on a booth serving trout with almonds and also sautéed grasshopper. They got a bit of the local cider and had just slung off their packs in a shady spot along the river when Bobcat saw an old squirrel staring at them. The squirrel was leaning on a gnarled wooden cane, his fur gray and patchy, his face lined and weathered. A bright red and purple knit beret had somehow settled itself over one of his wrinkled ears, and it struck Bobcat that he had seen that hat somewhere before.

Bobcat chewed his fish and thought about it. He had noticed the hat, he was sure, when he'd walked into the fairgrounds, it and the old squirrel sitting on a rock, the cane across the squirrel's lap.

But Bobcat had also seen the hat and the old squirrel leaning on his cane beside the trout booth, and now that same squirrel and hat were staring at him while he ate.

It wasn't very polite, and Bobcat looked pointedly at the old squirrel in the hope that he could get him and his hat to go away. But the squirrel only squinted some more, then began stumping forward, the cane making little squishing noises when it jabbed the ground. Bobcat poked Fisher, and Fisher looked up just as the old squirrel stopped beside her.

The squirrel raised his cane and shook it at each of them in turn. "Ye ain't welcome here," he rattled, "none of ye."

Bobcat just stared at him, and Skink spoke up: "But, sir, what have we—"

"Ye cain't fool a Kechetnin!" The squirrel's voice was suddenly very loud. "I knows ye! Me pappy al'ays said t' watch out fer a fisher an' a bobcat an' a skink trav'lin' togither, an' it were his pappy as tol' him, an' his pappy afore that! Yer cursed! Cursed by the Lady Squirrel to the Strangler's claw! An' ye ain't welcome here!" The squirrel raised his cane again and stabbed it down on Bobcat's paw.

It surprised more than hurt him, made him say, "Hey!" and pull his paw back. The movement wrenched the cane sideways, and the squirrel fell with a wail, the hat rolling from his head and skipping down the slope into the river.

"Help!" the old squirrel shouted. "For the love of the Lady, help!"

Bobcat held out a paw. "Sorry. Here, lemme—"

"Keep 'em away!" The squirrel was dragging himself backward, his eyes wide, fear a thick scent in the air around him. "Keep 'em away!"

Voices were rising up among the trees, and Fisher poked Bobcat in the shoulder. "Get your pack. Let's go."

"What?" Bobcat looked at her. "We didn't do anything, did we? It's not our fault this old guy starts—"

Fisher had already slipped her pack on. "This isn't our town, Bobcat, and we haven't got time to mess with whatever legal system they've got." She pointed her chin at the old squirrel. "He's all right—a little scared, but he'll get over it. Us, though, we'd better get ourselves gone."

Skink was already perched on Fisher's neck, his eyes spinning, the voices getting louder among the trees. Bobcat snorted, struggled into his pack, and took off after Fisher along the riverbank toward the bridge and the Meerkat Road ahead. He heard the old squirrel crying after them, his voice soon joined by a tangle of others, but couldn't make out what they were saying. The three reached the road without anyone trying to stop them, sprinted across the bridge, and Bobcat just had time to notice the red and purple beret caught on some rocks below them before they were over and heading into the hills to the west.

They kept a quick pace, Bobcat looking back every now and then to make sure they weren't being followed, till about midafternoon. The hills got flatter and flatter the farther west they went, the trees squatting closer to the ground, and by the time the sun was settling into a three-quarters position above and ahead of them they were stopped at the base of the last hill, their packs off and leaning against each other beside a little spring the road ran past.

Bobcat stared down the road, his cheek stuffed with walnuts. Not a tree stood on the plain there; not a hill rose above it, not a single roof poking into the deep blue of the sky. The Meerkat Road was a thin black line snapped straight out into a sea of yellow-green grass, rustling like a river as the wind combed through it all the way out to the flat of the horizon. "Charming spot," he said after he'd swallowed. "I'm starting to think that squirrel might've been right."

Skink stirred in the dirt next to him. "Oh, Bobcat, we are no more cursed than anyone else. But at least we now know our course is correct, and I must admit that that fellow has proven my contention far better than I could have dreamed."

"Oh?" Fisher was filling her canteen at the spring. "Which contention is that?"

"My belief that we are truly involved in a Cyclical Myth. The warning against a fisher, a bobcat, and a skink traveling together has become local folklore connected to the Plague Year, so the one Grandmother told us of could not have been the first. This must have all happened many times before."

"Yeah," Fisher breathed out. "Every hundred years or so we march through town, and the next thing anyone knows folks are dropping left and right. Terrific."

Skink raised a claw. "We don't know that every time it happens the Plague Year results. Grandmother seemed to imply that success was possible."

Fisher shook her head. "She just hoped it was, remember? 'An old story about a failure that leads to death,' she said, like no version she knew had a happy ending. And besides, it explains things so nicely." She rubbed her whiskers. "I mean haven't you ever wondered why there're so few folk around? Compared with the size of the continent, I mean?"

Bobcat cocked his head. "Whadda you mean?"

"Well, look." Fisher slid over to her pack, took out a map, laid it on the ground, and poked at it. "On the whole east coast, the only real cities are Lai Tuan and Ngyshen. There's Madison up by the Great Lakes, Beaverpool on the River, Kazirazif in the western desert, and Cayottle up along the northwestern coast. And that's it. Even considering towns like Ottersgate and Flatrock, that's not a whole lot. The archaeological data say folk've been on this continent for thousands of generations, but there's still so much room I've only ever read about such a thing as a property dispute." She looked up. "Makes you think, doesn't it?"

Skink's head was twitching from side to side, his eyes glassy. "We are killed off at regular intervals. I do not want to believe it, but . . . but . . . what if Grandmother's Plague Year was a mild one, the 50 percent dead reported by your great-great-grandfather an unusually light figure? What if we are but days away from a devastation never before known? How can such things be? How can the Curial powers—"

"Now wait a minute!" Bobcat made a referee's sign with his paws. "Time-out! Is it just me, or are we jumping to about fifteen assorted conclusions here?"

Fisher drummed her claws against her backpack. "You're the

one who saw her, Bobcat. You think the Strangler was just kidding around about all this?"

"Hey, don't ask me." Bobcat shrugged. "All I know about this stuff is what you've told me and some stories I barely remember hearing as a kit. The Blood Jaguar, I've got the scars to prove she exists, and your books prove that this Plague Year happened once. Maybe all that talk Skink was blowing around proves the Curials, but I'd say let's stick to the facts till we get some idea of what's going on. Taking things step-by-step saves wear and tear on the ol' glands, I've found."

Skink lay huddled in the dirt, wisps of sound drifting from his throat, and a little smile started curling through Fisher's whiskers. Bobcat shrugged again. "So we just gonna stand here?" he asked.

"Nah." Fisher folded up the map and picked up her canteen. "We wanna be at the crossroad before dark." She poked at Skink. "Don't we?"

The lizard stirred. "We must," he whispered. "We have no time to lose." He scuttled over to his pack.

They walked out into the grasslands then and on into the afternoon. Fisher and Skink talked between themselves ahead of him, but Bobcat scarcely noticed, the rustling of the stalks around him playing tricks on his ears, the sounds drifting into his thoughts and forming pictures as fleeting as cloud patterns. It got to be a game after a while; the sounds would almost remind him of something, almost form words, almost make some sense, and Bobcat would bat at them with a paw, try to catch them, try to hold them in shape before they were gone.

But every time, he would catch nothing but the pavement, would start back as if he'd been asleep, the road and the sky and the rustling grass all leaping into sharp focus, black and blue and bright yellow-green, Fisher and Skink still talking a few paces farther on. Bobcat would look around, would see that the sun had jumped a bit closer to the horizon ahead, but otherwise, nothing would've changed. He would half-listen to the conversation in front of him, but then the rustling would start popping things into his mind again, and he would be off on another round of brain tag.

* * *

At last, the sun licking at the horizon, the grass began to sink, the yellow in it taking over, and settle to the ground in patches on the reddish earth. Bluffs appeared ahead and off to the right, the land to the left starting to wrinkle and roll, and a sign came into view, brown and weather-beaten, by the side of the road: CROSSROAD AHEAD.

Bobcat read the words aloud and blew out a breath. "About time."

"What?" Fisher called back. "Tired already?"

About a hundred yards farther on, the strip of pavement they were walking on ran into two more, one coming straight down from the north, the other heading off to the southwest across the plains, three roads converging on a single spot. A stream gurgled along on the other side of the crossroad, its little ditch running south with the one road and passing under a stony bridge on the other. The area had been stripped clear of even the tufts of yellow grass, the earth hard-packed by generations of freight caravans pulling off the road to rest.

Bobcat had heard of minivillages appearing overnight when caravans met here, of impromptu festivals lasting for days when otters and foxes and others who plied the roads would find themselves together at the crossroad. Now, however, only a single figure lay curled against his backpack by the banks of the little stream: a graying kit fox, his canvas pack stained and frayed almost as much as he was himself. His snores sounded healthy enough, though, and Bobcat smiled, following Fisher a little ways down the southwestern road and over to the side of the stream.

Fisher glanced upstream at the kit fox. "I was hoping we'd meet somebody here. My info about the road's a few months old, and I'd rather not have too many surprises."

"I'm all for that." Bobcat crawled out from beneath his pack and flopped back against it. "We gonna let the ol' geezer sleep, or you wanna shake him down right now?"

Skink leaped from Fisher's back. "You'll do nothing of the sort, Bobcat! Why, the very idea—"

Bobcat held up a paw. "A joke. I was making a joke."

"Well, it was certainly a poor one." Skink slipped his pack off. "We who are travelers in strange lands must—"

"All right, all right, I'm sorry. I'll apologize to him when he wakes up, OK?"

Fisher rattled the pack Bobcat was lying against. "It'd be more helpful if you'd unload the gas jars and the pots. There's nothing like the smell of cooking to wake up a tramp."

So Bobcat pulled a number of things from his pack, and Fisher put them together into a trail stove. She had him fill some pots at the stream while she got it lit, and as the sun disappeared behind the bluffs to the west a stew began to bubble over the little fire.

True to Fisher's prediction, it wasn't long before the snoring stopped, and a rough voice drifted through the twilight: "Good evening to you, friends. Forgive me for not greeting you earlier, but a day's march seems longer now than even a few months ago. Would it be too much to ask for a share of your fire and your company?"

Fisher gave Bobcat a grin, then called out, "Not at all, friend, not at all! It looks like I've mixed up a bit more stew than we three can use; how would a bowl or two sound?"

"Friend," the voice answered, "how can I turn down so well put an offer?" The figure rose, shrugged on his pack, and loped across the road to the light of Fisher's fire.

The kit fox was old and gray, scars showing through his fur and standing out on his muzzle. The strands of one ear flopped down the side of his head, and the other was so torn Bobcat couldn't figure out how it kept upright. But the kit fox's eyes were quick and his smile infectious as he bowed to them each in turn, let his pack to the ground, and settled against it with an audible creak. "Thank you. It gets a little lonesome on the trail sometimes. It's nice just to hear the sound of other folk's breathing."

Fisher handed out bowls of stew, and they ate in silence while the dusk deepened into night around them. The kit fox finished first, set his bowl down, and bowed his head to Fisher. "Best stuff I've had in weeks. Folks on the road call me Rag Ears, and I think it suits me. Which way you all headed from here?"

Fisher gestured with her spoon. "Down to Kazirazif. Did you come up from that way?"

The kit fox didn't answer her, just looked from one to the other and rubbed his chin. "Y'know, there's some folks might get a bit nervous seeing a fisher, a bobcat, and a skink on the road to Kazirazif. A boy hears stories about things happening after folks like you pass through the Shasir gate."

Bobcat tried to keep his stew from going down the wrong way. This guy wasn't going to throw a fit on them, too, was he? The kit fox stayed quiet, though, his eyes on Fisher while she nodded. "Yes, you hear a lot of stories on the road."

Rag Ears settled back against his pack. "Best to keep that in mind, specially as you get closer to Meerkat Town. Things can happen to folks in the desert. If I was you, I'd go around the city to the Basharah gate and get there just before dawn. I knew a guard captain when I was down there; Tevirye was her name, the Raj Tevirye. She's about the only one I'd trust if I was a fisher, a bobcat, and a skink traveling down the road to Kazirazif. She gets off duty at dawn, and she'll take you right to the Ramon. If that's who you wanna see." His eyes seemed to sparkle in the firelight.

Fisher's did, too. "It's still the Ramon Sooli down there, isn't it?"

"Oh, yes. He's a tough old bird. Saw him speak a few times."

"Did you?"

"Oh, yes." The kit fox grinned. "I suppose you've heard about the death of the old Bison King, though?"

Fisher's grin faded. "No. No, I hadn't."

"Ah." The kit fox shook his head. "Sad, it was. One of his sons challenged him, and the old fellow didn't survive."

Bobcat blew out a breath. "Brains and eggs. That'll change things, won't it? We gonna hafta go around now?"

Skink rustled from where he sat. "Go around? Forgive me, but I'm afraid I do not see how this affects us. The road we travel does pass through the Kingdom of the Buffalo, but I am at a loss to understand how their succession to the throne would involve us."

Rag Ears raised a paw. "Ah, friend, it involves all of us who travel the roads. For you see, when the Meerkat Road was planned, it was to have connected Kazirazif directly with Beaverpool, but the bears who inhabit the woods and hills between the two cities would have none of it. So the only other course was to the north, through the Kingdom of the Buffalo. The Bison King was quite willing and only took a small toll from each passerby.

"But when a new Bison King took over some years after the Meerkat Road had been built, well, let's just say that a somewhat unusual aspect of buffalo law came to light. It seems that it's customary for the incoming Bison King to change every single law set up by his predecessor. And it was the new Bison King's fancy to take not stones or scrip or metals from each party, but a member of each party to be held as a slave in his palace.

"The traders along the road quickly took to bringing a fish or some lesser serpent, which had been duly registered as a member of the caravan, to give to the Bison King. And he took the creatures because it was his law and he wasn't about to change it." The kit fox shrugged. "That's how it's been ever since. Every time a new Bison King takes office, new rules appear for using the Meerkat Road."

Bobcat nodded. "So what is it now? The last time I went through, I just had to sign a paper saying I wouldn't take part in any plot to overthrow the king's government."

Rag Ears smiled. "That was over ten years ago; you must be older then you look, friend. No, the new Bison King is a nut for knowledge. Anything and everything interests him as long as he hasn't seen it before. Every traveler who enters his realm must show him something new, tell him something he hasn't heard, deliver to him some strange sort of a something that he cannot explain, something he can think about and muse over during the evenings. I understand," and he looked pointedly at Fisher, "that he has quite an extensive library."

Bobcat rubbed his chin. "Something he doesn't know, huh? What happens if you tell him something he's heard before?"

"Oh, he kills you."

"What?" All three of them sat forward.

"Oh, yes. Turns you over to his guards, they take you outside, and they trample you to death. Quite ugly, I've heard. Of course, I got through without any trouble."

Fisher narrowed her eyes. "Why? What did you do?"

"I had the sense to be born a fox." Rag Ears grinned. "One of the first groups through after this new Bison King took over was the Cayottle Acrobatic Circus, twenty of the finest vulpine aerialists you'll ever lay eyes on. And knowing their lives were on the line must've really inspired them, because when they were done the Bison King announced that no fox need ever show him anything again; their display had given him more to think about than the last twenty books he'd read." The kit fox's grin seemed to Bobcat to sparkle even more. "It's been quite a boon to those of us of the vulpine persuasion. The transport companies are hiring right and left."

"You cannot be serious." Skink's eyes were wide in the firelight. "This Bison King will actually kill us if we have nothing new to show him?"

Fisher gave a snort. "You better believe it. Once a Bison King comes up with something, he sticks with it."

"Oh, yeah," Bobcat added, "no matter how stupid." He turned to Fisher. "So now what? Up the Tundra Road past Madison, over Comston Pass, and down on Kazirazif like that?"

"Take too long," Fisher answered, rubbing her chin. "Unless I'm mistaken, we're on something of a schedule. We'll hafta risk it—go through at night and keep to cover—but we haven't got a lotta time to burn here."

The sparkle in the old kit fox's eyes seemed almost as bright as the stars starting to show themselves overhead. Bobcat blinked against the sight; he didn't feel so tired that his eyes would be playing tricks like this.

Rag Ears nodded to Fisher. "That's your plan then? To carry on?"

Fisher shrugged. "We haven't got too much of a choice." She gave a half-grin. "Have we?"

"There's always a choice." Sudden sparks appeared in the kit fox's fur, smoothing over his scars, knitting his ears back together, changing the gray of his fur to the sheen of burnished metal. "But sometimes the alternatives just ain't all that attractive."

"You can say that again," Fisher muttered.

Bobcat stared, the kit fox sparking and glowing until he grew into a thing of white fire, half-fox and half-star and still smiling at them. "You won't forget what I said?"

Fisher gave a shrug. "Have I ever?"

The thing turned its glowing eyes on Skink, whom Bobcat could hear muttering his whispery chants to himself; then the white fire was pouring over him. And such a different fire than that of the Blood Jaguar's eyes, not dark and murderous and full of hate, but a fire of warmth and of hope, a fire as sweet and welcoming as the fires Shemka Harr had built against the winter gusts in their cave so long ago.

Then the light was away from him, and Bobcat saw the kit fox turn back to Fisher. "You're one of my best," Bobcat heard a voice say to her. "If anyone has a chance at this, it's you. Just make sure you come back, hear?"

Fisher gave a little chuckle. "Well, I'm in no position to promise anything. . . ."

Wonderful laughter rang in Bobcat's ears. "You watch yourself, imp; you're not getting away from me that easily." The air gave a twitch then, and the kit fox shot up into the darkness, the stars seeming to dance around him.

And then they were alone, the three of them sitting by Fisher's little gas stove and staring at the sky. Bobcat thought he heard her sigh out a "good-bye," but when he turned to her she was taking another dollop of stew from the pot.

Bobcat wanted to say something, but he didn't know what. A part of him wanted to run screaming through the night, away from kit foxes that burst into flame, away from reptiles that coiled just beyond his vision and spoke without using words, away from cats of blood and death and smoke and fire and all the weird and twisted things that had happened to him in the past two days. And another part of him just wanted to start singing, to shout with the joy the fox's white fire had set in his heart and the deep and rustling rhythms he had heard at the kiva that morning.

It took him a few minutes to settle himself enough to choke out, "Who . . . What . . . That . . . You . . . It . . ."

Fisher looked over at him. "Problem?"

"Yes!" Bobcat burst out. "What just happened here?"

"You mean who have we had the honor of entertaining around our cook fire this evening? Is that what you mean?"

"No! I mean what in the bright blue above is going on in this place?"

"That," Fisher said with a shrug, "I can't say. But our visitor has been none other than the Curial Lord Kit Fox, my mentor and patron. You have heard of him, haven't you?"

Chapter Four

In the Hall of the Bison King

Fisher's bald statement surprised Bobcat, but not as much, he realized with a start, as it probably should have. Sure, he'd seen some pretty amazing tricks performed by magicians and conjurers at festivals and parties, but this . . . this had felt different somehow, as if the trick hadn't just happened in front of him but *inside* him as well.

No one said anything else that night. There didn't seem to be any need. Something hung in the air, a caressing breeze that was half the soft touch of an evening in early spring and half something beyond even that. It lulled Bobcat with such a gentle stroke that the dark fire of those terrible eyes seemed to sink to embers far in the back of his mind while Fisher dismantled her stove and Skink helped Bobcat wash everything up. Then they stretched out by their packs and fell asleep.

The feeling stayed with Bobcat the whole night, and at light's first touch against his eyelids he let himself drift awake, staying curled where he lay with his eyes closed, just lazing for a while. The stream chuckled past, the sun smooth on his fur, and he could almost forget that he was halfway between home and nowhere on a crazier mission than anything he'd ever dreamed up while under the catnip.

Catnip. He hadn't had a roll in how many days now?

A shiver iced through him, made him sigh and climb to his

paws, the sun suddenly too hot, the ground too dusty and dry, the stream too loud and murky. Even the blue of the sky was wrong, a sort of haze hanging around the horizon like dead moss. He rubbed at the ache starting up in his forehead; he had no reason to be here, didn't understand any of it, and the others thought he was an idiot anyway. Why shouldn't he just creep off, let them worry about this whole plague thing? It wasn't like he could help, and it wasn't any of his business anyway.

No, wait. He shook his head. It *was* his business, had become his business when the Blood Jaguar had kicked him into the Brackens. She'd picked him out for this, had left her eyes in his head, and he had to find out why, get some control over them somehow, or he'd go crazy. Wasn't that it? Hadn't he already decided this? Why was it bothering him again?

The catnip urge pulsed in his gut, a new, sharper edge to it than he'd ever felt before, and he swallowed against it, trying to figure out why it was so different. And when the answer came, bursting with a sudden cold fire into the back of his head, Bobcat couldn't stop himself from gasping; it was her eyes, the Blood Jaguar's eyes, boiling at his thoughts.

Those eyes were still doing things to him, digging in, somehow connecting themselves to his catnip cravings. Bobcat caught his breath, remembered Fisher saying something about the Blood Jaguar tearing folks apart from the inside without ever lifting a claw. He could feel it, could feel those eyes trying to slip up behind his own, trying to give him their hate-filled dirty, dusty view of things.

Bobcat shook his head again, took a breath, forced himself to look up, to see what was really there: the sky of a gorgeous spring morning, sharp as crystal and even bluer, a touch of mist dancing up from the prairie, the breeze holding just a whiff of sage. Bobcat shivered, those eyes ebbing down to embers again, took a few more breaths, and felt as normal as he had the past few days. He had to wonder, though, what else the Blood Jaguar's eyes might be doing to him.

The clanking of pots drew his attention to the side of the stream, where Fisher was once again stirring something over her gas stove. She waved a spoon at him. "Skink's already made the coffee. You want some?"

Skink's coffee was interesting, little twists and turns in it, places where it tasted almost like something, then spun off and tasted like something else. It went well with the scramble Fisher had mixed up, grains and nutmeats all stirred together like oatmeal. Bobcat had two bowls before bringing up one of the questions that was bothering him. "So, how're we gonna deal with the buffalo?"

Fisher chewed and swallowed. "Seems to me we should move down the road right about to their border. We rest there and stay out of sight till nightfall, then scoot across quick as we can. The moon's waning, but there'll be plenty of starlight out here. We shouldn't have any trouble finding our way." She shrugged and took another spoonful.

"Uh-huh." Bobcat looked at her. "It's four days across those plains at the best of times, y'know, and the way we're doing it, we're gonna need places to hole up each dawn."

"Yep."

"And just where did you have in mind?"

"Smugglers' caves; the first day, at least."

"Oh, sure. If those buffalo don't walk patrol too often. And if we can get to Council Bluffs before dawn. And if they haven't closed the caves off by now; I mean the cliffs above the Bison King's palace never seemed that good a place for a hideout to me. A whole lotta ifs, Fisher." He rubbed his chin and shrugged. "But I guess it'll hafta do."

"I'm so glad you approve."

"Forgive me," Skink said from his perch on the lip of his bowl, "but mightn't we just call upon the Bison King and explain the situation to him? If we can get him to understand the importance of our mission—"

Bobcat waved his spoon at the lizard. "Not likely. He's prob'ly heard the story about the fisher, the bobcat, and the skink; seems ev'ryone else around here has. And you remember what the Lord Kit Fox said last night: if the Bison King's heard it, you end up trampled."

He heard Fisher chuckle. " 'The Lord Kit Fox'? Do my ears deceive me, or is our friend Bobcat starting to believe what we tell him?"

"Yeah, OK." Bobcat looked away, his ears heating up. "Maybe some of it. I mean after everything that's happened, well, how many times can a guy get hit over the head before he starts believing in things like hammers?"

Skink rustled a laugh. "My goodness, Bobcat. That is almost a paraphrase of Iguana of Didris Kiva's argument in the third and fourth books of his—"

Bobcat held up a paw. "That's OK. Really. I'm sorry I brought the whole thing up." Something occurred to him then, something from Shemka Harr's stories. "Hey, but wait a minute. Isn't the Lord Kit Fox always going around messing with folk's minds? In the stories, I mean? Like the one where he gets that whole falcon hunting party to sit up to their necks in a river for three days trying to catch flying fish?"

"That is true." Skink cocked his head. "Though the Lord Kit Fox is technically one of the Seasonal powers in the Curia, controlling the aspects of summer, his trickery is well reported in the literature. Perhaps we ought to verify the information he has given us, if any way of doing so can be—"

"Nah." Fisher, pulling the stove apart, waved a length of pipe toward the sky. "Sure, he can get annoying at times, but I like to think I've developed a pretty good read on him over the years." She stopped, and a kind of sideways smile pulled at her whiskers. "When he's joking around, laughing and smiling and acting all relaxed, that's usually when he's being the most serious. And last night, well, I've never seen him try so hard to be cute and charming." Her smile faded. "I'm gonna take what he said *very* seriously."

She started stowing the stove parts in Bobcat's pack. Bobcat watched for a moment, his mind not quite turning over, then shook himself and began gathering up the pots and pans. It didn't take long to get everything loaded up, and then they were off, across the stone bridge and away over the prairie along the Meerkat Road, heading southwest.

Through the morning they walked, the road rolling with the hills over the hard red dirt. They passed a few prairie dog villages, little clusters of red-roofed holes surrounded by wheat fields, but the folk they saw just scurried away without even waving hello. More bluffs appeared to the left and fell away behind them as the grass came back in, poking itself higher and higher into the blue of the sky.

Just before midday, Bobcat thinking they ought to be pretty close to the buffalo's border, Fisher stopped and pointed ahead to a place where the road dipped down between two hillocks and was swallowed in the grass. She gestured for Bobcat to follow her off the road, then squatted down, the grass now over their heads. "We'll wait here," Fisher whispered. "The border station's just down that rise. After dark, we'll sneak around and go overland. Buffalo aren't too deft; we oughta be able to hear a patrol if it comes around. We keep our ears open and keep moving forward, we'll get to Council Bluffs just before dawn. That sound good?"

Skink was peering over her shoulder. "I know little of the arts of stealth, but we are comparatively small and should be able to stay out from underhoof of such as buffalo."

"Yeah," Bobcat said. "How much trouble could it be?"

So they lay there through the whole of the afternoon. Bobcat gnawed some trail mix, tried to ignore the way the sage scent made him think of catnip, did his best to sleep; after all, they'd have to travel all night if they wanted to make Council Bluffs by dawn. The grasses swayed around them, and slowly the light faded, shadows piling up among the stalks till it was dark. Fisher gave Bobcat a poke, and off they set, creeping around the hillock to the border.

They were caught almost immediately: Bobcat didn't even see the trip wires until he was setting a shaky paw right onto them. He tried to leap back, but cords wrapped his legs, hauled him up, twisted him back, and the next thing he knew, Fisher was flying into his face. Alarms screeched; searchlights swept the grass, Fisher cursing from somewhere over Bobcat's left shoulder. He couldn't tell if it was Fisher's fur or the strands of the net tickling his nose, so he figured not biting would be best. Skink he could hear chattering below him, so at least they were still together.

Something came crashing through the brush—several very large somethings, in fact. The alarms switched off, and the searchlight slowed to a stop, its beam shining right into Bobcat's eyes. "So, ho!" a voice boomed from behind the light. "Intruders, is it? His Majesty will be most pleased!"

The light clicked off, and Bobcat felt himself hoisted from the ground. "And try not to crush them this time, you moron!" the voice continued. "You know how His Majesty enjoys visitors! Take them away, and I'll get this thing set back up. There may be more of them out here."

Bobcat was jostled over sideways, which at least got Fisher out of his face, and then, with a thunder of hooves, they were off, swinging wildly, the net digging into Bobcat's cut-up sides. The thick scent of buffalo was everywhere, pressing even tighter than the ropes, and it was all Bobcat could do to keep himself breathing. On and on it went, rolling, bouncing, squeezing, till Bobcat just gave up and let himself pass out.

How long he stayed out he didn't know, but when he opened his eyes next, daylight streamed into them. Clenching his eyes shut again, he heard voices: deep and gruff, definitely buffalo voices. "His Majesty's in the Great Hall," one voice was saying. "He's expecting you." The rolling returned, slower this time, the clatter of their captors' hooves softer, echoing slightly.

Bobcat drifted in and out till something hard slapped up against him. A floor, he realized, squinting at it. They'd been dumped in a pile somewhere. A voice rang out: "Cut them loose that I might see what you have brought me."

The constriction around him eased with a snap, and Bobcat flopped to the floor, his legs tingling and unable to hold him. A grumbling voice from above said, "We caught them trying to sneak past the border gate, Your Majesty."

"Indeed?" came the first voice. "We shall see what they have to say for themselves."

After a minute, Bobcat's legs began feeling solid again, so he rose to see what was what. Light flickered all around, bouncing at odd angles, like he was underwater. But it was just the way the torchlight reflected off the golden sashes the buffalo along the walls wore, the tips of their horns also flashing with bronze points. Everything else in the room seemed to be brown, wooden panels interlocking over the floor and walls, the ceiling carved with arcs and waves that made strange shadows dance in the torchlight. These shadows seemed to draw Bobcat's eye over his shoulder, to beckon him to turn around, so he turned to see the other side of the room.

Bright as a lightning flash shone the throne of the Bison King, all blues and greens in the browns and golds around it; Bobcat almost staggered back. The king himself rested on a cushion the color of the sky after a summer shower, a mantle of fresh woven grasses draped over his back. His crown glowed silver-white in the torchlight, amethysts and emeralds gleaming between his horns. He looked down from his throne with large dark eyes, and a smile pulled at his beard. "Well, well. A bobcat, a fisher, and a skink. One hears many interesting stories about such folk traveling together. Perhaps we shall see if they contain any truth."

Bobcat saw that Fisher and Skink had gotten up and were now standing next to him. Fisher took a step forward and bowed. "Your Majesty, please forgive us our means of entry. We were in haste, and—"

The Bison King raised a hoof. "Please, my dear. Excuses are unnecessary and tiresome. You are here before me now, and that is all, under the Rules of the Road, that need concern us. So let us commence."

He lifted his head then and bellowed, his voice ringing through the Great Hall. "You will come before me one by one to present me with information, theories, stories, concepts: knowledge, that most ephemeral of commodities, the only truly ennobling element of our life upon this earth! All knowledge is welcome here, but that which serves me now can serve me in no greater measure! So give me not that which I already possess, for it would make you of no use to me or to the world! And what is of no use to me or to the world will be destroyed as all useless items should be! So speak!"

At that, the Bison King settled back onto his cushion and held out a hoof to Skink. "Good reptile, step before me."

Bobcat glanced at Skink, the little lizard still as a stone, his sides scarcely fluttering, but his eyes wheeling and spinning. After a few seconds, though, he snapped to life and bowed with a flourish. "Your Majesty," his voice squeaked into the silence of the hall, "I bring before you an item, an item of deep interest and concern to my own heart." Skink unslung his satchel and pulled his pebble from it. "It is an item to which a mystery is attached, Your Majesty."

The Bison King crashed his front hooves together. Two buffalo appeared and unfolded a table from the floor in front of him. "Please, good reptile, climb up that I may see more clearly that which you bring before me."

Skink put the pebble back into his satchel, scurried up the table leg, and settled down at the very nose of the Bison King. "Your Majesty," he said, holding the pebble aloft again, "this was my luck."

"The luck of a skink." The Bison King nodded his shaggy head. "I have read of it. But I take it you use the past tense for a reason."

"Just so, Your Majesty. For if Your Majesty will look closely, Your Majesty will see that my luck is no longer here."

"Indeed?" The Bison King brought an eye, nearly the size of Skink's whole body, to bear on the pebble. "That would truly be curious, if it were indeed so."

Skink's head twitched back a bit. "Your Majesty?"

The Bison King waved a front hoof. "I merely point out that one small pebble looks much like another. I do not impute any duplicity to you, friend Skink, for your luck has certainly deserted you if you have come before me with nothing more than a pebble. But I put it to you that someone has taken your luck, pebble and all, and has left this luckless pebble in its stead. Does this clear up your mystery?"

Skink stared at the Bison King, then down at the pebble, turning it over and over in his claws. His eyes went wide then, and his mouth dropped open. "This . . . this . . . this pebble, it has a lump here where mine did not, and this part is too rough, and . . . and . . . and I am a fool." The lizard looked back up at the Bison King. "Your Majesty is correct."

"I rather thought I was." The Bison King clashed his hooves together again, and the pair of buffalo appeared at his side. "Skink, you are sentenced to death, said sentence to be carried out at my convenience. You are to be held in custody here until I have dealt with your companions, on the chance that neither of them has any more to offer me than you had. Do you understand the sentence?"

Skink didn't move for some seconds, only his neck twitching slightly. But at last he stirred and said in a tiny voice, "Yes, Your Majesty." He climbed down from the tabletop, and a group of buffalo moved to surround him.

Bobcat stood, waiting for Fisher to do something, for the Lord Kit Fox to appear overhead, for lizards with those red collars and black rustling fronds to burst through the doors at the back of the hall, for a shout to go up from someone swooping down to rescue them. But Fisher just bowed her head and seemed to cower against the wooden floor—nothing flashed into being beside them; the silence of the place was not at all broken by the cries of angry reptiles.

Bobcat didn't know what to think. Weren't they on a mission here? Weren't they supposed to save the world? It wasn't supposed to end like *this*, was it?

Six buffalo stood in a ring, their heads inward and their eyes fixed on Skink, crouched motionless on the floor between them. The Bison King then turned and gestured with a hoof. "Good bobcat, step before me."

"Your . . . Your Majesty?" Bobcat blinked for a minute. What was he supposed to do? Show this buffalo something he hadn't seen before? Yeah, right; that seemed *real* likely. He glanced around wildly. Maybe he could make a break for it, run for the doors, slip out between the guards' legs before they stomped on him, get out and away from this place before—

But a picture jumped into his mind then, a picture of himself, younger but still seated on a floor in front of another someone who was so much bigger than him: not the Bison King, but the old lioness, Shemka Harr. The paneled wooden walls of the room became for an instant the gray stone of their cave, and the shaggy brown fur of the Bison King was suddenly her tawny coat. And she was giving him a challenge, a challenge she had given him before, a challenge to a game they had played many times that winter, a challenge to . . .

"A riddle game," Bobcat said aloud.

"A riddle game?" The Bison King cocked his head. "Do you propose a riddle game, good bobcat?"

Bobcat blinked once or twice, then gave a rough sort of bow. "Uhh, yeah, I mean yes, Your Majesty."

"A true riddle game? In the old tradition?"

"Well, yes, Your Majesty." And Bobcat realized that he almost knew what he was talking about. "By the Par Fang Rules, unless Your Majesty prefers one of the variations."

"No, no, the Par Fang Rules are fine." A smile twitched over the Bison King's face. "I have not participated in a riddle game since my days at the Cayottle Academy. Few in my kingdom," and the king cast his eyes over the buffalo standing guard, "possess even a modicum of wit, and none seems able to comprehend the least level of riddle combat." He turned back to Bobcat. "Sir, I do indeed look forward to this."

Bobcat gave another bow. "Your Majesty is too kind."

"Please, step forward so I may hear you better. On the table, if you would." Bobcat rose, jumped up onto the table, and the Bison King said, "Since I am here the challenger, the first couplet will fall to you."

The rules for Par Fang riddle games were poking back into Bobcat's head: riddles asked in related pairs, each pair building somehow on the last. He sat down, cleared his throat, bowed once more to the Bison King, raised his right front paw to show he was ready to begin, then spoke the first riddle that came to him: " 'Steps the stately, measured tread in fits and stops, stretches, breaks. Starts so slow, then off it's sped, but never varies, always straight.' "

"Well spoken." The Bison King had slid forward on his cushion, his hooves resting on a silver bar in front of his throne. "Your intonation, your rhythm, all most admirable, most admirable. The answer is, of course, 'Time,' but I haven't heard the riddle so well delivered in more years than I would care to mention." The king gave him a quick smile.

Bobcat swallowed against the lump in his throat and lowered his right paw. He knew there were six or seven riddles that were couplets for that one, but he could only remember one all the way through. Raising his left paw, he recited: " 'Twisting her head, his body outstretched, her head his body, his body their foot. Sweet and gentle to start, turbulent rushing ahead—' "

" 'Ending at last in a great wash of sweat,' " the Bison King finished. "Pray forgive me, but I was overcome with the spirit of the game. I knew the moment I laid eyes upon you that you were a classicist, and you have not disappointed me. I have never heard the 'Time and the River Flowing' couplet delivered with such aplomb, one might almost say virtuosity." The Bison King inclined his huge head slightly toward Bobcat. "A well-played opening move."

Bobcat lowered his left paw and sat waiting. Shemka Harr had tried to teach him the various strategies for these situations, and he thought maybe he could remember some of the classic couplets, but it had been—what—twenty years?

Sweat gathered on the pads of Bobcat's paws as the Bison King raised his right front hoof and recited: " 'Bundle balls that pierce the shuddering sky, rest your pinioned paws, pray, not on me. Yours is the throne of delight, scented and padded so bright 'gainst your prickling, venomous bite.' "

The words kicking up memories between Bobcat's ears, he was sure Shemka Harr had told him this one. He could hear himself asking her what *pinioned* meant, and she had said it had to do with the feathery look of the fur on their legs, the fur on the legs of . . .

"Bees!" Bobcat blurted out. "It's bees!"

"Well done," the Bison King said with a grin. He lowered his right hoof and raised the left. " 'Leap forward now, you champion of the light! Darkness falls away, the cold of night dispelled! Melt you the hearts and souls of all, the crimson orb its sad descent reversing! Wake, oh, wake; the tilted time is past, and all erupt and shimmer in your sight!' "

Bobcat's sides had begun to itch again. He wanted to say "The Sun Arising," but that didn't seem right somehow. He didn't think he'd actually heard this one before, and then and there, sitting before the blue and glowing throne of the Bison King, Bobcat drew a complete blank. He tried to remember the riddles that went with "Bees," but nothing kept coming to him. The Bison King was starting to tap his right hoof, and the *click, click, click* echoed through the hall and set Bobcat's whiskers twitching.

After another minute, the Bison King cleared his throat. "I'm afraid I must call time, good bobcat. Have you an answer for me?"

The throbbing in Bobcat's sides had moved to his head. "The, uhh, 'The Sun Arising?' "

The Bison King did not lower his left hoof. "Ah, my friend, I fear you fell into my trap. The riddle is, in fact, 'The Springtime Rising.' "

Bobcat said nothing, couldn't look up from the tabletop. He ran his tongue over his upper lip.

"Well played, though, my friend," the Bison King said, his voice quiet. "I am almost tempted to make it two out of three; you have no idea how much I've longed for someone to riddle with." He blew out a breath. "But no, that would not do. Precedents can be dangerous things, and I have no desire to get myself caught up in the various legal battles that would raise. Bobcat, you are sentenced to death, said sentence to be carried out at my convenience." He paused again. "I am sorry."

"Yeah," Bobcat muttered. "Me, too."

More buffalo appeared at the Bison King's side, and they shuffled Bobcat down from the table over into the circle where Skink was crouched, his eyes clenched shut, little rustling whispers rising up from him. Bobcat let himself be pushed into the space there and settled down to peer out between their legs. They were going to kill him here in a couple minutes, trample him to death, and bury whatever was left somewhere out here on the prairie.

The thought came to him easily, he could almost think he was dreaming, but he ached so much, he knew he had to be awake. He was going to get stomped pure and simple, and no one back home, not Lorn or Rat or Garson or anyone else, would know what had happened to him. Not that they would probably much care, except maybe Garson.

He hadn't even said good-bye to her, and for some reason that made him feel worse than anything else. The others he could leave without too many regrets, but to never see Garson again, never hear her voice, never tell her how much she meant to him, well, he just was *not* going to let that happen.

It sort of surprised him, the intensity of this feeling, but just thinking of her perked his whiskers up, set him looking around the throne room, trying to think of some way to get out of this.

And what Bobcat thought then made his ears rise and a grin cross his face. He looked out through the buffalo leg cage and saw the Bison King gesture with a hoof. "Good fisher, step before me."

Yeah. The guy still had to deal with Fisher.

Fisher sat in the same position, crouched on the floor where they'd been dumped. But at the sound of her name, she seemed to unclench, a bright smile flashing through her whiskers. "Your Majesty," she said, and she padded forward to settle at the foot of the Bison King's throne. "I propose nothing so grand as my friend Bobcat, nor anything as complex as my friend Skink's problem. I propose to demonstrate a simple mathematical principle." And Fisher bowed.

The Bison King arched an eyebrow. "Then perhaps you wish simply to join your friends now, for I am familiar with mathematics from set theory through differential calculus and beyond. I fear there is little you could show me."

"I am aware of that, Your Majesty, but, please, bear with me for a moment, and I will happily explain. You are, no doubt, acquainted with the concepts of the integer, the group of positive and negative numbers, and the additive inverse?"

"Most certainly. All very basic, I assure you."

Fisher gave another smile. "The idea of negative numbers has never disturbed Your Majesty?"

"Disturbed?" The Bison King's brow wrinkled. "Why should negative numbers disturb me?"

"Does it not set you to wondering, Your Majesty, how you can add something to something else and end up with nothing?"

The Bison King chuckled. "The additive inverse is but a mathematical convenience; it has no physical reality."

Fisher raised a paw. "Your Majesty is certain of this?"

That made the Bison King stop for a moment. He cocked his head. "Are you proposing that it does?"

"With Your Majesty's permission." Fisher bowed again.

"Well now." The Bison King's eyes lit up, and he waved a hoof at Fisher. "Please proceed, by all means."

"Your Majesty is too kind." Fisher shot Bobcat a look that sparkled in the torchlight. "I shall need your table, Your Majesty, and a plate with three apples on it."

The Bison King crashed his hooves together. After a moment, a buffalo stepped forward, a silver plate with three red apples balanced across her back. The buffalo let the plate slide to the table as Fisher jumped up onto it and bowed once more to the king.

"Your Majesty, I show you three apples." She patted each apple with a paw. "Three red apples on a plate. Now, three minus one," and she took one apple from the plate and placed it on the table beside her, "equals two." She patted the two apples still on the plate. "Is this not so, Your Majesty?"

"Most certainly," the Bison King replied.

"And two minus one," she took the second apple, placed it beside the other on the table, "equals one." She patted the apple left on the plate. "Nor should it surprise anyone that one minus one," and she took the last apple from the plate, set it down on the table next to the other two, "equals zero." She tapped the empty plate. "Your Majesty agrees?"

"Quite; there are no apples left on the plate."

Fisher raised a paw. "But, Your Majesty, is it not *also* true that zero minus one," and here Fisher reached down onto the empty plate and came away with an apple in her claws, an apple as big and red as the others on the table, "equals negative one?" And Fisher placed this other apple on the table beside the first three.

Bobcat stared through the legs of the buffalo around him. The apple had just appeared in her paw as easily as if she'd taken it from the plate.

The Bison King sat forward, his shaggy brow wrinkling.

"And in the same way," Fisher went on, "negative one minus positive one," and she reached down and took another big red apple from the empty plate, "equals negative two." And this apple joined the others on the table beside Fisher.

"What trickery is this?" the Bison King muttered, sliding farther forward on his cushion.

"Oh, no trickery, Your Majesty. It's simple mathematics. After all, negative two minus positive one, you will agree," and another apple came up from the plate to be placed next to the others, "must equal a negative three." Fisher looked up at the Bison King. "Mathematics, Your Majesty."

"Mathematics," murmured the Bison King. "Where did those other three apples come from?"

Fisher looked shocked. "Your Majesty, there are only three apples here."

The Bison King's eyes shot over to hers. "What? I count six altogether."

"But Your Majesty must remember the three negative apples on the plate. Six positive apples plus three negative apples equals three apples all told." Fisher passed a paw from the apples to the plate. "There can only be three apples here. That's mathematics, is it not?"

The Bison King looked from the apples to the plate and back again for a while without saying a word.

Fisher cleared her throat softly. "Perhaps if I did it in reverse." She picked up one of the apples from the table and held it out for the king to see. "A negative three plus a positive one," she lowered the apple onto the plate, and when her paw came away the plate was still empty, "equals negative two, you see? And the five apples left here plus the negative two apples now on the plate still equals three apples."

The Bison King had slid so far forward on his cushion, his nose was practically resting on the tabletop. Fisher picked up another apple from beside her. "And negative two plus positive one," the apple went down onto the plate and promptly vanished, "equals negative one." Fisher tapped the plate again with a claw. "The one negative apple still on the plate plus these four positive apples equals the three apples we had originally. Do you see, Your Majesty?"

Bobcat could barely hear the sniffling breath of the Bison King as he hunched his huge head over the table.

Fisher picked up another apple. "Negative one plus positive one will then bring us back." She set the apple on the plate, and again it disappeared; she smiled up at the Bison King. "Back to zero, Your Majesty."

The Bison King slid back a bit, his eyes wide under his bushy brow. Fisher held up a paw. "But, Your Majesty, just to be complete." She picked up the remaining apples and set them one after the other on the plate. "Zero plus one equals one, one plus one equals two, and two plus one equals three. Three red apples, Your Majesty." She patted them each and looked up with a grin. "Three red apples on a plate."

For a while, no one moved, the Bison King staring at the plate of apples for so long that several of his guards began shuffling their hooves, fear starting to scent up from them and tickle Bobcat's nose.

But the Bison King raised a hoof, and the shuffling stopped. It was another minute, though, before he spoke, and when he did his eyes stayed on the apples. "Never before," he rumbled, "have I witnessed such expertise. Truly, good fisher, your knowledge of mathematics leaves mine behind. It shall be some time, I fear, before I have such a mastery."

Fisher bowed. "Your Majesty is too kind."

The Bison King leaped forward then, clearing Fisher and the tabletop by a few feet, and clattered to a landing in the center of the hall. "Let this proclamation go out to all corners of my kingdom and to all who travel through it! I, the Bison King, decree that from this day onward, all fishers shall be exempt from the Rules of the Road, all laws and all regulations therewith set up by this administration! And further, any bobcat or any skink who passes through my kingdom need only present me with one red apple in remembrance of those apples that freed this bobcat and this skink! So it is proclaimed, and so it shall be!"

Every buffalo in the hall, all those surrounding Bobcat and Skink and all those that lined the torchlit walls, gave forth with trumpeting blasts that shook the floor and nearly tipped Bobcat over. And one buffalo at the end of the hall who had been writing furiously in big letters on a huge piece of parchment rolled the thing up and shouted, "The proclamation goes out!" before barreling through the doors and vanishing from sight.

The buffalo surrounding Skink and Bobcat curled themselves back and out of the way, and Fisher, all smiles, jumped down from the table and motioned to them with a paw. Skink scuttled across the floor to her side, and Bobcat followed more slowly, still not exactly sure what had just happened.

The Bison King turned to face them. "I will understand completely," he said, his voice suddenly very quiet, "if you wish to leave at once. However, I do invite you to stay for breakfast. I seldom have the honor of company at my table."

Bobcat was about to decline the offer in a loud voice, but the growling of his stomach made him stop. Fisher gave a laugh and replied, "I think that's a 'yes, thank you,' Your Majesty."

So the Bison King returned to his throne, clashed his hooves together, and buffalo appeared all around, balancing tables on their backs and pushing carts along in front of them. Some took panels from the walls, and sunlight streamed in, glowing over the polished wooden floor and setting the king's crown to sparkling. And the food: breads and fruits and cakes and cheeses, mugs of juices, milks, and coffees, all there for the taking and more than enough to quiet Bobcat's little doubts about eating breakfast with somebody who had sentenced him to death not ten minutes ago.

They ate in silence for a time; then the Bison King cleared his throat. "I still find myself wondering, though, if they are true, the stories I have heard about fishers, skinks, and bobcats traveling together."

Skink didn't have a mouthful, so he spoke up. "That's difficult to say, Your Majesty. For my part, I have not actually heard any of the stories that are told about us."

"Indeed?" The Bison King wiped at his beard with a green silk cloth. "There are several, none of them very complimentary, I fear. It seems that Death herself travels ahead of you, her claw reaching back along the road you have taken and tearing the land asunder. There are those who say you have entered into a covenant of blood with her, that you travel to Kazirazif to set her plan in motion. Other stories tell of your doomed and hopeless quest to stop this plan of Death's." He shrugged. "I have heard and read many variations."

Fisher nodded. "To tell you the truth, Your Majesty, we're sorta grasping at straws ourselves. I can't find the real story anywhere I've looked, so, I don't know, if you've had any insights, we'd really appreciate the info."

The Bison King drew himself up on his throne. "My conclusions will remain my own. For while I value the insights you have given me, I do not trade information. I gather it, and the fruits of my gathering are for none save myself." His gaze grew softer beneath his shaggy brows. "But this I *will* tell you." His eyes moved from Fisher to Skink and then settled on Bobcat. "If I had only these stories to judge from, I would have the three of you killed, right here and right now, all rules, laws, and regulations be damned. But I do not."

Bobcat blinked back into the Bison King's gaze, and the Bison King rose from his throne. "I must go now and attend to other affairs. You are all three welcome here for as long as you wish." He bowed to them each then and strode from the hall. Most of the buffalo followed, only two remaining at either side of the door.

The sudden silence seemed to snap something inside Bobcat, a cloudy wave rolling back to the stub of his tail, his sides itching, his eyes like cotton balls in his head. The food had settled strangely in his stomach, and all he could think about was lying down someplace for a good long while.

But Fisher was standing up and stretching. "We'd better get ourselves gone. We've wasted enough time around here."

Skink took another mouthful of peach and scuttled over to Fisher's side. "I agree. A place that first threatens death, then offers breakfast is not a place of calm reasoning. There is an air of unreality to this whole affair."

Fisher adjusted her pack and squatted down to let Skink clamber onto her shoulders. "Yeah, but if you'd gotten yourself stomped here, it would've been just as real as anywhere else. The sooner we put Council Bluffs behind us, the better I'll feel." She turned to look at Bobcat. "Shall we?"

It took Bobcat a minute before he could reply; the Blood Jaguar's eyes had risen up again, their dark, heatless flames skittering under his fur and licking at his sides. He almost wanted to scratch them, to roll around on the Bison King's inlaid floor, but he knew it wouldn't do any good. He made his thoughts turn to Garson, and that brought him enough warmth to stand and even give Fisher a little smile. "Yeah, OK. But only if you'll tell me how you did that."

Fisher cocked her head. "Did what?"

"Oh, c'mon. You know; how'd you make those apples appear from the plate like that?"

Fisher smiled then, turned away with a flick of her tail, and started toward the doors at the end of the hall. "Pure mathematics, my friend. Anyone can do it. You just hafta know where to grab."

Bobcat blinked at her. "What?"

Fisher was laughing now. "Or so the Lord Kit Fox would have me believe. Taught me everything I know about math and science. You coming?"

Bobcat shrugged his pack into place, hurried after her, caught up just as she was giving the buffalo at the door a little bow. Then through the corridors the three went, out into the courtyard, out the main gate, and back onto the road under a bright morning sky.

Chapter Five

Away across the Prairie

They put as much distance between themselves and Council Bluffs along the Meerkat Road as they could before Bobcat had to stop. It was only about midmorning, but he didn't think he could go another step. "Let's just set up here. I don't know about you, but I didn't get a whole lotta rest last night."

Fisher didn't look like she felt much better, and Skink had already curled up in the fur between her shoulder blades. "Yeah, OK," Fisher breathed out. "We wouldn't've gotten moving till tonight anyway if we'd stuck to our first plan."

So they stumbled off the road and stretched out in the scrub grass. Bobcat could scarcely push his pack off before he was down on the ground and asleep. His dreams when they came were mostly noises: crackling fires, hoofbeats, claws scratching against wood, shouts and purrs and words that he couldn't quite make out. He was able to sleep around them, though, so he didn't really mind them that much.

It was late afternoon when he opened his eyes again. Fisher and Skink were still breathing softly to themselves in the grass next to him, so Bobcat settled back against his pack and watched the patterns of birds flying overhead. He felt odd, tensed up but relaxed at the same time. Escaping from certain death could do that to you, Bobcat knew; he'd made it through some pretty narrow scrapes before. This one, though, this one had been, well, different somehow.

He was just wondering why when Fisher stirred, stretching a yawn from the tip of her nose to the end of her tail. "Ah, nothing like a little excitement to make you sleep. Get the stove out, will you? Might as well stir up some dinner." She gave herself a shake and stretched again.

Bobcat undid his pack and rummaged the various tubes and cans out onto the ground, his mind still brooding. And that was the problem. Like Shemka Harr had always said: "Thinking'll get you answers, Ghareen, but brooding only ties your mind up in knots. You start worrying about 'what ifs' and 'might've beens,' you're not gonna be any good to anyone."

Through all this, he was vaguely aware of Fisher putting the stove together and firing it up, of a sweet, spicy smell rising from the pan, of Skink shaking and blinking and saying with a yawn, "Ah. Lunchtime."

Fisher gave a little snort. "Dinnertime."

The lizard stood. "Good heavens. I didn't realize how tired I was."

"Yeah, well, adventure'll do that to you."

Skink blinked a few more times. "Adventure? Why, yes, I suppose this is an adventure, isn't it? It hadn't really occurred to me before; I've never been associated with anything adventuresome, you see."

"You've gotta have the knack for it." Fisher took a sip from her spoon. "Some weeks, I can't turn around without tripping over an adventure; they just seem to creep outta the woodwork." She put a pinch more of something into the pan and stirred it.

Skink nodded and scuttled over. "Yes, I suppose your line of work entails a great deal of adventuring."

Fisher shrugged. "It's a living." She sipped at the stew. "You ready for some of this?"

"Yes, thank you." Skink perched on the lip of a bowl as Fisher ladled a dollop into it. "It smells delicious."

"Thanks. It might be a little hot, though." She poured some

into another bowl and pushed it toward Bobcat. "You want some? Hey, Bobcat, you in there?"

Bobcat started back. "What?"

She tapped the bowl with the ladle. "Dinner?"

"Oh. Right. Thanks, Fisher." Bobcat pulled the bowl closer and settled onto the ground.

Fisher was still watching him. "You all right, Bobcat?"

Bobcat felt his ears heat up. "Yeah, I guess. I've just been thinking about some stuff. Sorta useless, I know, but, well, there you go."

"Thinking?" Fisher filled her own bowl. "About anything in particular?"

"Well, that's the problem. I'm not really sure."

Skink looked up from his stew. "Perhaps some of what we discussed the other day has taken root? The various aspects of the Curial powers can take you by surprise that way."

Bobcat quickly raised a paw. "No, no, nothing like that. It's, well . . ." He turned back to Fisher. "I mean I used to have adventures all the time, too, back when I was trav'ling. Brains and eggs, I once got chased halfway from Madison to Cayottle in the dead of winter by this wolverine who thought I'd been making eyes at his daughter! And the time I fell in with these squirrel brigands over past Timberline . . ." Bobcat stopped to gather his thoughts. "I've had scary stuff happen to me before, but this buffalo thing we just went through, it, I don't know, it's hit me all sideways." He looked from one to the other. "Y'know what I mean?"

Fisher licked the back of her spoon. "Maybe. Everybody changes, Bobcat, and you're not as young as you used to be. I mean when I think back on some of the things I did years ago, I've gotta thank the Lord Kit Fox that I'm even still around." She shrugged. "Everything's always different."

"Most certainly," Skink piped in, "especially after the Curial experiences you have had recently. I believe I can empathize with your feelings in this matter, Bobcat, for in leaving behind my home, my kiva, my family and friends, my entire world, if you will, I have entered into a world that would have been quite beyond my ken but a few days ago. The conceptual level upon which I have operated heretofore has been diametrically opposed to many of the realities I find here in the exterior world.

"In the same way, you have been recently exposed to a world beyond the habitual, to a Curial world not of your former experience. I would hypothesize that this exposure has had the same effect upon your way of viewing what would normally be the day-to-day realities of your life as my exposure to this world of danger and adventure has had upon mine. You have, if you will, been forced back a step to view your former world from another perspective, much as I have had to do."

Fisher gave a little chuckle. "Yeah, well, that prob'ly set him straight."

Skink looked at her, then back at Bobcat. "Oh, dear. Have I become carried away again?"

Bobcat wasn't sure. "Maybe," he said, "but I think you might've answered some of it for me." He brushed at his whiskers. "You said you had to leave your home and your friends and all. I haven't had a lotta places in my life that I've thought of as home, but that old tree stump by the River, all the folks back in Ottersgate . . ." He thought of Garson and had to smile. "This's the first time I've had something I want to go back to at the end of an adventure, y'know? The first time I could look forward to anything. I guess things *do* change."

"Yeah," Fisher said, dishing herself the last bit of stew from the pan, "and speaking of change, I've been thinking about the desert coming up. We might wanna start traveling at night even if we're not sneaking around; it'll be a lot cooler when we get farther southwest. Whadda you two think?"

Bobcat nodded. "I was gonna mention that, actually. I got no problem with it."

Skink stuck his head up over the rim of his bowl. "Normally, I would disagree, I being rather dependent upon the sun to keep my temperature up and my mind alert. But as I am not doing my own walking, I needn't be too energetic. The warmth of Fisher's fur is enough to keep me adequately awake, and I can drowse and meditate through the day while you two sleep. I think the situation will prove most satisfactory."

So Bobcat drank his bowl empty and sloshed a little canteen water into it while Fisher started pulling the stove apart. Skink licked his bowl clean and scuttled out; Bobcat washed it for him, stowed the bowls, waited for Fisher to tuck the stove parts away, then shrugged his pack over his shoulders. Fisher pulled on her pack, Skink climbed up into her fur, and they were off down the road and into the evening.

On they went, the night coming down around them. After a while, the stars came out, the whole countryside glowing in the gray of their light. Bobcat had gotten used to seeing them through the leaves of the trees at home, but out here there was nothing between them and him but empty air. They formed patterns he remembered from Shemka Harr's descriptions so long ago, the Old Bear of Winter settling at the western horizon and letting the springtime stars have their chance at the sky.

The shapes made Bobcat think of the black and white swirls of Garson's fur, and he felt a strange, warm loneliness settle over him. It had a sweetness to it he could almost taste, a sighing sweetness that rustled through his whiskers and settled somewhere in his chest, his eyes full of stars and the night filled with her remembered scent.

Midnight came and went, the moon sliding up the sky and shining its half-light over the prairie. Bobcat was lost in his own thoughts, but he did notice, whenever he came up for air, that Fisher and Skink were deep in their own conversation up ahead of him on the road. Bobcat didn't mind, though; he had Garson to think about.

The moonstruck landscape continued to roll him gently along, mountains rising black and jagged ahead and to his right, cricket calls shimmering through the grass beside him. The whole night ticked and pinged in Bobcat's head almost like catnip, and it wrapped itself so thickly about him that he didn't remember them ever stopping to rest. Everything was scents and sounds and sights and sighs, all bundled up around and inside him, and Bobcat floated along through it and beside it while the moon drifted up to the top of the sky.

A timeless time later, the black above began to grow gray, and Bobcat slowly came to realize that there were mountains around him, the road climbing and the ground all dirt and rocks. He followed Fisher and Skink around a bend in the road ahead, and the border crossing he saw there stretched across the road in the predawn coolness made him sure he was dreaming.

The searchlight blasting into his eyes and the bark of the sentry snapped him awake to its reality, though: "Halt! Who approaches the King's Crossing?"

"The border?" he muttered. "In one night? But how—"

In front of him, Fisher was answering the sentry: "We have passed through Council Bluffs on our way to Kazirazif."

The sentry strode forward, his golden sash sparkling in the searchlight's beam. "We've had no messenger from the king. How do I know you're not smugglers?"

Another buffalo appeared, blocking the glare, his eyes wide. "Captain! Look at them! The . . . the Pads of Doom, sir, sent by the Shadow herself!" His voice narrowed to a tiny squeak and choked off.

The first buffalo jumped back. "The Pads of Doom!"

Bobcat almost jumped himself when Fisher gave a hiss. "Yes, filthy mortals! We have returned!" She stalked toward the sentry, her back arched, her fur bristling. "Now open this gate lest you wish to feel the tickle of the Strangler's claw at your throats!"

The second buffalo had already leaped onto a treadmill and was straining against it. It squeaked beneath his hooves, and Bobcat saw the gate begin to rise.

"Go!" the first buffalo groaned, huddling against the wall. "Please!"

Fisher bowed and slipped under. Bobcat followed and found himself looking into a valley, the mountains high on either side, a series of switchbacks sliding along the slope below him. And there, down through a couple miles of air, the valley opened out onto a flatness that glowed slightly in the dim light.

Behind him, the gate crashed down, and Bobcat took a deep breath. "The desert. . . ."

"Fisher," he heard Skink saying, "I am shocked. I cannot approve of employing such a ruse. Playing upon the credulity of simple folk who know only the half-true story passed on through the—"

"Yeah, yeah," came Fisher's voice. "If they're gonna keep saying that stuff, I say we oughtta use it when we need to." Bobcat turned, saw Fisher gesturing down the valley. "We'll camp for the day at the bottom of these switchbacks."

Memories poked at Bobcat's mind. "Down by the spring?"

"Yeah." She shook her head and gave a little grin. "We made good time, didn't we?"

Bobcat could only stare for a moment. "Fisher, it takes three days to get from the Bison King's palace to the western border here."

She shrugged. "So we had a little help."

"Indeed." Skink's head peered over her shoulder. "Had we needed any further proof of Curial intervention, I would say we have just received it."

Bobcat couldn't think of a thing to say. Fisher gave him another grin and set off down the switchbacks.

The ridge to their left kept the sunlight from them until they were about halfway down, but at last it came pouring over into the valley, its heat washing past them and away along the rift. Back and forth down the valley wall they went, stopping more than a few times to rest, and Bobcat was very glad there was a spring waiting for them at the bottom.

As they went, he munched on trail mix from his pack and blinked at the dust in his eyes. He had avoided the southern desert as much as possible in the days before he'd come to Ottersgate, preferring the routes along the Tundra Road or the byways that twisted through the forests and swamps of the southeast, and the few times he had passed this way had only made him more determined to steer clear of it. It was too much like where he'd grown up.

They reached the bottom at about midmorning, found the

spring, and made camp beside a grove of piñon pines. Bobcat had never felt so tired in his life, slumping back against his pack without even taking it off. The last thing he heard was Skink muttering, "Of course, Curial intervention has its price;" then he was out. When he finally came awake late that afternoon, he didn't remember having any dreams at all.

Fisher was tending a little bonfire in a stone ring off to one side of the spring, and a moment's search showed him Skink perched on a rock not far from Fisher's fire ring. Bobcat stood, padded over, and Skink snapped his head up. "Ahh, Bobcat. Did you sleep well?"

Bobcat stretched the kinks from his legs. "Yeah, thanks. All that walking must've tired me out more'n I thought."

"Yes, I suppose, though I was equally tired and did not walk a step." Skink twitched his head closer to Bobcat's ear. "Our way is surely tended by Those Above."

"Yeah," came Fisher's voice. She slid over and stretched out in the shade of the piñon pines. "Anything to get somebody else to do their dirty work for them."

"Fisher!" Skink jerked back so hard he nearly knocked himself from his perch. "How can you say such things?"

Fisher laughed. "I've gotta get my little dig in ev'ry once in a while; the Lord Kit Fox expects it of me."

Bobcat cleared his throat. All this Curial stuff still made him feel like ants were crawling over him, and last night's impossible prairie crossing just made it worse. "So OK, we're ahead of schedule. Is that good or bad? I mean it's only a couple days to Kazirazif. Then what?"

"What else?" Fisher was scratching an ear. "We get to the Basharah gate at dawn and find the Raj Tevirye, she takes us to the Ramon, and we start asking questions. Simple."

"Simple," Bobcat repeated. "And what sorta questions might we be asking?"

Skink twitched his head to one side. "Why, questions about the end of the story, Bobcat."

"Story? What story?"

A little rasping sigh puffed from Skink's nose. "Good heavens, Bobcat, the story that we're involved in, the story that my grandmother gave us the beginning to, the story that everyone along our way has been familiar with and has alluded to time and time again! We have yet to hear, however, what transpires once we reach Kazirazif, so it is there that we must discover what our role is in the *ending* of the story and how we can, as Grandmother wished, change it."

Bobcat gave a sigh. "Oh, right. That story."

"Yeah," Fisher added, "and it's that changing the ending that we've gotta concentrate on. There's too much riding on all this for us to lose sight of that."

"So now wait," Bobcat said, holding up a paw. "All that stuff you were reading us about from that book, your grampa's book about the Plague Year—you think that's stuff's gonna happen again? I mean all that stuff? For real?"

Fisher closed her eyes and rubbed her forehead. "As real as half the folks you know back in Ottersgate, 'cause they're the ones who're gonna be dead, simple as that." She turned a cold stare onto him. "You were talking yesterday about your friends back home. Well, line 'em up, take every other one out, and plant 'em in the fields up north of Donal's Lake. And there's your Plague Year."

Skink rustled to another perch on his rock. "Fisher, please, I find this all distressing enough without your commentary. I've been mulling over this point for some time, and while I have to admit that there are certain in my kiva to whom a slight touch of plague might not be too detrimental, I shudder with apprehension at the merest thought of that cold paw stroking the flanks of some of my comrades.

"For I have begun to view it thus: I am nearly of age to begin attending the courtship functions at the kiva, and there are several in my social group with whom I would happily dance the steps of matrimony." Skink shrugged. "I find that by focusing my thoughts on the personal possible tragedy of the Plague Year reaching certain young ladies of my acquaintance I am able to muster the strength necessary to carry me on in our efforts to stop what is, in fact, an unimaginably large and terrifying possible tragedy for the entire world."

Fisher smiled. "Skink! You got a girlfriend?"

The lizard gave a clicking laugh. "Still potential girlfriends, Fisher, for some years. But you shall be the first to know of my eventual engagement." He cocked his head. "May I hope to be remembered at the time of your betrothal?"

"Mine?" Fisher rolled over in the shade of the piñon pines. "Sure. Just don't hold your breath; I've got enough troubles without throwing in kids and a husband as well. And anyway, from what I've seen of romance, I'd say I can take it or leave it, and leaving it has been a lot more convenient so far." Her eyes flicked to Bobcat. "How 'bout you, Bobcat? Anyone in your life we should know about?"

Bobcat felt his ears drop. His mind had been wandering while Fisher and Skink had talked, thoughts of Garson making up most of that wandering. "Well, I don't know. I mean, uhh, well, she's just . . . just a friend really, I guess. . . ."

Fisher sat up, grinning. "Well, well, now. I didn't know there were any other bobcats around Ottersgate."

Even in the shade of the pines, Bobcat's fur was heating up. "Well, she's, uhh, she's not . . . not exactly a bobcat. . . ."

For just a moment, the only sound was the bubbling of the spring. Bobcat looked up to see Fisher's grin spread wide through her whiskers. "Well, c'mon!" she said, rubbing her paws together. "Who? What's her name? Do I know her?"

Bobcat wasn't sure he wanted to go into the whole thing; it was none of Fisher's business, and he couldn't believe she was really interested. And besides, he'd never really talked to anyone about Garson before, had kept private whatever it was between them, something all his own that he could hold close on long, cold nights.

But he *had* been thinking about her almost constantly for the past few days, and he did love to tell the story to himself. . . . "I don't know," he said after a minute. "You might not know her."

"The name, Bobcat," came Fisher's voice from in front of him. "Just tell us her name."

Bobcat cleared his throat. "Uhh, she's, uhh, she's Garson Rix."

"Garson Rix?" Fisher's grin had gotten even wider. "You mean the field supervisor over at Brackens Farms? *That* Garson Rix?"

Skink twitched his head back. "Brackens Farms? But that would mean that she . . . she is a—"

"Yes, she's a rabbit, OK?" Bobcat glared from one to the other. "That a problem for anyone here?"

Skink raised his claws. "No, not at all, Bobcat."

Fisher was rubbing her paws again. "There has *got* to be a story to this, Bobcat."

"Yeah, well. . . ." Bobcat looked down at the pine nuts in the reddish dirt. "It's sort of embarrassing, really."

"Good." Fisher settled back. "Those're the only stories worth listening to."

Bobcat gave her a look but began anyway. "It was last year about this same time. I'd been sorta making it a habit to go over to the other side of the Brackens, finding rabbits out on their own and, well, chasing 'em around a little."

Skink's dry voice interrupted: "Chasing the rabbits? But whatever for?"

Bobcat could only shrug. "I dunno. It was fun, I guess, and I never really hurt 'em."

"Yeah, right," Fisher breathed.

"Well, I never meant to!" Bobcat ground his teeth. "I just, well, I got a little carried away sometimes, I guess, specially when I had a bad roll of catnip in me."

Fisher had turned to look at Skink. "Multiple fractures, contusions, lacerations—you know, the works."

"That's not true!" Bobcat burst in.

"But to our friend's credit, no one ever died, and most of his 'playmates' were treated for minor cuts and bruises, a certain amount of shock, and released." Fisher turned back to Bobcat. "I helped Leigh Thax treat some of 'em, y'see. Oh, I'm sorry, Bobcat; you were telling us how much fun it was."

Bobcat growled and set his ears back. "Now, look—"

"Please, Fisher, Bobcat, both of you!" Skink had scurried to the tip of the rock and thrust his head between them. "I am sure you will agree, Fisher, that none of us is above reproach for his or her past actions, but this is neither the time nor the place to bring such matters up. Bobcat is telling this story only because you asked him to, and it seems obvious to me that his embarrassment in telling it indicates a change of heart on his part. I feel that this story will be of great interest, so if there are no objections, I would like to ask Bobcat to please continue." The lizard's eyes stayed fixed on Fisher.

Fisher gave a snort and waved a paw in the air. "Oh, by all means."

Bobcat managed to bring his ears back up. "OK," he began again, setting the story back in place. "See, that's what I *used* to do. But one day, I was sneaking along north of Brackens Farms, and I came across a rabbit all by herself, munching away on some carrot greens. I was downwind of her, and I was able to get right up between her and the Brackens without her even noticing."

"Oh, good," Fisher muttered. "To cut off her escape route."

"Well, that's how I was thinking then. So I squeezed in, settled down, and decided I was gonna play it all cool and clever this time. So I say, in as deep and rumbly a voice as I can, 'A lovely afternoon, isn't it?' And this rabbit, she shoots straight up into the air, spins around, and plops right back down onto her carrot greens. Her eyes snap up to mine, and I can almost hear her heart thumping, it's so loud. I put on my best innocent face and say, 'Oh, did I startle you, rabbit? I'm terribly sorry.'

"Now, I was thinking she'd make a dash for it. I mean most rabbits woulda shot outta there like a flood was coming one way and a forest fire the other. But even though her eyes are bigger'n cabbages and her whiskers're jittering like they're ready to take off on their own, she answers in this clear, bright voice, 'Oh, not at all. You might want to announce yourself a little louder next time, though. Some rabbits are hard of hearing.'

"That confused me, I gotta admit, and this was the first time I'd heard a rabbit say anything except, 'Help!' But I figure I'll keep being clever, so I nod and say to her, 'You know what your trouble is, rabbit? You don't get enough exercise; I can tell just by looking at you.' I was just waiting for her to make her move, was watching for any little shift in her balance, any little dart of her eyes, to tell me which way she was gonna go.

"Well, she just brought her hind legs back underneath her like she was settling in for a chat or something, and she looks up at me with this, I don't know, this fascination in her face almost. 'Is that what you do?' she asked me, her voice high and sweet as honey. 'I didn't know we had any traveling physical education coaches around Ottersgate. It must be terribly interesting work.'

"It was too weird; she had this wide-eyed innocent look to her, and I started thinking maybe she was feebleminded or something—I mean more feebleminded than most rabbits. But I just couldn't tell, and I decided I'd play along for a while. 'Oh, sure,' I said. 'It's wonderful work. I specialize in rabbits and other small rodents, and I find that I can, oh, let's say motivate them strongly to pursue a personal phys ed program.'

"She batted her eyes. 'I'll bet you're very persuasive.'

" 'Oh, yeah,' I replied. 'Awfully persuasive.' And I give her my big grin, the one with all the teeth in it.

"Her eyes dart around a little, and I figure she's about to make a move, but she just starts in again: 'I've often thought about starting an exercise program, but you know how things pile up, what with the planting and getting the rotation schedules worked out and all.' And then, all at once, she cocks her head to one side, and she gives me the cutest little smile. 'Of course, that doesn't mean I don't get *any* exercise. Ever since they dug that bounce pit out by my house, I've been spending a few hours up there when I can.'

"By now, I was beyond surprised—I don't know, intrigued, I guess. I was sure she was gonna try something, knew that she was planning to make some sort of a move, but her eyes were so bright and her smile was so friendly, I didn't really know what to think. This had never happened before, and I gotta admit, I was hooked. So I kept it up. 'A bounce pit,' I said. 'I don't think I'm familiar with the term.'

"Well, her eyes just lit up. 'Oh, it's the latest thing in lepine aerobics. It's quite an exciting new technology. Would you like to see it? It's not that far from here. . . .'

"OK, I figured, if she wants to play, that's fine. I figured she's a rabbit, and what can a rabbit do to me? I figured I'd just play along and see what she was up to."

Fisher gave a little snicker. "Sucker."

Bobcat had to grin at that. "Yeah, I figured a lotta things. So I rubbed my chin and said, 'Not far, huh? Well, I should be keeping up with the newest things in my field. OK, rabbit, lead the way.' And I leaned forward just a little. 'I'll be right behind you.'

"She bowed her ears toward me. 'Oh, I wouldn't have it any other way. Follow me, then.'

"This was where I was expecting her to make her break, to shoot off and try to lose me. But all she does is turn and start loping along southward, just slow hopping, I mean, like she was out for a stroll or something. So I fall in behind her, but I keep my nose right on her tail so I'll be ready when she tries anything.

"But she doesn't; she just trots along, and I trot right behind her. After a minute, I get an idea, and I lengthen my stride a little, just enough to graze her right flank with my front paw. She jumps, and I call out, 'Oh, I'm *awful* sorry, rabbit! I guess I'm just used to traveling a little faster!'

"She gives a quick look over her shoulder, and I can smell a touch of fear washing back from her coat. But she calls out in a light voice, 'Well, we could jog, if that would make you more comfortable!'

"I do the grin with the teeth again. 'Good idea,' I say, 'and it would be so much healthier.' I was having fun with all this, more fun than I'd had in a long time.

"So she faced front again, picked up her pace to about a normal rabbit scamper. I sped up, too, kept my nose right on her tail so she could feel my breath, and I was so into the game that I didn't even notice how quick my breath was coming.

"I let us get past the farm buildings and all before I grazed her flank again. 'I *am* sorry, rabbit,' I said, 'but you can see why I was so concerned about your exercise program. This is not the pace of a healthy rabbit.'

"She called back then, and she was panting some; she even got her voice to crack. 'Well,' she said, 'I . . . I think I could go a . . . a little faster. . . .'

"I was so sure I had her. 'Do you think so?' I asked, and I graze her flank again, but a little harder this time.

" 'Oh, yes, I think so!' she calls back, her voice suddenly strong as ever, and, whoosh, she's off at a dead run. We'd come to the southwest corner of the Brackens by then, and she leaped away up into those little rocky bluffs they have down there.

"Well, I let loose a snarl and took off after her, my paws slipping on the gravel as she darts up and up between the boulders, and it suddenly hits me how much my legs ache and how I'm panting for ev'ry breath. And that's when I know she'd been leading me on just so she could get to these bluffs and lose me. But I just snarled again and set my sights on that fuzzy little tail flashing through the boulders ahead of me. She wasn't gonna get away from me.

"She keeps leading me higher and calling back, 'It's up here,' and I keep lunging after her, just missing that tail ev'ry time. 'Not much farther now,' she says. 'Just around this corner.' I'm panting, ev'rything getting steeper and steeper. 'Right up here!' she calls back, and she jumps up onto this little ledge on top of the rock pile. 'This way,' she says and scampers away. I drag myself up onto the ledge, and I could feel the foam at the corners of my mouth." Bobcat swallowed at the memory. "I, well, I don't like to think what I woulda done if she'd been standing there.

"But she wasn't. The ledge was this narrow thing curled around a knob of rock right at the top of the whole pile of boulders. I could smell her trail going along the ledge and around the other side of this little knob, so I start stalking her, following her scent out onto the ledge. 'That's it,' I panted out. 'Rabbit stew! That's all . . . you're gonna . . . gonna be . . . good for . . . when I . . . when I . . .'

" "I step past this knob of rock and I'm about to follow her around when something flashes on top of it, and she's standing up there saying, 'But you haven't seen the pit yet.' I try to turn, but the ledge is too narrow, and then she's jumping down at me, and wham! She slams into my left side while I'm half turned around. I stagger sideways with my breath whooshing out between my teeth. . . .

"But the thing is, there's no sideways to stagger to, and over I go into empty air. I tumble down and land with a thump at the bottom of this pit."

Fisher was rolling in the dirt. "I love it!" she whooped out, and even Skink was making dry wheezing noises.

Bobcat's ears were heating up again, but he had to admit it was sort of funny. "It took me a couple minutes before I could get upright again and another couple before I could breathe right. And then I hear her voice calling down, 'It's a nice pit, isn't it? You see, the exercise comes in jumping out. That shouldn't be too hard for you; after all, you *are* in such good shape.'

"I snapped my head up. It wasn't that deep a pit, but her head against the open sky still looked awful far away. 'Rabbit . . .,' I growled.

" 'The name is Rix,' she says, 'Garson Rix. You might want to remember that. Now, you go find someplace else to play, OK, kitty? Some of my field crew's in the hospital because of you, and they'll be there a lot longer than it'll take you to climb out of this pit. But you just go on your way, and we'll forget all about it. OK?'

"I couldn't believe it. I mean this rabbit was trying to make a deal with me! All the way along, she'd had this plan, coming up with it right when she needed it, and all to get me to leave the other rabbits alone! I couldn't think of a single thing to say.

"So I just sit staring up at her, and she says, 'Look, I'm not going to tell anyone about this, and you sure don't have to if you don't want to. So just leave the Brackens alone from now on, and everything'll be fine, all right?'

"She seemed to be waiting for something, but I couldn't find a word. I kept thinking about what would happen if this *did* get out, that this rabbit had kicked me into a pit and was blackmailing me into leaving the Brackens alone. I was, well, I guess I was still stupid enough to have an ego, and it had just been severely bruised.

"When I still didn't say anything, Garson clicked her tongue at me. 'Poor little kitty,' she says at last. 'It could've been worse, you know. I could've let you go on a little farther and kicked you off the other side of the ledge. That's a lot farther down. But you just keep your distance from now on, and it'll never come to that, OK?'

"I just stood there and stared up at Garson's little head peering over the edge. *Clueless,* I think, is the best word to describe me right then.

" 'OK,' she says with a shrug. 'I'll leave you here to think things over.' And her head disappears from the circle of sky above me.

"Well, I nearly panicked right then and there. What if she brought someone else? What if a whole bunch of little rabbit heads suddenly popped up around the rim of the pit and started laughing at me? She'd said she wouldn't tell anybody, but she was a rabbit, and ev'ryone knows that rabbits're the worst gossips anywhere.

"But then, ev'ryone knows that rabbits haven't got brain one in their heads, and ev'ryone also knows that no rabbit could ever outsmart anything tougher'n a carrot. This Garson Rix, I decided during the three hours it took me to climb outta that pit, was not your typical rabbit, nothing about her that'd make you think she was a rabbit except her long ears, fluffy tail, and twitching nose. I also decided maybe I would lay off the Brackens for a while. I mean she'd said she wouldn't tell anybody, and maybe she'd change her mind if I kept stumbling around. I was just completely dazed and confused, so I staggered home and went to bed."

Fisher was wiping the tears from her eyes. "I'm gonna have to look this Garson Rix up when we get back. I've heard good things about her from Leigh Thax, but nothing like this."

Bobcat held up a paw. "But you haven't heard the rest."

A grin curled through Fisher's whiskers. "There's more?"

"Oh, yeah." Bobcat shuffled in the dirt a little. "I almost wish there wasn't, but, well, you've come this far . . ."

"Certainly. By all means," Skink piped in from the edge of his rock. "I can hardly wait to hear."

Bobcat grimaced. "Yeah. Well, I sorta crept around for a few days, waiting for the comments and the snickering, but they never came. Even when I saw other rabbits in town or in the woods, nobody seemed to have heard the story. I got more and more curious about this Garson Rix; I mean you talk about your prime opportunities! This thing that Garson had on me has to be right up there on the list, and she wasn't doing anything with it, just like she'd promised she wouldn't.

"I got to thinking that no one was gonna find out, and I was sorta thankful to Garson for keeping her word. When I was sober, that is. And I guess that wasn't all that often, when I think about it. There was something bad in the catnip that year—I don't know, too much rain or something—but sometimes, when I'd had a roll or three, I'd get this burning lump in my gut, and I'd think about this Garson Rix and what she had on me. And the hate I felt for her, it was, gods, I don't even like to think about it now.

"And one morning just before dawn a couple weeks after the whole thing with the pit, after a really, really bad night and still higher'n the top of the Bailey Oak, I stormed outta my stump and tore off toward Brackens Farms. I'm not really sure what I was thinking, but I guess I figured if I went somewhere where there were lotsa rabbits, I could work my way through them till I got to her. I mean I was more than wasted, just completely gone.

"I remember getting to the Farms, and I remember tearing stuff up outta the ground and screaming a whole lot. It was still before dawn and I guess only the field supervisors were there, so I didn't do a whole lotta damage before Garson jumps out in front of me and shouts, 'Here we go, kitty! C'mon; let's play!'

"I took off after her like, well, like I wanted to kill her, more or less, and she raced away from the Farms and up into the woods. I threw myself at her, trying to snap off that fuzzy little tail, but, well, she was fast and I was all catnipped up and besides, it turned out she'd been planning for something like this ever since our first run-in.

"She leads me up into the woods to a place she's fixed up, runs between two trees, slips to one side, and slams a paw down on the lever she's put there. I go barreling past, the net underneath me goes snap, and I end up bundled into a little ball dangling from a tree branch, whap, out cold.

"Garson told me later that she left me hanging there, went back to the Farms, and told everybody she was all right. Her boss said she could take the rest of the day off if she wanted to, so she said OK, circled back around to where she'd left me, and sat there next to the tree till I came to.

"I couldn't figure out what was going on. The 'nip had run its course, the hangover pricking at the base of my ears, but when I tried to shift around to see where I was, I hear Garson saying, 'What am I going to do with you, kitty? I thought we had an agreement.'

"By this time, I'd figured out I was tangled up in a net. 'What . . . Who . . . What . . . ,' I managed to say before the fur at the back of my throat got too thick. But I knew who, and I knew what, and, well, I think you can figure out how much of an idiot I felt like.

"Garson came around to where I could see her. 'I kept my part of the bargain, kitty,' she says. 'I'd hoped I wouldn't have to use this little item, but you forced the issue, and so here we are. Now, are we going to talk like reasonable folk, or am I going to start selling tickets to my new pin-the-tail-on-the-bobcat booth?'

"Whatever stupid pride I'd had was gone. 'Yeah, OK,' I said, 'we'll talk. But can't you let me down, please? I . . . I don't feel so good. . . .'

"She goes back around behind the tree, and after a minute I'm sliding downward. Then the ground's under me, the net's loosening, and I flop forward onto the forest floor. I just lay there awhile, my head feeling like some giant bell just waiting to slam out a clang and snap my neck clean off. But pretty soon I hear leaves crackling, and Garson's standing next to me.

"She clears her throat, and, oh, how it echoed through my swollen head. 'All right,' I said without looking at her, 'you win. I give up. Go get your rabbit friends and staple me to the side of your barn; believe me, the way I'm feeling, I'd *rather* be skinned alive.'

"I hear her sigh. 'Well,' she says, 'I can see you're in no condition to talk right now. Can you walk any? It's not that far.'

"I didn't know what she had planned for me, but I didn't care. A rabbit had beaten me, chewed me up, and spit me out; whatever she was gonna do, I deserved every bit of it. I somehow got to my paws and trudged through the trees after her, my fur feeling like pins sticking into me and visions in my head of her taking me down to the Farms, all the rabbits gathering around, shaving me bald, burning my whiskers off, tying me up, and throwing me into the River. I couldn't've run even if I'd wanted to, and I didn't want to. All my stupidity had poofed away, and I saw that I was just this drunken idiot, not even a match for a rabbit.

"Well, Garson led me down and around the forest, and I had no idea where we were going. But at last she says, 'We're here,' and I look up to see this tree stump, all nicely carved and done up with awnings and flower boxes. 'You can stay in the guest room till you feel up to it, and then we'll have that talk.' And she opens the front door and ushers me in.

"The halls're big enough for me to walk through, and she opens a door into a cozy room that smells like lavender after a rain shower. 'Sleep it off,' she says. 'We'll talk this evening. OK?'

"I couldn't move, kept expecting the torches and pitchforks, but Garson just pushed me into the room and closed the door. The pillows and blankets in the corner were too nice to ignore, and I was curled up and asleep before I could wonder what was going on.

"And when I woke up I don't know how long after that, I just lay there on the blankets and looked at the little fern garden outside the window. It was late in the afternoon, and I would've thought I'd dreamed the whole thing if it hadn'ta been for, well, the room and ev'rything. I heard scratching at the door, and Garson poked her head in. She asked if I was feeling better and asked me to stay for dinner."

Bobcat stopped, his head full of words and feelings, and looked off down the dusty path along the bluffs to the end of the valley where the sands of the desert glowed in the late-afternoon heat. "And we talked—I mean really *talked*—something I hadn't done with anyone in years, and, well, I'd never in my life talked to anyone like Garson before. We ended up getting along, I guess; at least she doesn't seem to mind that I come visit her every few days." He looked down the trail some more. "Gods, I miss her. . . ."

Things stayed quiet for a while, the hot breezes chattering through the piñon pines, the sky a deep blue, sharp as the jags of rock poking up into it. Then Bobcat shook himself. "So, that's the story. Sorry I went on so long; it's just, well, I've been thinking about her and all that stuff a lot, maybe too much. A pretty good story, though, I think."

Fisher gave a chuckle. "I have got to meet Garson Rix when we get back. Anyone who tames wild beasts as a hobby . . ."

Skink laughed. "There is nothing," he declared, "like a humorous tale before dinner, and I would like, with your permission, Bobcat, to propose a toast to Ms. Garson Rix." He scuttled down from the rock and took up his little water bag. "May the Twelve watch over her and keep her from harm."

"Yeah," Fisher said, lifting her cup, "and maybe while they're at it they could spare a squint or two for a few other folk I don't think I need to mention."

Bobcat raised his canteen. "I'll drink to that." And he repeated Skink's phrase to himself as he drank, pretty sure by now that the Curials were out there somewhere and wondering if they were actually listening. He felt the hollow burning of those eyes, quiet at the back of his mind, and wondered if maybe the Blood Jaguar was listening, too. It struck him then, all at once and making him swallow more than just the water: the Plague Year, the Blood Jaguar, Kazirazif, everything they were heading toward and everything that was going down that trail into the desert with them.

And Bobcat couldn't help wondering if he would ever see Garson again.

Chapter Six

The Desert

So they ate and washed and filled their canteens and set off into the shadows settling around them. Down the trail between the bluffs they walked, the scuffling of the pebbles along the path sending echoes skittering over the walls.

The cliffs got higher and higher as the trail wound its way downward, got higher and drew away on both sides, the whole flat plain opening in front of them, and by the time the sun had dropped huge and angry red below the horizon ahead and to their right, they had come out at the base of the mountains and stood looking over the desert.

Bobcat had told himself he would be ready for it, but he wasn't. The desert to him would always be the place he had run out into so many years ago with no thought but to get away from where he was. It made him feel like a kitten all over again, the great plains rolling with nothing but sand and lesser serpents. And the sun glowered at the edge of it too much like those awful eyes that burned, squirming up behind his forehead. The whole idea made him shiver, there in the dry desert evening: sure, the Blood Jaguar was supposed to live on her Shroud Islands deep in the southern seas, but Bobcat could imagine her spending a lot of time in this place.

Fisher broke in on his thoughts: "If we keep up a good pace during the night, we oughtta get to Canyon Pienta just after daybreak. There's no water there, but there'll be shade, and we can camp for the day. Sound good?"

Skink rustled at Fisher's shoulder. "I know of this land only from my reading. The Lord Eft holds it in high esteem as many of my brethren call it home. But I can speak with no authority here; I will trust your judgment entirely."

"Yeah, whatever." Bobcat's sides were beginning to itch again. "The less time we spend out here, the better by me."

And so they started forward, the road still warm under Bobcat's paws, out into the desert. He concentrated on images of all the wonderful sunsets he had seen from the south parts of the Brackens when he and Garson would meet, all the evenings they'd spent there together, and that managed to keep those eyes at bay for most of the night, the breezes growing colder and slower till they dropped completely, the black quiet of the place settling like a sheet over Bobcat's back. Stars shone everywhere, crackling with the glint of shattered ice overhead, every once in a while sparking to life and tossing a shard to burn across the sky.

It could've been pretty, Bobcat told himself, and almost laughed aloud. He was shivering in the silence, scared to death that that growling would spring up behind him and he would turn to see that monstrous cat again. Every butte along the dark horizon seemed to be some huge crouching thing waiting quietly beside the road for any travelers stupid enough to be wandering around out there in the middle of the night.

Every time they stopped to rest, Bobcat could almost feel eyes resting on him, not just the eyes that guttered inside his head, but other, external eyes. When they were moving, it was all right; he had other things he could brood on and worry about then. But when they were stopped and he was taking a quick leak behind a boulder, or when they settled beside the road for a breather and a little trail mix, the feeling of eyes in the night would come itching along through his cut-up sides.

Finally, about midnight, Bobcat couldn't keep quiet. "Something's out there," he whispered toward Fisher's ear.

Fisher nodded slowly, cracking walnuts between her paws. "Oh, yeah. Ever since we hit the desert."

"You mean . . ." He stared through the darkness at her. "You mean you knew?"

"Sure. Stands to reason. The Lord Kit Fox said we had to be more careful the closer we got to Meerkat Town. There's a lotta things out in this desert, and some of 'em look to the Strangler herself."

Skink's gray head appeared like a ghost at Fisher's shoulder. "Indeed. In my readings I have come across numerous references to Death cults among the mammalian, avian, and even reptilian communities. The desert, due to its relative inaccessibility and extreme climate, is a great attractor of such groups. We must remain vigilant."

This conversation didn't do much to help Bobcat's jitters once they started back down the road. Those eyes were bright fierce points of red now, burning back behind his own. All around, the blackened silence of the night wore on, and Bobcat strained his eyes and ears for any scuffle, any little glow, any signal that whoever was out there was about to make a jump at him.

But the night went along just as it had, nothing more than vague feelings and stray scents ever reaching him. After a while, the crescent moon came wafting up, the rocky buttes and outcroppings taking the slight silver into themselves and making a few more shadows from it. The dribs of plant life spiking out of the sand seemed to shift every now and then, crackling quietly in the night, and Bobcat was glad when the sky behind them began to grow gray and the air began to stir with the approaching dawn.

Orange was just sparking at the eastern horizon, the first light of morning touching the arms of the joshua trees, when Bobcat followed Fisher and Skink around the jagged base of a tall, paw-shaped butte. Fisher was calling back, "Canyon Pienta's just up another couple of miles, seems to me, off to the right of the road," when Skink gave a sudden cry.

"Fisher! Stop!" The lizard had scurried to the top of Fisher's head and was clinging to her ears.

"Ouch! Skink, what in the—" She turned to face forward and stopped dead in her tracks.

Bobcat had already stopped; he'd seen the two things ahead in the road the same time Skink had shouted.

They were cobras, big cobras coiled in the shadow of the butte and swaying slightly in the heat of the sun's first breath across the sands. Bobcat had seen cobras before, stalking in groups along the streets of Kazirazif the times he'd been there; they always made his fur stand on end, their hissing voices, the way they managed to move without legs, and most of all, the lidless stare they turned on folks when they slithered by. That stare was settling even now on Bobcat, and their pale green eyes seemed to connect somehow with the red fiery eyes burning already inside his head.

For a few seconds no one spoke; then the larger cobra stretched his coils slightly forward, puffed his hood out just a bit, and said, his voice a slippery whisper, "So we are well met, we five, you, quester, brujo, and compages, we, the chosen desert-born, risen from the sands to greet you, ease your questioned steps and lead you onward toward your destined end, the end whose storied reach enfolds you, paws outstretched to soothe and comfort, warm and silken rest caressing, pleasure, rapt and all relaxing, soft and smooth her nestling stroke, soft and smooth her stroke. Tranquil calm in sleep beside her, downy, dreamless, languid sleep, soothe and comfort, warm and silken, rest caressing, all relaxing, soft and smooth her nestling stroke, so soft and smooth her stroke."

The words went humming, purring, rustling, fondling over Bobcat's ears, swaying gently through his fur, and spreading slow as sweetened syrup nuzzling at his tired mind. Eyes were everywhere around him: serpent eyes that ebbed and flowed with jaded greens and flinty grays; eyes inflamed with craft and guile, soft as hatred, hot as fear; and in between them, eyes that drooped with dust and distance, rattling somewhat in their frames. He knew these last eyes best of all, could feel them blink and almost close. For these last tired eyes were his, and soon the whispering rushing tide would wash them over, sink them down, and push them under, deep and drowned.

But then a voice came ringing out alarm clock loud, a rhythm jarring off its track the serpents' coiling inner hum. It tickled Bobcat, made him sneeze, brushed back his ears; he raised his head, and there stood Skink, one foot outstretched.

"I pray you'll forgive me my speaking so loud, and what's more to the point here, a bit out of turn, but you see, mine's a heart made of ivy and oak, made of thorny old rose bushes long gone to seed, and it prods me at times when a thing's not quite right. So I must in all conscience point out to you both that we have not yet properly been introduced. Now this may appear moot and perhaps even make me seem somewhat absurd in these modernish times, but I fear I must nonetheless hereby insist that before we begin what is likely to prove a protracted and obstinate course of debate, we ought to be known each one here to the rest in the manner and custom set down by our patron, the ancient Lord Eft, may his name always sing."

Skink had by now scurried down off Fisher and stood in the road with his eyes on the snakes. "For protocol shapes us," the lizard went on, "and all that we do. So with your permission, I'll take your lead and bend my measure to fit your own. I am Skink of Donalis Kiva, no one you should have heard of, I'm sure, but I am he. The Lord Eft follow and keep you both, and I shall speak for my colleagues here when I thank you for your kind concern. Now, whom do we have the honor of meeting, and who are you with whom I have the great good fortune of twisting tongues?"

The serpents seemed to hesitate, their careful hissing hum to falter; then at last the one who'd spoken turned to the other and breathed aloud a venomous voice like scuttling beetles. "Sister, seems it not to you that this slight creature spoke just now? I cannot think I heard aright, listening as I thought I was. Can it be that this slight creature hates itself to such extents that it would dare address us here? Can it think to use the old and dried-up name of absent Eft while here in lands where that one's name is less than dew on the morning sand? Can this be, my sister? And, if so, how can it hope to live?"

"Patience, brother," slid the words from out the other's swaying throat. "For we are here by duty bound, here to do the work assigned us, not to lose our focus getting pulled from our allotted course."

The larger cobra flared his hood, his eyes alive with pale fire; riding back upon his coils, first he fixed those eyes on Skink, then snapped them toward his sister's face. "This slight creature challenged me, my sister. That, I shan't ignore. These two mammals stand as good as dead right now; their transformation at our fangs is imminent. Just hold them here, dear sister, while I twist the tongue from this slight skink and show him in whose name is strength, is power, and might before he dies."

Bobcat saw through heavy eyes the smaller cobra start to speak, her tail twisting through the sand to settle on her brother's scales. But her brother shook himself away from her and slithered left, coils stalking 'cross the pavement, eyes now fixed on Skink alone. The swaying rhythm clung to Bobcat, made his paws all thick and useless, dumped its muddy weight upon him; down around his neck it drooped, forced his nose to tap the ground. But Bobcat pried his eyelids open, kicked his brain to concentrate upon the two now circling slowly, morning shadows long and stretching off across the desert sand.

"Simpering fool," the cobra hissed, his tongue a black and flickering thing. "Introductions are in order; yes, I must agree with that. For Death herself has sent us to you, not as faceless sneak-assassins, not like creeping, puffing adders. Not for you a death by stealth, but death with honor, open, regal, struck by poisons cobra borne, the highest form my mistress owns. But name? I have none, for I am not name, but function: deed, not word. I am but the agency by which she whisks you to herself, I, your guide and guardian, the coils that bear you on to rest forever 'neath her silken paw. Call me therefore what you will, for you are prey and nothing more."

"Guardian, then," the lizard said, his circling, shuffling claws upon the pavement clicking different rhythms, tapping counterpoint across the swaying hiss the cobras sang. "Greetings I bear from him whose name is blessing to all who speak his modality, shaping their speech as we do now in languages strange and measures incontinent, serving his will in thought and deed regardless of acts performed in another's name, she whom he cast from the warmth of the sun to lie quiv'ring in shadows beyond."

"Your bones will boil!" The cobra twitched forward a bit, his tongue lashing quick through the light of the dawn. "You will burn for your mockery, quartered and diced till I serve you as soup at my mistress's table!"

"That may be so," Skink said in return, "but hers is a fire that burns without heat, and who wants a soup prepared with cold fire? My Lord is cold, but he lives for the light, lets the warmth of the sun add its flow to his blood. Yours is a mistress that lurks in darkness, sealed in mists and clawing at shadows—"

"While yours is a master who's old and feeble, drier than bone with the life of a stone! She of the Cold Fire burns and consumes; vibrant and powerful, she conquers all!"

"All except beauty, true peace, and tranquility."

"All! She is everything, glorious, and bold! Hers is the triumph, the last conflagration, and we who would serve her—"

"Will die like the rest." Skink held a front foot up, suspended before him. "You who would talk of honor and duty, playing at both, but who function with neither—"

"Grasp at your straws, small skittering beast. Your Eft here is impotent, less than a word."

"Then how much less does your mistress bear, who dares not face my Lords and Ladies?"

"Dares not face?" The cobra drew back, the gold of the sun glinting wet at his fangs. "Your death will be painful, you—"

"What, is she here? Your mistress creeps out in the bright of the sun?" These last words were different, made Bobcat's ears twitch; Skink's voice seemed to deepen and ring through the air, an air that was thickened and rolling somehow. A gray undulation appeared around Skink, a strange solid something that Bobcat recalled from a glimpse through a distance some mornings ago: a sound taking shape, rumbling out from between and behind where the wind goes when no wind is blowing, a voice that was Skink's, and yet not his at all, a voice that went billowing out like a cloak, like a storm cloud, a flash flood, a thundering rock slide, pounding and shattering down through the air with a substance that added to Skink's tiny form.

"I ask you again," this huge voice exploded, its force making

Bobcat cringe back in alarm, "I who am earthly and like you a vessel in service to powers beyond and above! Speak, if you dare, in a voice of command! Let your mistress confront me through you, serpentine, as my master's least whisper slips out now from me!"

The mere breathy shadow cast down by that voice had been more than enough to turn Bobcat's skin cold, but the brunt of its sounding, the weight of its lash, the vast emanation that burst forth from Skink, from over and under, around him and through, had been aimed at the cobra, had torn through his hood, had slammed full and twisting straight into his face.

And down the snake tumbled then, felled like a tree, like a puppet whose strings had been suddenly cut. He collapsed all atwitch, flailing madly in place, a fish speared and plopped from the stream to the bank. For a minute or more he continued to writhe, till at last he had wound himself up in a tight little bundle of tail, a pile of snake, with his head lost from view in the depths of his coils.

And all around Skink, the flickering weight, the gray looming something that leadened the air, was suddenly gone with the softness of down being wafted aloft by a stray morning breeze, with a whisk, back to spaces that weren't there at all. Skink for his part sobbed out a slight sigh and seemed to deflate before Bobcat's dry eyes. But Skink shook himself, pushed himself forward again, and faced the she-cobra ahead on the road.

She had remained standing perfectly still during all this encounter, her hood slightly spread, her neck undulating the soft rhythmic hum that held Bobcat captive, set weights to his paws. She rose on her coils, returning Skink's gaze with cold stones for eyes, pale green and unblinking. "You speak with authority," she breathed at last, a soft, gentle curling of air from her lips, "an authority I cannot hope to endure. Yet I have pledged my heart to my mistress, she whose voice has summoned me here. So know I bear you no ill will, but promised deeds are deeds fulfilled to those whose work must need be true. En garde then, sir." And back she drew, her scales gleaming as she swayed.

Skink gave a bow. "Yes, it is said that duty to those above is a glorious, wonderful way to lead a life, and I wouldn't dream of ever disputing it. But it is also said by some that duty to self is just as important in taking responsible action and not laying blame where it does not belong."

The cobra lashed out, her hood a flash of light, and latched her teeth onto empty air. For Skink had thrown himself to the side, had skittered and slid through the sand on the road. The cobra gathered herself together, reared back again as Skink raised his voice: "The servants of Death and Destruction know nothing of duty and honor as you understand it! Duty in Death's rank serves as a mask, a cover for blind naked hatred and fear, for feelings of vengeance, not reasonable pride in a job that is honest, straightforward, and true! The servants of Death do her deeds out of pleasure, a sordid and vicious display for themselves, but, cowardly, never admit that they function for their own will and with their own reasons. 'It is my duty,' they snidely assert, when true sense of duty is just what they lack!"

The cobra held back, her swaying subdued, her hood giving forth with a slight sort of flutter. Skink raised a front foot. "What I'm telling you here is nothing you haven't yourself thought before. Your heart seeks to serve in an honorable cause, and the voice you heard calling was said to be Death's. But you have had doubts after seeing those ones who claimed to be hearing the same voice as you. For your blood flows with sterner stuff, and she who was calling you calls to you still."

"She does," came the cobra's voice, pale as her eyes. "She calls to me constantly, has called for days. I sought to ignore her, to listen to those who told me I'd found my true place in this desert." A shudder ran down to the tip of her tail. "A place among murderers, cheap toughs, and cutthroats, not royal assassins, none true to the call."

"Your call is not theirs," Skink quietly said. "They led you astray, and you know that, deep down."

"I do. I have known it, have know how my place lies farther off in lands I've not seen, lies in service to someone whose name I don't know."

"Dawn's broken." Skink turned his front foot, claws set upward. "The first light of morning for journey's first step."

The cobra looked down, and a flickering smile puffed up and was gone as her hood folded back. The tip of her tail slid forward and stroked into Skink's upturned claws, and there on the road, they danced a brief minuet, swayed a gavotte, gave a turn to the sun rising into the sky.

The cobra then bowed and stalked off through the sand where the shimmering start of the desert day's heat made the land seem to wriggle, horizons to jump. She coiled her way into it, grew indistinct and finally was lost through the glisten beyond. Her hum lingered on, though, a soft, tickling stroke, for some minutes, until like herself, it was drawn past the sands and was gone in the silence of dawn.

Bobcat found he could blink again, and he shook his head, trying to clear it. A groan reached him, and he looked up to see Skink collapse into the sand. He tried to move, but Fisher was faster, already at the lizard's side before Bobcat could find his paws. "Just take it easy," she was saying, pulling a bottle from her satchel and using the stopper to dab a few drops of something onto Skink's tongue. "Everything's gonna be okay."

Skink raised his head and gave a weak smile. "I think I would like to lie down for a while."

"You go right ahead. Bobcat and I'll get you to Pienta. You just sleep."

The little lizard nodded, his eyes rolled shut, and the quivering of his sides slowly relaxed. Fisher recorked her bottle, put it back in her satchel, then turned to Bobcat. "How you doing?"

Bobcat blinked at her. "Uhh, OK. I mean, I guess . . ."

"Take your time," she said with a tired smile. "After your first reptile tongue twister, you're liable to have a little trouble telling up from down for a while."

Bobcat could only blink some more. He gave his head a few more shakes, rubbed his nose between his paws, and bit by bit, got most of the fluff out from behind his ears. "I'm not even gonna ask what that was," he said when he could. His eyes came to rest on the rolled-up cobra still lying on the pavement ahead. "Uhh, shouldn't we do something about that?"

"Hmmm? Oh, he'll be all right."

"Yeah, that's sorta what I was worried about."

Fisher gave him a look. "He'll be out for a couple days; you don't recover all that quickly from the Lord Eft shoving himself down your throat. Help me with Skink, will you?"

Together, they gathered up the unconscious lizard and lashed him to Fisher's pack with some twine she pulled from a pocket. "Nothing a good ten or twelve hours of sleep won't cure," she said.

"Count me in, and quick: it's already hot out here."

"C'mon, then. We're just about to the canyon."

They left the bluff and the cobra behind to continue on through the rising morning. After a bit, they came over a rise, and there was the canyon, a jagged crack in the sand reaching back to the horizon. The road wound closer to it till the two were running side by side, the dark brown and red stone of the canyon's sides looking like layer cake to Bobcat.

The river only flowed through Canyon Pienta whenever it wanted to; Bobcat had heard stories of it suddenly crashing down on travelers camped in the shady caves along the bottom after forty or fifty years of no water for miles, the area blooming for a few weeks, then drying up again. Bobcat followed Fisher off the road and down the crumbling sides of the canyon with pricked ears—no flood rumblings, of course, but best to be safe—then turned his attention to his paws, the stupid pack trying its best to pull him over sideways.

A couple of shallow caves gaped nearby, and Fisher led the way into a fairly large one. Bobcat untied Skink, settled him into a hollow in the rock, then slung off his pack and dropped like a stone, not dreaming or coming awake until he couldn't ignore the shaking at his shoulder and Fisher's voice calling his name: "C'mon, Bobcat; the sun's almost down, we've got walking to do, and your chow's getting cold. C'mon, or I'll have Skink yell at you."

Bobcat mumbled, rolled upright, and stretched the kinks from his legs. A bowl was pushed into his paws, and he began spooning things out of it before he'd even opened his eyes. It was warm and nutty, and Bobcat had gulped the stuff down before he'd woken up enough to look over at where they'd left Skink. The lizard sat perched on the lip of his bowl, gnawing on something, staring out through the cave mouth at the gathering twilight. Bobcat looked from Skink to Fisher. "Is he OK now?"

Skink gave a dry chuckle. "There is often a feeling of loss associated with the Lord Eft withdrawing himself from such intimate contact. To have been so full, and now to be so . . ." The lizard sighed, turned to Bobcat, coughed another laugh. "I have read of it, but I had never dreamed that I would experience it. I have been . . . truly honored."

"But you're all right now?"

"I am, yes, and I thank you for asking, Bobcat."

"Hey, no problem." Bobcat grinned at him, then turned to Fisher. "So what's the plan for tonight?"

Fisher shrugged, swallowed her spoonful of stew. "Same thing as last night unless you've got a better idea. We walk. By morning we'll be at Fekadh, and we can set up camp by the oasis there."

Bobcat rubbed his chin. "We'll be kinda out in the open, won't we? I mean, if we're gonna have every cutthroat in the area out after us, shouldn't we—"

"Nah." Fisher poured a little water into her bowl, swished it around, and drank it. "I don't think we'll have much to worry about if we keep away from folks."

"You don't?"

"Nah."

"No more cobras sneaking up on us or anything? You really think she'll give up that easily?"

"She?" Fisher was taking the stove apart. "Who?"

Bobcat sighed. "The Blood Jaguar. Remember her?"

Skink immediately began muttering, tracing those same little patterns in the air with his foreclaws. Bobcat stared at him. "And why does he keep doing that? She's gonna pop in here just 'cause I mention her name?"

Fisher half closed her eyes. "She might. And that's exactly my point."

"Point?" Bobcat blinked. "What point?"

"The Strangler. She's Death incarnate, remember?"

"Hey, I'm the one who saw her: I'm not about to forget."

"Well, there you have it."

Bobcat blinked at her. "What? What do I have?"

She sighed. "Why would Death incarnate hire assassins?"

That stopped Bobcat, but only for a moment. "But those cobras, they said they worked for her, didn't they? Didn't you say something about death cults last night? Maybe she's got *all* her followers out looking for us!"

Skink raised a claw. "Well, actually, Bobcat, nothing in the literature indicates that She of the Cold Fire has anything but contempt for the cults that have sprung up around her. I've even read speculation that she reserves special places of torment for them in the Shroud Islands."

"Torment?" Bobcat had to grin. "I can't imagine that helps recruitment much. But how can you be sure no one—?"

Fisher set down the last bits of stove pipe and tapped her forehead. "Think about it. Anyone with half a brain could've figured out where we spent today, but nobody came to kill us." She shrugged. "Not that that proves anything. The Strangler might just be saving us for herself."

Bobcat saw Skink shudder where he sat. "Fisher," the lizard said, "you have quite a talent for gruesome thoughts. I feel I must point out, however, that I have never seen an example in the literature of such behavior on the part of the Cold Fire. She acts alone, indirectly, and from the shadows."

"Usually, I'd agree." Fisher leaned against her pack. "But everybody's been acting so strange lately. I mean we have the Lord Eft manifesting himself twice in the same week: he barely shows up for his own Grand Festival every year, and when he does, it's only a glimpse to the Hierophant. And look at the Lord Kit Fox, hardly pulling any of his stupid little tricks, just waltzing down and giving us information that's so far turned out to be pretty much correct. And, c'mon; Bobcat here's actually seen the Strangler and lived to tell about it. I've never even *heard* of that happening." She shook her head. "There's definitely something screwy going on."

"I had not considered that." Skink scuttled down from the lip of his bowl. "It is as if their roles are somehow reversing, those Curials who are normally shrouded in silence and twilight coming forward while those who are ever the most active in our sphere remain in the background. Consider: the Lord Tiger, who brings himself every day into the legal quandaries of earthly folk, has not flicked so much as a whisker. Nor has the Lady Squirrel, whose life blood is the redress of wrongs against the downtrodden." Skink twitched his head into a different position. "If this is indeed the case, I fear there is little we can count on with complete security."

Bobcat blew out a breath. "Brains and eggs."

Fisher laughed. "You said it. You wanna load up the stove here?"

So Fisher and Skink washed the bowls, and Bobcat settled the jars and pipes into his backpack. His throat was dry and his fur all prickly, an old, familiar tickling in the back of his head, jabbing all the harder in the guttering flame of the Blood Jaguar's eyes; he hadn't had so much as a quarter roll of catnip for more than a week now.

Sweat broke out between the pads of his paws just thinking about it. It wasn't bad enough he was stumbling around in the one place he hated more than anything getting zapped by mythical monsters and almost killed twice in as many days. But to have to go through it all without even a whiff of catnip; just a couple leaves to grind between his paws and bury his nose in . . .

Well, maybe he could pick some up in Kazirazif. Just a taste or two, that's all he would need, just enough to calm him down and get rid of this knot behind his ears. He could almost feel that first, sweet tingle, and a shudder curled down his back. Yeah, he'd get some when they got to town.

Skink was climbing up onto Fisher's shoulders, Bobcat wriggled into his pack, and they stepped from the cave out into the arroyo. Up the sides of the canyon they climbed, paws set carefully into the crumbling rock, until they reached the rim and hauled themselves onto the desert sands again. The sun had already set behind the mountains poking up at the distant horizon, and a warm and breezy twilight was spreading over the plain. Fisher led the way to the road, and they set off southwestward once again.

This night went by slow and quiet, exactly what Bobcat needed. Nothing blew up or burst into flames, no eerie rustlings in the scrub grass, the joshua trees and cacti didn't turn into monsters or anything; Bobcat just walked along behind Fisher and Skink, all nice and relaxed. He could almost forget where they were going and what they were doing, except when he heard scattered phrases from the conversation ahead. Not that he understood them, but some stuck in his mind like popcorn between his teeth: "Curial recognition," and, "The cyclical nature of reality," things he remembered from Skink's long speech the morning they had started out.

Bobcat slowed his pace a bit. Maybe with some more distance, he wouldn't hear so much. Sure, he couldn't really deny this Curial stuff any more, but the world had gotten along without him knowing about it for this long, so why upset things? A little catnip, a few bets on the water polo matches, an occasional evening with Garson: that's all he needed in his life. Of that he was sure.

But those eyes popped sparks in his head, reminded him that somewhere, some giant flaming cat monster had decided otherwise, and so here he was, stumbling through the middle of the night in the desert. Bobcat ground his teeth and aimed a few choice phrases at those eyes, sputtering their cold fire behind his own. This was all her fault, this Blood Jaguar and her Plague Year. Bobcat hoped he would have a chance to yell at her before she killed him.

The stars danced on above, spinning around the polestar to Bobcat's right and behind him. The jags of the mountains got steadily higher as the night went on, their black teeth rising from the western horizon: the Dyhari, a sight he hadn't seen in years, Kazirazif nestled where they rolled out into the southern desert and the Savannah beyond. Bobcat glanced southward then and thought again of Shemka Harr.

He had never visited the Savannah, had barely thought of it or the old lioness until recently, and he wondered what had happened to her. The last time he had seen her, the winter melting away outside their cave, the days growing warmer and longer, had been another sharp blue morning in early spring. Bobcat had woken to her calling him outside, and he had gone out to see her standing on their ledge. She had smiled at him, kissed him on the forehead, thanked him for his visit, and had begun strolling away down the valley.

He remembered clearly the panic that had stabbed through his chest, remembered running after her and asking where she was going, when she would be back, if he could go with her. She had just smiled over her shoulder, had said, "I'll think of you." And Bobcat had stood and watched her disappear among the rocks. He left the cave himself not long after.

There was so much pain in the memory, Bobcat almost winced. No wonder he had pushed that whole winter from his thoughts for so many years. How could she have just left him like that, just turned her back and walked away? Hadn't he meant anything to her?

The old resentment squatted in his mind, but it was so dry and dusty, Bobcat just sneezed it away. If he hadn't spent that winter with her, he knew, he wouldn't have survived the next winter or the winter after that. She had taught him to read and write almost without him realizing it, had showed him how to greet folks on the road, how to think on the run, how to listen and ask questions, pretty much all the things that he liked about himself. She would have had her reasons for leaving, and whatever they were, Bobcat figured he could live with them. Maybe he could look her up somehow, ask around Kazirazif when they got there.

And so the night wound on between the buttes and the mesas. The hours after midnight crept past, and the sky to Bobcat's left began to pearl with the shimmer of dawn. More joshua trees hunched themselves over the ground here, streams of purple and yellow blossoms peering out from around them. The first clear spark of sun showed against the palm trees ahead, and as Bobcat crested a slight rise behind Fisher and Skink, the white walls of Fekadh stood out before him.

It was almost like a splash of color, the sheer white of the adobe huts, after the yellows and browns of the desert. Sharp in the silence before morning had quite arrived, Fekadh glowed, its single street bending off the main road and leading down into the valley beyond, made green by the waters of the oasis. No one seemed to be stirring yet, and that suited Bobcat just fine. He remembered that the oasis was farther along, up the road a bit from the town itself, and that would be handy, too. The fewer folks they actually had to deal with, the better he would feel about it.

They followed the road past the white-washed buildings, up the slope, and around the bend from the town, the sand now alive with vines and flowers, till they came upon the grassy bank of the oasis, a shady pond bubbling up and trickling its way down into the Fekadh valley. Fisher led the way off the road, over the rocks around the oasis, and into a grotto of ferns that sloped down toward the pool.

"We shouldn't bother anyone camping out back here," she said, Skink scrambling down from her shoulders so she could undo her pack. "Most everyone who comes by this way stays in town anyway."

Bobcat nodded and started unpacking the stove. "The last time I was here, I managed to arrive right in the middle of some big festival honoring the Lady Dolphin for giving them the oasis or something. Pretty good food, I thought."

"Yeah," Fisher said, pulling a smaller satchel from her pack. "In fact, you get the stove together, and I'll gather up a few of the local legumes to put in the stew."

So Bobcat concentrated on the stove while Skink scurried down to the pond and back for the water to fill the cooking pot. Bobcat pulled a few packages from Fisher's pack and got the water bubbling before Fisher returned, her satchel filled with roots and leaves. These she washed off, cut up, and mixed in with everything else for a spicy breakfast that made Bobcat's eyes water as he spooned out a third helping. Then they cleaned up the dishes and settled back into the shade of the ferns to sleep through the heat of the day.

The dreams that shouldered through Bobcat's sleep were even more unclear than usual: folks he thought he knew but was sure he'd never seen before, snatches of garbled music, smells and sounds that didn't go together, like sweet honeysuckle and the chattering of teeth. Things did happen in these dreams, but he didn't pay that much attention and couldn't remember them when he woke up late that afternoon.

Something was splashing behind him, and he rolled over to see Fisher wringing a cloth out into the largest pot. She shook the water from her fur and gave him a grin. "I thought I'd clean up some before we got to town."

Bobcat yawned and sat up. "I could use a little of that myself. Too bad they don't let you paddle around the oasis."

"Impractical," Skink piped in from where he perched atop some small, spiny plant. "Since this water must serve all functions here, I imagine that the local authorities wish to keep the spring itself as clean as possible."

Another yawn stretched through Bobcat's whiskers. "You can say that again. They'll cut your paws off if they catch you swimming up here. Not pretty."

Fisher dipped the cloth in and tossed it to Bobcat. "Get washed, then, if you want to. We better get started early tonight if we wanna make the Basharah gate before dawn. The Lord Kit Fox was pretty specific about that, and I'd rather go with our clues than just stumble around."

The water felt good trickling through his fur, and Bobcat rubbed the cloth up, around, and over his ears, the dust from the past six days loosening and dripping to the ground. He dabbed a little at his cuts, pretty much healed but still tight whenever he bent back to lick his flanks, and thought dark thoughts about the Blood Jaguar again. But the smell of Skink's coffee was too sweet for him to dwell on such things, and he moved over beside the stove, Fisher beginning to tip the stuff from the pot into their cups. A pan had already taken the pot's place on the stove, and its spicy sizzle made Bobcat's stomach growl.

Fisher dished the stuff out, and they ate in silence for a while. Then Skink looked up from his bowl. "I have been meaning to ask the two of you about Kazirazif. Having never been farther from home than Beaverpool, I am curious as to what sort of city we are now approaching."

Bobcat had a mouthful, but Fisher was just swallowing. "It's, uhh, well, it's . . . different." She gestured with her spoon. "It's one of the oldest cities on the continent, and you can pretty much tell. See, Beaverpool was built by beavers, all of a piece and with a master plan, but Kazirazif more sort of just happened, folks coming outta the desert and settling at the foot of the Dyhari mountains wherever any water found its way out of the rocks. So instead of a Bailey Common or a Beaverpool Municipal Center with the town spread out around it, you've got about fifty old neighborhoods all twining in and out of each other.

"Then the Raj Canar came along, built a wall around the whole thing, and proclaimed himself the first caliph of Kazirazif." Fisher shrugged. "That's the history, but other than that, all I can say is you've gotta see it to believe it."

"That's what I'd say, too," Bobcat put in as soon as he could. "Meerkat Town's an accident all set to happen, but it's like it already has and no one's noticed yet. I dunno, but there's something about the place that made me wanna run for cover whenever I was walking down one of those twisty little streets, like someone was watching me or something. Nice catnip, though."

Fisher gave him a look. "You're not thinking of getting yourself all twisted up on us, are you?"

Bobcat didn't bother to keep his ears up. "Hey, maybe you can keep your whiskers on your own snout, you think? I don't go nosing around in your bottles and stuff, do I?"

Skink rustled from his perch. "Now, please, you two—"

"No, no," Fisher said, taking another spoonful from her bowl and looking through her eyebrows at Bobcat. "He's right. What he does to himself is his own business. Of course, as it *is* his own business, he can use his own cash to pay for it. That's only fair, I would think."

"Damn straight," Bobcat muttered, drinking down the rest of

his stew. It wasn't until he set the bowl back down that he realized that he didn't have anything of his own with him. "Hey, hey, wait a minute! All this stuff is yours! You wouldn't let me go home, wouldn't let me stop or anything! How'm I s'posed to buy catnip if I don't . . . if I don't . . ."

Fisher cleared her throat and turned to dip some water from the pot into her bowl. "Kinda late to think of that now, I'd say."

"You set me up." Bobcat glared at her. "Right from the start, you set me up. . . ."

"Let's just say I like to keep my bases covered." She crooked a claw at him. "We've each been included in this little excursion for a reason. Now I have no idea why the Strangler picked you as the bobcat for our turn at the story, but that's what she did, and our best chance for finding out, our best chance for living through this thing, our best chance for stopping the Plague Year, everything depends on us staying alert and being ready for whatever comes. You know that, Bobcat, and you know that catnip'll make you everything *but* that. Once we get through this, you can stone yourself under for a week; I don't care. But not now. You get me?"

A cold shiver twitched all the way down Bobcat's back, the stew in his stomach suddenly sour. "Then let's get this over with." he grumbled at last. "I'll get the stove apart."

Skink unfroze from the lip of his bowl and scuttled down to finish the last of his stew, Fisher dipping her scouring pad into the pot of oasis water, Bobcat wrenching the stove apart and clattering the jars. It all kept coming back to the Blood Jaguar and her stinking Plague Year and his paws were starting to hurt and his sides kept itching and the dust had turned to mud in his fur and, gods, he missed Garson and he didn't even have enough money for a lousy quarter-roll of catnip and he hated it, absolutely *hated* it, that Fisher was always right about everything!

Finally he got the stove packed away and struggled his load onto his shoulders. Fisher and Skink took the lead, and they clambered out of the grotto, over the rocks, and away down the road toward Kazirazif.

Chapter Seven

Kazirazif

Through another night they walked, the sun settling big and red behind the mountains to Bobcat's right and sucking all the blue from the sky. Long, glowing clouds stretched in from the west, their sharp pink fading to gray, thickening, and taking hold overhead. Then even the gray was lost, and solid night flowed down over them.

No stars tonight—Bobcat peered up into the empty darkness. The road from Fekadh had taken them back out of the foothills and was now skirting the first mounds of rock that eventually became the Dyhari, the mountains that had cuddled the sun to sleep.

Bobcat remembered Shemka Harr telling him six or seven different stories from around the continent about what happens to the Lord Lion after a long day of letting his mane shine down over the earth, but the one that had stuck in his mind was the Fekadh version: the Lord Lion's various attendants receiving him in a valley atop the Dyhari, fanning him with palm fronds, bathing him in fragrant waters till he was cool enough to rest, and the whole part where the Lady Dolphin carried him fast asleep through streams hidden beneath the earth to the eastern edge of the world so he could rise again, brilliant and fiery, in the morning.

Of course, Shemka Harr had also told Bobcat that the sun was actually a ball of fire many times larger than anything he would ever see on the ground, had given him another explanation of how everything followed natural laws, that the Curials were just characters in a bunch of old stories. "There's nothing wrong with stories," she would say, "but counting on the Curials is a sure way to end up dead, Ghareen."

Bobcat had no reason to think Shemka Harr had lied to him, but how would she have explained that kit fox who warned them what was ahead, then burst into flame and flew away? Or that weird reptilian whatever it was that Bobcat had seen humming its way out of the air twice already? Or that monstrous, fiery jaguar thing? . . .

The night went on and on, questions turning over in Bobcat's head. He wanted to ask Fisher or Skink about it all but couldn't quite bring himself to break the silence of the night; it lay so deep and thick around him that it clogged his throat whenever he thought about saying anything. Even the two on the road ahead were quiet, their usual conversation never quite starting up. All Bobcat heard was an occasional creak from Fisher's backpack, a lighter shadow jostling along through the darkness in front of him.

It was the longest night yet, the longest and the darkest and the least interesting to be out in. Bobcat's paws ached; his sides throbbed, the straps of his backpack chafing with each step. He was sure it wasn't even midnight, and he was ready to stop and make camp, his fur all frazzled and itchy and on edge, as if waiting for a thunderstorm to break.

More than that, though—and what was even weirder, what kept Bobcat alert and walking that whole long night—was the way another feeling kept pulling at him, a feeling he'd had before, usually after an especially hairy run with the catnip, right about this same time of night, too, when everybody else had gone to bed and left him alone, too wired to sleep. Like a rotted branch in the forest it would slam into him, bash him upside the head, leave him suddenly, terribly sober, the night snapping from warm, sweet, and fuzzy to cold, sharp, and clear.

And there it would be, this feeling, like thousands of faces turned toward him, faces he couldn't see, faces from every direction under the sun, faces with wide eyes, breath caught in their throats, their paws drawn up beneath their chins and balled into fists. And they were all waiting, waiting in hope or fear or kindness or hatred, waiting for something somewhere to happen.

But what that something was he just could never figure out. He would lie awake all night, long after the feeling had faded away, his pillow clutched between his paws, the blankets kicked to the floor, and just stare at the wall. It was something important, what all these folks were waiting for, but he had never had a clue; all he could do was lie there and stare till dawn started seeping up over the sky.

Bobcat shivered. Well, at least this time he was pretty sure he knew what everyone was waiting for.

On and on the night went, dark and cold and miserable. Bobcat thought he could smell rain somewhere in the distance. On and on they walked, and after more hours than Bobcat had thought a night could have a glimmer appeared ahead, a shadowy, guttering flame that had to be torchlight.

"Milestone," he said aloud, not really meaning to.

"Yeah," came Fisher's voice. Then the quiet folded back down, and they walked on some more, the flame growing slowly till they came up beside it, a large chunk of granite with an oily torch crackling in a holder on one side. Words were carved in the rock, words in several different languages. Bobcat recognized the blocky letters of Manx, the ottery rodent dialect that was spoken up and down roads and rivers all over the continent, and the shorter curls Shemka Harr had written her Savannah language in. And the words said: "This stone sitting one mile from the city marks the lands beholden to the caliph of Kazirazif."

Fisher gave a yawn. "Right. We'll leave the road here."

Bobcat nodded, but Skink stirred at Fisher's shoulder. "Leave the road? Would that be wise?"

"Very," Fisher said.

Skink blinked for a moment. "I fail to understand."

"I can live with that." Fisher headed left over the sand, the torchlight casting her shadow up into the dunes.

Bobcat followed. "It's just that the Meerkat Road leads straight up to the Shasir gate, and we were pretty much told to avoid that one. The Basharah gate's got less traffic 'cause the Coati Road just leads south into the desert down to the Savannah, and not a lot of trade goes that way. Anyway, we've gotta do a little off-roading to get there."

"I see," came Skink's voice after a moment. "But we will arrive before dawn?"

"We should." Bobcat looked around. "Kinda hard to say what time it is with this cloud cover."

Silence fell back over them then. The sand was cold under Bobcat's paws, crunched softly between his toes, made him think of a desert far north of here and a time long past and best forgotten. He shook his head and peered through the darkness; if they were on course, there should be another milestone poking its torch into the night somewhere ahead and to his right.

Around the dunes they wound, and Bobcat began to notice a slight gray sheen in the clouds above. "Maybe we oughtta pick up the pace?" he called to the dark figure in front of him.

"Nah," he heard Fisher say. "There's the stone."

Bobcat saw it now, a pinprick of orange against the slowly graying black. They padded along the sand till they reached it: a stone much smaller than the other but with the same inscriptions carved over its sides and the same oily sort of torch sticking from it. A road much rougher than the Meerkat Road ran into the darkness to the left and right. Bobcat blew out a breath. "I could really use a nap when we get wherever we're going."

"Whatever," Fisher said, scratching an ear. "Just, when we come to the gate, let me do the talking."

"No problem." Bobcat yawned. "I just hope there's a hotel open."

Fisher gave a snort and started down the road toward the black mass of the mountains ahead. Bobcat followed, and it wasn't long before he could make out more orange sparks of torchlight strung along the base of the Dyhari's jagged silhouette. The silhouette grew larger and larger, the washed-out light soaking into the clouds, and Bobcat began to make out the walls of Kazirazif, stretches of stone and spindly towers squatted against the dark of the mountains.

* * *

The walls got taller and taller, the flickering spots separating till only two remained directly ahead, mounted on either side of one of the towers. Soon Bobcat could make out the ridges on the tower, the arch of the gate through it, the smoke stains of the torches. Several thin figures were moving across the road before the gate—meerkats, Bobcat could tell by their upright posture; four of them, it looked like. He couldn't tell if the meerkats had noticed them approaching yet, but when one of them gave a short yip and pointed its spear he knew they'd been spotted.

Fisher just kept right on walking, so Bobcat followed her into the range of the torchlight, the wall now high enough to block out all but the peaks of the mountains. The meerkats had formed into a line, three with spears and wide eyes, the fourth in front of them, a cloak of rank around her shoulders.

Bobcat heard Fisher clear her throat. "Good morning!" she called. "Would any of you be the Raj Tevirye?"

"We would not." The one in the cloak stepped forward. "Who are you who asks to know?"

"Travelers," Fisher said, settling onto her haunches. "We've come quite a ways and were told to ask for the Raj Tevirye when we arrived."

"Were you?" The meerkat looked from Fisher to Bobcat and back again. "Well, I am the Raj's lieutenant. You will tell me what you want of her, and I will decide whether to bother the Raj with it."

"Parkash, no!" one of the meerkats squeaked behind her. "You mustn't! Do you not know these three? The Pads of Doom! They must be destroyed at once! At once!"

"Silence in ranks!" The lieutenant whirled. "I'll have none of that superstitious nonsense here!"

The meerkat who had spoken flinched, his claws gripping his spear, but he held his place. The lieutenant glared at the other two, then turned back, her eyes narrow. "Stay where you are," she said after a moment, then, over her shoulder, "Mekjir, fetch the Raj."

One of the meerkats gave a squeak, spun around, and scurried through the gate. The lieutenant remained in place, her arms crossed, but a steadily growing whimper from the two behind her finally made her turn with a growl. The whimpering stopped.

Bobcat settled down to wait, and after a few moments another meerkat came through the gate, a darker cloak at her shoulders, a sword at her belt. She missed a step, Bobcat saw, her eyes falling on him and Fisher, and he tensed, ready to run in case anyone started throwing spears.

But the meerkat only hesitated for a heartbeat before continuing forward to where the lieutenant stood. "Parkash," she said, her voice quiet. "Some trouble?"

The lieutenant tapped a paw against her chest. "Three storybook characters here to see you, ma'am."

The whimpering started again, but another glance from the lieutenant stifled it. "So it would seem," the other meerkat said. Her eyes on Bobcat, she bowed. "I am the Raj Tevirye. I feel obliged to warn you that four archers stand stationed on the wall behind me and they have been given their orders." She rubbed her whiskers. "It is odd, though: the story I heard as a kit always had you arriving at the Shasir gate." She gestured to the graying horizon. "That is at the east of the city."

Bobcat shrugged, and he heard Fisher chuckle. "Well, we hate being predictable," she said. "But we were hoping you might be able to take us to the Ramon Sooli."

Again the two started whimpering, and it took a shout from the lieutenant to quiet them this time. Bobcat thought he could hear a quaver in her voice, though, and she was looking a little pale around the eyes.

"The Ramon." The Raj blinked a few times. "And why should I wish to do that?"

Bobcat swallowed, got himself ready to run again, but Fisher spread her paws. "For all our sakes. We were directed to you by name, Raj Tevirye, as the best way to stop several misfortunes from occurring. We all know the story; all know what our coming to this city means. But we're convinced we can change the ending of that story this time around if we can consult with the

Ramon as quickly as possible." Fisher took a breath. "It's in your paws, Raj, all of it."

The Raj continued to stroke her stubby whiskers, and Bobcat couldn't even begin to guess what she might be thinking. When she turned to her lieutenant, fear clutched his gut, but all she said was, "Parkash, I commission you: when the Raj Eshtarif arrives with his squad at dawn, give him my regards and issue him a complete report." Her eyes fluttered back to Bobcat. "Use your discretion concerning our, uhh, visitors here; his ears only, I'd say. He will recognize the need to keep this situation quiet and under control."

The lieutenant tapped her chest again. The Raj laid a paw on her shoulder, then looked over at Bobcat. "If you'll follow me, sirs and madam."

Bobcat heard Fisher blow out a breath. He gestured for her to go ahead and fell in behind, padding past the two whimpering meerkats, then under the arch and into the city. "We will avoid the market squares," the Raj was saying, "and travel to the palace by side streets. The fewer who see you, the better for us all."

The city looked much as Bobcat remembered it, buildings of baked clay, two and three stories tall, their red tile roofs leaning over the narrow streets, shadows deep in the alleyways, the click of their claws on the cobblestones the only sound in the predawn stillness. He'd spent a lot of time stumbling through neighborhoods like this, wandering till the streets opened into a market square, hiring on at whatever odd jobs he could find to raise catnip money . . . but Bobcat forced that thought away, his stomach growling, his neck tightening, and his knees shaking.

As Tevirye had said, they didn't cross any squares. Very few meerkats were even out on the streets they passed over—vendors loading their pushcarts, mostly—and only a few of them squealed and rushed back into their houses after setting eyes on the little parade. They wound through alleys and foul-smelling walkways till Bobcat's bearings slipped away completely. The palace was on the west side of the city, he knew, but whether they were headed that way or not he had no idea.

The sky had been growing lighter and lighter, and an overcast dawn was in full swing when Bobcat followed Fisher around one more corner and found himself staring across the Great Square at the caliph's palace. It looked bigger than he remembered it, all gleaming marble and spiral towers glimpsed through a lush garden and a spiked iron fence, guards stationed at the gate. Tevirye had her paw up, Fisher staying behind her, and was craning her neck forward, her head moving to take in the whole square. Finally she beckoned, and Bobcat hurried after Fisher across the paving stones to the gatehouse before the palace.

Tevirye was flashing a badge at the meerkats standing guard. "Important visitors to see the Ramon," she said.

The guards stared from her to Fisher, to Bobcat, then back again several times before one asked, "Raj, have you lost your mind? You must know who these three are!"

"This is madness," the other guard muttered, his eyes wide. "Utter madness. The Pads of Doom. Here. On my shift. I knew I should've called in sick. My grandmother, she had a dream about—"

"Yes, I know." Tevirye spread her paws. "I've heard all the stories myself, Raj. But if you can think of a better place to bring them than to the Ramon, I would appreciate greatly your sharing it with me."

The first guard glanced at the second, and Bobcat blew out a breath. This could take a while. He turned to look over the square and blinked into the eyes of meerkats looking back, several groups of six or seven gathered murmuring around their pushcarts, more meerkats joining them with each passing second. "Uhh," he said, "excuse me, but we seem to be attracting some attention."

"Oh, my eyes," the second guard groaned. "Jarin?"

"So it seems," the first guard said. "Yes, then, take them to the Ramon. I'd rather have them inside with him than out here causing a riot. The Ramon will know what to do."

Tevirye nodded. "Exactly my thoughts." She gave a worried glance at the growing crowds. "Good luck with them."

The first guard nodded, taking keys from his belt to unlock the gates. "Good luck with *them*," the second guard said; then Tevirye was scurrying through, Fisher and Bobcat right on her tail. Ahead stretched a wide walkway, marble slabs set end to end and leading through the budding trees to a huge flight of stairs, massive golden doors set into the carved face of the palace's main entrance. Bobcat swallowed; just looking at it made him feel tiny. He couldn't even imagine walking up there.

But Tevirye didn't give the walkway a glance, turning to the left as soon as they'd passed the gate and setting off through the trees into the garden. Flowering hedges rose up, blocking the view of the square, and Bobcat followed Fisher and the Raj over the damp grass, past several small ponds and a topiary garden before he realized that they were circling the palace. Through what seemed to be a kumquat orchard Tevirye led them, the palace looming closer behind the trees until Bobcat found himself beside the marble wall itself.

Following the palace wall around some more topiary, the Raj turned, and Bobcat saw a small flight of stairs leading into a pit dug right up against the wall. A little wooden door sat among the ivy there; Tevirye padded down, stepped up to the door, knocked, and they waited for some minutes with nothing happening.

Tevirye scowled, knocked again, and this time the door came open. A wizened meerkat in a long red coat peered out, and Bobcat saw Tevirye, Fisher, and Skink all bow. The old meerkat stared a moment, then closed his eyes and nodded. "This day I have been dreading," he said, a soft lilt to his voice. "Please, all of you, come in."

The Raj raised a paw. "My thanks, Ramon, but I've stood watch all night." She glanced at Bobcat. "As it is, if what I remember from the old stories is true, there are some friends I would like to see before the end arrives."

Skink moved on Fisher's back. "Thank you for your assistance. And please, be assured that we will do all we can to keep the story from ending its usual way."

"Yeah," Fisher said, a tight smile under her whiskers. "Who knows? We may get lucky."

Tevirye looked over, her eyes settling on Bobcat, and he saw nothing there but doubt. She faced the Ramon and bowed. "Your pardon, sir." And with her cloak swirling behind her, she turned and hurried off through the hedges.

Bobcat watched her go, then looked back at the doorway. The Ramon was staring at him the same way, the same way everyone had been staring at him since he'd arrived in Kazirazif, it seemed.

But the old meerkat shook himself quickly and said, "Forgive me. I am the Ramon Sooli. Come in, please. Have you eaten yet this morning?"

That made Bobcat's stomach grumble, and Fisher laughed. "Lead on, sir, please," she said.

The Ramon's brow wrinkled, but he stepped back into the doorway. "This way, then."

Bobcat had to squeeze through the door, but the corridor on the other side was much roomier. The carpeting felt good under his pads, but the darkness made him blink till his eyes adjusted, the only light coming orange and flickery from oddly shaped lanterns—it took Bobcat a moment to see that they were little iron turtles clinging to the walls. The Ramon led them past door after door after door, all closed, turned left at a crossing corridor, also covered with doors and turtle lanterns, and then a brighter light was shining out from an open door ahead. The Ramon gestured for them to enter, so Bobcat followed Fisher inside.

What seemed like natural light poured in through a cloudy glass dome high in the ceiling, cushions filling the room, a long table piled with fruit and grain dishes. "Please, help yourselves," the Ramon said. "You may also sleep here, if you wish. A washroom is located directly across the hall. This evening, once you have rested, I shall call for you, for I am thinking we have much to discuss."

Bobcat nodded. "You bet we do."

Fisher bowed to the Ramon. "Thank you, sir. We look forward to your insights."

"Indeed," Skink added. "To take counsel from the Ramon of Kazirazif is a great honor, despite the circumstances that bring us all together."

Bobcat had already shucked his pack, moved over to the table, grabbed a peach, and was sucking it down when he saw the Ramon staring at him again. Uh-oh. "Uhh, yeah, sure. Thanks for everything. We'll, uhh, we'll see you later."

The meerkat blinked. "Yes. Yes, we shall. As I say, I shall call on you this evening." His brow still wrinkled, the Ramon turned and left the room, closing the door behind him.

Bobcat swallowed the rest of the peach. "Why does everybody keep staring at me? I mean it's not like they don't get bobcats through here all the time."

"No," Fisher said, coming over and picking up an apple. "But I'll bet most of them are a bit more polite to one of the foremost spiritual leaders on this continent."

"What? He said we could eat, didn't he?" Bobcat shook his head. "I don't know; this whole place just makes me twitch. I wouldn't be surprised if that guy came creeping in here later on with a knife."

"Bobcat!" Skink had scurried onto the table. "How could you possibly consider the Ramon capable of such an act?"

Bobcat shrugged, and Fisher rolled her eyes. "Don't you worry, Bobcat. I'm sure the three of us can handle one old meerkat. Besides, he's the only guy I can think of who can maybe tell us what we're supposed to do next." She stretched out on a cushion. "We might as well hang around, see what he has to say."

"Yeah, yeah, OK." Bobcat rubbed his eyes, his stomach still growling. It wasn't food he needed—he knew that—but he doubted this Ramon guy kept any catnip tucked away anywhere. Bobcat stuffed a few more peaches down his gullet, just for good measure, then collapsed back onto the cushions.

Whether he actually stayed awake or fell asleep and dreamed he was lying there awake he couldn't tell. Either way, it wasn't very restful, his back all tight and his paws all itchy, and he almost thanked Fisher when she started shaking his shoulder.

He rolled over, saw her and Skink already up. In the doorway stood a young meerkat wringing her paws. "There is no hurry," she said, her voice a high quiver. "The Ramon asks you to please take whatever time you need."

Fisher snapped her claws in Bobcat's face. "Nevertheless, let's get it together, shall we? Skink and I have already washed up. The bathroom's across the hall."

Bobcat grunted and stumbled past the little meerkat. The bathroom was pretty fancy: clean sand, lilac water in the washbasin, towels that smelled softly of lemon. Bobcat took his time, got all the grit out of his fur, gave himself a good licking, and came out to find the others standing in the hall. "Much better," he said.

Fisher blew out a breath. "With your permission, then, we'll be off to see our host. Is that agreeable?"

Bobcat waved a paw. "Perfectly. Lead on; lead on."

The little meerkat bowed, turned, and started up the corridor, Skink perched on Fisher's back again, so Bobcat slipped into his usual place at the rear. Down a couple hallways they went, more turtle lanterns flickering, then up several darkened flights of stairs, through another corridor, light and muttering voices trickling through holes in the ceiling, then up some more stairs. When the little meerkat opened one final door at the top of the last stairway, Bobcat wasn't all that surprised to find that they were walking out onto a roof.

Evening was just coming on, lights starting to sparkle up from the city below. The little meerkat gestured to the right, and Bobcat turned to see a table at the other end of the roof, various dishes set out, and the Ramon seated in a blocky chair at the table's head.

He didn't seem to notice them, his eyes focused out over the lights of the city, but the young meerkat cleared her throat. "Sir? Your guests, sir."

The Ramon turned then. "Ah, yes, of course. Please, join me for supper."

"Of course," Fisher said, Skink adding, "We would be honored, sir," and the young meerkat led them across the roof, indicating two large mats where Bobcat and Fisher could settle and a mat on the table itself for Skink. Bobcat sat where the young meerkat told him to, at the opposite end of the table from the Ramon, he noticed, Skink and Fisher both on the same side since the table was pushed right up against the stone railing at the edge of the roof.

Their plates were already filled; some sort of nut stew, it smelled like. The young meerkat poured dark liquid into glasses before each of them, a splash for Bobcat and Fisher, a drop for Skink, and four drops for the Ramon, then bowed and left through the door onto the stairwell. The Ramon picked up his glass, said something in a high, rolling language Bobcat was sure he'd never heard before, then set the glass down, picked up a fork, and began to eat.

Fisher and Skink, Bobcat saw, did the same, picking up their glasses, then setting them down before starting in on dinner, so he shrugged and did likewise. Night came on, stars popping in overhead, the quiet sounds of the city drifting up from the streets. The others ate in silence, not peppering the Ramon with questions, so, again, Bobcat followed their lead. These two had had more dealings with folks like this; maybe they knew what they were doing.

They didn't touch their glasses again, so Bobcat left it sitting there and cleaned his plate, the stuff nice and spicy, with just a little crunch to it. He was wondering what might be for dessert when the Ramon picked up his glass, sat back, took a sip, and let out a sigh. "It has been a bad month," he said. "All the signs spoke to me of the Blood Jaguar's prowling, but I, I would not believe it to be so." He took another sip. "Now, however, I must face facts. You are here, and the Plague Year is thus at my very doorstep." He shook his head. "And even earlier than the timetables had indicated."

Both Fisher and Skink had picked up their glasses, but at this they each stopped, Skink snapping his head over to stare at Fisher. "Timetables?" she asked. "You'll pardon me, Ramon, but . . . how can there be timetables for . . . for something like this?"

The Ramon looked over his glass at them. "Why, from the old accounts. The Ramons who preceded me long ago established the pattern. The last few thousand years have seen a decrease in the time between plagues, it is true, but even that change has been regular, incremental, following this pattern."

Skink's eyes were wide. "Last few . . . thousand years?"

"Yes, but now our figuring seems to have been in error. One hundred and fifteen years it has been since the last Plague Year. Our schedule gave us another eleven years. I had been hoping," and here his already-quiet voice dropped, "that I would be dead and my successor in place, but who are we mere mortals to hope against Curial planning?"

Both Skink and Fisher were blinking at the Ramon. Bobcat waited, but when neither one asked what seemed the obvious question he cleared his throat. "Excuse me, sir, but if you Ramons can predict these Plague Years, well, why don't you, I mean, why haven't you *done* anything about them?"

The Ramon stopped in the middle of his sip. "Oh, but, sir. Surely that is your job."

Bobcat stared across the table. "My job? What do you mean 'my job'? Who says it's my job?"

"Why, all the old accounts." The Ramon set down his glass. "They are very clear that it is the bobcat who has come to stop the Plague Year."

Now it was Bobcat's turn to blink at the meerkat, but Fisher spoke up: "Sir, you keep mentioning these old accounts, but we've been able to find almost no information about these Plague Years, and a matter of such importance . . . I mean, sir, I've been a shaman now for almost fifteen years, digging up just about everything from just about everywhere, and I've never heard of any secret accounts kept by the Ramons here." She turned to where Skink sat. "Skink, you?"

The lizard was shaking his head. "The Ramons are fabled for their knowledge of the arcane and esoteric, but to say that records exist, as you just did, sir, dating back a few thousand years . . . I have never even dreamed of such."

The Ramon looked from one to the other and then to Bobcat, his brow wrinkling again. "I do not understand. It is embodied in the very story of how the world began."

Fisher was absolutely still. "Uhh, which story would that be, sir? The one told by the reptiles, the one told by the otters, the one told by—"

"No, no, no!" Ramon Sooli sat forward, his eyebrows alive. "*The* story, the one story of how the world began, the basic story of all accounts, of all that we do here! You tell me you do not know this?"

"Uhh, well, I, uhh . . ." Fisher licked her lips. "I know the current theories: the gathering of the protostar, the accretion disk forming around it, the—"

"No, no, no!" the Ramon cried out again, whapping a paw against the table. "I speak not of *how* the world began! I speak of the *story* of how the world began, two very different things! Can you be telling me that you do not know?"

Bobcat saw Fisher glance down at Skink. The lizard shook his head.

"Ah," Fisher said slowly. "Well, I guess we don't know it, then."

The Ramon brought his paws to his mouth, and Bobcat could see that they were shaking. "Can this be?" his lilting voice came. "Then how can you hope to see . . . ?" A twitch passed over his face, and he set his paws on the table, his head bowed. "Very well," he said after a moment. His head came back up, and he crooked a claw at them each in turn. "Attend me now, all you three."

He settled back into his chair and began: "Many thousands of generations ago, the folk lived in the skies. But they longed to feel the solid ground beneath their paws again, so they gathered together and decided to build a new earth.

"For the work to get done in a reasonable fashion, it was decided that from each type of folk two would be elected, a male and a female, a Lord and a Lady, to serve in the Curia, the body that would decide the parameters for this earth. The Lord and Lady elected from each type of folk came together with all the other Lords and Ladies so elected, and the Curia was formed. The Curia scoured and scrounged, gathered the air and the dirt and the rocks and the water, set the land-to-sea ratios and the nitrogen content of the atmosphere, solved all the technical problems, and faster than you would think, the new earth was finished.

"The folk then left the skies and settled on the new earth, and it was the beginning of the Beforetime.

"The Curia, however, remained in session above in the skies to get the new earth up and running. And the physical laws for the new earth were passed in this fashion: the Lords and Ladies of the folk who lived in the deserts came together to decide how the deserts should be, while those of the forest folk set the rules for the forests, the river folk and the mountain folk and the plains folk all working on those parts of the new earth where their kin lived. The leaders of the committees would then present their recommendations to the Curia, and the members as a whole would vote.

"The leadership of these committees, and of the Curia itself, rotated, each Lord and Lady serving as chairfolk for a set amount of time, then surrendering the leadership to the next pair on the list. And so it went, laws getting passed and limits being set, with always the master plan in view: that the new earth would one day be completed, its chemistry self-sustaining and its geology running smoothly, so that the Curia might disband and its members join their own kinfolk down upon the earth.

"This master plan, however, had not been passed unanimously. There were those in the Curia who enjoyed the power of their position, the Curial Privilege that they were imbued with, and chief among these were the Lord Jaguar and the Lady Jaguar. They argued constantly against the dissolution of the Curia once the final rules were set in place, argued long and persuasively, trading favors and gathering support, looking forward to the time when they would assume leadership of the Curia and could put the question to a vote. And momentum grew for the idea, grew and grew until, in all likelihood, the motion would have passed. Had it not been for one problem.

"For the Lord Jaguar was convinced things would go much more efficiently if he were solely in charge of the Curia on a permanent basis, and the Lady Jaguar was convinced that she was the perfect one to permanently wield sole power. The thought of sharing the leadership even with each other was unbearable, so as they worked together to build support to pass their motion to keep the Curia in session for all time they also each worked separately to build support for his or her bid to take over as single permanent leader of the Curia.

"They were very clever and very determined, and by the time their turn arrived to lead the Curia three distinct parties had formed: those who backed the Lord Jaguar, those who backed the Lady Jaguar, and those who backed the original plan voted on at the beginning. This third group, by far the smallest, grew smaller with every meeting chaired by the Lord Jaguar and the Lady Jaguar, until only twelve in the whole Curia stood committed to that original plan.

"And these twelve sought to steer a middle course as debate in the Curial chamber dissolved into partisan bickering, the bickering into heated arguments, the arguments into sporadic violence, and the violence, finally, into civil war, the Lord Jaguar leading his followers against the forces of the Lady Jaguar.

"Battles raged through the skies, on the earth, and even in the sea, members of the Curia who had sat beside one another in deciding the laws for the new earth now tearing at each other's throats. Armies had even been raised among the earthly folk, drawn to the Lord Jaguar or the Lady Jaguar with promises of Curial Privilege shared, and death and destruction reigned over all.

"Until at last, as had to happen, the Lord Jaguar and the Lady Jaguar met in battle, just there," and the Ramon lifted a claw; Bobcat followed it upward and saw that the meerkat was pointing to the polestar, "at the very top of the sky. And those that remained alive of their partisans ceased fighting to stand on the battlefields and stare at the contest high above. On and on it raged, so fierce that not even the sun in its course could move them, the sky unable to turn, all time stopping to witness this last terrible battle.

"On and on they roared and raged, teeth tearing, claws rending, until the Lady Jaguar, torn and bleeding as she was, managed to close her jaws around the torn and bleeding throat of the Lord Jaguar. Her teeth clenched tighter and tighter, and with one mad burst of strength the Lady Jaguar tore the Lord Jaguar's head from his body.

"Yet that did not end it. The Lady Jaguar did not stop until she had ripped the Lord Jaguar's body to shreds, scattering the pieces far and wide over the sky. You can still see bits of him even now, streaking through the stars at times of a night. His head the Lady Jaguar devoured, howling her triumph, her teeth crushing the skull and her throat closing over the still-screaming face of the Lord Jaguar. His right eye, though, it is said, popped free and remains shining there at the top of the sky, all other stars circling around it.

"Only then was the Lady Jaguar sated, her furor spent; only then, the blood and bile flowing thick from her, did she fall from the sky, all the way down from the very top of the sky, fall fast and shrieking down, down to the earth, down to the very Savannah that had been her domain, fall down and slam unconscious into that land of grass, strike with a crash that shook the sky and the earth and even the sea. And there she lay, broken, bleeding, battered, but not dead, no, not dead. The Lady Jaguar lived, and slowly her Curial body began to heal itself.

"Then at last the sun could rise, hot tears falling from its face at the slaughter. Those Curials who had fought on one side or the other and had survived looked around at the shattered sky, the beaten earth, and the blood-soaked sea, looked around, struck dumb by what they saw and more by what they remembered themselves doing, and they ran and hid, as far as they could, as deep as they could, as quietly as ever they possibly could.

"The Twelve, however, those twelve who had taken no side in the terrible contest, stood in mourning, too numbed to weep at the carnage, until at last they met in the vast empty Curial chamber, and they agreed on what they had to do.

"The Twelve scoured the sky, the earth, and even the sea, and they hunted up every Curial still alive, dragged them out of hiding, no matter how far or how deep or how quietly each had run, and hauled them all back to the Curial chamber, all except for the Lady Jaguar, whose body lay motionless and healing down on the Savannah.

"All eyes were downcast as the Twelve took the floor, the Lord Lion and the Lady Lioness, the Lord Tiger and the Lady Tigress, the Lord Leopard and the Lady Leopardess, the Lord Kit Fox and the Lady Squirrel, the Lord Armadillo and the Lady Raven, the Lord Eft and the Lady Dolphin, and in the name of the Twelve the Lord Kit Fox and the Lady Squirrel pronounced their judgment upon the whole Curia:

" 'As of this day, the Curia is disbanded. The world will continue to function under the laws already passed, and all members of the Curia who took part in the battle, for either the Lord Jaguar or the Lady Jaguar, will be stripped of all Curial Privilege, will be sent down to the world, and will live the rest of their lives among their earthly folk.'

"And so it was done. The Twelve took the Curial Privilege from each member of the Curia, took it into themselves, and used it to place the former Curials down upon the earth, each in the proper area and among the proper folk. The Twelve then left the chamber, sealed it behind them so that no power in the sky or on the earth or even in the sea could ever possibly open it again, turned away, and descended to the Savannah where the Lady Jaguar lay motionless and healing.

"There the Twelve stood in a ring around the body of the Lady Jaguar, all in a ring around her body lying motionless and healing upon the Savannah. And in the name of the Twelve, the Lord Tiger and the Lady Tigress pronounced their judgment upon her:

" 'As the Lady Jaguar has caused and assisted death, chaos, and destruction, so she will become death, chaos, and destruction. As she has caused and assisted war, violence, and bloodshed, so she will become war, violence, and bloodshed. From this moment on, all power of death and darkness, terror and mayhem, vengeance and cruelty, all this will be invested in her. As she has lived, so she will now live, the Outsider, the Thirteenth among the Twelve, the Hated and the Feared. She will be, now and forever, the Cold Wind at Night, the Strangler of Laughter, the Shadow in the Grass: the Blood Jaguar.'

"And so the Twelve took from themselves and from the power of the whole Curia all that is lawfully given to death and destruction, and with those powers they invested the Blood Jaguar. And onto themselves they took the responsibilities of light and kindness, life and growth, harmony, beauty, and truth, and they pledged themselves to upholding the laws of the world. They would protect the rights of the folk against the Blood Jaguar, but also the rights of the Blood Jaguar against the folk, for Death does have rights, and they must be accorded her.

"And that was the end of the Beforetime, the beginning of our time here upon this earth.

"It is said then that when the Blood Jaguar awoke, saw the Twelve gathered around her, felt what had been done to her, she thanked them for it, thanked them for allowing her to become Death. She moved from the Savannah, rose through the skies, and settled far to the south in what she christened the Shroud Islands. There she established her new domain, her Kingdom of the Dead, where the spirits of the innocent dead she leaves to their leisure and those guilty she delights in tormenting.

"And that is who the Twelve are, and who the Thirteenth is, and how they came to be gods over our earth, ruling the cycles of nature and myth."

The Ramon stopped, took a sip from his cup, the sudden silence making Bobcat start back as if he'd just come awake from a dream. "There also," the meerkat continued, "according to all the accounts, the Blood Jaguar negotiated with the Twelve the terms for the first Plague Year. Among those agreed-upon terms is the provision that, at the start of any Plague Year, the Twelve shall choose a champion, visiting him in his dreams, and raise him up to face the Blood Jaguar on her old grounds, a hero with the strength and determination to stop the Plague Year from happening."

Bobcat felt his fur prickle as the Ramon raised his glass and crooked a claw at him. "You," he said, "Sir Bobcat, you are that champion, that hero, chosen by the Twelve themselves to defeat the Blood Jaguar's horrible plans."

Chapter Eight

By Southern Seas

"Wait a minute; wait a minute; wait a minute," Bobcat managed to get out after a moment of just staring. "Don't you point at me like that! 'Sir Bobcat?' Where're you getting this crap from?"

The Ramon's brow wrinkled. "But this is all . . . This is woven into the very fabric of the earth, part of the laws set up by the Curial powers! A bobcat is chosen by agreement between Those Above and the Blood Jaguar. She procures a skink's luckstone and retires to the great Savannah, and soon after, a bobcat, this luckless skink, and their fisher shaman arrive here in our city from the east, departing then for the great Savannah to the south. And in every account, it is the bobcat who is the leader, the driving force, the one who has received the visions, the True Dreams, the instructions from on high. Is this not the case?"

Bobcat almost laughed, but those eyes flared up in his mind again, made him swallow it before it got out of control. "Look, buddy," he said when he could. "If anyone's in charge on this little jaunt, it sure isn't me. I got kicked into a brier patch by this Blood Jaguar of yours, and if that's a deputation from on high, well, brother, you can have it. I'm not here under anything but protest, and I can't leave 'cause she left her eyes in my head to kick me again every once in a while! I've got no choice in any of this, haven't had any choice since day one, and I'll be damned if

I'm gonna take responsibility for something I've got no control over!"

The quiet sounds of the city drifted up around them, the old meerkat looking like a carved statue at the table's other end. Bobcat puffed out a breath and heard Fisher clear her throat. "It's, uhh, it's been kind of an unusual situation for us all around," she said. "We're operating without a lot of the standard equipment here, I guess you could say. So, sir, if there's, well, if there's anything you can give us, any information at all about what exactly we're supposed to do once we leave here and head out onto the Savannah, I know I'd certainly appreciate it."

The Ramon sat unmoving for another moment. "This . . . This cannot be. The accounts say nothing about . . ." He pressed his paws together, his eyes focused on the table in front of him. "The information you request, there is none of it. Yes, some centuries ago, it is recorded, the Caliph Rashur, against his Ramon's instruction, sent guards with the bobcat's party to report back what occurred. But, several nights later, the Ramon was visited in dreams by the Blood Jaguar herself, saw her laying the bodies of the guards at the city gates. They were found there the next morning, the first victims of that year's plague."

Again, silence fell, the Ramon visibly shaking now. Bobcat stared, then turned to Fisher. She was looking at him, and he could see Skink peering over from his mat on the table. "Well, now what?" Bobcat asked.

Fisher and Skink exchanged glances. "Well," Fisher said after a moment, "I guess we head south, then improvise."

"No!" came a bark from the other end of the table, and Bobcat saw the Ramon leap up, slam his fists against the arms of his chair. "No, this is not correct! This is *not* the proper way for the handling of these matters!"

Fisher shrugged. "Yeah, well, considering how 'these matters' have been handled in the past, maybe it's a good thing we're doing it differently this time."

The Ramon glared at her. "You speak with a loud tongue, shaman, and a fool's tongue, I assure you!"

Bobcat saw Fisher's ears go down. "OK, fine." She rose from

her mat. "I'm so sorry we wasted your valuable time, Ramon Sooli. If we'd've known you in your vaunted wisdom were as clueless as we are, we never would've bothered you." She looked like she was about to spit on the table, but instead she just said, "C'mon. Let's get outta here."

"Fisher, please!" Skink had scuttled over in front of her. "These are trying times for us all, and it's obvious that the expectations we held for each other are simply not going to be met! We can do nothing but make the best of the situation, not just for our own sakes, but for the sake of the entire world! Now, I suggest you apologize to the Ramon."

"Me?" Fisher shouted, but Bobcat saw the old meerkat slump back into his chair and nod.

"You touch truth, sir. My own stupidity shames me." He rose, bowed to Skink, then turned and bowed to Fisher. "It is I who should apologize. The Blood Jaguar's movement these past weeks has preyed so upon my mind, I was not prepared for the . . . for the unusual circumstances you have presented to me. Again, I am sorry."

Skink snapped his head back to Fisher, who blew out a breath. "Yeah, sure, me, too, whatever." She settled herself back onto the mat. "But, really, I don't know what more we can do here if there isn't anything in your accounts to cover our situation."

"I fear there is not." The wrinkle returned to the Ramon's brow. "I wish I could be of more help, but . . ." He spread his paws.

"Right." Fisher swigged down her drink. "I suggest we get going then, tonight; things were starting to look a little ugly out in the square this morning, and I'd rather get out of here before word spreads to the whole city."

"Yeah," Bobcat said. "That'd be just the right touch for all this, getting caught up in some riot or other."

The Ramon made a small clicking sound with his teeth. "I fear word has already spread; I understand that the palace guards were breaking up crowds outside all day." He tapped the table, then called out, "Kashas! Kashas, come here, please!"

The door opened, the young meerkat peering out. "Sir?"

"We have need of clothing for travelers heading south: traders'

cloaks and waterskins, suitable headgear, the sort of things anyone leaving the city would wear. Prepare the dressing room. We
shall be along shortly."

Fisher nodded as the young meerkat slipped back inside.
"Good idea. And if you've got any talcum, I can lighten up my fur;
I've passed for an otter before."

Bobcat had to laugh. "That I've gotta see."

She gave him a glare, then went on. "Skink can hide under my
cloak, and Bobcat, well, bobcats pass through Kazirazif all the
time. He shouldn't have any trouble if he's not out with a fisher
and a skink."

"Just so." The Ramon hopped from his chair. "Come along,
and we shall see how we may disguise you."

Skink scurried up onto Fisher's back, and with the meerkat in
the lead, Bobcat followed them all downstairs, his mind turning
the Ramon's story over and over. He didn't see how he could
have missed the Curials coming in his dreams to tell him he was
their chosen champion or whatever was supposed to have happened, but maybe somebody somewhere had made a mistake.
Just thinking about it, it seemed more likely that the bobcat they
had originally picked had fallen into a river or something and he
was being rushed in now as a replacement.

Those eyes flared up in his head suddenly, made him wince
and catch himself, almost losing his footing on the stairs.

OK, so maybe he was supposed to be here. Or, at least, the
Blood Jaguar wanted him here. Why, though, he still couldn't figure out.

Down darkened stairways and through shadowy corridors they
went until those odd little turtle lanterns began to appear along
the walls again. They rounded a corner, and a whiter light shone
out from an open door, making the Ramon stop, turn, and bow:
"If you will enter, we shall see what can be done."

Fisher walked in, Skink craning his head from her shoulder,
and Bobcat let out a whistle as he came in after them. Hundreds
of tiny candles burned brightly from inside little glass spheres,
their light reflected in the mirrors folding out from a huge dressing table against one wall. He stepped farther in and saw rack

after rack of clothing, fur of every shade—from black, brown, and dun to red, blue, and a vibrant electric purple—hung from pegs, jars overflowing from the shelves all around. "What is this stuff?" he asked.

The Ramon spread his paws. "Our caliph, Trajar—may the Twelve guard his steps—is always concerned to know the minds of his people. For his father, Ibrahim of great memory, charged on his deathbed that his son trust his advisers only so far, that he check their advice with his own experience as much as possible. Our caliph therefore often disguises himself here so as to roam the streets freely, to take the measure of his people's needs and fears. I often venture out so at his side. Only those most trusted know of this place."

"Really?" Bobcat looked around. "Should we be in here, then?"

The Ramon cleared his throat, glanced away, and Fisher rolled her eyes.

Bobcat blinked at her. "What?"

"Oh, nothing," she said. "Except that there's an even chance we'll all be dead in a week, and then it won't really matter what we know or don't know. Will it?"

Bobcat swallowed, and a silence followed until the Ramon clapped his paws. "Your disguises," he said. "We have much to choose from, so let us get started."

Skink jumped down off Fisher's back, and the Ramon took a jar from one of the shelves. He undid the lid, and the scent of talcum set Bobcat sneezing; he'd hated that stink since he was a kit. So when Fisher started patting the stuff over her face and paws, he moved away to clearer air behind the racks of clothing. He began pawing through them, the variety absolutely amazing, all sizes, styles, and professions represented, a simple beetle wrangler's shift too small for anyone but a mouse hanging next to the sort of embroidered vest and fez he'd seen lupine precious metal dealers sport.

None of them appealed to him, though, till he came to one, off-white and billowing, its black-edged head cloth tied to it, that he recognized as a bone dealer's cloak. It struck him as appropriate, so he pulled it down and tried it on.

It was almost too big for him, draping over his face and paws, and he was just tightening the black cord, fitting the head cloth between his ears, when he heard the Ramon calling, "Bobcat, have you found something?"

"Yeah!" he called back, padding to the front of the room. "Yeah, I think I have."

He came out from the last rack, and a figure in the plain black burnoose of a general trader spun around on a stool, an otter's wide grin flashing through her whiskers; Bobcat had to look twice to be sure it was Fisher. Her snout looked wider, her forehead rounder, her eyes sparkling the way an otter's always seemed to. It took some effort, but Bobcat managed merely to nod, to cock his head, and to say in a tentative way, "Well, maybe we can keep away from crowds."

Her smile bunched up a little, and that simple motion brought Fisher's own face closer to the surface. "Yeah," she said, even her voice somehow lighter in Bobcat's ears, "well, that was our plan anyway."

"Indeed," he heard Skink say, and the lizard scuttled into view on the dressing table. "Though I, for my part, continue to be amazed by your transformation, Fisher. Had I not witnessed it myself, I would not have believed it possible."

She slid from the stool with an otter's fluid motion and gave Skink a bow. "It's edifying to know that gentlemen of taste still walk among us," she said, and Bobcat couldn't help smiling at the lilt in her voice—just exactly right. She whirled then. "So, shall we gather the packs?"

The Ramon led them down the hall to the first room they had stayed in. "I have not yet had time to arrange a restocking of your packs. If you can wait a bit longer, I—"

"Nah." Fisher slipped into her straps. "Thanks, though. We've still got a few days' rations left, and I think it best we travel light and quickly."

Bobcat nodded, grabbed his pack, and watched Skink crawl up into the folds of Fisher's cloak.

"Yes," the Ramon said, tapping his jaw. "Come; I will show you to our exit."

He scurried from the room, Fisher following and Bobcat falling in behind, the meerkat's voice echoing slightly in the corridor: "Our caliph—may the Twelve guard his steps—has had built a passage beneath the palace that leads to the coal shed of a loyal blacksmith just off the Great Square. We shall take that route."

And then it was more flickering passages, more closed doors on either side. Bobcat blew out a breath; he'd worked at a termite farm along the eastern coast south of Ngyshen once, cutting the mounds open for the harvesters to dip the insects out, and he'd always been amazed at the mess of routes the termites carved. This place, though, was worse, corridors opening off at odd angles, seeming to double back on themselves, closed doors and little turtle lanterns everywhere.

After some time, though, they turned a corner and Bobcat saw a dark hole in the wall, the Ramon standing in its mouth. "The passage runs straight, yet you should duck your heads. It is our caliph's pleasure to keep the way rough-hewn that it might be collapsed at a moment's notice in case of emergency."

This was not exactly the sort of thing Bobcat wanted to hear about a tunnel he was even now entering, but he couldn't see that he had all that much choice at this point. It was a good thing Fisher reeked of talc; keeping his distance behind her even in the dark shouldn't be too much of a problem. The light faded from the walls, and he tuned his ears to the padding of paws, the meerkat's light and skittery, Fisher's soft but solid.

The darkness went on and on, Bobcat having to swallow whenever he blinked and those eyes sparked up, their afterimage seeming to flash in the space just ahead. Each and every time, his hackles rose, and he had to keep telling himself, *She's not here; she's not here; she's not here. . . .*

Finally, the meerkat's footfalls paused, and Bobcat drew back the step he was about to take.

"Just here," came the Ramon's voice. "If you will but wait, I shall open the hatch."

A scrape and a click, and a sliver of light appeared, then expanded into a gray rectangle, the meerkat's form dark against it. He gestured with a paw, and Bobcat followed Fisher out into a half-filled coal cellar, steps leading up at each end of the room. The meerkat scampered over the coal and up one set of stairs, peered through a crack in the door at the top, pushed it open. "Come now!" he called. "The way is clear."

Bobcat picked up his paws, trying to keep the coal dust off his cloak, and padded after Fisher up the steps. The Ramon stood waiting in the alleyway outside, the lights of the palace visible between the buildings behind him. "You know the way to the Basharah gate?" he asked.

Bobcat nodded, and Fisher said, "Just wander south and east, right? How hard can it be?"

The Ramon sighed and nodded. "How hard indeed." He reached up, and Fisher bowed her head so he could touch the side of her snout. Skink appeared from the folds of her cloak, leaned down to get a similar stroke; then the meerkat was moving over to Bobcat. Bobcat blinked, shrugged, lowered his head, and felt a brush like that of a moth's wing at his whiskers. "I give you whatever blessing I can," the Ramon's voice came to him. "And I pray that we shall meet again." A skittering of paws on the cobblestones, a creak from the door, and the old meerkat was gone.

They stayed still for another moment, the Ramon's worried face still floating in Bobcat's mind; then Fisher poked his shoulder. "Let's be off."

He blew out a breath. "Right."

Fisher headed toward the darker end of the alley, and Bobcat, after giving the palace one last glance, hurried to catch up with her.

The alley opened onto one of the thousand narrow side streets that wormed through Kazirazif. Fisher looked each way, then nodded right and looked at Bobcat. It seemed as good a direction as any till they found a market square and could get themselves oriented, so he nodded back, and they set off. The street wound around homes and shops, all dark and quiet, something Bobcat found a little strange. Kazirazif was usually a very nocturnal town, folk staying indoors during the heat of the day and coming out at night; he couldn't think where everyone might be.

Then they rounded a corner, and he saw where they all were. A market square lay before them, Keffiyah Square, he realized, the great fountain at its center unforgettable from all the times its water had been the only drink he could afford. Beside the fountain now, though, a large bonfire was burning, and around the bonfire had gathered folks of all sorts, meerkats and falcons, jackals and squirrels, serpents of every type, their voices a mishmash of sound over the fires' crackling. More folks were entering from the larger street mouths, coming into the square, groups forming and re-forming in the light of the bonfire.

Bobcat nudged Fisher and gestured to one of the street ends on the other side of the fire. "If we're where I think we are, that should be the Darb Mojambwe. We can take it east till we hit Hishafir Square, then cut over a couple blocks and meet the Coati Road. I think."

She turned, flashed that jarring otter grin at him again. "Well, nothing like wandering the streets of a strange city in the middle of the night, I always say. Makes a body glad to be alive." And she sauntered out into the square, her rolling gait making Bobcat wonder if she might actually have otter blood in her somehow.

He stepped out then, wove through the crowds, his eyes on the street end. Snatches of conversation reached him, things like: ". . . demons in the caliph's palace . . . ," and, ". . . woke up screaming, could almost still smell the blood . . . ," and, ". . . it was just that Granddad wouldn't stop crying, said it was the end of the world. . . ." Bobcat picked up his pace and kept himself focused on Fisher's dark cloak in the crowd ahead.

He got to the street and kept going, entering the traffic of folks out on the Darb. Here lamps burned, the cafés open, pushcarts moving up and down the street, but Bobcat didn't hear any laughing, no music, washing out from the pubs. The folks at their sidewalk tables talked in low voices, the scent of fear coming to Bobcat's nose under the stink of burning kerosene. And every cart, he noticed, seemed to be selling charms or totems—no snack wagons or drink merchants, no clothiers or hat dealers.

Down the blocks they went, Fisher staying a few paces ahead, until the buildings on either side pulled away and Hishafir Square opened in front of him, more bonfires burning, more crowds gathered. Fisher had stopped, so Bobcat moved up beside her. "There's a side street across the square," he muttered, "and it winds right down to the Coati Road." He shook himself, his sides itching under his cloak, the fear scent making his fur bristle. "Did you hear what folks're—"

"Yeah," she said, her voice suddenly her own again. "Real cheerful stuff." Then the otter lilt was back, and she slid forward, calling out, "Let's just get going, shall we?"

He wove through the crowds, trying to ignore everything around him, but . . . Two raccoons clutched their baggage, one assuring the other, "If we can just get out of town, we'll be all right." Among a few dozen meerkats, their jaws set, one was saying, "And if the caliph thinks he can keep us from knowing what's going on, then I say we go visit him tonight and take some good, hefty clubs with us." A fox, stinking of liquor, stumbled past, stopped, turned around, laughing, "Hey, yo, bone merchant! Looks like you're gonna be in the business here, don't it?" Bobcat almost sprinted the last few yards to the side street, Fisher a few steps faster.

This street lay as dark and deserted as the first they'd used, starlight making the way just bright enough; Bobcat let out a sigh of relief, his paws shaking with each step. It wound for a while, then ended at a larger street, lamps lit every few yards but also nearly deserted, only a few figures scurrying along. "This way," Bobcat said, starting down the street. "We shouldn't be too far from the gate." He looked over his shoulder. "Weird. I mean I heard folks talking about leaving the city, but there's no one here."

"Not weird." Fisher's walk still rolled a little, but her voice was practically her regular one. "After all, this road leads south."

"So?"

"So, south is the Savannah. No one with a brain wants to be heading into the Strangler's territory right now."

That sent a shiver through Bobcat's whiskers, and he let the conversation drop. A few minutes later, torches appeared ahead, and Bobcat could make out the tower of the Basharah gate. As they got closer, he recognized the Raj Tevirye standing with two other meerkats, and he shook himself, getting his head cloth to droop down a bit more over his face. He walked past quickly, thought he saw Tevirye's head turn . . . but she didn't call out, and he padded one paw after the other out through the gate, past the lieutenant and the other three guards, and onto the road again.

The night swallowed up the lights of the city, the sand dunes dark and quiet ahead, but the faces stayed: Ramon Sooli and his wrinkled brow, Raj Tevirye and the shake of her head when she'd left them that morning, all the wide eyes Bobcat had passed on the streets, the quivering voices, the bristling fur. The Ramon's story stirred through it all, and he realized with a shock, almost tripping, that all those folks back there, whether they knew it or not, were counting on *him* to stop this Plague Year, to defeat the Blood Jaguar, to save them all from her plan.

And so, he supposed, were Fisher and Skink. And Lorn and Rat and Shemka Harr, wherever she was.

And, gods, even Garson.

And he had no idea what he was supposed to do or how he was supposed to do it.

Bobcat didn't feel much like talking, so it suited him just fine when Fisher kept going through the flats outside the walls of Kazirazif and on into the dunes, down the Coati Road, and passed the milestone without stopping. Lightning flickered at the horizon to his left, thunder rumbling in Bobcat's ears, a whiff of rain on the breeze. Great. Knowing his luck, they'd end up trudging through the night in the rain, heading he didn't know where to do he didn't know what.

But the lightning kept its distance and the night wore on, Bobcat's thoughts making his paws heavier and heavier till he heard Fisher heave a sigh. "All right, let's take a rest. Skink's probably half-throttled by now." She padded off the road into the sand, stretched, and settled herself down between two dunes.

Something moved at her shoulder, and Bobcat got there in time to see Skink's head pop out. "Actually, Fisher," the lizard said, "I'm doing quite well."

"Glad to hear it. Watch out a minute." She heaved her pack off,

Skink ducking out of its way, and dug around till she pulled out some trail mix. Bobcat sat down beside her, slung off his own pack, found a little bag of something nutty, and started gnawing on it. The silence went on, broken only by an occasional roll of thunder thudding in the distance, till Bobcat couldn't stand it anymore. "So. What now?"

Fisher arched an eyebrow, her face still powdered but not an echo of otter anywhere in it. "Well, as I understand it, you're the one who's supposed to know."

Her voice was entirely hers now, too, and it made Bobcat's sides start itching. "And what's that s'posed to mean? You think I've been holding out on you?"

She looked away. "I don't know what to think anymore."

Skink rustled down into the sand, raised a claw. "Now, Fisher. We both know that Bobcat is as concerned about our success in this matter as we are."

Fisher barked a laugh. "Do we?"

"Hey!" Bobcat glared at her. "What, you think I *want* this Plague Year? My dreams never told me I was s'posed to be in charge here! How was I s'posed to know if—"

"You? Not know?" She fished a chunk of something out of her bag, took a bite of it. "I am surprised."

"Fisher, please." Skink had scurried up onto her pack. "We are all tired, and our visit to Kazirazif has thrown an entirely new light on our mission, a light none of us could have suspected. We must work with what we have been given." He twitched his head over to Bobcat. "Now, Bobcat, perhaps you *have* had some dreams of the sort the Ramon mentioned, dreams that made no sense to you when you had them because you had yet to understand the nature of Curial Manifestation. I have read of cases where True Dreams sent by the Lady Raven were not recognized as such until months later. Could this be the case here?"

Bobcat rubbed his chin. "Well, lemme think. . . ."

"Oh, gods." Fisher spat something into the sand. "You might as well ask a rock."

"Hey!" Bobcat felt his hackles rise.

"I mean c'mon, Skink; this's Bobcat we're talking about here."

She tossed her head. "Any True Dream that might've visited him would have to get through his catnip cloud, and I doubt even the Lady Raven could penetrate that."

The catnip urge rumbled up from his belly, those eyes simmering in his head, Fisher's voice grating over the cuts on his sides, and before Bobcat even realized what he was doing, just wanting to wipe that smirk from her whiskers, he had lashed out with a front paw and bashed Fisher in the face.

She jerked back, her stunned look gone almost instantly, her lips curling back. "Why, you goddamned little . . . ," she growled, and then she was leaping at him, her claws out, Bobcat jumping up to meet her; he'd taken all he was gonna take from her.

He tried getting his paws up to slash her as she came, but she was too quick, struck him straight in the chest and knocked him over backward. He heard cloth tear, felt her weight pressing him down, and kicked out with his hind legs, trying to rake her stomach. She was still moving over him, though, and all he ended up with was his paws tangled in her robes. But her dark fur stretched before his eyes, and he bared his teeth, ready to snap, when a huge light burst at the sky, thunder crashing at his ears. He blinked, and water swept cold and roaring over him, dashing him sideways.

Flash flood, he knew immediately, had seen more than one rip down across the desert after thunderstorms in the mountains. He tried to stop his tumbling, to get his head up, to breathe, but he was still tangled in Fisher's cloak, his paws bound in the cloth. Things slammed into him, mud filling his eyes and ears, every gasp giving him half a mouthful of water, the force of the flood knocking him from side to side. He couldn't tell if Fisher was still with him, couldn't tell which way was up, and he flailed through the raging torrent till he thought his chest would burst and his legs grew too tired to keep up their thrashing.

Just as they were giving up, though, the rush around him began to calm, the constrictions of the cloak seeming to melt away, his paws brushing ground for the first time in long minutes. He pushed off from it with as much strength as he could muster, felt his nose break the surface, managed to suck in a few coughing breaths. The flood was slowing, the water growing shallower, letting him stand this time with his head above the surface. He stumbled forward till his knees gave out, but by then the flow was a mere trickle, letting him drag himself up onto dry land.

He was alive, he could tell, because everything hurt so much, and he panted and heaved up water for he couldn't tell how long until the tightness crept from his chest. It took a while longer for his breathing to slow and his muscles to stop feeling like jelly, but then he raised his head, opened his eyes, and had to gasp.

A wide, crescent-shaped cove met his eyes, the darkened sea lapping at the sand that curved away in both directions, cliffs towering up behind. His hind legs still lay in wetness, the stream seeming to flow around him, along the left side of the knob of sand he had dragged himself onto, and into a large pool below, its water trickling in rivulets down the beach to the lagoon. A cold light flooded the whole scene, and Bobcat looked up to see the moon, huge and full, hanging overhead.

Which was odd, since the moon had been waning all week.

Everything stood out so clearly beneath that moon, too, the contrasts so sharp, that Bobcat shivered, the stark and shining silver and black of the place seeming somehow unreal.

A dark speck swung past the face of the moon then, moving quickly, across the moon and gone before Bobcat could more than notice it. He stared upward, and it swung past again, larger this time, seemed to be spiraling down through the sky, growing bigger each time it passed the moon's face, until Bobcat realized it was some sort of bird. A few more passes, and the wedge of its tail and the jagged feathers of its wings told him it was a raven.

It just kept getting larger, circling downward, and he could make out a dark sheen glowing from its feathers. Larger and larger and larger it came on, Bobcat's hackles rising, till it filled the whole sky, swooping past him and out over the cove, its wings seeming to brush the cliffs. He heard a gasp from his right, turned to see Fisher sprawled there, staring upward, Skink clinging to her head. "Oh," Skink breathed. "The Lady Raven."

Bobcat looked back, fur prickling, at the raven wheeling above the water. She glided down, stroked the surface with her wings, and Bobcat caught his breath as a slender silvery shape sprang up over her and knifed back into the sea. "The Lady Dolphin," he heard Skink say, but he'd sort of guessed that himself already.

The Lady Raven was still coasting, the gleaming figure of the Lady Dolphin again leaping up. But this time, the Lady Raven rolled, and the two flashed through a series of impossible spins and swirls, moonlight and darkness dancing through the water and over the whole sky, their music the splash of the waves and the stroke of night's wind on the sand. Again and again they circled and spun, up and around until Bobcat saw that they were headed straight for him, straight for the beach. But they were coming so fast, twirling so wildly, he flinched, expecting them to crash into the shore.

At the last second, though, they each gave one last flip, the Lady Dolphin sliding up the rivulets to settle into the pool below the knob of sand, her fins, tail, and bottlenose raised, while the Lady Raven somersaulted over her to land without a sound beside the pool, her wings spread, her head thrown back, her eyes closed.

They held that pose for a heartbeat, Bobcat afraid to breathe; then the Lady Dolphin yelled, "Wa-hoo!" and rolled over, slapping her fins in the pool and kicking her tail. The Lady Raven was laughing by this time, too, had fallen over onto her back, her wings draped over her chest. "Oh, sister!" the Lady Dolphin got out after a moment. "You never could do that last double reverse, could you?" She bent her tail and splashed water up over the Lady Raven.

"Hey!" the Lady Raven cried, brushing a wingful of sand into the pool. "You're the one who comes out of your turn too high, sister."

"Oh, I like that! The bird's complaining about the fish flying too high!"

"I see. Suddenly you're a fish?"

The Lady Dolphin kicked out some more water. "You get technical on me, sis, and, oh, I'll give you such a pinch!"

Their laughter, gentle in Bobcat's ears, made him think of the crystal chimes he'd heard while wandering among the temple rows of Lai Tuan, all pure tones and clearer than any sound had a right to be. He pressed himself lower against the sand and hoped they wouldn't notice him.

But the Lady Dolphin's eyes had already darted over, and she waved a fin. "But then it's been so long since we've had an audience, sister o' mine, I'm surprised you didn't pass right out from stage fright."

A smile somehow curled the corners of the Lady Raven's beak, and she turned toward him, too. "Well, at least it's stopped them fighting."

"Excuse me?" The Lady Dolphin scooped water up with her tail and let it run down her back. "My flood did that. And quite nicely, too, I might add."

The Lady Raven heaved a sigh. "I shall apologize for my sister, since she certainly won't." She raised a wing and beckoned. "Please, the three of you, come down and sit."

A movement to Bobcat's right made him look, but Fisher was already gone, the crunch, crunch, crunch of her paws in the sand passing behind him and to his left until he saw her wading across the little stream. She stopped, bowed to the Ladies, Skink bowing from his perch on Fisher's back; then the lizard scuttled down, and they both settled beside the pool in front of the Lady Raven.

Bobcat didn't move, didn't want to move, the pounding of his heart shaking him all the way to the tip of his tail. Yet their laughter was so wonderful, their voices so smooth, cool as evening's touch in his fur, sweet as springwater on his tongue, that when he glanced up, saw the Lady Raven still beckoning, her dark eyes still shining, he couldn't deny her, couldn't keep himself from rising on quivering paws, creeping down through the stream, and inching up beside Fisher.

Both the Ladies were looking at him now, and Bobcat could only stare back, completely unsure how he was seeing them. The Lady Raven seemed to be huge, vast, the spread of her wings covering the whole night sky, the stars just glimmers reflecting from her feathers, but she was also right here, right in front of him, not that much bigger than he was, in fact. And the Lady Dolphin, lolling in her pool, seemed to flow in place, water entering her, becoming her, then turning back to simple water again as it washed down into the sea.

The Lady Raven spread her wings, and the awful beauty of the whole sky seeming to unfold almost made him break and run. "Welcome," she said. "I hope we weren't too rough on you. Have you calmed down a bit?"

Bobcat heard Fisher sigh, saw her nod.

"Good." The Lady Dolphin rolled over in her pool. "Though if it were up to me, I'd just start this whole thing over. I can't remember a group being this much trouble. Of course, if *I* were in charge, I'd make sure some otters were involved, maybe replace all three of you. No offense, but otters are just a lot more interesting to watch than most other folk." She puffed through her blowhole. "That otter stuff you were doing back in town, shaman, now that was fun." And her smile spread so sweet and broad along her snout, Bobcat couldn't help grinning back.

He heard Fisher breathe out a little laugh. "Thanks. I've been working on it."

"Oh, it shows, believe me."

The Lady Raven was tapping her wings in the sand, glancing sideways at the Lady Dolphin. "Finished?" she asked.

The Lady Dolphin waved a fin. "Oh, please, do go on."

"Thank you." She cleared her throat. "As I said, we're sorry about all the water—"

"I'm not," the Lady Dolphin muttered.

The Lady Raven cleared her throat again. "I repeat, we are sorry, but, well, we couldn't just let you tear each other to bits, could we?"

"Yeah." Fisher dug at the sand, then looked back up. "If I might ask, though, have you been watching over us long?"

"No, just tonight." The Lady Raven waved a wing upward. "Brother Kit Fox asked us to look in on you."

"That's right." The Lady Dolphin flashed another of her grins. "Kit really seems interested in you, shaman; there something going on there we should know about?"

"Sister. . . ." The Lady Raven clicked her beak. "Can we stick to the subject here?"

"No, we can't." The grin faded from the Lady Dolphin's snout. "And you want to know *why* we can't?"

The Lady Raven reached out a wing. "Sister, please—"

"I'll tell you why we can't!" The silvery sheen of the Lady Dolphin's flanks deepened to storm-cloud gray. "Because every time I think about how the fate of billions of earthly folk is riding on the pads and paws of these three morons, it gets my stomach churning!" The water in the pool began to swell and ripple. "It gets me thinking about how much I like earthly folk, the stroke of their gratitude when I rain where they need it or don't rain where they don't! And it gets me thinking that I might not have to worry so much if these idiots would just get their act together!"

"Sister, you know it's not their fault; they're—"

"Oh, really? Then I'd like to know whose fault it is!" She smashed her tail into the pool, and thunder came to Bobcat's ears. "You sent the dreams like you were supposed to, Raven, but this guy doesn't seem to have picked up a one!" The clouds rose from her flanks into the air, the whitecaps in the pool eating away its sides, stretching it across the sand right toward Bobcat, the Lady Dolphin rolling toward him like a cold front, lightning in her eyes. "You! You're supposed to be our champion, the world's last, best hope! And look at you! What a mess! It makes me sick, and I for one would like to know just what you've got to say for yourself!"

At the back of his head, the Blood Jaguar's eyes flared up, twisting the ever-present claws in his gut, the tearing grip he knew only catnip would loosen, and Bobcat almost snarled at the Lady Dolphin, almost leaped up, almost shouted in her face that maybe they didn't try hard enough, maybe they should've thought a minute before settling on an idiot like him, maybe they should've picked a bobcat somewhere who actually knew something about this stuff, who understood and could do whatever it was they expected him to do.

Almost he shouted this out, but the Lady Dolphin had slid right up in front of him now, and as he opened his mouth to snarl he saw a glimmer behind the lightning of her eyes, a shimmer like sunlight sparkling off drops of summer rain . . . or like tears. And when her thundering voice shook him again—"What have you got to say?"—Bobcat could hear a quiver behind it, could hear a catch in her throat.

Bobcat stared, his mouth still open, the words bunching up behind his tongue. She was trying not to cry. . . .

Her raw emotions filled the air, the electricity prickling his fur, and he swallowed his anger, swallowed his words, lowered his head, and said the only thing he felt he really could say: "I . . . I'm sorry."

The clouds seemed to flinch, the storms over her to pause. "You're what?"

"I'm sorry. I'm sorry I'm not a hero or a champion or whatever you need me to be. I'm just a guy who got kicked into a brier patch, and I . . . I don't know how to be whatever I'm s'posed to be." He ventured to look up, saw the lightning still frozen in her eyes. "All I know is that this is the Blood Jaguar's show, that she's still rattling around inside my head, letting me know that she's still waiting for me. I don't know why or where or what, and to tell you the truth, I don't think I could take knowing anyway. So, I mean, sure, I'll try, but I'm just stumbling around here the best I know how, and I'm sorry, but . . . that's all I can really do."

The clouds rolled a little over her head, then began clearing up, the lightning dissipating with a few fizzles. The Lady Dolphin blinked, shook herself—Bobcat winced, but the drops that hit him were warm—and reached out a fin to take Bobcat's paw. "You're an idiot," she said, her voice as quiet as the waves lapping on the sand. "But at least you're an honest idiot. And that's better than nothing, I guess." She let his paw go then and just seemed to melt into the pool, the water dropping out of her shape and flowing back against the banks with barely a splash.

A throat cleared, and Bobcat looked up to see the Lady Raven. "Again, let me apologize for my sister. Dolphin's heart's in the right place, but she does get a bit carried away at times." A sideways smile touched her beak. "You'd never know she was older than me, would you?" She shook her head, looked back at Bobcat. "I think she's so upset because, well, when this most recent round started she was telling me that she had a good feeling about you, thought you were the best champion we'd had in millennia."

Bobcat stared at her. "Me?"

"Yes, you." She cocked her head. "Can't imagine why, myself, but, well, that's Dolphin for you." She spread her wings. "You ought to find your packs back up the stream a ways, but feel free to spend the night here."

She turned, seemed about to take off, then paused and glanced over her wing. "She misses you, your Garson does. I'll visit her dreams tonight, let her know you're thinking of her." She looked upward again, flexed her legs, and leaped, the whole night sky embracing her.

Bobcat stood, stared up at the stars, unable to turn away for several moments. "Wow," he got out at last, tearing his gaze away and moving it to the others. "What do you think she—"

They were both asleep, curled up in the sand, their sides gently moving. Weariness washed over him then, made his eyes droop, and he settled into sleep beside them.

Chapter Nine

On the Savannah

A high-pitched squeaking made Bobcat's ears twitch, brought him awake, his whole body aching. He blinked at the little hill of sand in front of him, wondered where and what for a while before deciding to sit up and take a look around.

The cove still curved away in both directions, the waves still lapping at the shore, the stream trickling into the pool next to him, the cliffs and the beach shadowed in the light of early dawn, the sky and ocean as clear and blue now as they'd been dark and silvery last night.

All of which meant that it was possible the things he was beginning to remember about last night might, in fact, be true.

Bobcat thought about that for a moment and was a little surprised to find that he didn't want to start screaming. Weird things were going to be a part of his life now, it looked like, and he didn't see what else he could do but learn to deal with it. He was involved in an ancient reptile prophecy, was the one the gods had sent out to stop Death's plan for the world; the Ramon and the two Ladies had pretty much told him that straight out. He didn't like it, but, well, if everyone was going to be saying it, he might as well get used to hearing it.

The squeaking was still going on in his ears, more like a cawing now that he was awake and listening, and it seemed to be coming from above. He tipped his head back and saw birds, dozens of them, gray and white and spiraling in slow circles up in the blue over the cliffs, the light flashing from their wings and making Bobcat squint down in the shadows of the cove. The shadows were lessening, though, crags along the cliff face becoming balconies and window ledges, awnings stretched over crevices, and Bobcat realized that he was looking at a seagull village among the rocks above the cove.

A moan drew his attention back to the ground, and he saw Fisher standing and stretching. "Whew," she said with a yawn. "It's been a couple years since I last fought a bobcat. I'd forgotten how sore it makes me."

Bobcat felt his ears go warm. "Uhh, yeah, I'm a little stiff, too." He swallowed. "I guess I should apologize—"

She was pulling the sandy remnants of her cloak off. "Forget it. We were both acting like idiots. We should just be thankful the Lady Raven was here to keep the Lady Dolphin from frying us both. Then Skink would've had to carry on alone."

Bobcat heard the lizard's dry little laugh and turned to see him crouched atop the sand dune.

"That would have been the worst possible outcome. I, luckless, going to confront the one who has apparently taken it?" He shook his head.

"Hey, that's right." Bobcat tapped a paw on the sand. "But why would the Blood Jaguar need to take your luckstone? Can't she just wave a paw, do whatever she wants?"

Skink spread his claws. "Cyclical Myths often focus on artifacts, items that must be gathered before an action can be pursued. Symbolism plays a large part in the—"

"Yeah, OK." Fisher had gotten to her paws. "Maybe we can get into the underlying metaphors after we find the packs, you think? We don't know where we are or where we're supposed to be headed, so I'd like to know if we have to start worrying about rations, too."

"The packs?" Bobcat stood up, gestured up the stream. "The Lady Raven said they were up there a ways, I think."

Fisher raised an eyebrow. "Yeah? Well, let's go see."

The stream wound up the beach and into a brush-choked

crevice that curved back into the side of the cliff, and that made Bobcat blink. The flood should have smashed all that brush to kindling, but Bobcat couldn't see any sign of damage at all. He turned to Fisher and gestured with a paw. "Hey, how do you s'pose we got down that canyon without leaving a mark? I mean that was some flood last night."

"What?" Fisher was tugging at what looked like a strap sticking out from a pile of sand. "Oh, we didn't come down this stream."

Bobcat blinked at her. "But . . . but last night. I dragged myself out of this stream back there above the pool. It was . . . It was right there, and I—"

Fisher let out a sigh. "Look, when that flash flood hit us, we got pulled into a . . . Well, I don't wanna get technical. Just look at it this way: it was night, and we were in water. The Lady Raven *is* Night and the Lady Dolphin *is* Water, so it's not too much of an exaggeration to say that they could've done anything they wanted to us. And what they wanted was to pluck us up, plop us down in this cove, and have that little chat." She stopped, closed her eyes, and rubbed them. "Now, let's gather up the packs and get back to Skink, OK?"

Bobcat stared at her some more, then at the stream canyon, his resolve to accept all the weird things in his life wavering slightly. When he looked back, Fisher had already dug out her pack, was shrugging it on, so he grabbed his own and followed her back to the dune where they'd left Skink.

There she had him pull out the stove parts, and she peered into them, blew them out, even filled a few with water and sloshed it around before she shrugged and put the thing together. "I'll say this for the Curials," she muttered, striking her flint and steel together. "When they want you to kill yourself for them, they sure do take care of you."

"Fisher," Skink said from the dune, "I realize that the shaman's relationship to the Lord Kit Fox allows for these comments, but—" He broke off then and was suddenly gone. Bobcat blinked, saw movement between his paws, looked to see the lizard there, his eyes wide. "Above!" he whispered.

Bobcat stared down, then up, and saw several seagulls winging down to land on top of the little dune. They cocked their heads, each pointing one yellow unblinking eye at him. "Uhh, Fisher?" he said.

"Hmmm?" She had a twig burning, was poking it at the top of the stove. Bobcat heard the gas catch with a *foomp*.

Another group of gulls landed—surrounding them, Bobcat realized—more birds settling with each passing second, a few dozen standing in a circle before he could get out, "We, uhh, we have visitors."

"Really?" She was grinning when she raised her head, but it disappeared immediately. "What in the—"

"Infidels!" came a cry from above, and one more seagull fluttered down to land inside the ring of birds, a seagull wearing a cap of black feathers. "You have no business here! We have been given sovereignty over these coves, we who follow both the Lady Raven and the Lady Dolphin, and we guard these sacred lands in their names! Now be off with you, vagabonds, or face our wrath!"

Bobcat held up a paw. "Well, if that's all, the Lady Raven told us we could stay, so I don't see—"

"Blasphemers!" The gull in the black hat leveled a wing at him. "In these sacred lands, such impiety is treated most severely! You may think it all very amusing to mouth such phrases, yet we who have known Her Ladyship, who have met with her favor, we do not find any humor in—"

One of the other seagulls, her eyes wide, her feathers ruffling, began tapping the gull in the black hat. "Hrati! Hrati! Look at them! Look who they are!"

"Silence!" The gull in the hat spun around, slapped at the other with his wings. "I'm Hrati this month, so I get to deal with this! It's my jurisdiction, isn't it?"

"But, Hrati!" The other seagull had her wings up, shielding her face. "But, Hrati, look! They're a bobcat, a fisher, and a skink! Look at them, Hrati; look at them!"

Bobcat folded his ears back; he'd been wondering how long it would take someone to notice.

Hrati's wings froze. He wheeled around, cocked his head, and looked with one eye from Bobcat to Fisher to Skink. He clicked his beak together, turned his head, squinted with the other eye, and looked at them all again. "So," he said, then threw his head back, spread his wings, and let out a caw like a rusty gate creaking, repeating it over and over till the others took it up and joined in.

This went on for a few minutes, Bobcat trying to hold his ears closed against the noise, until Hrati lowered his wings and silence slowly fell again. "Minions of Death," he said at last. "My authority does not extend to act alone concerning you. Therefore, it is my judgment that you be held here in custody until such time as I can get word to the other gull councils along the coast. We shall all have to meet, and there we can decide whether to imprison you for life or just plain kill you."

"Uhh, excuse me." Fisher was stepping forward. "If I might suggest a—"

"Silence!" Hrati sprang his wings, looked like he might be about to leap at Fisher, when a commotion started among the seagulls behind him. "And you, too!" he shouted, spinning around, and with him out of the way, Bobcat could see something slinking through the gathered birds. The front rank of gulls jumped aside, and a cobra slid out onto the sand in front of Hrati. "What do you want here!" he demanded.

"Surely you know." The cobra's voice made Bobcat's ears flinch, a shiver of that hypnotic thrum reaching him, and he glanced around, wondered if he could push his way out through these birds.

But the snake never looked at him, just swayed there, staring at the gull, her tongue flicking in and out.

Hrati snapped his beak a few times, then lowered his wings. "Of course," he said, his voice quieter. "I'm sorry, Seer. It's been such a long time, I had forgotten the stretch of your jurisdiction."

"Understandable," the cobra hissed. "Please leave me now to my work. I shall notify you of my judgment."

The gull cocked his head, squinted at the cobra with one eye, then with the other. "Of course." He raised his wings and rushed past her, slapping at the birds in the crowd. "You heard her! Go on! Let her get on with her work! Go! Go! Go!"

Caws broke out from the crowd, birds spreading their wings, leaping and flapping away. Bobcat squeezed his eyes shut, flinched against the swirling sand that pinged against his nose, waited for the storm to die down before he ventured to take a peek.

The beach stood empty of birds now, only the cobra curled in place, eyes unblinking, hood slightly flared. After a moment, she started slinking toward him, and Bobcat took a step back. Something remained in the sand where he'd been, though: Skink squatting still as a stone, not even looking at the oncoming serpent. Bobcat hesitated. Was Skink summoning up the Lord Eft again or whatever he'd done the last time? He was just sitting there, the snake coming closer and closer, but Bobcat didn't want to yell, run up, and grab him or anything in case it might break his concentration.

But the cobra stopped next to Skink, the tip of her tail sliding over to hover beside Skink's head. "I am pleased to meet you again, Skink of Donalis Kiva," her voice came soft and buzzing to Bobcat's ears. "I, Cobra of Jen-hrati Cove, your former opponent."

Skink snapped his head over, reached out, and took her tail in the claws of one paw. "I am pleased as well. May I guess that you have found the voice that called you?"

"I have," she said, and Bobcat almost thought he saw her smile, a strange shifting of her facial features that was gone immediately. "I wandered after I left you last, followed the sound of my Lady's voice till at last I was brought down the cliffs to this cove. And here lay my Lady Dolphin sweetly singing the song that had drawn me on." She stopped suddenly, looked down, then back up. "Forgive me. It is hard speaking without rhythm, but my Lady proscribes it except on certain occasions. I am not yet accustomed to a meterless measure."

Skink nodded. "I find it difficult myself at times, the plain speech of this common tongue, and I know my dialect of the Lord Eft's language is nowhere near as lyrical as cobra."

Cobra bowed her head. "This language is the only tongue common between myself and these birds, among whom my Lady has set me to be their Seer. Long they have been without one, she said, long, for I was foolish, not listening to the call that would have drawn me here. Several disputes I have already arbitrated successfully, devouring those against whom my judgment fell." Her hood fluttered. "I have never known such joy as now embraces me, fulfilling the role Those Above have assigned. And I owe this all to you, friend Skink."

Skink bowed to her. "I am honored to have been the instrument though which Those Above could reach you. Am I to understand that we three fall under your jurisdiction here?"

"You do." She slid her tail from Skink's claws. "For the Seer flows forth from the Curial powers, and all that concerns them is matter for me." She stopped, swayed in place for a moment, then said, "You move toward Death at Death's behest, rendering my poor judgment moot." She shook herself and bowed to them each in turn. "I cannot let you eat here, but my Lady would offer you the hospitality of the waters if you wish to bathe or refill your canteens before you continue. The steps you follow sink deep into the earth, and I wish you all luck with them." With that, she turned and slithered away into the rocks.

Bobcat waited until he couldn't see her anymore before he dared blow out a breath. "I thought we were in real trouble there for a minute."

He heard Fisher chuckle. "What makes you think we're not?" She flicked the stove off. "Guess we'll have to eat on the march." She rummaged around in her pack till she pulled out a little jar of soap. "A bath sounds like a good idea, though. Anyone else?"

Sand itched all through Bobcat's fur. "Yeah, I guess."

Skink scuttled around. "In a pool frequented by the Lady Dolphin, it will be quite an experience."

Fisher waded in, and Bobcat followed. The water did feel good, warm and flowing like the River at Crawford's Bend south of Ottersgate, a wide wooded place Bobcat liked to visit on the hotter days of summer. He splashed himself, bent around to lick his fur down, stubble already bristling in the deeper cuts along his sides. He took his time again, managed to get most of the sand out of his coat, and when he waded out of the pond Fisher and Skink had already packed everything up.

He took the towel Fisher held out to him, ran it once or twice over his face, but the scent of the air made him think it was probably going to get hot today; he decided to leave his fur wet, let the evaporation cool him down. "So," he said, stuffing the towel into his pack. "Where do we go from here? That little canyon the stream comes out of seems to be the only way off this beach."

"Yeah." Fisher squatted beside the stream, her canteen bubbling beneath the surface; she brought it up, recorked it, strapped it onto her backpack, and slipped the thing on. "We work our way back inland, I guess, see where we come out."

Skink scurried up onto her back. "Our way is tended by Those Above. I have no doubt we shall find our way."

Bobcat shrugged, filled his own canteen, and pulled on his pack. "Well, you want to go first again?"

"Sure." Fisher shook a paw, then started up the beach along the streambed, Bobcat falling in behind. "From what we saw of that canyon," she went on, "I think it might be easier if we wade upstream. The current's not too fast, and the brush up in there looked mighty thick."

Bobcat had to agree, especially after they followed the stream around the curving rock face and came into the mouth of the ravine, all the brush making him think of the Brackens, the weathered crack running back into the cliff not much wider than the stream but tangled with brambly vines and things that looked to Bobcat like tumbleweeds. Fisher waded out into the stream, and Bobcat followed, the water barely reaching his ankles. He lowered his head against the brush closing in around him, and they started up the canyon.

It was still shadowy down here, sunlight occasionally striking the layered cliffs rising on both sides of the stream winding into the rocks. They were climbing, Bobcat was sure, just not very quickly, and as the day wore on, the creek bending and twisting, midge flies buzzing at his nose and ears, the air thickening, heating, getting stickier and stickier, not a breath of wind stirring, Bobcat started hoping they wouldn't have to spend a night down here.

But around midmorning the canyon began widening, the brush not crowding in on them anymore. The cliffs stopped towering overhead, started pulling away, sloping off into hills, the sun finally showing itself over their tops off to the left. Other canyons branched off theirs, other creeks carving their own ways to the sea, but they stuck with the main flow, getting larger and quicker the farther inland they went, until they finally had to crawl out and walk beside it.

The heat got worse, too, the sun rising higher, and by the time it stood burning at the top of the sky the hills were flattening out, the stream they followed fast and deep. Around one last low hill it led them, and there stretched the grasslands of the Savannah, green and yellow and swaying off toward the horizon as far as Bobcat could see.

Fisher had stopped, and Bobcat settled down beside her. "Wow," he said.

"Eloquent," Fisher replied. "How 'bout lunch?"

His pack felt alarmingly light when Bobcat shrugged it off. "Yeesh. I'm starting to think we should have reprovisioned back at Kazirazif when the Ramon offered."

Fisher had rummaged one of her little sacks out and was pulling nuts from it. "I'm sure he was just being polite. I mean remember the track record here; we may never need another meal, y'know?"

Skink raised a claw, swallowed the sip of water he'd just taken. "Not necessarily, Fisher. After all, both my grandmother and your great-great-grandfather did return."

"True." Fisher's eyes slid over to Bobcat.

"Hey!" Bobcat crooked a claw at her. "Don't you look at me like that! Don't forget: the Lady Raven said that the Lady Dolphin thought I was the best bobcat they've had in a long time!"

Fisher's brow wrinkled. "She said what?"

"Yeah, last night. After the Lady Dolphin left. She said that the Lady Dolphin had gotten so mad at me 'cause she thought I had a good chance of pulling this off."

Fisher blinked. "Last I heard, the Lady Dolphin had just called you an idiot."

"What?" Bobcat sat forward. "But . . . the Lady Raven! She said it! You . . . you *must've* heard! I mean . . ."

Skink was cocking his head from side to side. "I myself was struck with slumber after the Lady Dolphin dematerialized, awakening again only this morning."

"Me, too." Fisher had set her sack down. "Did the Lady Raven say anything else?"

Bobcat looked from one to the other. "Well, uhh, no, I mean, she, uhh, she said that she would send Garson a dream to let her know I was thinking about her, but, uhh . . ."

Fisher was rubbing her whiskers. "Did she say she agreed with the Lady Dolphin's assessment?"

"What, uhh, what do you—"

"Did she say that *she* thought you were the best?"

Bobcat flicked at a pebble. "Not, uhh, not really, no."

"Thought not." Fisher picked out another nut, cracked it between her paws. "The Lady Dolphin's great to spend time with. I mean it just recharges your batteries being in the same place with her. But, well, she's a little, uhh . . ." She looked over at Skink. "Help me out here."

Skink shifted on his rock. "I believe the Lady Dolphin's youth is what Fisher is trying to convey here. The second youngest of the Curial powers, she is nonetheless in many ways the most idealistic, the most emotional. Her blessing is a tremendous honor, Bobcat, but she is vast and ever-changing. Cottonmouth of Selmir Kiva put it best when he wrote: 'In all ways and in every thing, she is Water.' "

Bobcat blinked at him. "What does that mean?"

Fisher tossed her bag of nuts to him. "It means she can be ice one minute and steam the next. Pinning her down is like trying to put a nail in a river. Now eat something, will you? We've gotta be getting along here."

Bobcat caught the bag. "OK, I get it. You're saying the Lady Dolphin's a little flaky."

Fisher rolled her eyes. "Just forget it. I mean, if you have to, look at it this way: The Lady Dolphin paid you a compliment. That's all. She likes you, but that doesn't change anything, and we've still got work to do." She jerked a thumb over her shoulder. "Now, seems to me we should head due east. The Coati Road runs straight through the Savannah to the cat collectives and the towns of the hoofed folk farther south, so if we head east, we'll eventually hit the road again. I can use that as a fixed point, maybe try some scrying to find out where exactly we're supposed to go to meet the Blood Jaguar. What do you guys think?"

Skink was nodding. "I understand your reasoning, Fisher, but I feel we should continue south from here. That is, after all, the only direction the Ramon could give us, and it seems likely to me that the Ladies diverted us to this part of the Savannah with some purpose in mind. Although, of course, it may be that since we are, so to speak, following the story line, the direction of our travels will make no difference. Whatever is supposed to happen to us *will* happen regardless of which way we choose to go." He spread his claws. "I can only conjecture on this point, but the nature of our journey being that of a Cyclical Myth, I—"

Bobcat held up a paw. "Yeah, fine, but can't we stick to the stream here?" He pointed to the track it made winding out into the grass. "It looks like it's coming out of the southeast, so, hey, we can go with both your ideas. And who knows? The water might keep things a little cooler." He shrugged. "I mean if Skink's right and we're gonna run into the Blood Jaguar no matter where we go, then, well, we might as well be a little more comfortable while we're walking, you think?"

The other two blinked at him, then at each other, and Fisher shrugged. "Sounds good. You ready to go?"

Bobcat gave her back the bag and shouldered his pack. Fisher did the same, Skink taking his place between her shoulders, and they set off along the stream bank into the grass.

For a time, everything went along well enough, Fisher and Bobcat traveling side by side. But with each step they took out onto the plain, the grass grew taller and taller, bunching thicker and thicker, until Bobcat found himself in front, shouldering through the grass, over his head and standing in clumps; before long, sweat dripped from his whiskers at the effort of trying to push through what sometimes seemed to be a solid wall ahead of him. Every once in a while he would stumble into a little clearing and be able to take a breather, but mostly it was just probing and digging, forcing a path in the right general direction if he couldn't find one.

"Wait a minute; wait a minute," he panted out after less than half an hour, collapsed against the side of one of the clearings, his paws aching. "This isn't . . . Can't we . . . Can't we take the stream again?"

"Doubt it." Fisher cocked her head. "Take a listen."

Bobcat held his head up. He could hear it rushing past through the pampas grass somewhere off to his left, and it sounded like a real river now. He nodded.

Fisher was looking up. "I don't know what else we can do but push on."

"Well," came Skink's voice from her back, and he scuttled down to the moist dirt. "As I am smaller than either of you, I might have less trouble moving through these canebrakes. I propose that I scout ahead until I find a clearing, at which point I will call back to you and give you directions. I doubt that we will make any better time, but it is certain to save wear and tear on poor Bobcat."

"I like this plan." Bobcat gave him a grin.

Fisher nodded. "All right, but you be careful, Skink. We won't really be able to come running if you need help."

"I understand." He scuttled around. "I shall keep us close to the river." The grass rustled, and he was gone.

A few minutes passed, Bobcat getting his breath back and waiting with pricked ears for Skink's voice. The sun beat down, the grass still and silent, not a breeze moving the air, until Bobcat heard the lizard calling: "Fisher! Bobcat! Push through from the end of your clearing and move toward the river! The way is fairly passable for about five yards; then you will have to cut right to the side of a large clump of pampas grass! I am in a clearing just past there!"

Fisher grinned. "Gotcha, Skink! Be there in a minute!"

Bobcat staggered to his paws, clawed at the grass at the end of the clearing till he could push through, and found the grass much thinner on the other side. He homed in on the sound of the river and headed toward it, Fisher padding along behind, till another stand of the stuff blocked the way. He squeezed around to the right of it, found a gap, and stumbled into a clearing where Skink was waiting.

Grass rustling, Fisher popped through behind Bobcat, and he saw Skink scamper to the other end of the clearing. "Off again!" he called, and disappeared into the pampas.

This went on for the rest of the afternoon, some passages short and easy, some long and complex, Skink guiding Bobcat and Fisher halfway sometimes, then leaving them to wait among seemingly solid walls of cane while he tracked another route. Hour followed hour till the sun settled behind the tops of the grasses and a strange premature twilight fell, the sky above still bright and blue when Bobcat could glimpse it, but the grasses filled with shadows, nothing but the rush of the river to give him any sense of direction at all.

Bobcat just felt tired all over, the uneven intervals of sitting and moving and sitting and moving and then sitting some more making him drowsy, letting him doze off, not paying that much attention. So it wasn't until after one long, nasty push through close-pressing pampas, as he shouldered his way into the clearing Skink had been guiding them to, that he first realized he wasn't hearing the river anymore.

He blinked, took a few steps toward the center of the clearing, stretched his ears out. Skink had already moved to the far side, and all Bobcat could hear was the rustling of Fisher shoving her way into the clearing after him. "Hey!" he called out. "What happened to the river?"

He saw Skink cock his head, saw his eyes go wide. "I . . . I don't understand. I am certain I heard it mere moments ago."

"Me, too," Fisher said, and Bobcat watched her prick her ears by the wall of pampas they had just come through.

"Oh, great." Bobcat looked up, tried to get his bearings, but he couldn't tell where the sun was. A sharp, uniform blue spread above him, the grass all in shade, nothing to tell him where the light might be coming from.

A gust of wind burst into Bobcat's ears then, sudden and cool, the first wind he'd felt all day. It staggered him, it was so unexpected, made him turn in its direction, and there in the clearing before him sat three huge fiery cats.

The shudder that wracked through him almost made him bolt for the grass, but in the next second he saw that none of the three was the Blood Jaguar. The largest, lying just in front of him, glowed with a light more golden than the raging reds he remembered in the Blood Jaguar's fur, while the one to his right reclining before Fisher burned bright orange, black stripes somehow running through its fire. The third, to Bobcat's left on Skink's side of the clearing, shone white-hot and brilliant, black circles floating over it. Or, rather, Bobcat realized, over *her*. For he saw they were female, all three unmistakably, now that he was actually looking at them.

Huge, glowing female cats, and it came to him all at once: the Lady Lioness lay in front of him, the Lady Tigress to his right, the Lady Leopardess to his left.

Skink, he noticed, had his head between his claws and was muttering more of his little chants, while Fisher had taken a step back, was staring wide-eyed, her ears down and her legs bent like she was about to leap. The three Ladies, though, didn't seem to be paying any attention, their paws stretched out, their eyes closed, just lolling in the shade of the tall grass. Bobcat knew there was nowhere he could run to, so he just stood there, waiting.

Time went by—whether minutes or seconds Bobcat couldn't tell. Then the Lady Lioness opened her eyes, let loose a yawn that showed every one of her gleaming teeth, and said, the ground rumbling under Bobcat's paws, "Tell me, sisters; why do you suppose earthly folk would wander onto our Savannah? I can't imagine they thought anything good would come of it."

The white fire to Bobcat's left flared, and the Lady Leopardess opened her eyes. "Seems unlikely," she said, her words making the air colder around Bobcat somehow. "Maybe they've taken leave of their senses."

"No," came a grumble from his right, a sound so close to the Blood Jaguar's growl that Bobcat felt his knees buckle; the Lady Tigress had opened her eyes. "I can't think that even someone gone crazy or stupid would come out here on their own. I wonder if perhaps they are under the protection of any of our various brothers and sisters. At least, for their sakes, I certainly hope so." Bobcat felt the raw heat of her eyes pass him, her gaze moving from Fisher to him and on to Skink. "Consequences would ensue otherwise."

"Indeed." The Lady Lioness stretched one massive paw out and turned to the Lady Leopardess. "Sister, is yours under someone's protection?"

The Lady Leopardess rose, the blinding white of sunlight on snow the only thing Bobcat could think of, and stepped toward Skink, still rustling his chants. She sniffed, cocked her head, and said, "Yes, sister. This one has been a shadow cast by the voice of our brother Eft."

"Ah, brother Eft." The Lady Lioness smiled, like the sun breaking though the clouds after a shower. "It's been too long since we've seen even his shadow here." She turned to the Lady Tigress then. "And yours, sister. Is she under someone's protection?"

The Lady Tigress rose, a lightning strike, a scattered spark, every blazing fire ever struck moving on her paws. Fisher bowed, but the Lady Tigress reached out, touched a huge paw to Fisher's chin, and murmured, "Let me see your eyes, child." Fisher's head came up, the two stood with eyes locked for a moment, and the Lady Tigress smiled. "Yes, sister. This one is a shaman in the service of brother Kit Fox."

"Ah, brother Kit Fox." The Lady Lioness's smile rose slowly, dawn in late spring. "He and his are always as welcome as a summer afternoon."

The other two Ladies had turned now, their eyes hot and cold on Bobcat's flanks. "And yours, sister?" the Lady Leopardess asked.

"Yes," the Lady Tigress added. "Is yours under anyone's protection?"

The Lady Lioness rose in one smooth motion, clear and unhurried as the sun at high noon, and padded toward Bobcat. She loomed before him, and Bobcat's throat closed up; he wanted nothing more than to break her gaze, but the golden fire of her eyes held him fast, and he knew she was gazing right down to his insides. "I . . . ," he started to stammer. "I . . . don't think . . . I'm, uhh . . . under anyone's, uhh . . ."

But her eyes went wide, their unearthly glow vanishing, a pair of regular lion eyes staring down at him. "No," she whispered, and her voice didn't shake the ground, didn't send his fur shivering and his whiskers jittering; in fact, it reminded him of someone. "It . . . It can't be," she said a little louder, and her face was a lioness's face, tawny and beautiful and old and . . . familiar? "Ghareen?" she asked.

A scent tickled Bobcat's nose, a scent he hadn't smelled in decades, and all at once he knew her. "Sh . . . Shemka Harr?"

Then paws were around him, hugging him close, her voice laughing in his ears: "I never thought I'd . . . I mean how did you . . . Where did you . . . It can't . . . Oh, Ghareen, Ghareen. . . ." Just as suddenly, though, her voice stopped, the paws going rigid across his back. Bobcat felt the ground under him again, and when the lioness stepped back he could see that everyone else in the clearing was staring at them.

The Lady Leopardess and the Lady Tigress now looked more like actual folk, still larger than anyone Bobcat had ever seen, but they weren't glowing the way they had been. The silence lingered for a while then, the Lady Tigress finally clearing her throat. "Perhaps," she said, still rumbling deep and scary in Bobcat's ears, "you can explain, sister, what all this ad-libbing is about?"

"Yeah," said the Lady Leopardess, her fur still bright white but her voice now higher. "I mean you can't just break the rules like this, can you? The bobcat's supposed to defy us, push on unprotected, you know, give that big speech they always give. What're you doing? How can you—"

The Lady Lioness's ears went back, her lip curling, and the Lady Leopardess pulled her mouth closed, her eyes going wide. The Lady Lioness put a paw up to her mouth, looked down, then back up at the Lady Leopardess. "I . . . I'm sorry, Pardess; it's just . . ." She stopped again, and the fear in the look she gave Bobcat made him even more confused. "Someone's made a mistake somewhere."

"What?" The Lady Tigress padded over, looked down at Bobcat with a wrinkled brow for a moment, then sat back, her brow clearing suddenly. "Oh, Nessie, no. You don't mean . . ." She looked from the Lady Lioness to Bobcat and back again. "This is *that* bobcat?"

The Lady Lioness nodded slowly, her eyes on the ground.

"Oh, Nessie. . . ." The Lady Tigress stroked a paw over the Lady Lioness's back, and the silence fell again. "Well, we're going to have to do something," she said at last. "Whatever you want, you just tell me."

"But I don't know." The Lady Lioness looked over, and Bobcat could only gape at the tears he saw in her eyes. "I . . . oh, Gressa, I . . . I really don't know. . . ."

The Lady Tigress blew out a breath. "All right. As much as I hate to say it, I think you'd better take these three to Himself." She coughed a little laugh. "I can't believe I'm actually recommending someone go see him. . . ."

The Lady Lioness sniffed, shook her head, and looked up. "I suppose that's the only thing we can do." Her eyes wavered toward Bobcat again. "But . . . But do you think he'll help?"

"I doubt it." Something very close to a snarl touched the Lady Tigress's face. "Not if it means breaking his precious rules and regulations."

"Really?" The Lady Lioness smiled. "Not even for you?"

The Lady Tigress held up her paws. "Especially not for me." She shook her head. "You take them over there; Tiger's much more charming when I'm not around."

"Gressa . . ." The Lady Lioness closed her eyes. "You know that's not true."

"Go on." The Lady Tigress rose and strode over to where the Lady Leopardess sat, her mouth still closed. "Come on, Pardess; let's head off somewhere a bit cooler."

The Lady Leopardess licked her lips. "I'd still like someone to tell me what's going on here."

"Oh, Pardess. . . ." The Lady Lioness reached out a paw. "I'm so sorry. I'll tell you the whole story as soon as this is over; I promise you."

The Lady Leopardess stayed where she was for a moment,

then gave a sideways smile, padded over, and rubbed a cheek against the Lady Lioness's paw. "But I want to hear it *all,*" she said, crooking a claw. "Every detail."

"I promise, kit."

"Well, OK." The Lady Leopardess turned and moved back to the Lady Tigress's side. "How about Tyurnan Peak, Gressa?" And the two Ladies vanished into the grass.

Bobcat watched them go, his mind not quite working, not then and not when he finally turned back to the Lady Lioness, still sitting there and still looking just like Shemka Harr. The questions whizzing through his head tangled with each other, and all he could get out was the single word, "How?"

She gave a sigh, swallowed, and nodded. "You'll want the truth, then," she said. "From the beginning." She raised her head. "And please, Fisher, Skink, come closer."

Bobcat didn't notice if they did or not, his eyes only on the Lady. She swallowed again. "You see, many thousands and thousands of generations ago, we all lived on another world, a world much like this one in many ways." A smile pulled at her whiskers. "Lion and I grew up there, married, saw our children and their children grow up, and then it all went . . ." The corners of her smile twitched. "Well, anyhow, after that, they decided to build this world, and when they asked us to be the Lord and Lady Lion we were both overjoyed, and we worked very hard to see the new world to its completion.

"Then, well, then came the end of the Beforetime, as Eft named it, and we were forced to divide things up among the twelve of us. I picked the duties of spring, always my favorite time of the year, the flowers so lovely, I remember thinking." She shook her head. "I had no idea, of course.

"For, you see, I had forgotten that spring, at its very core, is the dragging of the world back from the near-death of winter. And Pardess did such wonderful winters that every year my duties seemed to get harder and harder, century after century of straining to pump life back into the planet, pouring my heart and soul into reviving all creation, only to get it up and running and then turn it over to Kit Fox, who had taken on the duties of summer. And knowing that each and every year of every decade of every century all my efforts would come to nothing: Leopard's autumn would cripple the world, leaving it open to the death blow of Pardess's winter.

"And I would have to start all over again." She stopped, took several breaths. "As millennium followed millennium, I began dreading it more and more, certain I would never be able to do the thing again but somehow always pulling myself together in time to perform my duties.

"Until one year." She turned away, her eyes focused off over the pampas grass. "I just chucked it all, decided to let the whole thing go hang. I left in the dead of night, slipped away so not even Raven saw me go, found myself a cave in some faraway mountains, and let my Curial Privilege ebb out into Pardess's winter.

"I had planned it all so carefully: my Privilege would go to swell Pardess's winter so there would be no real way the others could trace me, and out I let it, fed it into the winter. In less time than it takes to tell, I was as earthly as any lioness, a thousand times as old, and ready to die. I had abandoned my post, and I had nothing left to live for."

She sighed. "I had planned so well." A smile touched her whiskers. "But I never counted on some poor bedraggled bob-kitten stumbling in on me." She turned to Bobcat. "And I couldn't just let you freeze, could I?

"So I put my plans on hold and set about getting you back on your paws. I was shocked at how ignorant you were, and I found myself telling you the old teaching stories, stories I had told my own children and grandchildren, all long since dead. And as I told you these stories, I began to realize that that was why I was here in this cave: not because I couldn't manage the springtime, but because I couldn't manage my memories, the absolutely crushing fact that all my children, all my grandchildren, nearly everyone I had ever known, my entire world, Ghareen, all were dead, dead and gone so long I was just about the only one who even remembered them.

"And I came to realize, there in that cave, telling you the old stories, that there were still cubs and kittens in this world, this world I had helped create, and that I had the ability, the power, the duty to make this world as wonderful a place as the world I remembered. So, once you were well, I regathered my Privilege and went off to start the springtime." She stopped again. "But I never forgot, Ghareen, that in a very real sense, you saved my life that winter."

Silence came down over the odd near-twilight, and Bobcat could only stare at her for a long moment. "But," he finally got out, "but wait. You always told me the Curials were a bunch of made-up characters, that I shouldn't believe in them, that . . . that they were all just stories!"

"Yes, well." She looked away. "I was a little bitter." She turned back. "But everything I told you about figuring your own way out of a problem rather than waiting for anyone else to do it for you, that I'll still vouch for."

An old something started bubbling in Bobcat's gut, older than the catnip urge that had been clenched there for days. "Yeah, all very nice," he spat out, the hardness in his voice surprising him. He shook his head, started again. "But why did you just leave? I was so convinced that I'd done something wrong, that I'd made you go, that I couldn't . . . I could barely . . . I mean why couldn't you tell me?"

She looked down at him then, her face exactly as he remembered it. "Oh, yes. I can just hear it: 'Sorry, Ghareen, must run. Have to get the trees sprouting, you know.' " She squatted down, looked him straight in the eye. "I had to make a clean break, Ghareen, for both our sakes. I would make a horrible mystical guardian, and having me at your shoulder would have ruined your life, believe me. I wanted so much to look in on you, see how you were doing, but I knew it would reopen all my old feelings for you, and I'd start meddling. I didn't want that. And you wouldn't have wanted it, either."

A troubled look tugged at her whiskers, and she straightened up. "Well, I guess we'd better get along to see Tiger, find out, uhh, what's what." She turned, padded to the wall of grass, and it parted before her. "This way, please," she said. "All three of you."

Bobcat rose, saw a dark movement at the corner of his eye, heard Fisher fall in behind him, and followed the Lady Lioness into the pampas.

Chapter Ten

The Blood Jaguar

The grass kept parting before the Lady Lioness, a little bubble of clear air that made Bobcat's whiskers hum. Then the pampas pulled away to reveal another large clearing, and Bobcat caught his breath at the sight of the huge tiger lying there with paws crossed. "Ah, sister," he rumbled, his voice smoother than purest catnip. "I've been waiting for you and your . . . companions." He arched an eyebrow. "I certainly hope you have no other possible conflicts of interest lurking about in your past."

The Lady Lioness sat down, waved a paw. "Oh, now, Tiger. You know I only wanted to make your job more interesting."

The Lord Tiger's ears flicked ever so slightly, and his eyes moved to regard Bobcat. "Well, sir, I must say, you have certainly managed to make a mess out of what is really a very simple situation."

"Tiger . . ." The Lady Lioness rolled her eyes.

"Forgive me, sister, but it's true." He tapped a paw on the ground. "All the bobcat has to do is sit still and receive sister Raven's dreams, dreams that all come into sudden focus when the Blood Jaguar attacks him. He, his fisher, and his skink pursue those dreams across the continent, overcoming all obstacles to arrive here. You and your sisters separate him from his companions, and he proceeds alone to meet his fate. All very straightforward, I've always thought."

His voice deepened, something Bobcat wouldn't have thought possible. "Now, however, sister, you seem to be invoking your protection based on this winter you spent together some years ago. Do I understand the case correctly?"

The Lady Lioness didn't say anything.

"By your silence," the Lord Tiger said after a moment, "I take it that I do. Very well, my Lady. If you have no objections, court will now come to order." He flicked a dagger of a claw, leaving a gash in the earth before him. "Those who have points to raise in the case of the Law versus the Lady Lioness will kindly address themselves now to the bench."

Again the Lady Lioness said nothing.

The Lord Tiger narrowed his eyes. "If no statements are made from the floor, my Lady, the court will have no choice but to render judgment based on the few facts so far at paw."

The Lady Lioness drew herself up, gazed down at the Lord Tiger. "The court knows all the facts it needs to," she said, her voice almost brittle in Bobcat's ears. "You know me, my Lord, and you know of my relationship with this bobcat. I have refrained from intervening on his behalf in the past, but now I cannot sit idly by while he is offered up in this pointless ritual!"

The Lord Tiger flexed his claws, his eyes pure ice. "You are out of order, madam."

"This world is out of order, sir!" She didn't break his gaze. "How I have been able to stand by and watch this happen for so long I will never know! But no longer, sir!"

The air crackled between them. Bobcat looked up at her, then over at Fisher and Skink before turning to the Lord Tiger and raising a paw. "Uhh, excuse me, sir?"

Both the Lady Lioness and the Lord Tiger started back, looked down at him. "Ghareen!" the Lady Lioness whispered, but the Lord Tiger had already turned.

"You wish to address the court, sir?" he asked.

"The court? Uhh, yeah, yeah, I guess I do, sir."

The Lord Tiger waved a paw. "Please proceed."

Bobcat swallowed. "Well, sir, it's just that I don't think I understand all this about the Lady's protection. I mean, sure, twenty years ago she let me spend the winter in a cave with her, but I didn't even know she was a Curial then. And, yes, Shemka Harr, I mean the Lady Lioness, yes, she taught me a lot, and I wouldn't have made it this far if it hadn't been for her, but, sir, for better or worse, I've really been on my own since then. She turned me loose, left me behind. I mean she said so herself, not just today before we came in here, but in everything she ever told me.

"I mean Fisher here hobnobs with the Lord Kit Fox all the time, and Skink had the Lord Eft right inside him or whatever. But me and the Lady Lioness, that all happened years ago, back when we were both different folks, and I don't want her to get in trouble because she thinks she owes me something." He looked up at her. "Maybe I saved your life back then, Shemka Harr, I mean my Lady, but I know for a fact that you saved mine. We're even, I'd say, and thanks for trying to get me out of this, but, well . . ." He couldn't think of anything else to say, so he stopped.

The Lord Tiger had been tapping the ground the whole time; Bobcat wondered if he'd even been listening. Silence followed until the Lord Tiger flicked a final claw at the ground. "Yes," he said. "You raise a cogent point."

That startled Bobcat. "I . . . I do?"

"Indeed. For the Lady Lioness was someone different when she took you in. She had allowed her Privilege to dissipate and was therefore technically not a Curial. The protection she would claim is Curial protection, and as she was not a Curial during the time in question the matter becomes moot. This court is adjourned." He tapped a quick rhythm on the ground. "You, Bobcat, are therefore here without protection and must go to meet your fate. Are you prepared?"

A chill rustled through Bobcat's fur. "Uhh, I guess so. I, uhh, don't suppose you could give me any idea what that fate might be?"

The Lord Tiger just waved a huge paw toward one side of the clearing. Bobcat looked in that direction, saw nothing but more grass, then turned to the others. Skink was peering over Fisher's shoulder, and Fisher was standing, her mouth opening. But the Lady Lioness was suddenly beside her, whispered something in her ear; Fisher's eyes darted back and forth, and Bobcat thought he saw water in them, but she sat, looked away, and the Lord Tiger's voice was rumbling: "I have already bent the rules as far as I am willing. Now go."

Bobcat looked at them all again, tried to think of something to say, but he couldn't. So he just turned and walked off into the grass.

It closed behind him, and he found himself on a different sort of pampas terrain, the grass in much sparser clumps, bare earth visible in large patches. Strange silvery flowers blossomed from the grass into the solid blue afternoon, the sun still nowhere to be seen in the near-twilight all around.

Bobcat blew out a breath. At least it would be easier getting around.

Not that he had any idea where he was supposed to go. If Skink was right, though, it didn't much matter which way he went; the Blood Jaguar would find him when she wanted to. So he shook himself, picked a direction, and started walking.

The silence settled over him, made him breathe through his mouth and tread carefully over the dry, spongy soil so his pack wouldn't rustle. Nothing moved anywhere, and he found himself choosing paths that had the least amount of reeds blocking the way so he wouldn't disturb the quiet when he pushed through them.

He walked on for he didn't know how long, the sky never getting any darker, and found nothing but more grass and more dirt. Which just didn't seem right. After all, wasn't he here to confront the Blood Jaguar or whatever? Weren't they at least supposed to meet? Wasn't that what everybody kept telling him?

But more walking only got him more pampas. He sat down after another period of timelessness, tried to think what he should be doing, the silence so thick his own thinking seemed too loud. He blinked then, and it struck him how quiet the fiery eyes in his head had become. They barely flickered now, and he realized he hadn't really been aware of them all day while tromping through the canebrakes.

That seemed a little odd, too. Hadn't she left her eyes in his head to keep him moving toward her, to prove that she was really out here waiting? Shouldn't they be blazing right now, guiding him on to her lair or something?

So where were they? Bobcat concentrated on the Blood Jaguar's eyes, felt for them like he would for a sore tooth, but they barely smoldered at the very back of his mind, nothing he tried making them flare up. He sat there trying for a while longer, but he just couldn't figure it out. So he got up and began walking again.

More time went by—at least, it felt like time went by. Nothing kept changing around him, and he was just starting to think that nothing ever would change when he came around a canebrake and heard a trickle of water. A stream cut through the grass ahead, sparkling in the shadow of the pampas. He padded forward, squatted down to sniff at it. It was too small to be the one they'd been following all day, but maybe it was a tributary. The canteen hanging from his pack was still pretty much full, but, well, as long as he was here . . .

He lapped up a mouthful, wondering what to do next, when a crackle behind him made his ears cant back, those eyes blazing up like prairie fire in his brain. His legs twitched, he lost his balance, and before he could catch himself he had pitched face-first into the water. It was only about ankle-deep, but it still took a moment of sputtering and flailing for Bobcat to get to his paws, spin around, and see the thing he already knew was there behind him.

Lying on her stomach, paws resting in front of her, her fur shimmering with just a trace of the raging fire he had seen before, the Blood Jaguar stretched and yawned, and the terrible red blackness of her eyes made the pair floating in Bobcat's head snuff to dead cinders. The stream water swirled around his paws, dripped from his fur, but all he could do was stand and stare at her, those eyes focusing on him.

Bobcat couldn't look away, couldn't speak, didn't have a single clue as to what he was supposed to do now. The Blood Jaguar blinked slowly, and after a moment of silence she cocked her head, a strangely sweet voice, rich as honeyed wine, rumbling out: "You enjoy sitting in creeks?"

"Uhh . . ." And that was all Bobcat could say, his throat clenching tight. His every hair felt like it was sticking straight out, trying to get away from him, biting like thousands of fleas all over his body.

"And another thing," she went on, tapping a black claw in the dirt. "I don't appreciate you making me wait like this. I've got a lot of work ahead of me the next few weeks, and all this nonsense just takes up too much time." She yawned again. "But you're here now, so let's get started, shall we?"

Again, all Bobcat could do was stand and stare. He didn't know what she was waiting for, why she didn't just leap on him and tear him to shreds. He couldn't move, couldn't look away from her, couldn't even remember how to blink.

The Blood Jaguar raised her smoky eyebrows. "What? No big speech? No attempts to appeal to my better nature, to get me to see the error of my ways?"

Bobcat couldn't imagine what she was talking about. She watched him for another moment, then shrugged her massive shoulders. "Well, have it your way." And she rose to her paws, flowing like wildfire up a hillside, took a step toward him. "Let's just get this over with, then."

And that did it, her movement unfreezing his paws: Bobcat scrambled backward out of the stream, bashed right into the canebrake, hard as stone and just as impenetrable, pressed himself against it, unable to think of anything but getting away from her.

Another step, and she rolled her eyes. "Oh, come on." She stopped, sat back down, and lifted her chin. "Here. I'll give you a free shot." She patted her neck with one huge paw. "If you're quick, you might just get my jugular."

At last, his confusion overcame his terror. "What?" he blurted out.

"Sure." She turned her head and leaned forward, the ash black rings in her fiery coat seeming to pulse in Bobcat's eyes. "I won't lay a claw on you; let you get the first hit in. OK? Honest."

"What . . . What . . ." The thought of getting within five yards of her made his stomach cramp up, and she wanted him to hit her? "What are you talking about?"

This time she blinked, her whiskers shifting back. "I'm talking about you. You *are* here to fight, aren't you? To defeat me and my plans to destroy the world?"

"Fight?" Bobcat couldn't stop a laugh from bursting out. "You've gotta be crazy!" he said before he remembered who she was, and he winced back against the canebrake, expecting those black claws to come slashing down at him.

They didn't, though. The Blood Jaguar just sat there and stared, the fire in her eyes flickering slightly. "You are the right bobcat, aren't you?" she asked after a moment. "The one who's supposed to be here? You've heard all about my Plague Year and everything?"

"Yeah, that's, uhh, that's me." Bobcat swallowed. "But, I mean, nobody ever said anything about having to fight!"

"What?" The Blood Jaguar blinked. "Well, then, why are you here?"

"I don't know!" he announced and, with a rush he couldn't stop, everything he'd been feeling all week, the pent-up anger and resentment he'd been reserving in his mind for the Blood Jaguar, welled up through his fear like sudden heartburn. "I have no idea! I don't know what's going on, didn't know a thing about all this until you came along, kicked me into the Brackens, put your eyes in my head to push me along every step of the way! How should I know what I'm doing here? This is all your fault! I've got nothing to do with it!"

The Blood Jaguar sat with her brow wrinkled. "Excuse me?" she asked after another moment.

But the cork was out of the bottle. Bobcat let his ears fold down, pushed himself up onto his paws, and marched across the creek, his eyes never leaving hers. "I was just minding my own business, going along with my life! Sure, maybe it wasn't anything special, but, hey, I was nothing special, just another bobcat, nobody at all!

"And then *you* came along, turned everything I ever knew into a lie, booted me into a brier patch, and left your eyes inside me so I couldn't just roll over and forget about you! You forced me to come here, forced me every goddamned step of the way, almost got me killed at least twice, twisted me up inside, and all because I'm apparently supposed to do something that I can't even begin to figure out!" He stopped in front of her, her half-closed fiery eyes making him shiver all over. "So why am I here? I'm here because I want to know before you kill me why you ruined my life!" He swallowed again, sat still, and waited for her claws.

But the Blood Jaguar just sat, looking down at him. "You really don't know what's going on, do you?" she asked after a moment.

Bobcat made his head shake. He was doomed, but maybe she would give him some answers before she diced him. He stared up at her . . . and saw a grin curl at her whiskers. The fires in her coat jittered, and before Bobcat's startled eyes the Blood Jaguar threw back her head and laughed—real, humorous laughter, not the fiendish sort he would have expected, deep and ringing and making the grass waver all around. She clutched her sides, stomped a paw, actually rolled over onto her back, her legs kicking at the air, tears falling from her eyes and sizzling when they hit the ground.

This went on for at least a minute, and after she finally got ahold of herself, wiping a paw over her fiery eyes and turning to face Bobcat again, it took another moment for her to get a word out. "Oh, gods," she said, still chuckling. "I haven't had a laugh this good in millennia."

Bobcat waited while she straightened up, blew out a breath, and focused on him. "Look, kitten, it's nothing personal. It's just, well, it's just the way things are. See, to do a Plague Year, the rules say I have to go out and get a certain skink's luckstone." She waved a paw. "Don't ask me why. The whole thing gets a little complicated, and I don't see these stones making skinks any luckier than anyone else.

"Anyway, every time I go out to get the stone, no matter how I do it, when I grab the thing and turn around there you are." She shrugged. "I mean not *you*, but some bobcat or other; this time it just happened to be you."

Bobcat couldn't move, wouldn't believe what he was hearing. The Blood Jaguar shrugged again. "This bobcat's been set up, y'see, his head pumped full of all this weird stuff, and with it, he finds out about my Plague Year. He decides he has to save the world, comes out here, challenges me, and I have to pound him into the ground before I can get on with things." She spread her paws. "I know it sounds kind of stupid, but, well, I don't make the rules."

"This is crazy," Bobcat heard himself muttering. "You don't make the rules? I thought . . . I mean of course you make the rules!"

Her head drew back. "Who told you that?"

"Well, everybody!" Bobcat found he had leaped up. "The Ramon and Fisher and Skink and all the stories and everybody! You're Death! That's what you're in charge of!"

Her mouth went sideways under her whiskers, and she raised a paw. "Look around," she said, moving the paw from one side of the clearing to the other. "Does it look like I'm in charge of anything here?"

Bobcat looked, saw only the pampas grass, not even a breeze ruffling it. "Well, I mean, but what about the Shroud Islands? The Kingdom of the Dead?"

"Oh, gods." She closed her eyes, rubbed her forehead. "That story's still floating around? You can't tell me you really believe all that crap?"

"Uhh, well . . ." Bobcat swallowed. "I didn't even believe in you till about a week ago."

She laughed again, but it was a tired, breathy sound, not anything like her earlier laughter. "Well, let me set you straight, kitten. There are no Shroud Islands, no Kingdom of the Dead, no nothing like that. I mean what would I do with it if I had it?"

Bobcat shook his head, tried to clear his thoughts. "I, well, I always heard that we all go there when we die. You come, and . . . and you take us there, and . . ."

Her eyes were dark, more smoke than fire. "You want to know?" she said, her voice a rumbling whisper. "I'll tell you what happens, what it is I do, and then you can tell me where your Shroud Islands fit in.

"Because I bounce, kitten. That's all I do. Bounce from place to place all over this whole goddamned world. And for an instant, I'm standing above someone old or sick or broken. Their eyes go wide, and the stink of their fear, it just . . . I can't . . . It's like trying to not breathe. I have to tear it out, have to make it stop. I rip through their bodies and out comes this thing, all limp and wet and cloudy." She stared past him. "And it's them, it looks just like them, only not old or sick or broken, and for that instant I'm holding them, there in my claws, dangling and helpless, as the life flickers out of what's left of their body.

"But then, in the next instant, this . . . spirit, it flickers, its eyes open, its limbs flex, and it drifts through my paw, drifts off without a backward look, without a nod, without any sign that it's noticed me at all. And then, whoosh, I'm bouncing again, coming to rest over another dying body, and it goes on and on and on and on, just bouncing and slashing, bouncing and slashing." Her paw flashed up, black claws spread. "Every living thing ever born I have held in this paw, every living thing for thousands of generations. And every one of them has drifted away, flittered off, and I've got no idea of where or why or anything."

She lowered her paw, turned her fiery eyes toward Bobcat again. "And you tell me I'm supposed to be in charge?"

Bobcat felt himself cringing all over at the solid menace in her quiet voice. "But . . . But wait," he got out after a moment. "I mean you're all gods, aren't you? You and the other Curials? How can you—"

She burst like lightning before him, knocked him backward, her fiery face filling his eyes. "I am *not* a Curial!" she snarled, her paw heavy and cold against his chest, her claws pricking at his fur. "You call me that again, and I'll rip you apart right here! You understand me?"

Bobcat could hear his own breath rattling in and out of his throat, but that was the only way he knew he was still alive. "I'm sorry," he managed to squeak.

She had already risen, was pacing from one side of the clearing to the other, her tail lashing. "Those twelve idiots probably *believe* they're gods, but they're nothing, no more in charge of their little realms than I am! But they prance along, pretending not to notice how the earth spins just fine on its own, how the sun burns and the moon rises, how the plants grow and the weather changes and all of it, all of it, would keep on if they never lifted a paw again! We're nothing but slaves to this damn whirling clock-work!"

The Blood Jaguar stopped in her tracks, looked back at Bobcat. "You thought we were gods? Well, let me tell you, kitten: if there are gods out there anywhere, I've never met them, and I've been out there, been there in a way you could never even remotely begin to understand."

She shuddered, the fire flickering over her pelt, then stretched her whole enormous body, settled down into the dirt of the clear-ing, rested her head on her paws. "I used to enjoy thinking, though," she said after a moment, her eyes not focused on any-thing, "thinking that maybe when I slashed their souls free they drifted off to wherever the gods were, somewhere like in the old stories." She raised her head, gave Bobcat a look. "Somewhere like your Shroud Islands, I guess." She blew out a breath, laid her head back down. "I've come to kind of doubt it, though."

Bobcat felt a little surer by this time that his legs could hold him up, so he rolled over and got to his paws. He had to sit almost immediately, though, the memory of her paw against his chest making his shakes break out again. The Blood Jaguar stayed where she was, lying a few yards across the clearing, her eyes still unfocused, a flick at the very tip of her tail the only motion he could make out.

None of it made any sense. This was the monster that had kicked him into the Brackens, he was sure of that, but how could she be the Death Goddess of Shemka Harr's stories? She seemed so . . . so forlorn that he had to swallow against the lump in his throat. "I'm sorry," he said at last; he wasn't sure why. He just felt like he should say something.

"Oh, yeah, really." She didn't look up. "For yourself, I'll bet."

"No! I mean I just . . ." He spread his paws. "It just doesn't sound like much of a life. For you, I mean."

"Life?" She raised her head, and her glance set Bobcat shaking again. "I've got nothing to do with life. Nothing at all."

"Oh. Yeah." Bobcat felt like his fur was shrinking. "I knew that." A phrase popped into his head, and he had to stifle a laugh.

She cocked her head. "What?"

He felt his ears go back. "Oh. Well. I was just thinking how stupid it would be for me to tell you you should try to look on the bright side of things." He couldn't stop from hiccuping a little giggle.

The Blood Jaguar blinked, and Bobcat froze, waiting for the flash of her claws. But a smile touched her whiskers, and she said, "Yes. Yes, that would be stupid."

"Well." Bobcat risked a glance at her, felt a grin on his snout. "Good thing I didn't say it, then."

She put a paw to her forehead, shook her head, and Bobcat heard her chuckle. "You are such an idiot," she said, slight laughter still in her voice.

"Yeah, well, I've heard that a lot recently."

The Blood Jaguar put her paw down and gave him a sideways look. "This is weird, just talking to someone." Her whiskers twitched. "I don't get a chance to do it very often, you understand." She tapped a claw on the ground, pulled at her upper lip with her teeth. "Look, I know you're not really into this whole thing, that you just got caught up in circumstances, so how 'bout this: when I come around to Ottersgate, I won't slash you and any ten folk whose names you give me. Heck, I'll even give you back your skink's luck. I won't need it once I get the plague started." Her paw flashed out, and she set a pebble on the ground in front of Bobcat.

Bobcat looked at her, then at the pebble. Could it really be that easy? Just pick up the pebble, give her a few names, and head off through the pampas? Would that be it?

His paw moved toward the pebble, but a sea of faces burst into his mind: Raj Tevirye, Ramon Sooli, all those folks he'd passed in Kazirazif, bathed in fear and torchlight.

And what about back home? Sure, he could tell the Blood Jaguar to spare Garson and Fisher and Skink and Lorn and Rat, but what about all those mice, Kily and Pol and the little Nibblers, Mernin and Patil and Deece and the rest? And Trec Sinpatclin, Ewell and Forst and Lally, all the otters from the transport company he had drinks with every other week? And Crow, Doc Mallard, Ma and Pa Jaybird, everyone in Ottersgate, the folks he knew but didn't really know. . . .

His throat had gone terribly dry. He couldn't meet the Blood Jaguar's gaze, kept his eyes fixed on the pebble. "Uhh, thanks for the offer. Really. But, well, I guess I don't know ten folks. . . ."

"No?" Her voice was quiet. "Well, I'll remember you, your fisher, and your skink at least." He heard her rise, a sound like beetles scuttling under fallen leaves. "I've enjoyed this, and I hadn't expected to at all. It's usually more annoying than anything else, going through this whole rigmarole. You can find your way out, can't you?" She stood still for a moment, he could tell without looking; then the shuffle of her turning reached his ears, the pad-pad-pad of her paws, the rustle as she reached the grass at the other end of the clearing. . . .

"No," he said, still unable to look up. "I mean no, I . . . I can't . . . can't just let you . . . *do* this. . . ."

All sound ceased. "You what?" her voice rumbled.

"I can't." He felt like he'd swallowed a rock. "I mean everyone keeps telling me that I'm the one, that I have to do something, that I have to . . . to stop you somehow, and I can't just . . . just walk away." He looked up. "Can I?"

She was standing at the very edge of the clearing, only her head turned to look at him, and the way her whiskers twitched back from her teeth made Bobcat's stomach clench even further. "Well, I can't see why not. No one can blame you for bowing to reality." She pointed with her chin. "Look around; the dust of your predecessors' bones lies thick over this Savannah. For all their posturing, they weren't any more successful at stopping my Plague Year than you were."

The fire in her eyes burned almost gently. "All their efforts got them was dead, but your efforts have saved two of your friends and yourself. You've done more than all the others put together, and I don't see what more you can do. Besides, what do you owe the rest of the world, anyway? Why should you be concerned about what a bunch of old lizards and meerkats say?"

"But that's not it!" Bobcat found he had leaped to his paws. "I don't care about the rest of the world! I just care about my little part of it! I mean I couldn't stand there and watch all those folks die knowing I was here and didn't do everything I could to stop it, could I? How could I live with myself?" He forced himself to swallow, took a breath, and sat back down. "No. It turns my knees to water to say it, but I can't . . . just . . . leave. . . ."

The Blood Jaguar sighed and settled onto her haunches. "So. You *do* want to fight, then?"

"Um, well, uhh, isn't there . . . Isn't there some other option? Maybe, I don't know, some sort of deal we could make or something?"

She brushed at her whiskers. "I rather doubt it. You have to understand, kitten: a Plague Year is the only thing I can really do anymore, the only bit of control I can still exercise. I plan it, put it together, pull it off, make the choices of who dies and when and where, actually get to do something with all this garbage they've dumped into me instead of just bouncing around." The Blood Jaguar cocked her head. "I really can't see that you could make me much of an offer in exchange for that, I'm afraid."

Bobcat blinked at her. "Yeah, I . . . I guess so." She was right, of course. He didn't have anything anyway, nothing of any real value: a rotted-out tree stump, two threadbare blankets and a pillow, a mattress he'd found ten years ago at the city dump, a couple chipped plates, and a cup, and besides, those were all back in Ottersgate.

He was still trying to think when the Blood Jaguar got to her paws again. "You've done a terrific job, kitten, tried everything you could think of, and I'm still not angry at you. Now take your skink's luck and go on home." She turned for the canebrake again.

"Yeah." Bobcat put a paw on the pebble, rolled it around under his pads. "I mean even all this stuff in my backpack is Fisher's." He shook his head. "I guess the only thing I could really put up in any offer would be me."

The Blood Jaguar froze, her nose not quite touching the pampas grass, the wavering of the fire inside her suspended for just an instant. Then she looked back slowly, her molten eyes half-closed. "I must advise you to think carefully before you speak again."

"What?" He blinked at her. "No, see, I was just saying that I don't have anything but me." He had to smile. "Like you said, not much of an offer, is it?"

"On the contrary." She had padded back around to face him again, her fire somehow darker to Bobcat's eyes. "A willing death is worth many hundreds of thousands of unwilling deaths." Her lips curled, her teeth gleaming. "But again, I must urge you to think carefully before you speak. I won't even begin to consider an offer of a willing death until it's been made a third time."

"Whoa, whoa, wait a minute." Bobcat wasn't sure he was hearing correctly. "Death? Who said anything about death? I just—"

She turned, shaking her head. "I knew you weren't making a serious offer."

"No, no, wait!" Bobcat jumped a few steps forward. "Please! I just want to know what you meant! I mean willing death? Unwilling death? What's the difference?"

Her tail lashed, and she stopped, still facing the canebrake. "To me, there's an enormous difference. So, unless you're making an offer—"

"But wait." He tried to gather his thoughts. "All those other bobcats you were telling me about, my predecessors or whatever. Didn't they come out here willingly? I mean they knew they were going to die, didn't they? That they didn't have a chance?"

Her ears folded back, and she shot a look over her shoulder. "Actually, they were stupid. Every one of them thought he was quick enough or clever enough or strong enough to stop me. They tried every trick, every argument, every decoy, every deal they could think to pitch at me for the suspension of my Plague Year, and when none of those worked it always came down to tearing throats: me tearing out theirs while their teeth were trying for mine. Unwilling deaths, each and every one, screaming and crying and fighting till the end." Her eyes flared. "Does that answer your question?"

His heart crashing against his ribs almost knocked Bobcat over. "Yeah, I . . . I guess. But what . . . What exactly is a willing death, then?"

Her voice crackled in the afternoon stillness. "A willing death is one freely given to me, a death that is mine to do with as I will, offered in place of the hundreds of thousands of unwilling deaths that my Plague Year will generate." Her eyes smoldered. "Death, after all, is the bottom line here, and I mean to have it—the juicier the better. And a willing death is the juiciest of all." Those eyes fastened on him. "So, if that's the offer you're making . . ."

The air had turned to thick liquid in Bobcat's lungs, a steaming syrup that choked and burned his insides.

The Blood Jaguar shook her head. "I didn't think so," she mumbled, and she turned away, raised a paw to part the grasses.

But there stood Garson in Bobcat's head, the cool evening shadows in the white swirls of her fur, the twitch of her nose, the chirp of her laughter. Then sores burst over her sides, her face growing thin, the spark fading from her eyes, her body collapsing into the fern beds. "Wait," he coughed out. "It is. It is what I'm offering."

Huge and fiery, those eyes flared against him, her voice low and quiet. "What is?"

"Me." He could barely hear himself. "My life for all those other lives."

"Life?" Her eyes blazed up, and Bobcat couldn't help but shrink back. "I have no interest in life; I told you that! It's your *death* I would want!"

Bobcat blinked at her. "Well, yeah. I mean it's the same thing, right?"

"Not in the slightest." She didn't turn away. "Now, for the last time, is that what you are offering?"

He tried to shrug and nod, found he couldn't quite lift his shoulders or move his head. "Yes," he finally whispered. "That's . . . that's it."

The Blood Jaguar sat back and rubbed her chin. "Interesting." She stood, padded across the clearing, stretched herself to settle before him, her paws very close to his. "Let me see if I understand your terms. I am to call off my Plague Year in return for your death, given freely to me and for my own use. Is that your offer?"

Bobcat scooted away from her a bit, his throat convulsing, and felt the pebble beneath his paw. "Oh, and . . . and Skink's luck, too, I guess. I mean since you wouldn't . . . wouldn't need it for anything anymore. . . ."

"Interesting," she said again, and Bobcat couldn't look up, left his eyes on the pebble, waited for her decision.

He concentrated on breathing, and after a stretch of time he heard her say, "Yes. Yes, I think I'll accept your offer." He saw one of her huge, guttering paws rise into the air; then it crashed to the ground, thunder cracking the sky and her voice shaking Bobcat from ears to tail. "Elements, scatter, relinquish your claim, and witness your mistress here swear and aver that by the conditions agreed to herein my pursuit of this Plague Year has come to its end."

The thunder faded into her breathy laughter. "Well, I never thought I'd hear myself use *those* words. But there you are, my own. No more Plague Year. And I won't be able to summon another for, oh, I'd say at least the next four earthly generations. Well done."

Bobcat let his head drop, found his paws, pressed his face into them. He would never see Garson again, and she would never know why, never know what had happened to him, never know how much he loved her.

And he did love her, he realized then, though it wasn't really much of a shock; he'd suspected it for a long time now. He'd just thought that, well, that he could always be there with her, that they could grow old together, enjoying each other's company without having to put a name to it, without weighting it down with words.

But now . . . He felt his paws getting wet where his eyes were rubbing against them. At least she'd still be alive back home, and maybe she would think about him every once in a while. Or maybe Fisher and Skink and the Ramon and those guys would be able to figure out what had happened, and they could go and tell Garson a little of how much she had meant to him. Yeah, maybe. . . .

He felt a tap on his back, looked up through blurry eyes to see the fire of the Blood Jaguar's face, her brow wrinkled. "Are you all right?" she asked.

Bobcat sniffed. "Yeah. Yeah, I'm fine, I guess." He pushed himself up. "So. What now?"

She blinked at him. "Now? Well, my own, we're done here. You might as well be on your way."

"On . . . my way?" He couldn't help staring.

"Well, yes." She took the pebble from the ground, held it out, pinched between two black claws. "I'm sure Skink is anxious to get this back."

Bobcat looked from her to the pebble, reached out, and plucked it from her claws. "But . . . but . . . ," he managed after a moment. "Didn't we just make a deal here?"

"We did, yes." She cocked her head. "You look a little uncertain, my own. It's too late to back out now, you know."

"No, no, I didn't mean . . . I just . . . just . . ." He felt the fur prickle on his neck. "Aren't you going to kill me?"

"What?" The Blood Jaguar stared at him, then laughed and rolled her eyes. "I've already told you: I'm not taking your life from you. I have nothing to do with life. It's your death you've given me."

"Uhh, yeah, that's . . . what I . . ." He stopped and shook his head. "I guess I don't get the distinction again."

She put a paw to her eyes and shook her head. "What am I going to do with you?" She lowered her paw then and said, "After you've lived your earthly life, however long or short that might be, I'll appear to you the same way I appear to everyone. I'll slash you free from your body the same way I slash everyone, and you will dangle from my claws the same way everyone dangles.

"But—and this is the deal we've just made—you will *not* then drift away from me the way everyone else does. For you will be mine, mine to do with as I will." A smile touched her lips. "Someone to talk to while I'm bouncing, maybe."

Bobcat felt his shoulders loosen with such a snap, he almost staggered sideways. "Then . . . Then I can go?"

"For now," she replied. "Oh, one more thing." She reached out, took his head gently between her cold, dry paws, and pressed her muzzle against his forehead, set it to tingling like an itch being scratched. "There. Now anyone with eyes to see will know that you're mine." Her claws stroked the fur below his ears, and Bobcat stared into her half-closed eyes, not quite sure what he was seeing there—sparks, flares, shooting stars. "I look forward to our next meeting."

The fire of those eyes wrapped close around him, and Bobcat swallowed. "Yeah. I'll, uhh, see you around."

Her laughter swirled the fire, gouts of flame washing over him, not horrible this time, though, not trying to devour him as they had before, but dancing, almost warm, a distant bonfire on a winter night. Into the air the fire whirled, spinning the afternoon light, and then it was gone.

Bobcat stared at the empty clearing, watched the little flowers on each stalk of pampas grass sway until they stopped and the whole place settled back into silence. He looked down then, smiled at the pebble, pushed it up between his claws, turned around, and walked through the curtain of grass he had come through earlier.

He didn't even try to retrace his steps. He was alive, and he was going to see Garson again; nothing else he could think of even remotely mattered. So he wandered under that eternal early-evening sky without a thought in his head except Garson Rix until he came out into another clearing and saw the Lady Lioness waiting alone in the slight shadows.

She looked over and smiled, so Bobcat padded across the clearing to her side. He couldn't think of anything to say, but the quiet didn't seem to be the sort that needed filling. He just sat there with her, glad to be sitting anywhere.

Finally he heard her take a breath. "How are you feeling, Ghareen?"

Bobcat let a little laugh out. "I don't know, Shemka Harr, I mean my Lady. I just can't really believe the whole thing's finally over."

She raised a paw. "You don't need to keep correcting yourself, Ghareen. I know I'm not really Shemka Harr anymore, but I do so love the sound of the name."

He smiled up at her golden eyes, then had to look away, something still gnawing at him. "It's just . . . all that stuff the Blood Jaguar was saying about herself and you and the other Curials, about how you're, well, not really gods or anything, how the world would keep going without you. It's the same sort of stuff you told me in the cave, kind of, but, well, everyone else has been telling me how you're all in charge and like that."

Her well-remembered laughter rolled over him, and Bobcat raised his head again. "Well, now, Ghareen, you tell me: if you hadn't come along that winter, and I'd gone through with my plans and died in that cave, what do you think would've happened?"

Bobcat blinked. "Uhh, well, I s'pose . . . I s'pose winter would've just kept on going. Spring wouldn't've come."

"Ah." She held up a paw. "But what did I tell you about the way the tilt of our earth's axis causes the seasons to come and go?"

Something about it glittered in his mind. "Oh, yeah. Since we're not directly up and down, when we're tilted toward the sun we have the warmer seasons, and when we're tilted away things get colder. But how does that fit in with—"

"Just remember this." And it was Shemka Harr's voice he heard, exactly as if he'd never left their cave. "The only lie I told you was when I said there were no Curials."

"But . . . but how does that fit with—"

"We exist," she went on. "We have influence. Anything else, however . . ." She shrugged her massive shoulders.

Bobcat considered. "But wait. I mean Fisher and Skink and the Ramon and everybody, the way they were talking, it's like . . . like they all think you *are* gods." He stopped. "Are you saying that they're all, I mean, that they don't know what they're talking about?"

Her smile was radiant. "All I'm saying, Ghareen, is that you were exactly right a bit earlier."

"Me? Right?" He had to grin. "When?"

"When you said you couldn't believe the whole thing was over. Because it's not, not by a long shot."

Bobcat blinked. The sky was growing dark, the afternoon light fading, and she seemed to be fading with it. "What? Shemka Harr, I don't know what you—"

"Go on," she said. She raised a dimming paw, pointed through the canebrakes, and Bobcat say the glimmer of a cook fire. "Your friends are waiting for you. Have a wonderful life, Ghareen. You've made your old teacher proud. . . ." Her voice trailed off, and when Bobcat looked back she was gone, the shadows so thick he could barely see the pampas grass anymore, night finally falling around him.

A breeze rustled the grass. Bobcat took a breath, then turned and started toward the firelight.

Chapter Eleven

Returns

The light flickered through the pampas grass, drew Bobcat on through the sudden darkness, until he came out into yet another little clearing, and around a burning heap of reeds sat Fisher and Skink, one on each side, eating silently and staring into the flames.

Bobcat had never thought anything could look so good; he rustled the grass with a paw and grinned when Fisher snapped her head over. He heard her sharp intake of breath, saw Skink scuttle around on the rim of his bowl. "Hey," Bobcat said, padding forward. "Any stew left?"

Fisher just blinked for a moment. "Uhh, no, actually. You went off with the stove and the pots in your backpack; we've been eating trail mix." She stared some more, her eyes focused on his forehead, Bobcat realized. "You . . . What . . . What happened out there?"

Bobcat rubbed the still-tingling spot above his eyes and shrugged. "We made a deal. Do you have a mirror or something anywhere?"

It took another second or two of staring before she shook herself. "Uhh, yeah, yeah. Gimme a minute."

She began rummaging through her pack, and Bobcat turned to see Skink squatted on the ground, his head bowed and his mouth moving. Bobcat felt his fur prickle, his ears going down, and he poked Skink in the back. "Will you cut that out? It's really getting on my nerves."

Skink froze, his claws splayed. "Forgive me, Bobcat," he said after a moment. "It was my surprise at seeing Death's Mark upon you. I could not help myself."

The scuffling from Fisher's side of the fire stopped, and he heard her say, "Here. I suppose you'll be able to see it; I mean it's on your head."

She was holding out a circle of metal and glass. Bobcat took it in his paws, held it up, and saw himself looking back, tufted ears, bushy cheeks, drooping whiskers, everything as usual except . . . except for a large dark-ashy circle in the fur halfway between his eyes and ears, right in the center of his forehead. He scooted around, used the mirror to reflect the firelight, and the mark showed clearly: over his regular brown spots lay one of the Blood Jaguar's black rings, square with rounded corners, unmistakably the same sort of spot that floated over her fiery sides.

He reached up, rubbed at it some more, but it and the tingling behind it didn't go away. "So," he heard Fisher say. "Is that a good thing or a bad thing?"

"A good thing, I guess." Bobcat blew out a breath and gave her the mirror back. "I mean the Blood Jaguar's canceled the Plague Year, but I . . . I don't think I'm quite ready to talk about it yet, if that's OK."

She took the mirror, and Bobcat almost expected her to launch a barrage of questions anyway. But she just shrugged, tucked the glass back into her pack, and said, "Well, I know I'd like a hot meal. Get your pack off, and I'll put the stove together."

He nodded and shrugged out of the pack, but the movement made a strange pressure poke at the inside of his paw. "Oh, yeah." He plucked the pebble out from between his pads. "She gave me this for you, Skink."

The lizard's eyes went wide; he reached up, took it, stared at it, his mouth open. "Oh," he said. "Oh, Bobcat. My luck. I can't . . . it's really . . . Oh, Bobcat, thank you."

"Yeah, well . . ." Bobcat looked away, started pulling the stove parts out of his pack. "Next time, you might wanna hold onto it a little tighter."

There wasn't much left in Fisher's little bags, and she had to tap her oil flask to get even a few drops into the pan, but the stir-fry she mixed up smelled and tasted better than Bobcat knew he could've managed. Whenever he made anything from odds and ends, it ended up weird, lumpy and greasy and cooked only part-way through. He was really going to have to learn how to cook, he decided, when he got home.

Home made him think of Garson, and he had to close his eyes at the wonderful warm rush that shimmered up his spine. He was going to see her again; that he swore to the stars starting to flicker in overhead.

Then he and Skink cleaned up the dishes and they all settled down for the night. Any dreams Bobcat might have had were so gentle they didn't make any impression on him at all, and he came blinking awake the next morning feeling nothing but rested. His forehead still tingled slightly, though; he touched it with a paw and guessed he'd have to get used to it.

The sky above the pampas grass had a smoky-blue cast to it that Bobcat knew meant more heat. Dawn had only just broken, though, the air still cool, and he rolled over to see Fisher yawning, Skink perched atop her pack.

"I woke early," Skink said, "to dedicate a thanksgiving ritual to the Curial powers. I found granola for you each as well." He waved to two waxed bags beside the ashes of last night's fire.

Fisher raised an eyebrow. "Breakfast in bed. We should save the world more often."

So they ate, the crunch-crunch-crunch the only sound till Bobcat couldn't stand it anymore. "So now what? I mean do we just go home?"

Fisher looked at him, swallowed her mouthful. "Unless you'd like to hang around here a little longer."

Bobcat looked at the clumps of pampas grass standing motionless everywhere, and even the rising warmth couldn't stop him from shivering. "No, I, uhh, I think I've seen enough of this place for a while."

"Suit yourself." Fisher looked sideways at him, then went on. "The best I can figure, we should head east till we find the Coati Road, then take it north back to Kazirazif. I'd rather not have to, but we *are* running low on just about everything but water, and there really aren't any towns in this whole part of the Savannah."

"Indeed," Skink said from his perch. "As we have seen, this area is somewhat sacred to the Curial powers. I also feel I must point out that we have no idea how far south we actually are. After all, the cove in which we met the Lady Raven and the Lady Dolphin could conceivably have been anywhere along the western coast."

"Whoosh." Bobcat looked from Skink to Fisher. "How bad are we fixed for food?"

"We're OK." She shook her canteen, uncorked it, took a sip. "If we take it easy, we can stretch things for a couple days, maybe four, and I can't imagine it's that far to Kazirazif." She jerked a thumb over her shoulder. "This pampas grass doesn't grow this thick any farther south than about two days outta town, seems to me."

Bobcat lapped at the mouth of his own canteen. "Might as well get started, then." He got up and started pulling the stove apart.

Skink rustled down, and the three of them got everything stowed, Skink pulling the counterfeit pebble out and setting his actual pebble in its place. Bobcat took one last look at the place, the tingling between his ears making him feel certain that he would see it again someday; then he turned away and set off after Fisher, heading through the grass into the rising sun.

The grass wasn't nearly as thick here as it had been the day before; Skink only had to scurry ahead to scout a path three or four times as the sun bulged up to midmorning. The day did get hotter and hotter, though, Bobcat trudging along and glad for what little shade the stalks overhead provided. He tried to concentrate on the path, to keep his mind off the things he'd heard the night before.

Because it just didn't make sense. Everything that had happened to him this whole trip had seemed geared to getting him to believe that these gods were real, that the old stories about them, the stuff they did, the parts of the world they controlled, were all true. But now he'd been told pretty much flat out by two of these gods that they weren't gods, that they weren't in control.

So where did that leave him? Everything works the way Shemka Harr had told him it did, except that there are these Curials running around? Where had they come from? How did they do what they did? And how could he tell Fisher and Skink that the world they seemed to be operating in wasn't the world as it really was? Would they even believe him? Did he even believe it himself?

He tried very hard not to think about these questions during that whole long morning stumbling along beside Fisher and Skink. Around midmorning, though, a smell reached him from ahead. "Hey." He gave a few sniffs. "Is that asphalt?"

Fisher's whiskers twitched. "Yeah. Nothing in the world like the stench of hot tar. We must be getting close."

Another few minutes of weaving through the pampas, and Bobcat pushed through a wall of grass into a strip of clear dirt. The asphalt stink coated his throat, made him cough, and he looked forward to see a wide stretch of blacktop running along to his left and to his right. He padded out onto it, the surface squishy beneath his paws, and looked off to his left. "North, then, I guess."

Fisher stepped up next to him. "Might as well."

He bowed and gestured, she puffed out a breath, and they began heading up the road toward Kazirazif.

And they walked and they walked and they walked, the road cutting straight through the grasslands, nothing but pampas everywhere. When the sun climbed to stand directly overhead, Fisher led the way off into the grass to get a little shade and trail mix. Then it was back to the road and the plod-plod-plod northward.

Bobcat found himself dozing off as he walked, his head drooping down, his mind going fuzzy, till he would almost tumble forward, coming awake with a jerk. On and on into the afternoon, the stink of the tar making him feel all sticky inside and out.

It wasn't until the sun started flirting with the grass to his left that Bobcat could see for sure that the pampas was thinning. Rocks appeared, small ones along the road at first, then outcroppings surrounded by bare dirt glimpsed through the curtains of reeds. The sun sank lower and lower, and so did the level of the pampas grass, the soil growing sandier, until Bobcat could see more of it between the smaller clumps. By the time the sun had bloated, huge and orange, and begun disappearing at the horizon, Bobcat had no doubt at all that they were coming up to the desert, nothing but empty sand already apparent in the distance ahead.

He blew out a breath. "I never thought I'd be glad to see this place."

Skink made a clicking noise from Fisher's shoulder. "Perhaps. But I must say I cannot wait to see an actual tree again, just growing on its own along the side of a hill."

"Yeah," Fisher said. "Let's take a break here, OK? I gotta take a leak."

She shrugged off her pack and hurried behind one of the last low clumps of grass. Bobcat settled down beside Skink and looked out onto the flats ahead. "So, you wanna just keep going? Maybe an hour more and we'll be in town."

Skink was nodding. "Spending a night in comfortable surroundings would be a welcome change of pace."

"Sounds good." Fisher came trotting back. "I just hope they've been able to keep a lid on things. It was plenty ugly when we left, and that was what? Two days ago now? We should probably try to get word to the Ramon so he can tell everyone the plague's not coming after all."

"Whoa." Bobcat had been padding around the clump of reeds but stopped himself. "I hadn't thought of that." He moved back to his pack. "Maybe we'd better just get going."

Fisher nodded, shouldered her own pack again, and they set off down the road. The night came down quickly, the afterglow fading along the horizon . . . except, Bobcat noticed as it got darker and darker, for a glow dead ahead. Kazirazif always lit up the sky, but not from this distance; he hadn't even seen the milestone yet. How could so much light be coming from the city that . . .

A chill rattled his fur even in the warm air. "Hey. That light. You think maybe the city's been torched?"

"I don't know," he heard Fisher mutter, and she picked up the pace.

The horizon get brighter, Bobcat now able to make out the little orange speck of the milestone torch against it. At the speed they were moving, they reached the milestone fairly quickly, and Fisher stopped so suddenly beside it, Bobcat almost stepped on her tail. "What?" he asked.

She looked back. "If the city's been gutted, who'd've come out this afternoon to light the torch on the milestone?"

Bobcat blinked at her, then at the stone, its little torch sputtering away. "But . . . But the glow. . . ."

"Yeah." Fisher was facing the brightness. "Come on."

Another few minutes of walking, and Bobcat still wasn't quite sure what he was seeing. The entire outline of the city shone, fires burning everywhere. But once he got close enough to make out the towers, he was amazed to see that all the light came from torches, set so close together, the whole wall was traced out in their light. Even where buildings stuck up above the wall here and there, their roofs blazed with light. "What the . . . ," he heard Fisher mutter in front of him.

By this time, smells were reaching Bobcat across the sand, incense and food frying, mesquite smoke and fragrant oils burning, and he could hear laughter, music, voices raised in song. Had a carnival broken out?

The walls rose up to hide the city beyond as they got closer, most of the sounds and scents fading, but even the tower around the little-used Basharah gate stood festooned with torches. Bobcat followed Fisher up to the gate, and the two meerkats posted there he recognized at once: the Raj Tevirye and her lieutenant. The Raj was stepping forward, her arms spread, a smile on her face. "Welcome! In the name of the caliph, all travelers are welcome to the festival!"

She stopped then, blinked, and gave a little bow. "Welcome back, I mean. Though, again, I certainly did not expect you here. As you are returning in triumph, I assumed you would feel free to follow the stories' dictates and enter at the Shasir gate."

"Triumph?" Fisher was blinking at her. "But . . . But how did you know? What's going on?"

Tevirye spread her paws. "The Ramon announced this morning that the Strangler had appeared to him in a dream. She informed him that, due to extenuating circumstances, she would not be pursuing her Plague Year at this time. The tension caused by your arrival had been building so all week that at the Ramon's announcement the city went mad with relief. The caliph proclaimed the festival, and—"

"Wait a minute." Bobcat's ears pricked at two of her words. "All week? We . . . We've only been gone two days."

Tevirye tapped a paw against her chest. "Forgive me. It is just that, since your arrival was eight days ago, rumors have flown all week about—"

"Eight days?" Bobcat stared, his stomach rolling, his knees suddenly going weak and making him sit. "We left the night we arrived! I mean the night after. I mean . . ."

He looked over, saw Skink's eyes wide. A shudder ran through Fisher's fur. "Uhh, OK," Fisher said. "I should've expected a little time dilation. Raj, would it be possible for you to sneak us to the Ramon again?"

"Sneak you?" Tevirye blinked a few times. "But you would be given a hero's welcome, received as honored guests in the caliph's palace!"

Fisher raised her paws. "No, not yet. We . . . I . . . We're gonna need some sleep here, real quick."

"I see." The meerkat stroked her chin. "I think it unlikely that I could get you unnoticed through the streets; I have never seen such crowds in the city before."

"Great." Bobcat's eyes had started itching. "Maybe there's a hotel or something nearby, somewhere we can crash?"

Tevirye shook her head. "I saw nothing but 'No Vacancy' signs in the windows on my way to work this afternoon." She tapped her nose. "All I can offer you is the spare guardroom. It's somewhat cluttered, but there are mattresses."

"Uhh . . ." Bobcat looked at Fisher.

She was looking back, the dark fur of her face ashen. "Whatever," she said.

Tevirye nodded. "Then this way, please." She started toward the gate. Fisher fell in behind, Bobcat dragging himself after, but the meerkat didn't actually go through into the city. Instead, she stopped under the gate's arch beside an iron door set into the wall, pulled a key ring off her belt, worked a key into the door's lock, and pushed the thing open. "As I said, it's not much, but you should be able to get some sleep."

Fisher squeezed past her, and Bobcat peered in. The room inside was dark, two small windows letting in just enough light to see a table covered with broken spear parts, rusted armor hanging from the walls, and a couple dingy mattresses. "Thanks," he mumbled. Tevirye got out of his way, and he stumbled in. Fisher had already crawled out from under her pack, was curling up on one of the mattresses, and Bobcat was only awake long enough himself to hear the door close.

Sounds kept tripping over him in his sleep, though, clatterings and mutterings and something that reminded him of bubbles popping, sometimes shaking him so much that he was fairly sure he had woken up. But his eyelids were too heavy to lift, and none of the sounds seemed worth the trouble to investigate; he felt tired enough to think that he actually had missed a week of sleep.

Finally, though, a smell washed over him that made his stomach rumble: chili, it was, a scent spicy enough to make his whiskers sweat just whiffing it. *That* was worth waking up for, he decided, so he rolled over and opened his eyes.

If not for the soiled mattress under him, the same little windows, and the same narrow shape, Bobcat would've sworn he'd woken up in a different room. Lanterns now hung from the walls, the broken spears and rusted armor cleared away, and several meerkats were hovering over some wonderful-smelling pots on a stove that now rested beside the door. A carefully embroidered cloth covered the table, and Bobcat saw that the Ramon Sooli sat in his chair at one end talking in low tones with Fisher and Skink. When Bobcat sat up, the three of them looked over.

The Ramon smiled. "Good afternoon, Bobcat. You slept well, I trust?"

"Yeah." His tongue felt dusty. "Afternoon?"

Fisher nodded and tossed something at him. His paws weren't quite up to that, though, the thing striking him in the chest and rolling to the floor: a wicker-covered bottle. "Apple-grape juice," Fisher said. "If you feel half as dry as I did when I woke up, you'll need it."

"Thanks," he croaked out, raising the bottle and sucking it all down, shaking the last sweet drops onto his tongue. He set the bottle down and blinked at the light slanting in from the windows. "How long have I been out?"

Skink rustled from his mat on the table. "We slept through all of last night and most of today. Curial time is not our own, and the transition from one to the other, as we saw crossing the prairie, can be quite draining." He jerked his head into another position. "All in all, this has been a most intriguing experience."

Bobcat blew out a breath. "Uhh, yeah." He rose to his paws and was a little surprised to find them steady. He felt pretty good, actually, sort of quiet inside, nothing jabbing or flaring up behind his eyes. Even the buzz at his forehead had sunk to a sort of whisper. "I've got to tell you, Ramon: that chili smells incredible." He padded to the nearer end of the table and settled at the place set there.

The meerkat inclined his head. "It is a favorite recipe of mine. I thought perhaps it would be best for you to eat something before the festivities begin."

"The what?" Bobcat blinked at him.

The Ramon's eyes had lit up. "Oh, yes. I have been discussing my plans with your associates, but I will happily go over them again with you. From here, I will call upon our caliph, Trajar—may the Twelve guard his steps—and inform him that you have arrived. You, I am thinking, can use that time to move around the city to the Shasir gate, and I know our caliph will be overjoyed to lead a grand procession out to meet you. The three of you will then accompany him back to the palace, where you will be his guests at a celebration of the Strangler's defeat. I will arrange—"

"Uhh, you'll pardon me, Ramon." Bobcat raised a paw. "But is this all really necessary? It's not that I don't appreciate the gesture and all, but, well, I mostly just wanna get back to Ottersgate as quick as I can."

"What?" Fisher leaned forward. "You don't want a big party?"

Bobcat shrugged. "Well, if you guys really want one, then I'll go, but—"

"Me?" Fisher gave a laugh. "Hey, I was only agreeing 'cause I figured *you'd* want to eat a lot and get all drunk." She turned to the Ramon. "It's a great offer, you understand, sir, but huge state-sponsored social gatherings give me gallstones." She rubbed her flank.

"Yes, Bobcat." Skink shifted again. "You are the hero of the hour; in a very real sense, you have saved the world. You deserve something in recognition, do you not?"

"It's OK. Really." Bobcat did his best to keep his ears up. "I don't wanna get everything in an uproar. I'm glad I could give you folks a chance to have your festival and all, but me, I just wanna get reprovisioned and get back on the road home."

Fisher had narrowed her eyes, and Bobcat looked away. How could he go to some party with the caliph? It was bad enough the Ramon was here, probably was going to start asking questions that Bobcat would have to dance around, trying not to blurt out that the world didn't work the way the Ramon had said. "It's just," he said, running for an excuse, "it's just that meeting Death, well, it's made me want to get back to my life as soon as I can."

He looked back, saw the Ramon nodding. "Perfectly understandable," the meerkat said. "I would be honored, though, if you would at least stay for supper."

Bobcat's stomach growled some more, and he had to grin. "Hey, the way the chili smells, you'd have to kick me out to keep me away from it."

The Ramon laughed, raised a paw, and called something to the meerkats around the stove; they bowed and hauled one of the pots off. In the bustle that followed, chili being ladled out, condiment bottles and seasonings appearing on the table, Bobcat tried his best to keep his eyes from straying anywhere near Fisher's furrowed brow. Back home, he'd always gotten the feeling that she could look right through him, tell what he was thinking almost, and he didn't want to give her the chance to do that now if that was possible.

It got harder and harder as the meal went on, though. The Ramon wanted to hear all about their journey south to the Savannah so he could write it up for his accounts, and Skink seemed more than happy to go into all the details: their dash through the crowded streets, Fisher and Bobcat's fight and how the Lady Dolphin and the Lady Raven broke it up, the encounter with the seagulls, the trek across the pampas, meeting the three Ladies, and all that followed among Bobcat, the Lady Lioness, and the Lord Tiger.

Bobcat kept his head down the whole time, concentrating on the spicy bite of the chili and dreading the story's end. He was just about done with his bowl when he finally heard: ". . . and Fisher and I watched Bobcat disappear into the reeds. The Lady Lioness led us from the Lord Tiger's clearing to another nearby and told us we should wait. 'Start a fire,' she said, 'so he may find his way here. If, however, he has not arrived by the time full night has fallen, then he will not be arriving at all.' She turned away quickly then, the grass opening before her and closing behind her."

Skink stopped for a moment. "Fisher and I waited, and the sky grew darker and darker. I had nearly given up hope when Bobcat came out of the reeds."

Silence fell, and Bobcat kept his eyes on the last chunks of tomato in his chili. A throat cleared, and he heard the Ramon say, "Bobcat, I would much appreciate your tale as well for my accounts. You are, after all, the only one on record to have met the Blood Jaguar face-to-face and lived. With your defeat of her as well, your story becomes even more—"

"I didn't defeat her." Bobcat had to interrupt. "We made a deal. All that talk about having to stop her, facing her down and all, that was all a crock of . . ." He swallowed the rest with the last bits of his chili.

"Indeed?" Bobcat could hear the excited quiver in the Ramon's voice. "Could you elaborate? If we can come to—"

"No!" Bobcat hadn't meant to shout, but he couldn't stop himself once he'd started. "Just drop it, OK? The Plague Year got canceled! That's all that matters! Not the way I stumbled around, not the way I had no idea what was happening, not the way I behaved like an idiot the whole time! Everything turned out all right despite me, so can't we just talk about something else?"

Everyone in the room was blinking at him, and after a moment the Ramon nodded. "How did you like the chili?"

Bobcat swallowed, took a shaky breath. "It was fine. Thanks. Really."

The others turned back to their bowls, and the meal ended quietly, the Ramon dabbing at his whiskers with a napkin before getting up from his chair. "Feel free to remain here as long as you wish; I shall post my assistants outside to see that you are not disturbed. You may take with you any of the provisions I have provided, and I wish you the safest of journeys. May the Twelve keep and follow you."

Fisher and Skink accompanied the Ramon and his assistants to the door, exchanged murmured parting comments, but Bobcat stayed put, gnawing a paw, his ears burning. When the others returned, Bobcat couldn't make himself look at them. "I'm going back to sleep," he said into the silence. "We'll be walking all night, right?"

"Yeah," he heard Fisher say. He winced at her tone, waited for her to start yelling, but she didn't. After another minute, he decided she wasn't going to, so he rose, padded back to the mattress, and flopped down onto it.

He slept some—at least, he was fairly sure that he did. Music began in the distance after a while, the daylight from the little windows turning to torchlight, and Bobcat figured it must be evening. He rolled over to see Fisher drowsing against her pack, now stuffed as full as he had seen it back when they had left her sycamore.

How long ago had that been? he wondered suddenly. A week to get to Kazirazif and another week, apparently, out on the Savannah. With a week now to get home, this whole thing would take the better part of a month. It felt like years already.

Bobcat got up, stretched, saw Skink scuttle out between the mattresses. "Ah, Bobcat. Fisher and I have seen to our provisions, and I have made certain we have two apples for our crossing the Kingdom of the Buffalo. We are prepared to depart."

Fisher stirred, blinked, scratched at her back. "Yeah. Might as well get ourselves gone."

"OK." Bobcat padded over, shrugged on his pack. "I . . . I'm sorry I yelled and everything."

"Hey, don't tell me." Fisher was adjusting the straps on her pack. "Tell the Ramon. Come on, Skink." The lizard scurried up onto her back; she moved to the door, pulled it open, and walked out.

"Well, I will." Bobcat followed her outside into the arch of the Basharah gate. Two meerkats stood there, one of them the little meerkat Bobcat remembered leading them up to the roof of the palace. She bowed to him, and he surprised himself a little when he bent his knees to bow back. "Please tell the Ramon that I'm sorry I snapped at him earlier. Tell him . . . Tell him I'll send him something for his accounts after I, well, after I figure it all out. OK?"

"Of course, sir," the little meerkat said. "I shall be honored to bear your message."

"Uhh, yeah. Well, thanks." He tried another bow, then headed for the outer gate.

Fisher was standing there. "Manners. I'm shocked."

He gave her a glare, but a call from the other side made him turn, the Raj Tevirye coming up. "What is this? You're not staying for your own festival?"

"Nah." Fisher tapped her snout. "Remember? We hate being predictable."

The Raj laughed. "Well, I predict that I will be getting some mileage out of this story for a number of years to come." She held out her paw, and Fisher shook it, Skink reaching down to tap his claws against hers. She turned to Bobcat, but just as he was raising his paw she rushed forward, threw her arms around his neck, and gave him a little peck below the ear. "Thank you," she said quietly.

Bobcat rubbed his check and blinked at her. "You . . . You're welcome."

Tevirye stepped back, snapped out a salute, spun, and scurried to her post beside the gate, Bobcat only able to stare after her. "Come on," he heard Fisher say then. "Let's go." He turned, saw her disappearing into the darkness beyond the torchlight, and he had to hurry to catch up. "We might as well keep on to the milestone," she was saying. "We can cut across the desert again to the milestone on the Meerkat Road and avoid most of the traffic around the city that way." She looked over her shoulder. "Sound good?"

"Yeah." Bobcat shifted his pack, heavier again, into a better position. "Avoiding traffic sounds real good to me."

On into the night they walked, coming to the milestone along the Coati Road before cutting left and starting off across the sand. They wove in and out among the dunes, the city a constant glow on their left, until Bobcat caught sight of a pinprick of torch flame up ahead. It appeared and disappeared, getting larger and larger, until he followed Fisher out into a flatter area, the milestone clumped just ahead. Fisher padded past it, onto the road, and continued off into the night.

But Bobcat had to stop and turn. Kazirazif sat shining like a jewel, light everywhere, snatches of music still reaching his ears. He smiled at it, then spun around and loped up the road after Fisher.

The night passed quietly, the sliver of the moon sinking early in the evening, the desert trudging past, and the stars drifting overhead till Bobcat saw the horizon to his right grow gray with the dawn. Fisher left the road at the fern grottoes around the spring above Fekadh, and they camped there in the same secluded spot, sleeping all day and setting off when evening came down. Bobcat saw lights glowing in the little valley as they passed the outskirts of town; then they were off into the darkness again.

A larger slice of moon hovered along behind them, still sinking fairly early, and Bobcat couldn't help thinking about the Lady Raven, about Fisher saying she was the Night, about the old story of her working the phases of the moon, about the way she had promised to send Garson a dream telling her he was thinking about her. But if the Curials weren't gods, if the world worked despite them, what did the Lady Raven really do? What did any of them really do? Whom could he even ask?

But this night passed, too, the sun coming up over the plateaus of the eastern desert. A little more walking brought the road to Canyon Pienta, and they slid down the sandstone walls to settle for the day in one of the caves there. Bobcat pretended to be more tired than he was, curling up after eating a few pawfuls of trail mix, ignoring the mutters of the other two till he finally fell asleep.

Around the stove before they set off that evening, and again the next morning after they'd trekked all night to the grove of piñon pines at the base of the trail leading up to the western border of the Kingdom of the Buffalo, Bobcat waited for the questions to start, for Fisher to do more than look sideways at him, for Skink to do more than make comments about the favorable weather.

But it never happened. And lying in the shade of the pines, Fisher and Skink stretched out in their places, their breathing making him think they were asleep, Bobcat wondered why. Were they waiting for him to bring the subject up? He knew they had to be curious about what had happened between him and the Blood Jaguar, but what could he tell them?

He drowsed through the day, no way of telling them the basics without telling them the whole thing occurring to him, so it was quiet again around the stove as they ate Fisher's stew. The way that night led up the switchbacks into the mountains, and they arrived at the buffalo's western border station while the moon was still in the sky.

They had no problem getting through this time, Fisher just smiling while Bobcat got the two apples out for himself and

Skink. He couldn't tell if these were the same buffalo sentries they'd spooked the last time through; they just took the apples, nodded their shaggy heads, and walked the treadmill that raised the gate.

They were just coming out of the mountains into the short grass of the plains when the sun started sparking the horizon ahead. Bobcat grimaced. No Curial magic this time; it was going to take them the regular four days to cross the kingdom.

Which meant more mornings and evenings of sitting and eating in silence, Fisher's face getting more sour, even Skink giving up his attempts at conversation the farther they inched their way across the face of the prairie. It got worse and worse, Bobcat feeling the weight of Fisher's glare even when she was in front of him, and on the third night they passed the lights of the Bison King's palace without Fisher even slowing, though Bobcat didn't feel much like stopping either. So on they stalked, camping in the grass beside the road when dawn came up, not a word passing between them.

Sleeping that day wasn't easy, Bobcat tossing till noon, Fisher's narrow eyes and mouth floating behind his eyes. But what could he do? What could he say? Not a thing came to him, not then and not that evening when they set off, the only sound the rattle of their packs. The sky spun above, the moon nearly a quarter full in the sky behind and just settling at the horizon while they waited in silence for the bison sentries to bow them through the northern border station.

Things had slowly begun smelling more familiar to Bobcat, and now, the grass waving under the stars, no bluffs standing up against the horizon ahead, it would've been nice if he could've started relaxing a bit. But Fisher and Skink weren't even muttering to themselves in front of him, and the quiet seemed to cling to Bobcat's fur, made him want to shake himself with every step.

It just kept on all night, and the first gray strokes of dawn found Bobcat wrung out and constipated, a familiar sign coming into view: CROSSROAD AHEAD.

Before him lay the streambed, the bridge carrying the Meerkat Road over it to meet the Tundra Road rolling down from the north, the third road slicing toward the growing dawn and heading off across the plains. For a moment, he thought the place was deserted, but the rising light revealed a single figure in the dirt just this side of the bridge: an old kit fox with ragged ears leaning against a stained pack, his eyes closed, his paws crossed over his chest.

Bobcat stopped in his tracks, but Fisher padded over and looked down at the figure. "I should've known," she said, her voice almost strange in Bobcat's ears after so long. "The least you could've done was have breakfast waiting."

The kit fox scratched his side. "Ah, but you've tasted my cooking."

"Oh, yeah." She shrugged off her pack. "Beetle gravy plays a large part in it, I seem to recall."

A grin tugged at his whiskers, his eyes opening. "Well, it's good, and good *for* you." He sat up and rubbed his paws together. "So, tell me all about it! What happened? I know you pulled it off—Dolphin was positively turning cartwheels—but I've *got* to know the details!"

Oh, no. Bobcat took a step back and heard Fisher snort. "Wouldn't we all!" She gave him a look, then waved a paw at the kit fox. "It was apparently too horrible for words; we've been on the road a week now, and he hasn't said a thing!"

"Really?" The Lord Kit Fox's grin sparkled.

"Yeah! After everything I've done, the closest thing he's got to a friend, dragging him every step of the way, and now he won't even deign to tell me what went on out there!"

"Hey!" Bobcat couldn't help barking out. "It was . . . I just . . . I don't want everyone to make a big deal out of it, that's all." What could he possibly say, and with the Lord Kit Fox standing right there!

Fisher snorted again. "Oh, yeah, right. You're modesty itself, you are. We all survive the greatest transplanar event of the century, and out of spite you hold out the final information from me! That's what it is!"

"Spite?" Bobcat blinked at her. "What are you—"

"Yes, spite! I get you through this, keep you sober, share my knowledge and experience with you, finally educate you enough so you have a chance, and when it all finally comes out right, you—"

"Now hold on, Fisher!" Bobcat tried to keep his ears up. "You've been so high-and-mighty, telling me what's best for me through this, well, maybe I'm trying to do what's best for *you* for once!"

Fisher's jaw dropped. "You what? You expect me to believe that you have any idea about—"

A whistle split the air, and the Lord Kit Fox's raggedy head popped up between them. "Children, children, please! Some decorum, I must insist!"

Fisher glared, but she pulled her mouth shut. The Lord Kit Fox nodded to her, then padded over and put a paw on Bobcat's shoulder. "Now, Bobcat, I've known this young fisher for a number of years, and if there's one thing she can't stand, it's being left out of a secret."

Fisher gave a little laugh. "Look who's talking!"

The Lord Kit Fox cleared his throat. "In my opinion, I'd say you'd better tell us the entire story before my favorite pupil pops a vein or two."

Bobcat swallowed, couldn't look up at him. "But—"

"It will be for the best." A paw touched his chin and pushed till he had to raise his head, had to meet the Lord Kit Fox's old eyes, bright and clear and friendly. "Believe me," he said quietly. "Just tell it as you remember it."

The warmth of those eyes calmed him, made his shoulders unclench and his heart's pounding slow. "Well, OK. But don't blame me if you don't like it!"

"Just tell," the kit fox whispered.

"Well, I went out there and wandered around till she found me. And it turned out she was expecting me to fight. She said all those other bobcats had tried to beat her by fighting, had tried tricks and bargaining and stuff, sure, but, well, it had always come down to her fighting them. And she had just torn them all to bits."

He looked over at Fisher. "Which I guess is why you couldn't find anything about the last bobcat, whoever he was. He went out there, tried to fight with her, and got shredded." He shrugged. "Well, I wasn't *about* to do that, so we talked for a while, and . . . and I was trying to think of something I could offer her, you know, some sort of deal I could make. And I made a little joke, sort of, about it, saying the only thing I had was my own self but that I couldn't imagine she'd be much interested in some mangy old bobcat hide."

He swallowed. "Except, it turned out, she was. And, well, she agreed to take me instead of . . . of all those others."

Nobody said anything, and Bobcat felt his neck tense again. Had he managed to tell them what had happened without getting into all the weird stuff? A smile pulled at his whiskers, but when he looked up he found Fisher looking back with narrow eyes. "That's it?"

"Well, yeah. Basically."

She squinted at him. "I don't know how to tell you this, Bobcat, but she hasn't taken you. She's marked you, yes, but, as far as I can tell, you're still all here." She looked at the Lord Kit Fox. "Am I missing something?"

The Lord Kit Fox shrugged and crossed his paws across his chest.

Bobcat cleared his throat. "Well, see, she's going to take me after I die."

He heard a rustle in the dirt, saw Skink raise a claw. "Forgive me, Bobcat. I know these memories must be painful for you, and I hope you will take my words in the spirit of one who is trying only to assist, but She of the Cold Fire takes us all after we die. That is her function, the domain over which she reigns. How is her taking of you to be any different?"

Bobcat licked his lips, tried to think, but Fisher giving another snort interrupted him. "Oh, this is just great!" She waved a paw at the kit fox. "He still won't tell us!"

"I'm trying! But it's just . . . I don't know how to—"

"Oh, gods!" Fisher spun away. "Why do I even bother! Any information in that head's gonna be locked up like diamonds in shale! We'd have to blast it out!"

"Hey! I'm just trying to—!"

She wasn't looking at him. "I'd have a better chance of teaching a pygmy shrew to talk than of getting anything useful outta this idiot!"

"Shut up!" Bobcat leaped for her, but she slipped to the side, a double pawful of dirt suddenly dashing into his face; a crack at his knees knocked his paws out from under him, and he slammed into the ground, the teeth jarring in his head. "All right, damn it!" he found himself shouting. "Fine! I don't care anymore! You wanna know how wrong you were, you and Skink and the Ramon and all your stories and your talk, that's fine with me!"

And he let it all burst out, the dirt in his eyes turning to mud. "It's all a lie, Fisher, all of it! That's what I learned out there! There are no Shroud Islands, the Blood Jaguar doesn't rule over any Kingdom of the Dead, doesn't have any say over who dies or how, and when she slashes them free of their bodies she doesn't even know where they go drifting off to! She doesn't know, isn't in control, isn't a god! And neither are any of the other Curials! All that stuff about their realms and ev'rything, it's lies! Nobody's in charge, Fisher! Nobody really knows anything!"

He let himself collapse, wiped furiously at his eyes with his front paws, finally getting his vision clear, and when he looked up Fisher and Skink were staring at him, the Lord Kit Fox sitting beside him and smiling, his ragged features knitting up, a liquid silver smoothing over his scars. "There now," he said, and Bobcat felt a paw cool as river water stroke his back. "That wasn't so hard, was it?"

Bobcat raised his eyes to the Lord Kit Fox's. "You . . . you knew? You knew what I was going to say?"

"Well, of course. I *have* been doing the Curial thing for several thousand generations, you know, and I'm not quite as enamored of our godly image as certain of my brothers and sisters." He glanced around and lowered his voice. "Just don't let word get around, all right?"

"What?" Bobcat stared at him. "I don't . . . I don't understand. . . ."

Only laughter shone in those silvery eyes. "That's all right. Just take my advice and don't take the whole thing too seriously."

"What? You . . . You think this is funny?"

The Lord Kit Fox grinned. "Everything is, my friend, if you look at it right." He tapped Bobcat on the nose. "Be seeing you." The air twitched around him, and he shot upward into the rising dawn, a streak of silver against the gold.

Chapter Twelve

Bobcat's Bet

Bobcat stared at the shining trail arcing overhead, then turned and looked at the others: Skink huddled to the ground, his eyes wide, Fisher leaning back against her pack. She gave a half-smile. "OK, so I'm sorry. I should've guessed; it's not easy when you first learn nobody really knows anything."

Bobcat blinked at her. "You mean you . . . you already . . ."

Fisher shrugged. "It's the first lesson a shaman has to learn. When we get back to Ottersgate, I can set up some time with you, help you talk this through, if you want."

"Talk?" The week's worth of silent fretting overflowed, and Bobcat just let it out. "What good's that gonna do? Nobody knows anything, remember? And far as I can tell, that means you, too!"

"Excuse me?" Fisher sat forward.

"Yeah! All this time you've been acting like you've got all the answers, and now I find out you're every bit as clueless as your precious Curials! You drugged me, dragged me away from my home, rubbed my nose in how everything I ever thought I knew was a lie, and now it turns out you were just as stupid and brainless as me!"

"Oh, no!" Fisher's hackles were rising. "Nobody could be as brainless as you, not if they tried! If you'd just think for one minute—"

"Think?" Bobcat waved a paw. "That's all I've been doing this whole trip! And look where it's got me! Nowhere!"

"Well, maybe if you had a little sense, you—"

"Fisher, Bobcat, please!" Skink's voice burst like a gust of wind into Bobcat's face, and he started back to see the lizard crouched in the dirt, his head twitching back and forth between the two of them. "If you will both calm down, I believe I can clear up this misunderstanding. For, if you recall my discussion when we began, the essential relationship between the Curial powers and earthly folk hinges upon—"

"Oh, gods!" Bobcat clenched his paws into fists, spun away before he felt tempted to use them on Skink. "All your talk, your schools, your theories, and what good is it? Why should I listen? Your Curials don't know what's going on, you don't know what's going on, Fisher doesn't know what's going on, and I sure don't know what's going on! If we're all just stumbling around like idiots, what even is the point?"

"And yet," Skink said from behind him, "your stumbling around managed to save at least half the world's population."

The words struck Bobcat, made him stop and turn back. "What?"

Skink raised a claw. "The words you used in describing yourself to the Lady Dolphin, I believe: 'just stumbling around.' And that is, essentially, all any of us are doing, all any of us can hope to do."

"What?" Bobcat crooked a claw at him. "You told me the Curials were in charge! You told me that they knew—"

"What I told you," Skink said, "and what you heard seem to have been two very different things!"

Bobcat had to blink at the force in the lizard's voice; he glanced around to see if the Lord Eft had come creeping in again, but only Skink sat before him. "Now, please," the lizard went on, "sit quietly, and I will once again try to explain.

"You claim that we do not know what is going on, that we are just stumbling around. In a sense you are very right. Yet in our stumbling, we uncover useful bits of information: that certain foods work well together; that fire, when used prudently, can be lifesaving; that killing one another tends to lead to unfortunate consequences. None of this information is ordained from on high, as you seemed to have thought. It is learned, discovered in our stumblings."

"And it's always changing." Fisher held up a paw. "I mean we could be sitting by a riverbank tomorrow and a fish could step out and explain to us that we've been wrong all these generations about fish not being intelligent, that for thousands of years we've been killing and eating folk just like us. Sure, everything we've ever learned about fish says it's not likely to happen, but, hey, it could." She grinned at him. "It's what makes life exciting."

Skink was staring at her. "An odd analogy," he said after a moment, "but it does illustrate the point." He turned back to Bobcat. "Everything we think we know is based on observations and assumptions. Every answer we find can be questioned, until at last we can only reply that we believe in the things we do because they seem to work. That is why school is important, why the lessons passed down from fisher to fisher have validity." He shrugged and fell silent.

Bobcat looked from him to Fisher and back again. "But . . . But wait. You told me that the Lord Eft had explained to the elders of the first kiva how everything worked, that those stories were all the things I heard when I was a kit. And, I mean, every one of those stories talks about the Curials being in charge. What? Did the Lord Eft lie to them?"

Skink looked away, and it was Fisher who answered. "Oh, no. It's just that when the elders come out of the kiva to give the gathered reptile communities the Lord Eft's words, no two of them could agree on what he'd said. They'd all heard such different things; some even contradicted each other."

"What?" Bobcat looked from her to Skink.

The lizard rolled his eyes. "Several theories have been advanced to explain—," he began, but Fisher cut him off:

"Yeah, but the *story* says that they each heard only those things they wanted or expected to hear, disregarded the rest, and each came out convinced that their way of looking at the world was correct, stamped with the Lord Eft's approval. The story ends by stating that the Lord Eft was so disgusted, he withdrew into his current seclusion." She shrugged. "He gave it his best shot, but the poor saps couldn't handle it. Now, who wants breakfast?"

Bobcat's stomach growled, and Fisher smiled. "I'll take that as a yes. Get the stove out, Bobcat."

Questions continued to swirl as Bobcat undid his backpack. "So, now, wait. The Curials, then, are . . . are what?"

Skink gave a rustling laugh. "The age-old question. Many in my kiva would answer that they are the true inhabitants of this world, that we are but creatures who developed accidentally. They hold that our devotions to Those Above are useless, that Those Above have no need or concern for us.

"However, certain rituals done in the Curials' names can be efficacious. Prayers for rain, recited in the proper way to the Lady Dolphin, oftentimes lead to cloud formation, all meteorological data to the contrary. Of course, the very nature of the Curial mind is such that these prayers grant no certainty, but after this trip I believe that I will be able to add my voice constructively to those who argue for Curial concern and intervention."

Bobcat shook his head. "So, then, the stories—"

"Are mostly just stories, like I said before." Fisher was taking the pipes as Bobcat set them down and fitting the stove together, but now she stopped. "The Shroud Islands, though . . ."

"Indeed." Skink scuttled up onto Bobcat's pack. "How true do you believe your information to be?"

"Me?" Bobcat thought. "Well, Shemka Harr—I mean the Lady Lioness—didn't deny it. And the Blood Jaguar agreed to give up her whole Plague Year just because I said she could keep me when I died instead of letting me go." He shrugged. "Why would she do that if the Shroud Islands really existed?"

Skink's eyes seemed to whirl. "This will bear much meditating on," he said after a moment.

"Yeah, well, you go right ahead." Bobcat could almost smell Garson now on the breeze from the east. "Me, I wanna put this all behind me and get started on my life."

Fisher looked up from her flint and steel. "Now that's the best idea I've heard yet. Get the pan, will you?"

Then the fire was burning, and soon Fisher had something simmering away. Bobcat swallowed it down, his yawning almost interfering with his chewing. He managed to keep his eyes open long enough to help Skink with the dishes, then settled back against his pack and dropped off.

After a while, though, things began shaking him: voices, wheels creaking, rope on canvas. He tried to ignore them, but they just kept at him till he found his eyes were open.

It seemed to be about midafternoon, and all he could see from where he lay was the open sweep of the prairie, a few wispy clouds stretched through the blue above; the mutterings and clankings all seemed to be coming from behind him. So he rolled over to take a look.

Wagons filled the space across the bridge, at least a dozen, otters and foxes hammering stakes into the ground, stringing up awnings, laying out tables, pennants of green and gold and burgundy fluttering in the breeze. Bobcat sat up, watched otters hauling buckets up from the stream, foxes in chefs' hats squirting fluid over several barbecues.

A vixen popped up from the boxes atop one of the wagons, a satchel bulging over her back. "Hey! You! Riverdog!" she shouted. "Where d'you want these dishes?"

An otter scurrying by on the road stopped, and Bobcat couldn't believe his eyes. It was Trec Sinpatclin. "Well," Trec said, looking up at the vixen with a paw on his chin, "I rather thought down here where the tables are might be best."

The vixen shrugged, wrapped her paws around the satchel's mouth, and hurled it into the air, plate flying out. "Any available paws!" she shouted; then she leaped off the roof, tucked into a roll, and tumbled into the awning of the wagon across the road. Cables groaned, the framework creaking like a tree about to give way in a windstorm, but the thing held, bounced her back out toward the wagon she'd jumped from, and she snapped out of her roll, slid through the dirt on her knees, and jerked to a halt right under the spot the plates were dropping toward.

Her head came up, she gave a sharp whistle, and foxes were suddenly surrounding her, serried in ranks, their eyes fixed on the falling dishes. Bobcat hardly dared to breathe as the foxes snatched plates out of the air, somehow getting themselves out of the way of the others behind them until each one held two plates, the vixen, still on her knees in their center, clapping her paws closed above her head and catching the last plate between them. She rose then, wheeled to face Trec, and asked, "Down here, you said?"

Trec still stood with his paw on his chin. "Yeah," he said. "On the tables, if you wouldn't mind."

"No problem." The satchel had fluttered down by now, and she tucked her plate into it, then held the thing out in front of her.

The other foxes trooped past, setting the plates in so carefully, Bobcat could scarcely hear them clatter, until the satchel was bulging again. The vixen gave Trec a dazzling smile, slung the satchel over her back, and started for the wagon where the fires were just starting to smoke.

Bobcat shook his head and padded across the bridge. "They're all bloody acrobats," he heard the otter mutter.

"Tell me about it."

Trec turned, and the astonished look on his face made Bobcat grin. "Bobby?" And then Trec had slid up next to him, was pounding him on the back. "What're you doing here?"

"Just on my way home." Seeing Trec brought so many memories bursting over him, Bobcat couldn't stop grinning: late nights at the pubs along the West Channel; water polo games won and lost; the songs and the laughter and the company, at least when he wasn't too catnipped up to join in. "How's town? I've, uhh, I've been away awhile."

Trec nodded. "Thought I hadn't seen you about of late. Town's much the same, though; least it was when we scurried off this morning." He waved a paw at the wagons. "Another rush job, civilization coming to an end if these crates don't reach Meerkat Town by yesterday. Just the sort of thing I relish getting punted out of bed before dawn about."

"Oh." No ride back, then. "You're off to Kazirazif?"

"No, no. Only foxes through the Kingdom of the Buffalo these days. We meet a crew of 'em here with a load bound for the Beaverpool docks, swap wagons, party all night, then head back into town." He stroked his whiskers. "If I'd had a bit more notice, I'd've brought the good china."

An accordion off in the direction of the cook fires broke into a rolling hornpipe; a mandolin and fiddle joined it, and Trec's paws began shuffling on the pavement. "You're invited, of course, Bobcat, and whoever you're traveling with, but if you'll excuse me, I've got to put on my host hat now." With that, he slipped past Bobcat and between two of the wagons.

A buzz of voices began rising from beyond the caravan to Bobcat's right. He chuckled, then turned and headed back across the bridge to where he'd left the others. Skink was already awake, staring at the camp with wide eyes, Fisher just starting to stir. "What . . . ," she said, sitting up and blinking. "What on earth . . ."

Bobcat laughed. "A party's breaking out. Interested?"

Fisher smiled, rubbed her eyes. "Friends of yours?"

"Some of 'em." He turned to Skink. "You coming?"

The lizard was moving with the music. "I have never been able to resist a well-played accordion, I'm afraid."

Bobcat stuck out a paw. "Climb on, then."

Skink scurried up and settled in the fur at his shoulder blades; then Bobcat hurried to catch up with Fisher, already crossing the bridge. The largest awning was stretched over the barbecues, a few tables and the little bandstand there, a cleared area before it for dancing. Foxes of every type mixed with the otters, the laughter and the music and the smells of the fish frying almost overwhelming. Bobcat had to stop at the edge, let it all wash over him for a moment.

Fisher's paws were tapping. "Now *this* is a party."

Trec came sliding up. "Fisher! Gods! You hanging about with this character?" He thumped Bobcat on the back.

"Trec . . ." Fisher passed a paw over her brow. "It is a long, weird story, one that, I believe, will soon be coming to an end. What's it take to get some food around here?"

All it took was Trec pushing them through the crowd. "Beer

and wine are at the next wagon up!" Trec called over the din. "You're my guests here, so anyone gives you guff, well, you give it right back to 'em!"

And by the time the afternoon had turned to evening, Bobcat had eaten, danced, put away a few beers, and was generally feeling pretty good about this whole adventure. He was lying behind the band, out under the stars slowly winking overhead, the smoke from the fires bringing delightful scents of more food, and was just thinking about home, about rushing out to see Garson, sweeping her into his paws . . . when a slight spicy scent started tickling his whiskers, made his ears cant back and his stomach muscles clench.

Catnip. Somewhere. And getting stronger.

"Ah!" a sloppy voice called behind him, and Bobcat jumped straight up, his whole body twitching. He landed, spun, and a red fox was standing there, a knotted shawl over his shoulders, a wide grin on his muzzle, an unmistakable smell wafting from him, stale wine and damp earth mixed with it. "Well met, my friend!"

Bobcat tried to move, tried to back away, but the scent, the scent, the . . . scent . . . It ruffled his fur like soft claws, caressed the ache he'd almost forgotten. The fox staggered forward, flopped a paw over Bobcat's back, fumbled at his shawl with the other, and pulled a sweet, spicy bag from it. "Choice Santiran, cut in the fields this week." He squeezed the bag, a cloud puffing over Bobcat's whiskers like a cudgel slammed into his face. "Special caravan price, my friend."

The blood pounded in his ears, the urge twisting his insides, and Bobcat's last effort to pull away was just failing when a sudden tingling swept down from between his ears, a rush of pinpricks that shocked him, let him stumble back, shake his head, and scramble off into the darkness.

Spots pulsed before his eyes, something like a scream echoing beneath his fur, and it wasn't until the ground sloped under his paws and sent him tumbling into the stream that he even knew where he was. His stomach yawed and flipped, a hot pressure at the back of his throat, and he just managed to get his face out of the water before he threw up, muscles heaving and heaving, all the way down to his toes.

The tingling stayed, and he clung to it, clung to it with all his desire not to slip back and become what he'd been before. The rest of the night he lay there, the tingling finally pushing the urge far enough away so he could fall asleep.

Sunrise woke him, light creeping between his eyelids and making him blink. He sat up on the stream bank, winced at his own stink, and waded in. When he crawled out, he shook himself, padded up the slope, and caught the more welcome smell of Fisher's stew in the air.

Half the wagons were already gone, only otters milling about the six or eight that remained. Most were busy pulling up stakes and taking down awnings, but another group stood off to one side gathered around five or six little stoves, Fisher and Skink among them, Fisher stirring a pan over her stove while Skink supervised a large pot of coffee nearby.

His paws actually carried him all the way, and he slumped to the ground, heard Fisher's chuckle. "Well, I've seen you look worse."

"Thank you so much." He cleared his throat and spat off into the field. "Now that you mention it, I've felt worse." Sure, he was bleary-eyed, his sides ached, and his throat still burned a little, but his fur wasn't too tight around him, his brain nowhere near as shaky as a night of catnip always left it. And all because of the Blood Jaguar's mark. . . .

Fisher interrupted his thoughts. "Trec's invited us to join the caravan back, if we want."

"Definitely." Bobcat rubbed the sleep from his eyes. "I've had enough of walking for a while."

"Indeed," Skink said from his perch overlooking the coffee. "I am anxious to see my family again, and the chance to arrive in time for vespers is more than enticement enough."

Otters were starting to wander over now, Trec weaving among them. "Eat up, all!" he called out. "We're to be in Flatrock by midmorning." With a cheer, the otters converged, dipping bowls into the pots, grabbing the coffee dishes from Skink's station as they passed. Bobcat waited for the rush to settle a bit, then got himself some breakfast, found a spot that didn't have too many otters lolling over it, stretched himself out, and had just taken a mouthful when Trec slid up next to him, his own bowl balanced in one paw.

"Ah. . . ." The otter took a deep whiff of the steam rising from his stew. "Nothing like chowder on the open plains of a morning." He took a few slurps, then looked over at Bobcat. "You have a good time last night?"

Bobcat chewed and swallowed. "Yeah. Not bad, I guess."

"Good." Trec nodded. "When I heard there was a catnip dealer traveling with those foxes, I pointed him in your direction. I know how much you like the first taste of the new crop when we bring it into town."

It took some control for Bobcat not to smash his bowl over Trec's head. "I'm off the stuff now, Trec," he said when he felt steady enough. "For good, I hope."

"Really?" Trec cocked his head. "Well, glad to hear it. Never have understood why folks muddy themselves up with anything like that. I mean unless it's beer, of course."

Bobcat had to laugh. "Of course."

Trec drank down the rest of his stew. "Well, must dash, things to do and all. We'll be off quick as we can."

Otters were leaping up everywhere, dropping their bowls into a pot of water, other otters grabbing them out, rubbing them over with scraps of towel, flinging them back toward the nearest wagon, where an otter jumped and spun, catching them and shoving them into a box strapped to the wagon's side. Whoops rang through the morning, otters scrambling over the crates, tossing canvas over them, tightening ropes through eyelets and weaving them around the whole stack.

"Bobcat!" he heard Fisher shout. "Let's pack up!" He slurped down the rest of his breakfast, tossed his bowl to the wash crew, then hurried back to where Fisher was stuffing the stove parts into his pack. "Once otters finally get moving, I've never seen anything yet that'll stop 'em. Tie this off, will you? I've gotta get my own stuff."

He had the drawstring knotted when three high shouts drew his attention: Trec standing on top of the first wagon, his orange vest bright against the blue of the sky, a wrinkled fedora over his ears. Six other otters in orange vests rushed up, each with a hat crumpled in one paw, the other paw coming to rest on the haulers' yoke at the front of the wagon. For a moment, they stood, the only bit of stillness in the entire camp; then Trec gave a huge whoop, tore off his hat, and thrust it the air. The otters below yelled, jammed their hats on, and sprinted to the other wagons.

Fisher jostled Bobcat's elbow, her pack across her back. "You ready?"

"What? Oh, uhh, yeah." He slipped his pack on, got to his paws. "Where's Skink?"

"Here, Bobcat." The voice came from beside him, the lizard squatting in the dirt. "These preparation rituals are most intriguing. I wonder what studies have been—"

"C'mon." Fisher padded around, held out a paw to Skink. "You can ask all about them after we get our seats."

The otters were shouting back and forth, slipping under the carts and tapping the boards, greasing the axles and poking the shocks. Bobcat walked past staring, had forgotten how big the things were, each wheel wider than he was and nearly taller than he could reach standing on his hind legs.

They reached the front wagon, eight otters already in their stations at the yoke, four on each side of the thing, their front paws gripping the grab bars as they stretched into their warm-up exercises. Someone whistled above, and Bobcat looked up to see Trec grinning down. "All passengers aloft!"

Bobcat snapped out a salute. "Aye, aye, sir!" Fisher was already halfway up the rope lattice covering the sides of the wagon, so Bobcat leaped on, hauled himself to the top.

Three other otters lolled about in the early-morning sunshine. Bobcat recognized them all, but he only knew one by name. "Lally! How you been?"

"Can't complain." She slid over with a grin. "Bosun'd fire me if I did."

Trec was bent over the side, pounding on a few crates. "I could never fire a muscular lass like you, Lally. How'd we get through the hills east of Flatrock?" He looked over, blew her a kiss.

She clasped her paws. "Oh, sir, you make my heart race!"

"I should hope so." Trec rubbed his paws together. "So, passengers, prepare for departure." He rose up, grabbed his hat, lifted it into the air. The whoops everywhere died all at once, silence falling before Bobcat could even blink. Trec stood still, then gave a whistle that cut right through Bobcat's ears, whooped, and slammed his hat back into his head.

Yells exploded all around, and the cart jerked under Bobcat's paws; creaking loudly, it rumbled forward, the shouts slowly taking on a rhythm, speeding up as the ride smoothed out. Bobcat looked over the side to see the ground sliding by, the haulers' chant starting to take shape in front of him, and when he glanced back he saw the next wagon lumbering onto the road. The caravan had begun.

Trec was just starting his part of the chant, a deep melody line that wandered over the base provided by the haulers. These chants were the only times Bobcat had ever heard otters using their native language, and though he couldn't understand a word, he really liked the sounds, the clicks and squeaks and long held notes all combining to give the sense of rushing to get somewhere without ever hurrying at all.

As the morning rolled along, the others got into it, too, Fisher humming first, then letting fly with a countermelody, twining around Trec's without ever colliding. A bit later, Skink began a whistling, wordless rhythm that darted in and out of the chant, highlighting one part, then scuttling away and playing around with another side of it.

The grasslands flashed by beneath, swaying all the way out to the horizon wherever Bobcat looked, but in what seemed like no time at all he saw hills coming into view ahead, growing rapidly while the grass shrank. Trec changed the chant, slowing it down, reeling it in, and the wagon creaked to a halt, the grass dropping to dirt and the first bend in the road visible there beside the little spring; with a whoop, the haulers leaped from the yoke and dove into the water.

Bobcat smiled, uncorked his canteen, and winced at the smell of it. Trec and the other otters were clambering down, so he followed, figuring a little fresh water wouldn't hurt.

"Right," Trec was saying when Bobcat reached the spring. "It's two hours to Flatrock; then we've got the hills pretty much straight through to Ottersgate. Treps, Clobber, Mavis, I'm gonna need you then, so you take this shift topside."

The otters pulled themselves from the water and gathered around Trec, so Bobcat took the opportunity to take a few licks. A moment later, a paw touched his back, and he looked up to see Trec. "Fancy a quick stretch in harness, Bobcat? Penn had a bit too much last night, and I wouldn't mind giving him a little sleep before we get to the hills." Trec turned and scowled over his shoulder. "Course, I also wouldn't mind strapping him in and making him run the whole way."

One of the otters, stretched out in the dirt, an arm across his eyes, let out a groan, and the others immediately lined up and began trooping past, wiping their snouts and saying, "He looks so lifelike," and, "Such an untimely end," and, "Somehow, I thought he'd outlive us all."

Bobcat couldn't help laughing. "OK, sure. Tragedy always makes me soft in the head."

The otter on the ground rolled over. "Oh, bless you, friend. I'll never be able to repay your—"

"Yes, yes." Trec waved a paw. "Haul his carcass topside before the ants carry it off." He turned back to Bobcat. "All right. You can take port side third. Lally!"

"Who?" She broke away from the procession carrying the limp otter toward the cart.

"Help Bobcat get placed, will you? Port side third."

"No problem." Lally gestured to the front of the cart. "Welcome to the ranks," she said, Bobcat padding to join her.

"Thanks." Bobcat eyed the yoke, maybe four yards long, with

crosspieces sticking out every yard or so at about shoulder-height. "What do we, uhh, do?"

Lally shrugged. "Grab on and run. Fairly simple." The others were coming up now, and she showed Bobcat to the third spot on the left side of the yoke. She took the space across from him, and the other otters filled in the rest. "At the whistle," Lally was saying, "you rear up and grab on. And when he whoops, you dig in and shove for all you're worth. Getting started's the hard part; then you just let the chant carry you." She smiled. "Easiest two hours you'll ever run."

"I'll keep that in mind." The whistle shrieked down from above, and the otters all snapped into place, Bobcat grabbing the bar and hauling himself onto his hind legs. He was trying to figure a good grip when the whoop sounded; the otters echoed it. Bobcat gritted his teeth and pushed. The cart pushed back, forced a grunt out of his throat, but then it was moving, slipping away from him, and he had to start trotting to stay with it. The chant began slowly, the pace picking up till Bobcat was running, the song all around him.

And it wasn't that hard, Bobcat found, once he got into the rhythm; with these other folks pushing, he felt like he was just along for the run. The chant really helped, and after a while he found himself sort of joining in, recognizing by the way the otters ahead of him straightened up and bent forward when certain sounds were going to be made.

Turning took some getting used to, the otters in front wrenching the yoke over, Bobcat feeling the whole thing slide, shifting his weight to pull it one way, then push it back the other, and even though the hills were gentle, as the road flashed by under his paws and his breath started coming faster and faster it got to be all Bobcat could do just to hang on.

Finally, the chant started to slow, the yoke pushing back at his paws, and he looked forward through hazy eyes to see a huge rock slumped off to one side of the road, buildings visible around it and against the hills farther on. The chant kept slowing, Bobcat straightening his back and arms the way the otters in front of him were, trying to imitate the way they skipped more than ran, the cart slowing till he was just trotting again, past the boulder and a few isolated buildings, then across the bridge and into downtown Flatrock.

Folks waved and shouted, the otters grinning and waving back, but Bobcat didn't think he could pry his paws from the crosspiece. Everyone seemed to be heading in the same direction, and when the otters in front of him hauled the yoke over, the wagon rolling into the shady park where the festival had been, Bobcat guessed from all the folk in white shopkeepers' aprons setting up booths that it must be market day.

The wagon trundled to a halt, and Bobcat slumped forward. After a moment, he wrenched his paws free, staggered around to the shady side of the wagon, and collapsed, sweat dripping from his whiskers.

Lally came scooting by and shoved something cold into his paw: a bottle, he realized after she grinned, waggled her thumbs, and swigged down her own. Bobcat got it to his lips, and it turned out to be some bubbly lemon-lime drink. He gulped it down as quickly as it would pour into him.

Above him, Trec and several other otters were casting lines off the wagon, some mice and a couple squirrels standing around watching. "So, yeah," one of the squirrels was saying, "got the packages wrapped after you came through yesterday. Everything's ready to head out."

Trec wiggled a crate free from the cart. "I understand we've got a couple cases of cola nut in here for you, Rits."

"Yeah?" One of the mice strode forward, took the crate from Trec, and set it down. "Can't beat that."

Bobcat lay back, concentrated on breathing, but then Trec said something that almost made him sit up. "So where's old Kechetnin? I didn't see him by the bridge prophesying doom as we went by yesterday or this morning. He all right?"

The mouse scowled. "He was never all right."

"True." Trec paused, wiped his brow. "Old squirrel's gotten to be a regular feature of the trip, though. Didn't fall in and drown, did he?"

"Nah." The mouse gestured vaguely toward town. "About a week ago, he just stopped, let his grandkids take him home." He shrugged. "I guess Doomsday's been postponed."

They both laughed. Bobcat almost asked if this squirrel always wore a weird red and purple hat, but he decided he needed his breath for breathing, so he stayed put in the cart's shadow.

The sounds of voices swirled around him, and the next thing he knew, Trec was shaking him awake. "We're all loaded up, Bobcat. Climb on, and we'll be off."

Bobcat shook his head, got to his paws, his legs feeling like chunks of wood, and somehow pulled himself to the top of the crates.

Fisher and Skink were there, and Fisher smiled. "Having a good time?"

Bobcat flopped himself down. "If I start to slide off, just toss a rope over me or something."

"Or something," she agreed.

Bobcat nodded, rolled over, and fell asleep again. The whoops and the whistles all echoed in his dreams, and he was strolling the decks of some riverboat down in the Gulf south of Beaverpool, Garson beside him, Fisher and Skink walking along ahead.

Then the water got choppy, the boat rising and falling, folk screaming, tossing Bobcat so hard he woke up . . . and found himself sprawling over the crates, one paw knotted among the ropes, the whole cart rushing downward at such an angle, for a second he thought they must've gone over a cliff.

But there was Trec perched in his place, Fisher beside him, and the screaming from Bobcat's dream became the whoops of the hauling crew. He raised his head as much as he could and saw trees flashing by, wooded hills stretching into the distance, the sun behind and settling into afternoon.

The hills. Between Flatrock and Ottersgate.

The wagon bottomed out, Bobcat's stomach lurching; then the front end rose, the ride slowing down. Trec gave three quick shouts, and the cart jerked, sent Bobcat tumbling toward the back, only the knot around his paw stopping him. He dug his claws in, rolled himself over, and when he felt secure undid the knot with his teeth. He started to pull himself forward but stopped when he came across Skink clinging close to the canvas, his eyes clenched shut. Bobcat lowered his head and asked, "You all right, Skink?"

The lizard's eyes rolled open. "This sensation . . . They tell me the way will smooth the closer we come to Ottersgate, but they have been saying that for some time now."

"Well, hang on." Bobcat patted Skink's back, then continued to crawl. The chant was still going, but he thought he heard a different rhythm from the haulers, a different counterpoint from Trec. Bobcat clawed uphill, had almost reached the front when a whoop rang out and what had been uphill slowly rolled over to become downhill. He dug in, peered over the edge, saw the haulers all clinging to the yoke, pounding and whooping and laughing like loons, the road seeming to fall straight down into a wooded valley.

The cart teetered at the crest for an instant, then pitched over and down, started picking up speed, and Bobcat couldn't help but scream along with the otters, his sense of gravity going haywire, wind rushing into his face. Down and down and down it sped, trees whipping past, Bobcat's eyes watering, till again the tilt gradually lessened, flattened, and tipped back, the wagon slowing down. Trec gave his three shouts, and the otters tumbled down from the yoke, dug in at their stations, and the cart began moving up the next hill.

Bobcat took a deep breath, and the smell of home hit him so hard he almost lost his grip. He sat up, sniffing, and heard Fisher call, "Bobcat! How could you sleep? It was incredible, all those hills! We're practically there by now!"

He looked across Trec, still perched at the edge of the crates, still chanting away, and saw Fisher looking back.

"How close?" Bobcat called to her. "How close are we?"

She shrugged, faced forward, and he saw a smile burst through her whiskers. "That close!" she cried, raising a paw.

Bobcat turned. They were coming to the top of the hill, and rising in the distance beyond the crest Bobcat saw the crown of an enormous tree, an oak, branches spreading wide. The Bailey Oak. It had to be.

The otters whooped and leaped up onto their beam. The wagon topped the hill, the whole forest spread before him, the road running straight through it, and they started down the slope, Bobcat letting his eyes rest on the roofs and windows of Ottersgate, nestled up under the Bailey Oak and shining in the afternoon sun.

The cart couldn't go fast enough for him then, and he leaned forward, trying to see it all, smell it all, let it all wash over and around him. Closer and closer the wagon sped, the Bailey Oak towering, the woods whipping by, till on his left Ree's Meadow opened up and Trec gave a huge whoop.

The otters rolled off, the wagon jerked, cries ringing out, the air full of creaking, and the cart slowed, turned off the road, settled snugly into a space between two of the Ottersgate Transport Service warehouses.

"All off!" Trec shouted, and the otters sprang from the yoke, disappeared through the warehouses, a splash reaching Bobcat's ears, but all he could see was the West Bridge crossing the Channel, the houses rising up the slope of Ottersgate island to the roots of the Bailey Oak, its branches broad and protective overhead.

He vaguely heard Fisher saying, "Well, thanks for the lift, Trec. Can we help off-load?"

"Ah, it's no problem, Fisher. I'll just let the crew cool off a bit, and they'll be happy to get to it. It's what they get paid the big bucks for, after all."

"Indeed," Bobcat heard Skink say next to him. "Hazard pay, I'd wager."

A paw on his shoulder tore Bobcat's gaze away from Ottersgate. Fisher smiled at him. "Well, let's go, then."

Bobcat shook himself, everything so quiet after a whole day of rattling along the road. "Right, yeah." He turned to Trec. "I'll see you, OK? And thanks."

"No problem," the otter said again, and he slipped down the side of the cart.

Fisher stuck out a paw to Skink. "Shall we?"

"Most certainly." Skink scurried up into her fur, she went over the edge, and Bobcat followed.

Somehow, the dirt felt different between his toes, and when Fisher had padded through the warehouses and down onto the beach along the West Channel, Bobcat could barely keep from flipping over and rolling around in the sand, it felt so wonderful against his paws. The otters were leaping about in the water, but a whistle from among the warehouses sent them rushing to shore, streaming past Bobcat, and vanishing from sight. The quiet closed around him again, and all he could think about was Garson.

He heard Fisher yawn. "So, what do you want to do now?"

His ears went warm, and she laughed. "Never mind. I think I've got a pretty good idea."

Skink chuckled, scuttling into the sand. "Give Ms. Rix our regards. I, for my part, must make a report to the Elders." He raised a foot, sniffed, grimaced. "Though I think perhaps I should stop at home first and freshen up a bit."

Fisher nodded. "In a few days, though, I'd like to get together, go over this all with you both."

Skink cocked his head. "An excellent idea."

"Yeah." Bobcat rubbed his chin. "You could write it up, a *Journal of the Plague Year That Wasn't* or something." He shrugged off the backpack. "You want this now, or should I—"

Another whistle shattered the quiet, this time from across the Channel. Bobcat looked over and saw Lorn Gedolkin tumbling down the beach. He sliced through the water, leaped up the bank, and slammed right into Bobcat. "Bobby, Bobby, Bobby! Where have you been hiding yourself?"

Bobcat tried to catch his breath, but Lorn had already spun off to Fisher's side. "At least you've been keeping some excellent company." He took her paw and pressed it to his lips. "My dear Fisher, my invitation to dinner still stands."

Fisher smiled, pulled her paw from his. "Thank you, Mayor, but I prefer my food a little less greasy."

"Ooooh!" Lorn grabbed his chest. "That rapier wit!" He

turned, whacked Bobcat on the shoulder. "And you, Bobby, now that you've joined the moneyed class, what will become of you? How will his newly acquired fortune change our old Bobcat?"

Bobcat stared at him. "My newly acquired what?"

"Oh, Bobby. . . ." Lorn pressed his paws together. "Don't tell me you've forgotten."

"Forgotten? Forgotten what?"

"Your bet? Last month? At the water polo game? You asking me to put fifteen on Ewell holding Coll Belverdeen to less than three goals? Any of this ringing anything?"

Slowly, it came back. "Oh. Yeah. You mean she—"

"Stopped him cold." Lorn wrapped his arms around himself and shivered. "It was an absolute pleasure to watch. But imagine my shock when I couldn't find you after the game." He shrugged. "So, as president of the Ottersgate Commerce Bank, I had to open an account in your name. You've got nearly 500 gold castors waiting for you, Bobby."

"Gold?" Bobcat stared. "Wait. Gold? But . . . but how?"

Lorn frowned. "Well, the bookies had Ewell at thirty to one. You asked me to bet fifteen gold castors, and acting as your agent these past few weeks, I've managed to increase—"

"Fifteen *castors?*" Bobcat grabbed him by the scruff. "I haven't got that kind of money! Lorn, I was talking about scrip! Greenbacks, not gold!"

Lorn blinked. "Well, good thing you won the bet, then."

Bobcat let the otter go, his head spinning: five . . . hundred . . . in gold. . . . But Lorn was going on. "Of course, for a mere 10 percent I'll be happy to stay on as your financial manager should you not care to sully your paws with arcane fiduciary matters." He grinned and stuck out a paw. "Deal?"

"What?" Bobcat shook himself, then took Lorn's paw. "Uhh, yeah, Lorn, sure. You, uhh, you do that."

"Wonderful!" Lorn clapped him on the back. "Come by my office tomorrow around tenish, and I'll have all the papers ready for your signature. Must dash now; I'm speaking at the Mouse Lodge this evening. Lovely to see you again, Skink, and Fisher . . ." He sighed, pressed a paw to his chest. "I am, as always, blinded by your radiance. Farewell, all." He slid back down the beach, into the water, scooted out onto the other bank, and disappeared into the streets of Ottersgate.

The quiet seemed even quieter, Bobcat staring after Lorn, the backpack still hanging from his paws. "Five . . . hundred . . . gold . . . castors . . . ," he heard himself mutter.

After a moment, he realized Fisher was calling his name; he forced his eyes up and saw her grinning. "I can take care of the pack if you wanna just leave it. Let's say day after tomorrow, you and Skink at my place for lunch. Right now, though, seems to me you might have someone to see."

He blinked at her for a moment, then dropped the pack and leaped to his paws. "Fisher, you're absolutely right. Skink, day after tomorrow, I'll pick you up." All he could do was smile. "And thanks, both of you. For everything."

"See you," Fisher said.

"Indeed." Skink jerked his head over. "We shall."

Bobcat spun around and took off down the riverbank, his mind buzzing. He cut right, weaving through the trees till he came out into the cleared area north of the Brackens, the briers rising up like a wall in front of him. He sprinted along the wall till it turned left, turned with it, and the woods to his right opened onto the Brackens Farms, fields stretching away from the Brackens and out into the valley.

Rabbits, their straw hats bobbing up and down, worked out among the crops, and Bobcat barely noticed their heads stop and turn as he barreled past, his eyes intent on the south part of the Farms, the cabbage fields that Garson was in charge of. He cut through the carrot patches, rabbits shrinking back, their ears flattening, and started shouting, "Garson! Garson, you out here?"

Several hats ducked down among the cabbages, but one rose straight up, a black and white figure beneath it. And then she turned, was looking back at him, her nose twitching, her long-imagined voice saying, "Bobcat?"

He cleared the rows of cabbages between them in several leaps, scrambled up the row, and skidded to a stop in front of her, his heart pounding, her sweet scent stroking his whiskers, not wanting to close his eyes even to blink. It took him a moment to get out a, "Hi."

"Hi yourself," she said, her ears spreading. "I've been having some fairly weird dreams about you. What've you been up to? Where've you been?"

He couldn't stop a laugh bursting out, and before he even knew what he was doing, he had swept her up in his paws and started spinning with her down the row of cabbages. He only took a few steps before he tripped over himself, tumbled back into the dirt, Garson across his chest, a confused look on her face. Bobcat drank it in, then gave her nose a kiss. "Garson Rix, will you marry me?"

"What?" She started back a bit, but, Bobcat noticed with absolute glee, she didn't hop off, didn't scream, didn't pull herself away; she just lay there, warm against him, and blinked. "Where did this come from all of a sudden?"

"I want to tell you everything." He wasn't really sure what he was saying, only sure that she was right there, her fur soft in his. "Everything that happened, how much I love you, how you saved my life out there, how much you mean to me, how I've been thinking about you so much, and . . . and . . . and . . ." He stopped, lost in her smiling eyes. "Will you marry me?"

Garson looked down at him, tapped his chest gently with a paw, her smile slight beneath her whiskers. "I'll think about it," she said after a moment. "I also think the boss owes me a half-day off, and I think I'll go ask him for it. I've got to give you a chance to persuade me, after all." She leaned forward, pressed her nose to his. "Shall we, Bobcat?"

"Ghareen." His heart was pounding so hard, he could feel himself shaking. "My name's Ghareen." He lifted her up, set her on the ground, rolled to his paws, and set off with her through the fields.